"Author Regan keeps the tension alive from the first page. Her psychological insight into her characters makes the story as intriguing as it is real as today's headlines. This is a well-written and thought-provoking novel that will keep you riveted until the conclusion."
—*Suspense Magazine*, September/October 2013 issue

"Readers should drop what they're reading and pick up a copy of *Finding Claire Fletcher*."
—Gregg Olsen, *New York Times* bestselling author

"*Finding Claire Fletcher* is truly a story of our times and magnificently told . . . it is superbly written and moves with intense, page-turning speed."
—Nancy S. Thompson, author of *The Mistaken*

"The writing shows a maturity and control that many far more experienced writers lack. The characters—even the minor ones—are well developed and three-dimensional. Expect to hear a lot more of Lisa Regan."
—David Kessler, author of *You Think You Know Me Pretty Well*

LOSING
LEAH
HOLLOWAY

OTHER TITLES BY LISA REGAN

Aberration
Hold Still
Cold-Blooded
Finding Claire Fletcher

LOSING LEAH HOLLOWAY

LISA REGAN

THOMAS & MERCER

Text copyright © 2017 by Lisa Regan
All rights reserved.

Published by Thomas & Mercer, Seattle

www.apub.com

Amazon, the Amazon logo, and Thomas & Mercer are trademarks of Amazon.com, Inc., or its affiliates.

ISBN-13: 9781503942998
ISBN-10: 1503942996

Cover design by Damon Freeman

Printed in the United States of America

For Shihan Robert Tomaino—you made me a better person.

CHAPTER ONE

SATURDAY

Leah knew she was driving fast enough when the children started screaming. Their shrieks punched through the air, careening off the interior walls of her SUV. Even baby Tyler wailed, the kind of purple-faced cries that not even a bottle could soothe. Still, her foot pressed harder against the gas pedal, pinning it to the floor and holding it there until her toes ached. The I-5 stretched out before her. Ahead she saw the overpass that crossed the American River. Her fingers tightened around the steering wheel. The numbers on her dashboard's computerized screen that showed her speed jumped higher and higher.

Her daughter's voice broke through the cacophony in the back of the vehicle. "Mommy," Peyton said. "Slow down!"

Leah kept her eyes on the road. "I can't, honey," she mumbled under her breath. "Mommy needs all the speed she can get."

"Mommeee, please."

As she neared the overpass, Leah spoke loudly enough for the children to hear. "God help me."

CHAPTER TWO

The sun glinted off the surface of the river, a thousand diamonds winking at her. Claire smiled and sucked in a deep breath, focusing on the feeling of contentment that had settled in her chest. A cool breeze lifted her curls from her neck. She had just looked down at her Roughneck boots, sunk into the mud along the American River, when the moment of perfect, silent peace was shattered by a great splash of water that fell on them. The culprit, her golden retriever, Wilson, raced past, followed by her sister's shouts.

"Wilson! Get out of here!"

Brianna appeared at Claire's side, her fishing rod in hand. "Damn dog," she muttered. "If there were any fish in there, they're gone now."

Claire laughed and glanced over her shoulder at Wilson, busy sniffing something out beneath the I-5 overpass. He had wriggled between the large concrete pillars, probably ferreting out a squirrel.

"Now help me get the worm on the damn hook," Brianna said, thrusting her fishing rod at Claire.

With a wry smile, Claire grabbed a small container of mealworms from her fishing vest and expertly attached the fat white body of one of them onto the hook of Brianna's rod. Her sister gagged as the worm's brown pus-like guts squirted out and onto her pants. Claire laughed, her eyes drawn to her sister's feet. "Flip-flops? Really?"

Brianna arched a perfectly plucked brow. "There was a dress code?" She glowered at the scene around them. "I don't see why we have to do this."

"You *wanted* to come."

Brianna sighed. "I wanted to spend time with you. I mean, we never see one another. It's like we're not even living together. I see Mom more than I see you, and she lives a half hour away! What I had in mind was a mani-pedi, not a mud party with stinky old Wilson in the middle of the damn wilderness."

"This is hardly the wilderness," Claire scoffed, then loaded her own hook with a mealworm. "Now go farther down—you're too close to me for us both to cast."

Grumbling, Brianna picked her way over some rocks farther down the bank. "How long do we have to stay out here?" she called.

"Bree, really!"

Brianna held up a hand in concession. "Okay, okay. I'm sorry. Let's fish. I want to spend time together."

Claire smiled and cast her line. "Thanks." She began reeling it in a little at a time, dragging the mealworm across the bottom of the river, hoping to draw the attention of any bass lingering nearby.

"But you owe me a mani-pedi," Brianna shot back.

Claire rolled her eyes. She reeled the line back in and cast again. Another breeze swept across her bare calves. The temperature had been hovering between fifty and fifty-five degrees all morning. It would warm up as the day went on, but Octobers in Sacramento meant cooler mornings. Claire didn't care. It felt good to be outside.

She glanced back at Brianna about to cast and noticed the overhanging limbs of a tree above her sister's head. "Bree, wait. Don't cast there. Your line will get—"

Between the gurgle of the river and the rush of cars passing over their heads, Brianna must not have heard her. Or maybe she did and just ignored the warning because she cast high, and her line got caught in the tree overhead.

"Oh, for fuck's sake," Brianna griped, yanking hard on the rod. The fishing line pulled taut, completely snarled in the mass of branches.

Claire rested her rod on the bank and went over to where Brianna stood, pulling the line like she was in a game of tug-of-war with the tree. Claire put her hand on Brianna's forearm. "Stop," she said. "You won't get it down. I've got to cut the line."

"What about my hook?" Brianna said, crestfallen. She didn't really enjoy nature, but she also didn't like to fail at anything. She may have protested the entire morning, but Claire knew that Brianna fully intended to fish—and probably wouldn't be satisfied until she caught the biggest fish in the river.

"I'll tie you a new one," Claire said, patting the left breast pocket of her fishing vest. "I've got a whole box of extras right here."

Brianna groaned but Claire noticed the smile fighting to burst forth from the corners of her mouth. "Oh my God, you're like a real-deal fisherman. Fisher person. Whatever. You really love this, don't you?"

"I do. It helps with my anxiety. Now hold the rod." Beaming, Claire extracted her Leatherman tool from the side pocket of her cargo shorts. She loved the thing and used it frequently when fishing. Though it fit easily in her pocket, the multitool was fitted with different types of knives, screwdrivers, pliers, and a number of other features she had yet to find a use for. Reaching overhead, she used it to cut the line.

Brianna pointed to the tool as she handed Claire her rod. "Isn't that Connor's?"

Without looking at her sister, Claire nodded. Even after all this time, just the mention of his name caused a small ache in the pit of her stomach. His face flashed into her mind. Those blue eyes—her perpetual oasis in a broken, damaged world. Sense in a world of senselessness.

She squeezed her eyes closed and snapped them open again, trying to rid him from her mind. It didn't work. It never did.

Connor Parks was a detective with Sacramento's Office of Investigations, formerly known as the Major Crimes Unit. He had been instrumental in solving Claire's cold abduction case. It was, in large part, the connection between them that had given Claire the courage to finally escape her abductor. They had dated for a few years after Claire's return.

"How long have you had that?" Brianna asked as Claire slipped it back into her pocket. Her fingers worked nimbly to tie a new hook onto Brianna's line.

"When's the last time you guys tried to get us back together?"

Brianna put a hand to her chest, batting her eyes in feigned innocence. "Me?"

Claire raised a brow. "Yes, you. All of you. Mom, Dad, Tom."

Brianna cast her eyes downward and jammed her hands into the pockets of her shorts. "We can't help ourselves," she mumbled.

Claire laughed loudly. "I know!"

Brianna met Claire's eyes. "We love Connor."

Claire sighed. "I know." *I do too*, she almost said aloud.

A moment passed in silence. Claire handed Brianna her rod back. "Last year, when we went on the family fishing trip, and you ambushed me by bringing Connor along, he gave it to me."

Brianna thrust a hip out. "He *gave* that to you?"

Claire matched her sister's pose. "Yes. He did. How do you even know it was his?"

Brianna rolled her eyes. "How could you forget how excited he was about it? Mom got one for him, one for Tom, and one for Dad. It was that first Christmas after—" She faltered. It had been five years since Claire had been reunited with her family after being held captive by a pedophile for ten years, but Brianna still had trouble talking about it.

"After I came home," Claire said pointedly.

"Yes," Brianna said. "Don't you remember the three of them doing those dumb poses by the tree, all lined up, flexing their arms and holding their Leatherman tools?"

Claire smiled even though the thought pained her. She did remember. The photo was still tucked into her bedroom mirror—only, for the last few years, Connor had remained covered by the edge of another photo.

"Yeah," she said. "I remember."

She looked away from her sister. She reached into her pocket and pulled the Leatherman out again. Brianna caught Claire's hand and turned it so that the tool rested in Claire's open palm. Brianna traced the handle with an index finger. "Besides, Connor cut a notch here so he could tell his from Dad's and Tom's."

Claire stared at the tool, a lump growing in her throat. "Dammit," she muttered, although she hadn't meant to say it out loud. This was supposed to be a nice day. Fun, relaxing. She couldn't stop the tears from stinging her eyes. Brianna wrapped Claire's fingers around the tool and relinquished Claire's hand. She put her rod on the ground and pulled Claire into a hug. Sighing, Claire nestled her head against her sister's neck. She would never get tired of her family's affection after having been deprived of it for so long.

Brianna waited a long moment before asking, "What happened?"

It was the one thing Claire never talked about. She had told her sister all the horrible things that had happened to her in captivity, but she could never bring herself to talk about why things hadn't worked out between her and Connor. She disentangled from Brianna and wiped her eyes with the heel of her hand. With the other hand, she deposited the Leatherman back into her shorts pocket. "I couldn't—we couldn't—"

She took another step back from her sister and threw her arms into the air. "Men don't like having sex with women who cry," she blurted.

Immediately, she thought of the man who had kept her prisoner for all those years, of all the times she'd cried and begged him to stop.

6

"Well, normal men don't," she added. "We couldn't have sex. I always started crying, and I couldn't stop. Connor said he would wait as long as I needed, but I couldn't do that to him."

She met Brianna's eyes. They were frozen on her. Brianna's entire body was stock-still like she'd encountered a deer in the woods, and the slightest movement might send it running off.

"I don't know if I'll ever be ready for sex. You know, real sex."

Brianna let out a breath, her posture relaxing somewhat. "But, Claire," she said carefully. "You've had sex with men."

"It wasn't the same."

Brianna's mouth twitched, a snicker fighting to stay hidden. "Not even with Too-Concerned Todd?"

Claire raised an eyebrow. "Brianna," she admonished.

Brianna rushed over to Claire and shook her lightly by the shoulders. She thrust her neck forward and peered into her face with wide eyes. "Are you okay? Are you feeling okay? Is this okay?" she teased.

Claire brushed Brianna's hands away, shaking her head but trying not to laugh.

Brianna smirked. "And don't even get me started on Comb-Over Charlie."

Claire had dated two men since she and Connor parted ways. Both had been incredibly kind, but very ill equipped to deal with her past. The chemistry was nil, and it didn't help that the Fletchers ridiculed them mercilessly. The would-be relationships were doomed from the first date.

Claire sighed. "When I slept with them, I wasn't really—I didn't—I wasn't there. I shut down. It was like I was out of my body. I felt nothing, emotionally and physically."

Brianna grimaced. "Claire, I'm sorry."

Claire waved a hand and retrieved her own fishing rod. "It's okay. That was my coping mechanism all those years. After I'd been raped so many times"—Claire saw Brianna flinch at the word, but went on—"I learned how to disconnect. To remove myself mentally from the act."

Brianna drew a deep breath. "Go on," she said.

"With Connor, it's real. It means something. I'm really there when I'm with him. I feel everything."

Brianna swallowed, the pale skin of her throat quivering. "Isn't that a good thing?"

Claire shrugged. "Well, yeah, I guess. I mean, I want to be present when I'm with him, but I can't do certain things without thinking about—" *Without thinking about how damaged I am.* She sighed again, shoulders slumped. "I may never be able to have a sexual relationship with a man. A normal one."

Brianna put one hand on her own hip and, with the other, poked Claire's shoulder with her index finger. Her blue eyes darkened. "What happened to you is in the past, Claire. It's over. The person who hurt you is gone, but you are not. Don't let him take this from you. Not one more thing."

Claire opened her mouth to speak, but the sound of car horns blaring and the squeal of tires froze her. She turned and looked up at the I-5 overpass. Wilson barked.

They couldn't see anything from where they stood, not even the roofs of passing cars, but the clap of an impact followed by the sounds of metal screaming and glass shattering seemed to shake the ground beneath their feet.

"Oh my God," Brianna murmured. "Is that an—"

The concrete guardrail of the overpass shattered; huge chunks of it launched out into view along with the black undercarriage of a vehicle that revealed itself to be a red SUV as it sailed over their heads toward the river.

CHAPTER THREE

"You want to get a what?" Connor asked. He leaned back in his desk chair and laced his hands behind his head, studying his colleague.

"A forensic odontologist," Stryker repeated. He waved several pieces of paper in the air. "It's a forensic dentist who studies bite marks." He thrust the pages at Connor. "There's one in Southern California who's available to help us out with the Strangler case."

Connor took them and glanced at what appeared to be a curriculum vitae for Stryker's forensic odontologist of choice, then put the CV on his desk and looked again at his friend, who was worrying the knot of his tie, loosening and tightening it. "The coroner's word isn't good enough for you? He says the bite marks on all four victims were from the same person, right? So why do you need an otologist?"

"A forensic odontologist. Well, I'm saying if the case goes to trial. I mean, this is serious shit. It's not every day I get assigned to lead a serial killer task force."

Connor laughed. "Yeah, no shit."

Stryker loosened his tie again. Connor stood and gave Stryker a pat on the shoulder. "Stop fucking with your tie. You look fine. Let's do this briefing before you strangle yourself."

Stryker rolled his eyes but pulled his hands away from his throat. He put them at his sides, but Connor saw him clenching and unclenching them into fists as they walked side by side through Sacramento's

Office of Investigations, headed to a conference room where Stryker was about to give his first briefing as a task force commander.

Connor had known Stryker for over ten years. He was a good friend, a good man, and a damn good detective. Connor had no doubt he'd be an excellent task force leader but convincing Stryker of that was another matter. "All I'm saying," Connor said, "is I don't think you need to start throwing experts at this case until you've got a suspect. Getting a forensic odontologist is not going to solve this case. Good old-fashioned police work is what you need. Run down the leads, work the evidence, talk to the witnesses. That's what you're good at. Well, that and your knitting."

Stryker was so tense he didn't even respond to Connor's lame attempt at humor. Normally, Stryker had more bravado than a Vegas act. Come to think of it, he hadn't said *fuck you* to Connor once all day.

What was the world coming to?

As if on cue, Stryker stopped in the hall and turned to Connor, his brown eyes dark pools of worry. "Oh shit. I called in an FBI profiler. He'll be here tomorrow. Do you think I should call him off?"

"Stryke," Connor said. "You need an FBI profiler right now. You don't need a forensic dentist. Now let's go. Everyone's waiting."

Captain Danny Boggs had poked his head out of the conference room and was beckoning the two of them. "You girls gonna make out in the hallway all goddamn day or can we start this briefing?"

His stern look lasted until Stryker crossed the threshold. He grasped the younger detective's shoulder and squeezed, giving him a gentle shove into the room. He winked at Connor and pulled the door closed behind them.

The room was packed with bodies. Plainclothes detectives, uniformed officers, public-relations people, FBI liaisons, and a few investigators from the Sacramento sheriff's office. Someone had opened the windows but it didn't help. The air in the room was hot and close. Connor could smell a strange mixture of sweat, cologne, and perfume.

Stryker pushed his way to the front of the room. Connor stood by the door, fully intending to be the first one out until three more officers squeezed into the room, pushing him farther inside.

At the front of the room, Stryker held up the day's issue of the *Sacramento Bee*. In huge black letters, the headline screamed, "Soccer Mom Strangler Strikes Again." Below that were grainy photos of the first three victims. At press time, they hadn't yet gotten a photo of Ellen Fair, the fourth victim, but Connor would bet his house that if he checked the *Bee's* website right then, they would have found one, lifted from one of the woman's social media accounts, no doubt, once they confirmed that they had the right Ellen Fair.

"This is today's paper," Stryker said, his voice hard, all business now. His nervousness vanished. He looked like the bulky, chrome-headed nightclub bouncer he usually resembled. "'Soccer Mom Strangler' wasn't my first choice, but I didn't get a say in the matter. The press is whipping the city into a frenzy right now—with good reason. As most of you know, a forty-one-year-old woman named Ellen Fair was found strangled to death in her minivan in Pocket last night. She's the fourth victim in almost six months. Based on the evidence—four victims, all women between the ages of thirty-two and forty-three, all mothers of young children and all owners of minivans, killed in exactly the same way—we believe that we have a real live serial killer, and he shows no signs of slowing down. Right now I need all hands on deck running down every lead we've got so we can catch this guy before he kills again."

CHAPTER FOUR

The vehicle bobbed in front of Claire and Brianna. It was a large SUV, red with tinted windows along the back. They stared at it for what seemed like an eternity. The world had gone silent for Claire. She looked at Brianna, who was saying something, and then at Wilson, who stood at the river's edge, barking, though she couldn't hear him. Her limbs felt thick and heavy. Even her head seemed to swivel on her neck in slow motion as she turned back to look at the SUV just as it began to sink, its front end bobbing down into the water and not coming back up. Beyond it, the Jibboom Street Bridge loomed, one of its massive concrete pillars directly in the path of the vehicle, which was being carried by the current.

Then the world rushed back at her like a cold slap to the face. Claire threw her rod to the ground and ran. Her boots splashed in the water, sending a cold spray up her bare legs. She darted past Wilson, who kept barking loudly, and dove into the water. Her arms and legs were pumping before she even had a chance to register the cold. Her boots pulled like lead weights against her legs. Should she have torn them off? Too late now. Even fighting them, it took her only seconds to come up on the rear of the vehicle, which remained above the water. She peered inside but couldn't make anything out. She paddled up to the next set of windows—the back seat, passenger side.

The girl who stared back at her couldn't have been older than six. Her pale, round face was framed by blonde hair cropped in a pixie cut. Her brown eyes were wide with fear. Claire and the girl stared at each other for a frozen moment. As it had on the riverbank, time seemed to stop. Then the girl reached a hand up and pressed it against the window. Her mouth formed the word *help*.

Claire's ice-cold fingers tried the door handle—to no avail. The girl pounded on the window, two hands this time. "Locked," she said. She gestured down, where Claire could see her struggling with the door handle on the inside.

"The windows," Claire yelled.

The girl appeared to be working on the buttons that would unlock the door or lower the window, but nothing happened.

Claire couldn't see if there was anyone else in the vehicle. The sun's glare made it impossible to see behind Peyton. She pulled herself to the front passenger-side door. That door wouldn't open either. Inside the car, the seat was empty. In the driver's seat slumped a heavyset blonde woman. Her arms lay slack at her sides. Her head rested against the steering wheel. Claire banged against the window, shouting, but the woman didn't respond. Water had already begun to fill the front of the vehicle as the SUV continued to lower into the river, covering the passenger-side seat and the driver's lap.

The girl climbed into the passenger's seat and tried the door handle, the locks, the window.

Nothing happened.

The girl's pale face reddened. Tears streaked her cheeks. She looked right at Claire. "Locked," she said again, the word silent from inside the sealed car.

"Childproof," Claire said. "There's an unlock button on the driver's-side door."

That had to be it. Unless some mechanism had been damaged when the SUV crashed through the guardrail and off the side of the overpass.

Claire had been bested by the damn thing herself after her return from captivity. She and her mother had been arguing as her mother drove her home from a therapy session. Claire had gotten so angry that she tried to get out of the car the moment her mother stopped. But she couldn't. She couldn't even roll the window down.

The girl inside the SUV looked over at the unconscious driver, then turned to try to rouse her. Claire moved again toward the back of the car. From her periphery, she saw that the Jibboom Street Bridge had come up much more quickly than she anticipated. As she scrambled to the driver's side, the passenger's side of the vehicle slammed into one of its pillars, stopping there. The current kept it wrapped around the pillar.

Claire was moving toward the driver's window when the bright pastel colors of a baby toy inside caught her eye. It dangled from the upright handle of an infant car seat. The hood was pulled over part of the rear-facing seat. Claire couldn't tell if there was an infant in the seat or not, but she could see three other children in the vehicle. A boy sat behind the driver. Stunned, he stared blankly ahead. He looked only slightly younger than the girl. In the seats behind him were two identical girls. One was unconscious, head lolling against the window, mouth open, eyes at half-mast. The other sobbed, her face red and twisted in pain or fear, or both.

"Oh my God," Claire gasped. She froze, hanging on to the ineffectual door handle, staring at the children.

If there was indeed an infant in the vehicle, then that was five children. There were five children in the vehicle.

She felt herself separate—her consciousness breaking away from her body, which wasn't able to hold her panic. It hadn't happened to her in nearly a decade. Not since her abductor held her prisoner in a desolate shack in the woods, torturing her in ways that no human being should have to endure. She'd gotten past that. She'd gotten through the rest of her captivity, her escape and recovery whole, taking things as they came—even panic.

But now she floated above the river, watching the SUV sink into the water as her panicked body pressed its face against the unyielding window, trying to figure out how she was going to get five children out of the vehicle and to safety.

"No," she said, not sure if it was the Claire in the sky or the Claire in the water who spoke.

"No," she repeated. She wouldn't do this. She would not separate from herself. Her abductor was gone and Claire was free. She needed to be present for every second of this. She knew what she was capable of. She could do this.

"No!" The voice this time was her body's—joined now with her consciousness. She snapped back, and the jolt sent her scrambling to the driver's-side window. The woman was coming to, responding finally to the girl's pushes, pokes, and screams. The water was almost to the woman's throat. The impact of the vehicle on the pillar worried Claire—she didn't know how badly the children were injured—but the pillar was now giving them precious seconds, keeping the SUV from sinking too quickly.

Dazed, the woman's head rose. She looked around slowly, not seeming to see Claire or the girl on the other side of her. By her second pan of her surroundings, the reality of the situation seemed to hit her, her brown eyes growing sharp and scared. She looked at the girl and, in one movement, pushed her away, sending her into the rising water. Claire's stomach plummeted. She watched the girl's head disappear under the water, but the girl quickly emerged, gasping. Thankfully, she moved once more to the back seat. The driver turned back and looked at Claire.

Claire motioned to the panel on the inside of the door. "Unlock it," she shouted.

The woman stared. Her eyes were clear and alert. She was lucid. Claire could tell by the terror in her face. Claire recognized the emotion. She hadn't encountered it in many years, but she knew it well. She also knew fear, panic, desperation, and anxiety. But this was something entirely different.

The woman had been terrorized.

And she knew exactly what she was doing.

Claire pointed to the locks again. "The kids," she shouted. "We need to get the kids out. Unlock the doors and windows. Now! We don't have much time. Unlock the doors!"

The woman met her eyes, desperation in every terrified line of her face. "No," she said.

As the water rose to the woman's chin, she kept her eyes on Claire's. Then she slid down in the seat, submerging her head in the water.

Claire slapped a palm against the window. "No!" she screamed.

But the woman opened her mouth wide and drew in great lungfuls of water. Her eyes bulged as her body responded to her drowning. She fought it then, her arms and legs flailing, body convulsing, face contorted in pain.

"Son of a bitch," Claire shrieked.

She turned away. She couldn't watch. Her consciousness tried to separate from her body again as visions of the last time she'd watched a woman die flooded her brain.

"No," she said, although she couldn't be sure what she was saying no to anymore—the separating, the old images, or the fact that the desperate woman before her had just chosen to take her own life with five children locked in her vehicle.

The SUV was sinking deeper into the water. Claire had to do something. There was no way the girl would be able to get past the woman's convulsing body to take the child-resistant locks off. As the top of the vehicle came into view, Claire noticed the sunroof. She fought to get herself and her insanely heavy boots onto the roof and peered down into the sunroof, balancing precariously on all fours. She could see the top of the girl's head facing the front of the SUV. Claire observed her lifting her small hands over her head, working at something out of Claire's view. The sunroof buttons, no doubt. Of course, they didn't work.

The water was inching up over the bottom of the infant seat now. Claire could hear the screams of the other children, muffled though they were. With both palms, she smacked the sunroof's glass. The girl looked up at her. "Get away from the window!" Claire yelled.

The girl understood. She expertly unhooked the car seat from its base and moved off to the side with it. First, Claire tried standing like a surfer, arms extended to keep her balance as she stomped on the glass with the heel of her boot. After her third attempt, she nearly tumbled into the water. She lay on her back, scooted herself into position, then with arms wide to grip the cargo racks on either side, raised her leaden boots high and slammed her heels down as hard as she could onto the window.

"Come on," she screamed. Tears stung her eyes, frustration tensing every muscle in her body. "Goddammit!"

For a split second, the question flashed in her mind: *What if I can't get them out?* But she shook it away. She was not going to watch five children die before her eyes.

She kicked the window again and again. Her arms and shoulders ached. The muscles in her legs burned. Her feet were numb. The Leatherman tool dug mercilessly into her hip.

The Leatherman tool.

She flopped onto her stomach like a landed fish, fumbling to pull it from her shorts pocket with numb fingers. It was small enough. She needed pinpoint force against the pane of glass. She flipped the Leatherman so the point of the Phillips-head screwdriver was out. Rising to her knees, she used both hands to bring the point down onto the window. After several tries, a small crack could be heard above the muffled screaming of the children, the movement of the river, and Claire's own labored breath. Then fine spider-vein cracks traveled from the center of the glass outward. She brought the Leatherman down a few more times, and more cracks webbed the glass. Pocketing the tool, she gripped the roof rack again and brought her heels down once more. This time the glass gave way, falling into the interior of the car in one malleable sheet of cracked glass.

Already ahead of her, the girl inside had begun unbuckling the other children, and they gathered in a knot beneath the open sunroof. Claire lifted the boy out first and set him down on the roof, what little of it remained above water. He too was blond, and tears streamed from his dark eyes. "I want my mommy," he whimpered as Claire instructed him to hold on to one of the cargo racks.

The girl handed her the car seat next. Inside it was an infant—a boy judging by his blue dinosaur-covered shorts. He stared at her silently, his little hands in his mouth. He gnawed with his gums, saliva dripping down his chin. She placed him next to the boy and put the boy's other hand on the infant-seat handle. "I need you to hold on to this while I get the girls out. Can you do that?" The boy nodded.

Claire pulled each one of the girls out—the girl who had helped her was last. Claire held on to her once she was free of the sunroof. She smiled down at the girl, trying to look as reassuring as she could. "What's your name?"

"Peyton," the girl mumbled.

"Peyton, you did a great job in there."

The girl looked forlornly at the sunroof. The water was nearly to the top. "My mom?" she said.

Claire's smile turned to a grimace. She shook her head and squeezed Peyton to her. "I'm so sorry, sweetie."

She looked at the other two girls, both with thick brown hair in braids, curly tendrils surrounding their faces. Twins. They clung to each other. The one who had been unconscious in the vehicle had a large gash on her leg. Claire looked beyond them to the shore and almost wept with relief. Several people had made their way to the bank from the bridges. Two men were swimming out toward them and another was on the bank, pulling his shoes off.

She looked down at Peyton. "Let's get out of here."

CHAPTER FIVE

Stryker brought up the PowerPoint presentation he'd prepared for the Soccer Mom Strangler briefing. Near the door, Captain Boggs flicked the lights off. In the back, several people moved to lower the miniblinds, plunging the room into semidarkness. Stryker moved his fingers across the tablet before him and brought the first slide up on the white screen.

A blonde woman in her midthirties beamed at them. Two young boys clung to each of her legs. Her hands rested on their backs. They stood in front of a mustard-yellow single-level ranch home. The woman was large breasted and curvy.

"This is Hope Strauss," Stryker said. "Age thirty-six, mother of two young boys, ages four and six. She lived in the Pocket area. She was our first victim. Her murder took place in April. She had taken her children to Parkway Oaks Park for a playdate with a friend. She left her phone in her minivan, so she left her children in her friend's care and went back to her minivan to get it. She did not return. After about a half hour—the other mother is not sure how long it was, since she was playing with the kids—this same friend finds Hope Strauss dead in her minivan."

Stryker swiped his tablet and, this time, Hope Strauss appeared in death, partially clothed and lying across the first rear seat of her minivan. Her shorts and underwear had been torn from her body, her tank top and bra had been pushed up over her breasts. The killer had left her upper body partially propped against the far smoke-glassed window. One of her arms was flung over her head, the hand twisted in the seat belt. One of her legs lay straight, the other bent at the knee, her foot flat on the floor. Her eyes were fixed, staring glassily at the ceiling. There were deep-purple bruises around her throat and angry red bite marks on her breasts.

The silence in the room grew heavier with each close-up that Stryker swiped across the screen. "Hope Strauss was sexually assaulted. There was evidence of one type of semen in her vagina. Tears and abrasions consistent with rape. She was manually strangled, and, as you can see, the perpetrator bit her three times on the breasts. There were hundreds of different prints in the minivan. Most could be accounted for by working our way through her family and friends. There are two fingerprints that we cannot match to anyone in her life, but we can't say for certain that they belong to the perpetrator. We ran them through AFIS and got nothing."

He swiped the tablet again and another woman appeared on the screen. Her hair was longer and more sandy brown than Hope Strauss's blonde locks. This woman smiled from the driver's seat of a vehicle, giving a thumbs-up to the camera. "Sofia Hapi," said Stryker. "Mother of a fourteen-year-old girl and a seven-year-old boy. Resided in Midtown, which is where she was killed. Almost the same story. Ms. Hapi was at her son's soccer practice, which was in September, before the season started. She smoked, so she snuck off to her vehicle for a cigarette and did not return."

The death photos were nearly identical to those of Hope Strauss except for the interior of her vehicle, which was beige instead of gray. Stryker swiped through her death photos a little more quickly. "She too was raped, strangled, and bitten on the breasts. No prints this time, looks like he hastily wiped the vehicle down—everything was smeared. The same with Faith Stine."

He swiped to another photo of a smiling, curvy blonde woman. Her hair was pulled back in a tight ponytail as she stood beside a young boy outside of the Sacramento Zoo.

"Faith Stine, victim three, was the mother of a five-year-old boy. Lived in North Natomas. Same MO. The perpetrator attacked her while she was alone at her minivan during her son's soccer game. The game was in North Natomas. This happened two weeks ago. Stine was raped, strangled, and bitten on the breasts. We've got bite impressions, DNA, but no prints."

Another round of graphic crime scene photos—these so similar to the first two sets that they were almost interchangeable. Then Stryker pulled up the photo of the last victim, introducing them to Ellen Fair, who had also been at her daughter's soccer game, this time in Pocket, when she was murdered in her SUV after having returned to it alone for some minor item. Fair had had brown hair, but she had the same figure as the other women, and she had been raped and murdered in exactly the same way as the women before her. Again, the perpetrator had made a halfhearted effort to wipe prints away, even though he had left his DNA all over the crime scene. For their purpose, it really didn't matter that he had wiped his prints away, because they'd be able to match him via DNA and dental impressions—it would just take longer. As Stryker went over the details of Ellen Fair's murder, Connor swallowed, his throat dry.

Stryker lingered on an up-close photo of Fair's breasts where the perpetrator had bitten her hard enough to break the skin. "The coroner has concluded that the bite marks on each victim came from the same perpetrator, so we're looking for one guy. We had been keeping the biting from the press. Unfortunately, the press caught wind of it this past week, which means we have a leak. Not sure if it's here or somewhere else, but if I find out someone in this room is leaking sensitive information to the press, I'm going to have your ass. We need to catch this guy. Yesterday. And we need all the help we can get, so I expect everyone to keep their fucking mouths shut about this case. No one but me talks to the press from here on out.

"I want four teams," Stryker continued as he swiped to the last slide in his presentation, photos of all four victims side by side, as they were in life. Smiling, happy, hopeful. Connor's stomach burned.

"Each team will be assigned to a victim," Stryker went on. "You'll run down the leads. Talk to every person who was on the scene the day of the murders. Talk to every person who lives in that area. Every person. Even kids if their parents will consent. Reinterview everyone who's already been talked to. No stone unturned. We're putting cameras and undercovers on every soccer match in the city until further notice. I've got someone compiling a list of every youth soccer player in this city and cross-referencing to see if any families were at all three games, in case this is a relative or friend of one of these kids. The press has a tip-line number they'll be running on every newscast for the foreseeable future. Someone will be manning that number 24-7 until we catch this guy. We've got to shake down every registered sex offender within five miles of each crime scene. Tomorrow we'll have an FBI profiler here to review our evidence and give us an idea of who we're looking for. As soon as he is ready to present his profile, we'll all be back here to get briefed on that. Team leaders—you know who you are—you will check in with me every hour from six a.m. until eleven p.m."

A collective grumble went up across the room. Stryker extended a finger, pointing toward the mass of bodies in the center of the room. "Yes. Every hour, every day. Those are everyone's absolute minimum hours, every day, until this piece of shit is found. Now, on the conference room table to your left, you will find boxes of files on each victim. Everything you need to know will be in there. Teams, get your boxes and get to work. Thank you."

Connor saw Captain Boggs nod with satisfaction in the doorway as he watched Stryker conclude the meeting. Boggs suppressed a grin—there wasn't much that satisfied him. Just as he was about to turn to hunt up Stryker, one of the Office of Investigations' younger detectives, Matt O'Handley, stepped past Boggs and poked his head in. He panned the room until he found Connor.

"Parks," he called.

Everyone else had moved toward the file boxes, but Connor headed toward the door where Stryker and Boggs now stood. "What's up?" Connor asked O'Handley.

"It's about Claire."

CHAPTER SIX

By the time they got all the children to shore and in the capable hands of paramedics, the riverbank was teeming with police officers, emergency responders, bystanders who had stopped to help, and even a few members of the press. What had been an oasis of peace only an hour ago was now complete chaos.

Claire left Brianna talking to a uniformed police officer while she slogged her way back to the Jeep with Wilson. She was soaking wet, her boots still three times as heavy as they'd been before she had gone into the water. She knew she had a blanket in her own vehicle. It was the one she put over her back seat so Wilson didn't shed all over the place. She would smell like wet dog but she didn't care. She was shivering, even though the sun was now high in the sky and the temperature had increased.

Wilson followed close beside her, not stopping to explore the myriad smells she knew were tempting him. She had her head down, concentrating hard on each step so that she wouldn't think about all the memories being in that river had brought back. She wanted to get in her Jeep and drive home, retreat to the quiet of her house. It was tempting, but she knew that like Brianna, she would have to speak to the police. She would have to tell someone about the driver.

Claire was so focused on her boots that she collided with a wall of a man, bouncing back away from him and nearly falling flat on her behind. Firm hands gripped her shoulders. She looked up, an apology on her tongue.

It was Connor.

"Claire," he said. "You're okay."

She stared up into his blue eyes. She knew the look—knew all of his looks. He was relieved to see her upright and unharmed. He looked her over as Wilson tried unsuccessfully to get his attention. He had grown a beard since she'd last seen him. It suited him.

The swell of emotion that she'd been pushing back since she saw the children in the car hit her hard and fast, propelling her into his arms like she was some kind of jumping spider.

"Whoa!" he exclaimed, but caught her and folded her into his arms, his touch, as always, firm but gentle. He held her close, and she pressed the length of her wet body against his, reveling in the feeling of calm that flooded through her. She had forgotten about this. How he could make her feel safe, how his embrace could keep the memories at bay.

His chin nuzzled her scalp, his facial hair catching on her unruly curls. She inhaled deeply, smelling him instead of the river, instead of fear and panic and death. She could tell by the smell of coffee, pastries, and the hint of stale sweat covered by copious amounts of deodorant that he had likely been working for a few days straight with little or no sleep.

"You okay?" he murmured into her ear.

She shook her head but said "Yes" anyway.

Why shouldn't she be okay? She'd just saved a bunch of kids from drowning. But the image of the suicidal driver's face and her silent refusal to spare her own children wouldn't leave Claire.

She kept picturing the woman's mouth forming the word *no*.

Claire knew she should end the embrace with Connor. She had sent him away from her. She told herself to let go, to back away, but she couldn't.

Lucky for her, Wilson could no longer be ignored. He jumped up, pawing at Connor's arms, emitting a needy whine that matched Claire's internal cries. Connor let go of her and bent to pet Wilson, working over the dog's back and sides until Wilson settled, swooning, against his legs. Connor stood and looked at her again, a half smile on his face. Claire motioned to his suit, which bore an imprint of her. "I'm so sorry," she said. "Your suit . . ."

Connor looked down at the wet spots and laughed. "It's okay," he said. "It'll dry."

Claire was vaguely aware of someone approaching them from behind Connor, although she kept her eyes on him. Then she heard Stryker's voice. "You found her?'"

Stryker, who had been trotting, pulled up short beside the two of them. He gave Claire a once-over, his usual hard features softening into a smile when he realized she was all right. "You're okay," he said. He touched her arm and leaned in to kiss her cheek.

Claire smiled at him. She had always adored Bobby Stryker. He looked and acted the part of pit bull, but beneath all that was a whole lot of soft and fuzzy. "Hi, Stryke," she said.

"I saw your sister," Stryker said. "She's still talking to the uniforms. We heard over the scanner that there was an accident. Someone said you two were here, so we came to—"

A female voice interrupted him. "Bobby Stryker, don't you have a serial killer task force to run?"

The woman came from behind Claire. Given the notebook in her hand, the gun at her waist, and her Spartan clothes—black slacks and a white polo shirt—Claire pegged her as a detective. She looked to be in her midthirties: thin but ample chested, tall for a woman, her brown hair pulled back tight in a ponytail. She smiled sunnily, her face lighting up even more when she noticed Connor. "Hey, Parks," she said.

Connor nodded in her direction.

"Stand down, Webb," Stryker said. "It so happens I'm in command of the task force as we speak." He held up his cell phone. "This is my command center right here."

The woman chuckled. EMTs wheeling an empty gurney back to their ambulance passed by them, and the woman moved out of their way, shifting so she was next to Connor. She raised a brow at Stryker. "Mobile command, huh?"

Stryker nodded and used his phone to motion toward Claire. "Miss Fletcher here is an old friend. I came to make sure she was okay. Claire, this is Detective Jade Webb."

The detective stuck her hand out and Claire shook it numbly. "Miss Fletcher—just who I'm looking for!"

Before Detective Webb could say more, Stryker cut in. "What've you got on this?"

Webb flipped a page in her notebook. "We received a few calls about a woman in an SUV on the I-5 driving erratically and way too fast. The SUV collided with two vehicles up top." Webb pointed toward the overpass. "Four fatalities. The SUV crashed through the guide rail and into the river. We know there was an adult female driving with five children in the vehicle. According to witnesses, Miss Fletcher here went into the river and pulled the children out of the vehicle with some people who had been driving by and stopped to help. All the kids were pulled out of the river alive and taken to Mercy General for evaluation.

"The vehicle is registered to Leah Holloway, a thirty-seven-year-old woman who lives in Pocket. I've already sent uniforms to her home."

"Jesus," Stryker said. "Four fatalities."

"It could have been so much worse," Brianna said, joining the circle. She quickly hugged Connor and introduced herself to Detective Webb. "If Claire hadn't acted so quickly, those kids would be dead. She had to break the glass in the sunroof." Brianna nudged Claire with her elbow. "What did you use, by the way?"

Claire met Connor's eyes. "The Leatherman."

"No shit," Brianna said.

"She wouldn't unlock the doors or windows," Claire went on stiffly.

Detective Webb's brown eyes zeroed in on Claire like a hawk on a small rodent. "She was alive when you got to the car?"

Claire licked her dry lips. She could feel all their eyes on her. She looked down at her boots, then back up into Connor's eyes again. "She was unconscious when I got to the vehicle. I tried the passenger's side first. By the time I got to her window, she had come to. The child safety lock was on. I yelled at her to unlock the vehicle, and she wouldn't do it."

Webb's brow furrowed. "What do you mean she wouldn't? She refused?"

Claire looked at the woman. Webb had put a hand on Connor's arm, balancing as she lifted one of her feet and swiped a large insect from her pant leg. The intimacy of the gesture caught Claire off guard. Connor didn't seem to notice. He kept looking at Claire expectantly.

"Claire?" Brianna prompted.

Claire shook her head briefly, bringing her focus back to Webb's question. "I told her to unlock the car so I could get them all out, and she said no. Then she—she drowned herself. She opened her mouth and purposefully took in the water."

Claire realized she was hugging herself. Brianna wrapped an arm around Claire's shoulders. The three detectives looked momentarily stunned.

"Well," Webb said, flipping pages in her notebook. "That changes things, doesn't it?"

CHAPTER SEVEN

"You've got a mass murderer on your hands," Stryker said to Webb.

Her easy smile had been replaced with hard lines, pursed lips, and a set jaw.

"She was going to kill her own kids?" Brianna said incredulously.

"We're looking at homicide," Webb agreed.

Connor swiped a hand through his hair. His gaze hadn't left Claire.

"What kind of woman tries to kill her own children?" Brianna asked.

A desperate one, Claire thought.

Only Claire had seen Leah Holloway's face, looked into her terror-stricken eyes, and recognized what was there. Claire didn't have children. She had no frame of reference for what it meant to be a mother, let alone what it would take to drive a mother to do what Holloway had that day, but whatever it was—it was bad. Very, very bad.

"Maybe she was mentally unstable," Connor offered.

"Seems a fair bet," Webb said drily.

"More likely drunk," Brianna said.

Stryker shrugged. "Or both."

Webb shook her head as she pulled her cell phone from her pants pocket and punched in a number. "Excuse me," she muttered as she stalked off, phone pressed to her ear.

Brianna's arm fell away from Claire's shoulders. She touched Claire's forearm, her fingers coming away bloodied. "Claire, you're bleeding."

Claire lifted her right arm to see a small gash on the outer side of her wrist. Blood trickled from it. It had been running down her hand and dripping from her index finger.

"Jesus," Connor said. He pulled a tissue from his pocket and pressed it gently against the cut, keeping her arm upright. Claire watched the blood seep through the white tissue. Connor always carried tissues with him, she remembered. His mother had taught him that before she died, that he should always have a tissue on him in case he happened on a person in need of one. It was old-fashioned, but Claire had always loved that about him, and let's face it, it came in handy.

"You might need stitches," Connor remarked.

"It's fine," Claire said. "It's just from the glass in the sunroof."

She concentrated on Connor's warm palms wrapped around her arm. She couldn't feel anything in her body—not the gash, not the wetness, not her aching muscles—yet she knew the next day she would be hurting.

"You really should go to the hospital," Brianna said.

Claire shot her a look. "No hospitals."

Brianna put a hand on her hip. "Claire."

"No. Hospitals," Claire repeated through gritted teeth.

She had spent some time in the hospital after her escape from captivity. They always brought back bad memories, and Claire had had enough for one day.

"Claire," Connor said gently. "Someone has to look at this." He raised one of his hands at her anticipated protest. "But no hospitals, I promise."

Stryker cleared his throat as Webb rejoined them. She pointed toward the incline that led to the overpass. The uniforms had begun cordoning it off to keep the press and other onlookers out. "Your girlfriend is up there," she said to Stryker.

"Oh shit," Stryker said. "Noel?"

"You have more than one?"

Noel Geary was a reporter for KCRA 3. She and Stryker had met five years earlier while Connor was investigating Claire's cold case. Their relationship had moved at a glacial pace, since they both put their careers first. Claire knew that early on they had had several fights because Noel wanted Stryker to give her the scoop on stories involving the police. Claire also knew Stryker was very careful about what he told her, and that it put a strain on things.

Webb looked at Claire. "I'm afraid the cat is already out of the bag. They know a Fletcher got those kids out of the car. They'd like to talk to you."

Claire felt the color drain from her face. "No, Detective Webb," she said firmly. "No press."

"Call me Jade, would you?" she said. She squinted at Claire. "Not even Noel? I mean, you guys were both victims of that guy—"

"We're not friends," Claire said quickly. Before Reynard Johnson abducted Claire, he had struck up a romantic relationship with Noel's mother to gain access to young Noel. While Noel's mother uncovered the abuse and put a stop to it, she didn't turn Johnson in, leaving him free to abduct and victimize Claire for ten long years. During the media frenzy following Claire's escape and Johnson's capture, Noel held more news conferences than a presidential press secretary. Constitutionally incapable of wrapping her mind around the notion that someone could *not* want to be on television, it took the blessed arrival of the next news cycle to put a stop to Noel's incessant requests for Claire to join her in front of the cameras. Claire had wanted to like her for Stryker's sake, but she just couldn't trust her to keep anything Claire might say in confidence and not use it for a story.

Jade sighed. "Okay, well, look, the press isn't going to back off. This woman just killed four people and drove her SUV packed full of kids into a river." She looked toward Stryker. "It will take the heat off the Soccer Mom Strangler investigation at least for a day or two. They could use the break."

Before Claire could open her mouth, Connor exchanged a look with the female detective. "Jade, she's not doing press."

Jade shrugged. "She's a hero, Parks. People could use a story about a hero right about now. How many hero stories do you see on the news where they don't get to interview the hero?"

"I'm not doing it," Claire said.

"She's not doing it," Connor and Stryker said in unison.

Brianna sighed. "For Chrissake, I'll do it."

They all turned to stare at her. She tugged at her brown curls. Since growing her hair out, she did look remarkably similar to her little sister. "You said they know *a* Fletcher did it, which means they don't know for sure it's Claire. The people who helped won't know the difference and if they do, maybe Stryker can talk to them. I'll say it was me."

"No," Stryker said immediately.

"Not a good idea to lie to the press," Jade added. "That will come back to bite us in the ass."

Brianna folded her arms across her thin chest. "Well, then no one is doing press."

Gently, Connor pressed a hand to Claire's lower back, nudging her away from Brianna and the other detectives. "I'm taking Claire to get this cut looked at."

"Parks," Jade implored. "She wouldn't have to say much. Claire?"

"No," Claire said. "No press."

Brianna rolled her eyes. "Come on. Just let me do it. No one will know."

"Oh shit," Stryker said, his eyes drawn to the top of the incline. Claire followed his gaze to see Noel Geary making her way down the riverbank in six-inch heels, her cameraman following her, one hand holding his camera and the other outstretched toward Noel as though to catch her should she fall. Noel's eyes were fixed on the ground ahead of her, probably to avoid mud, Claire thought.

"Who the hell let her down here?" Jade grumbled.

At her lower back, Claire felt Connor press harder, pushing her now up the riverbank, veering away from Noel Geary. "Let's go," he said.

Claire glanced over her shoulder as they walked briskly up the incline. Brianna stood grinning at Stryker and Jade.

CHAPTER EIGHT

Connor drove Claire's Jeep. Wilson sat in the back, his head between them, panting, his tongue hanging out.

"Keep that arm up," Connor instructed.

Claire lifted her arm and peeled back the gauze that Connor had gotten from one of the EMTs on the riverbank. "It's stopped bleeding," she said.

He kept his eyes on the road, driving slowly, more slowly than necessary. She watched him, studying his profile, admiring his new, well-groomed beard. Her first crush. He had been her first real crush. Her only real crush. She'd been attracted to him in spite of all the horrific things that had been done to her. He had wanted her, had been willing to wait for her, had not been afraid of her baggage. He knew every single sordid detail of her past and he wanted her anyway.

And she had pushed him away.

She really was a fucking idiot.

Staring at him, she kept coming back to Detective Webb touching his arm, leaning into him. The touch had been so familiar, almost intimate. She'd told Connor many times to move on. He deserved better. He deserved more. Claire could give him nothing but baggage. Tons and tons of it. More than the cargo hold of a packed international flight. She couldn't even fulfill his most basic needs as a man. But she had never given any real thought to what it would actually mean if he moved on. Had never thought about how it would feel to watch another woman touch him.

Oh God.

Had he kissed Jade Webb? Had they had sex? Did he trail little kisses along her collarbones the way he had always done to Claire? Had Jade been able to do all the things that Claire hadn't?

Connor's quiet laughter broke through her silent panic. He glanced over and met her eyes for a brief moment before turning back to the road. "Claire, Jade and I are just friends."

A hand flew to her chest. A stinging heat enveloped her face. "I didn't—I wasn't—I mean I—" she stammered. "Wait. Was I thinking out loud?"

Even in profile, she could see the grin on his face. "No," he said.

"Then how—"

"I know you, Claire," he explained. "And I'm a detective, remember?"

She humphed and looked away from him, folding her arms over her chest. She tried to think of a witty reply but nothing came.

"Jade and I worked a very big case last year," he said. "We spent a lot of time together. We became good friends. That's all."

"Okay," Claire said. She watched the scenery passing by—hotels and motels along the flat expanse on either side of Jibboom Street, which gave way to the tree-lined banks of the Sacramento River on her left, then downtown Sacramento's high-rise buildings reaching toward the azure sky in the distance. He turned right, away from the I Street Bridge, and got on to I-5, heading south. They were well below the Holloway accident, and the highway was deserted. The northbound side was jammed across all lanes. A gaper delay, no doubt, people staring in horror at the carnage that Leah Holloway had caused on the southbound lanes just a few miles ahead.

An image of Holloway's mouth, opened wide to take in water, flashed across Claire's mind. She gave her head a small shake, as if to rid her brain of the memory. It was easier to think about Connor and Detective Webb than to relive the encounter with Holloway.

She realized Connor had gotten off the highway and was cruising down the wide streets of Midtown. It was where she had first lived after returning from captivity. She had moved in with Brianna, who had an apartment right in the heart of the district. Claire had loved it, loved the energy of it. Things were always in motion. People were everywhere. There were restaurants and coffee shops and many other busy places for her to explore. After ten years in isolation, she couldn't get enough of noise and crowds and near-constant activity. But by the time their lease was up, she had rescued Wilson, and he needed more space and a yard. They had found a lovely Tudor-style house for rent in Land Park, which was only ten or fifteen minutes away from all of Claire's favorite Midtown haunts, including the veterinary clinic she now worked at, which they were getting closer to with each block.

"Where are we going?" she asked.

"Someone needs to look at that arm."

She felt a small tick of anxiety. "You promised no hospitals."

He smiled at her, and her anxiety melted. God, she missed him. "That I did," he agreed.

"Then who's going to look at my arm? I hate doctors too."

Connor laughed. "You like Dr. Corey."

Dr. Corey was Claire's boss. Claire had worked for her all through college. She had helped Claire get into veterinary school. "Dr. Corey is a vet. She's not going to give me stitches."

"True. But her son is a physician's assistant. He's more than qualified to do stitches, and any old sterile environment will do for him."

Claire raised a brow. "You've already texted him, haven't you?"

The Saturday morning office hours were over, but Derrick Corey usually worked Saturday afternoons, sometimes into the evening, watching over the animals that had to stay one or more nights. During the week, he worked for an orthopedic practice. The regular office hours allowed him time on evenings and weekends to help out at his mother's clinic. He waited for them outside of the building, smiling as they pulled up. He was dressed casually in jeans and a T-shirt, his wavy brown hair slicked back with gel. Wilson jumped over Claire to reach him, greeting him eagerly. "Hey, boy," Derrick said, scratching behind the dog's ears. After he let them in and locked the door behind them, he led them past the reception and treatment areas to Dr. Corey's office.

"Sit," he instructed Claire.

She pulled out one of the padded guest chairs and plopped into it.

"Connor said you didn't like exam rooms," Derrick explained.

Connor stood in the doorway, leaning his shoulder against the door frame. A small smile played on his lips, although he pretended not to pay attention to them. Instead, he bent his head to his phone, typing something in every now and then.

"Ow!" Claire exclaimed.

She turned to Derrick, who had positioned himself in a chair directly across from her, their knees touching. He held her wrist between two gloved hands, using one to dab her wound with alcohol-soaked gauze.

Derrick frowned. "Sorry about that. There's really no way to keep it from stinging. So," he said, as he rummaged through the first aid kit he had placed on the desk. "Who was this lady? What's her deal?"

"We're really not sure what her deal is yet," Connor said. "Her name was Leah Holloway. Looks like she lived in Pocket. But her name hasn't been released to the press, so keep it to yourself."

"Of course," Derrick said. He laid Claire's arm across their laps and pointed to it. "You don't need stitches. Steri-Strips and bacitracin should do the trick. We'll cover it up with a piece of gauze to keep the greasy stuff from rubbing off on your clothes."

Claire's shoulders slumped with relief. "Thank goodness," she breathed.

From the door, Connor asked, "Did you or Brianna call your folks?"

"They're on a cruise for two weeks in the Caribbean, but Brianna left them a message."

"How about Mitch? Is he still back East with his daughter?"

Mitch Farrell was a close family friend of the Fletchers and had helped Connor crack Claire's cold case five years earlier. "Yeah," Claire said. "He's in Arlington, Virginia. Brianna talked to him."

"I'm sure this has made national news already," Connor muttered.

Derrick worked quickly and deftly, applying a row of Steri-Strips to the thin four-inch slice on her wrist. "It's sad," he remarked. "Those children. You know, Mrs. Holloway brought their dog in a few months ago. I don't know how many Leah Holloways live in Sacramento, but the Mrs. Holloway we had in here was also from Pocket, so I'm guessing it's the same lady."

Both Claire and Connor's eyes darted to Derrick, but his attention was on bandaging her arm.

"I don't remember her being a client," Claire said.

"No, not a regular client. This was an emergency. Weekend. Her regular vet was closed. It was after hours, but you know my mom, she couldn't say no. I was here, as usual. Mrs. Holloway was pretty distraught. Kids loved that dog."

Connor put his phone away. He folded his arms across his chest, watching Derrick with a slightly raised brow.

"What kind of dog was it?" Claire asked.

"Oh, it was a mutt. A rescue dog. Some kind of collie–German shepherd mix."

Connor said, "What was wrong with it?"

"Somebody poisoned it. Gave it raw meat with Xanax in it. Large dose. Really sad. At least the poor thing didn't suffer for long. But Holloway, oh boy, she was a mess."

Claire glanced at Wilson napping in the corner of Dr. Corey's office. As usual, he had found the one square of sunlight in the room and was passed out in it, snoring loudly. "Of course she was," Claire murmured. She started thinking of Leah Holloway in a slightly different light. Regardless of what the woman had done that morning, it must have been devastating to lose her dog in such a way.

"She said she was going to file a report with the police," Derrick added. "But I don't know if she actually did."

Claire glanced at Connor. He was back on his phone, fingers flying over the tiny keyboard—texting Jade Webb, no doubt. Claire's face flushed—part jealousy and part embarrassment at having been so transparent to him in the car.

"Anyway," Derrick said, taping a piece of gauze over her cut and patting her arm. "I'm glad you're okay. Call if you need me."

"Thanks," Claire and Connor said in unison.

"I'll let you guys out when you're ready." Derrick gave Connor a mock salute on his way out of the office. Alone together, Claire and Connor gazed at each other. Connor dropped his phone into his pocket and made his way across the room. He took the chair Derrick had just vacated, pulling it closer to her, his knees knocking against hers. The proximity made her heart race—not in the usual, anxious way, but in an excited way. Claire put her hands on her thighs and looked down at them. Connor waited. In the corner of the room, Wilson yipped in his sleep. When Claire looked back at Connor, he said, "Tell me about today."

Involuntarily, Claire shuddered. Shoring herself up, she said, "That woman—Connor, I told her to unlock the doors so I could get them out of the car, and she said, 'No.' She knew what she was doing. She killed herself. She was terrified. She was—the last time I saw that look on someone's face, the life was being strangled out of her."

"Sarah?" Connor said, using Claire's name for the girl her abductor had murdered in the woods. It wasn't until Claire had escaped and Sarah's body had been recovered and properly identified that Claire had learned her real name: Miranda Simon.

Claire nodded. The tears came fast and hard—the kind she usually only cried during therapy sessions. A sob shook her whole body.

"Claire," Connor said. He reached for her, taking her face in his hands. He pulled her in until their foreheads touched. She tried to stop the tears, but they came anyway, and Connor wiped some of them away with the pads of his thumbs. Their breath intermingled, and she felt a strong urge to close the distance between their mouths and kiss him.

The vibration of his cell phone made them both jump. He held on to her, but the moment had passed. She reached up and gently pulled his hands away. "You have to get that," she said.

With something between a growl and a sigh, he fished his phone out of his jacket pocket and glared at it. "Captain Boggs," he muttered. He answered, listening momentarily, then uttering a series of "yeahs" and "uh-huhs" and "okays." After about two minutes, he hung up, dropping his phone back into his jacket pocket. He swiped a hand through his hair. "Boggs is pulling me off the Strangler task force and putting me on Holloway. The twins in her car weren't hers—they were her neighbor's kids. And one of the people she killed on the overpass was the mayor's father-in-law."

"My God," Claire said.

Connor grimaced. "Yeah. It's worse than we thought."

She pushed her chair back and stood, calling for Wilson. "I'll drive you back," she said. "Or wherever you need to go."

"Claire, I—"

She touched his face, laid a palm on his bearded cheek. It was softer than she imagined. He looked up at her. She thought about Jade Webb. They'd probably be working the Holloway case together. The thought made her gut clench.

"When you have time," she said, "stop by my place."

CHAPTER NINE

Claire dropped Connor off at Mercy General Hospital where he found Jade waiting inside the ER. He caught her eye as he entered, and her face brightened. "I thought we lost you, Parks."

He shook his head. "Nope, I'm here," he said without enthusiasm.

Jade eyed his suit, which he knew still bore wet spots from Claire's unexpected hug. Connor shifted uncomfortably beneath her gaze. "Don't start," he told her. "I'm here to work."

"Okay," Jade said with what Connor knew was feigned indifference. "Did you get a statement from Miss Fletcher?"

"Of course I—" Connor stopped abruptly. Of course he had not. He had been too busy worrying over her. He could tell from the moment he saw her on the riverbank that the Holloway thing had messed with her mind, upset the delicate balancing act of her recovery. And frankly, as usual, he'd been intoxicated by her. He always thought he was over her until he saw her again. But today had been different. Today there was something decidedly missing—the wall she always put up between them.

Jade's noisy sigh brought him back. She pushed herself off the wall she'd been leaning against and started walking away. "Thought so," she said. "By the way, I got your text about the dog. Had someone at the division pull up the report. Your friend was right. Dog died of Xanax poisoning. Almost three months ago. It was in their yard, so someone either snuck into the yard and gave the dog the meat, or they threw it over the fence. No suspects. No movement."

"Suspicious, though," Connor said as he followed her down a hallway to where two rooms sat side by side, walled in glass. In one of the rooms, Connor saw two gurneys, each holding an identical little girl. Their parents sat between the gurneys, the mother holding the hand of one of the girls, and the father holding the hand of the other.

"Those are the Irvings," Jade said. "Apparently, Mrs. Irving and Leah Holloway were besties. The families live next door to each other. The Irvings' twin girls are six and in the same youth soccer league as Leah Holloway's six-year-old daughter. Docs say the one girl has a concussion and the other a fractured ankle."

Connor studied the girls' faces. They looked exhausted. The curly brown tendrils that had escaped their braids hung limp and stringy from the river, although they'd both long since dried. They each had several Band-Aids on their arms. One girl's eyelids sagged as she fought sleep beneath her mother's watchful eye. The other smiled wanly at something her father said, then looked up and saw them at the window. Connor smiled and gave her a small wave as he followed Jade to the next room, crowded with a man and three kids, one of them a babe in arms.

"That the husband?" Connor asked.

Jade nodded. "Jim Holloway, age forty-two. Those are his and Leah's children."

Jim Holloway was short, stocky, and about thirty pounds overweight. His sandy-brown hair was shaggy and hung in his brown eyes. He wore a moustache and goatee, a green polo shirt, and wrinkled khaki shorts. His eyes were bloodshot. His children were not happy. The infant screamed loudly in Jim's arms, his tiny face nearly purple with rage and indignation. For a man with three kids, Holloway looked very much out of his element. Connor wondered if he was always so inept at handling his kids, or if it was just shock over the news about his wife.

Given what Leah had done that morning, Connor was inclined to give him the benefit of the doubt.

Holloway shifted the baby from one hip to the other as he watched his older son throw a full-blown tantrum on the floor. The boy looked like a miniature version of Jim, sans facial hair. The boy lay face down, little arms and legs pounding against the tile.

"I want my mommy!" he screeched.

Jim held the infant against his chest as he knelt to his other son. He spoke in low tones and touched the boy's head, but it didn't help. He looked helplessly at his daughter, who sat curled into a ball on one of the gurneys, rocking back and forth. She hugged her knees to her chest and looked straight ahead, her gaze blank and far away.

"Peyton!" Jim called, but the girl didn't acknowledge him.

"Word is the guy's mother is on the way. Flying in from Nevada," Jade said.

"I hope so," Connor muttered. Then he headed to the nurses' station. "First things first."

Fifteen minutes later, a nurse was bottle-feeding the extremely hungry baby while the other boy watched *SpongeBob SquarePants* on the television affixed to the wall. It had taken two nurses to get him tucked beneath the covers of one of the gurneys, where he continued to scream and cry until he wore himself out. He watched the television with the vacant expression of someone who had been through a war. Either he would fall asleep for a while, or he would experience a fresh onslaught of tears in a few minutes.

Connor knew Jim Holloway was in shock, but he didn't know how the man could go without scooping the kid up and holding him until he fell asleep.

Jim stepped out of the room and looked around as if he were trying to locate someone in the small but crammed ER.

"Mr. Holloway," Connor said. He and Jade moved toward the man, Jade with her notebook out, Connor ready to take point on questions. The man looked at them dumbly, uncomprehending.

"My mom should be here soon. She's coming from Reno."

"Mr. Holloway, I'm Detective Parks. This is Detective Webb. We need to ask you some questions about your wife."

He seemed to look through them. He put both hands in his hair, rubbing until it stood out in every direction. "My wife," he said, his voice husky. "My wife."

Connor decided to start with the easy stuff. "What time did your wife leave the house this morning?"

Jim shook his head slowly from side to side. "I don't know. She was gone when I woke up. She always takes the kids to soccer. I mean, she doesn't always take Rachel and Mike's kids, but she always takes our kids."

"What time did you wake up?" Jade asked.

He scratched his head. "Don't know. Ten? Ten thirty? I work four to midnight at Ranger Heating Supply, so I get home late and sleep late. Leah was already gone when I got up."

"How old are your kids?" Connor asked.

"Oh. Well, Peyton is six. Hunter is four, and the baby, Tyler, is five months old."

"And it was Peyton's game?" Connor asked.

"Yeah, I guess. I mean yeah. Hunter doesn't play soccer."

"Did Leah always take all of the children to Peyton's games?" Jade asked.

Jim's eyes went to her. "What?"

Jade smiled warmly, using what Connor always thought of as her calming look. "Did Leah ever leave the boys with you on Saturday mornings while she took Peyton to soccer?"

"Oh no," he said. "The kids—you know—they were Leah's thing. She always took them with her."

Connor didn't miss the sour look that crossed Jade's face. "So, Leah was a stay-at-home mom?"

Jim looked momentarily puzzled. "What? No. She works for a radio station. She's in charge of advertising."

"And what do you do at Ranger?" Connor asked.

"I work on an assembly line. We manufacture heating elements."

"So your wife took your three kids and the Irving twins with her sometime before ten a.m. this morning to go to a soccer game?"

Jim nodded.

"When is the last time you saw your wife?"

Jim shrugged. "Last night, when I got home from work."

"Did the two of you talk?" Connor asked.

"Sure. She, uh, waited up for me. Heated up a dinner plate for me, and we sat at the kitchen table and talked."

Connor and Jade looked at one another again. "What did you talk about?" Jade asked.

Jim shrugged again. "Work, the kids. The usual stuff. Hunter got in trouble at preschool. Rachel had some recipe she wouldn't give Leah. I don't know. Just talk."

"Did she seem distraught to you?" Connor asked. "Tense? On edge? Distressed?"

Jim shook his head to every word Connor threw at him.

"How was your wife's mood?" Connor asked. "Had she been depressed?"

Again, Jim shook his head. He looked at the floor. "No," he said. "She was good. Things were good. She was always in a good mood. Everyone loved her. She's a—she was a great mom and wife." Tears leaked from the corners of Jim's eyes, and he wiped them away quickly. "I don't understand," he mumbled, so low that Connor had to strain to hear him.

"Mr. Holloway," Jade said. "Did your wife drink?"

His head snapped up. "Drink? No. Leah never drank. Not a drop. She was always—she always said she needed to be sober and clear-headed 'cause of the kids. Even after they went to bed, she wouldn't have a drink. She used to say what if one of the kids woke up with a really high fever in the night and she had to take them to the ER? She couldn't be drunk in case something happened. In case—" He looked over his shoulder at his children on the other side of the glass. Mercifully, Hunter had fallen asleep. Peyton hadn't moved at all.

"So, your wife never drank?" Connor clarified. "How about socially?"

"No," Jim answered. "Never."

"And you weren't having any marital problems?"

Jim's head shake was more vigorous this time. "No. We never had marital problems."

"You never fought?" Connor added, trying to keep the incredulity out of his voice.

"Well, sure we had fights like any couple, but we never had prob-lems. I mean our marriage was fine. It was great."

"Were you having any financial problems?" Connor asked.

"No," Jim said. "I mean it's tough sometimes with three kids, but we were doing good. Leah got a raise last year, and we were doing fine."

"How about at Leah's job?" Jade asked. "Was Leah having problems at work?"

"No. Like I said, she just got a raise. Work was good."

"How about family and friends?" Connor said. "Was there anyone she was having trouble with? Anyone she was maybe feuding with?"

"Feuding? No. No way. Leah is good to everyone. Everyone loves her."

Connor could tell by the way Jade drummed her pen against her notebook that she was growing frustrated with the man. A woman who was loved by everyone, who never drank and had zero stress in her life—not at work or at home—didn't kill four people with her car

47

and then crash a vehicle filled with kids into a river. A woman like that didn't drown herself.

"Any mental illness?" Connor asked. "Was Leah taking any medications? Did she have any medical conditions?"

"No. She was fine. She was healthy. I mean, she had problems with her stomach sometimes, and heartburn. She took pills for that sometimes, like Tums or whatever, but other than that, she was fine."

"There was an issue with your dog a few months ago, wasn't there?" Jade asked.

Jim looked momentarily confused. He touched his forehead. "Oh, the dog. Yeah, the dog died. He got into something in the yard or whatever. The kids took it hard."

"Do you know what the dog got into?" Connor asked.

"I don't know. It ate something bad, I guess," Jim said.

"Did Leah tell you what the vet said?" Jade asked.

"She just said it was something toxic."

Jade made a notation in her notebook. She was probably wondering the same thing that Connor was: Had Leah not told her husband that their dog was poisoned, or was Jim Holloway simply minimizing what had happened?

"Did your wife have any social media accounts? Facebook? Twitter?" Jade asked.

Jim shook his head. "No. She wasn't into any of that stuff. She always said she was online all day at work. The last thing she wanted to do when she got home was get back on a computer. Plus, she said she doesn't—didn't like to broadcast every detail of her life. Rachel always wanted her to go on Facebook, but she wouldn't."

"Did she have an email address?" Jade asked.

"Yeah. I don't remember it, but yeah, she had one."

"Did she have a computer at home?"

"Yeah, but she hardly ever used it."

"Would you allow us to have a look at it?"

Jim shrugged. "Sure, but what's that—what's that got to do with anything?"

Connor and Jade had once been tasked with investigating a woman's death after she fell from the Tower Bridge. Her friends and family insisted it was an accident, but when they checked her email account, they found a half-dozen unsent messages to her family explaining why she had chosen to kill herself. This was not something that Connor was prepared to explain to Jim Holloway, nor anything Holloway appeared prepared to hear, so Connor kept his voice friendly and soothing and said, "It's really just routine. We can send someone to your house to pick it up to make it more convenient."

"Uh, sure, okay," Jim said.

"Mr. Holloway," Connor continued, "can you think of any reason why your wife would try to kill herself and your children?"

This time, Jim couldn't hold his tears back. Tremors shook his body as he sobbed into his hands. "No," he said through his tears. "No, I can't."

CHAPTER TEN

"You think he's lying?" Connor asked Jade. They had stepped outside so they could check in with Captain Boggs by phone.

Jade pocketed her cell phone and shook her head. "No. I think he is just your typical oblivious male."

"Typical oblivious male?" Connor echoed. "Should I be insulted?"

"Nothing typical about you, Parks," Jade said with a wink. "You heard him, though. The kids were 'her thing.' Everything was great. He's a figurehead husband. He donates his sperm, hands over his paycheck, attends social functions, and maybe, just maybe, he cuts the grass or fixes a few things around the house. He has very little real function."

"Yikes," Connor said. "Don't you think that's a little simplistic? And unfair?"

Jade slowly shook her head. "Don't be naive, Parks."

"That's exactly the kind of attitude that's going to land you a great husband one of these days."

Jade's look darkened. "Don't make me punch you, Parks. I'm really not into workplace violence."

Connor laughed and walked away from her. "Let's interview the best friend," he called to her over his shoulder. "She'll give us the real picture of Leah Holloway's life."

Rachel Irving stood outside her daughters' room, arms tightly folded over her chest. She looked like she had just come from working out—brown hair pulled back in a ponytail, black yoga pants, Nike sneakers, and layered tank tops over a sports bra. She was flat chested and thick around the middle, but her skin was soft, supple, and evenly tanned. She had an attractive face—high cheekbones, large blue eyes with long lashes, and a straight, thin nose. Only a small white star-shaped scar on the very bottom of her chin marred her complexion. A gold chain with a heart-shaped "#1 Mom" charm hung around her neck. She reached up to fidget with it as Jade made introductions and pulled out her notebook and pen.

Rachel looked over her shoulder where she could see her family through the glass. The twin she had been sitting with had fallen asleep. Rachel's husband spoke softly to their other daughter, his back turned to them.

"Is it true?" she said, turning back to the detectives. "Is it? What the other officers said? Did Leah—did she do this on purpose?" Rachel said the word *this* carefully, as if she were using code that might easily be misinterpreted, as if the word itself might coax something awful into being. But something awful had already transpired, and as Jade spoke to the woman, Connor could see tension drawing Rachel's shoulder blades together.

"We are extremely early on in our investigation, Mrs. Irving," Jade told her, "but at this juncture, by all initial accounts, the only conclusion we can come to is that she purposely crashed her car with the children in it. When given the chance to exit the car, she chose to stay in the water. She was deceased when we recovered the vehicle."

Rachel shook her head as if she were refusing something being forced upon her. "No, no, no. Leah wouldn't do that. My kids—she had my kids in the car." She waved in the direction of the Holloways' room. Her voice went up an octave. "All of our kids were in the car. This has to be a mistake. You don't understand. Leah, of all people, would not do something like this."

"So you and Mrs. Holloway were quite close, then?" Connor said.

51

Rachel chewed her bottom lip. "She was my best friend. I knew her better than anyone."

"When was the last time you spoke to her?"

Rachel shook her head once more, closed her eyes momentarily, and opened them again. "This morning. She took the kids to soccer. They left around seven thirty. Mike had to work, and I was waiting for a delivery. She was fine."

"Did she always take your children to soccer?"

"No. Usually, we went together. If one of us didn't feel well or had to do something, the other would take them. We helped each other out. We were *friends*."

"Mrs. Irving," Connor said. "Can you think of any reason Leah might have been upset or stressed? Was there anything going on in her life that was causing her a great deal of trouble? Any recent stressors?"

"No. Nothing major. Nothing that would make her—I mean, she has a five-month-old. Tyler has been teething. She hasn't—hadn't been getting enough sleep lately. Jim was no help, but that's nothing new. We've both been there before. That's motherhood."

"You said Jim was no help," Jade said. "Were the Holloways having marital problems?"

Rachel barked a dry laugh. "Besides him being oblivious as usual? No, they were fine. I mean, it's the usual shit we all deal with—the mom gets stuck with the brunt of the childcare while our husbands do whatever the hell they want, but it's always been that way. If Leah was going to leave Jim for that kind of thing, she would have left years ago."

"Had she ever planned to leave him, or did she ever talk about leaving him, to your knowledge?" Jade asked.

Rachel shook her head. "No. Never."

"Had they been fighting recently?" Connor asked.

"No, no. They were fine."

"Did Leah love her husband?" Jade cut in.

Rachel made a *puh* sound. "Please. If she didn't love him, no way would she put up with all his shit." Fingering her "#1 Mom" charm, she moved down a few steps and looked in on the Holloway children. "Oh my God, he's never going to be able to handle those kids on his own." Her voice grew squeaky. "Oh my God. This is a mistake. Leah would never leave her kids."

"Mrs. Irving," Connor said, trying to bring her back from the brink of hysteria. "What kind of shit was Leah putting up with?"

"Was Jim having an affair?" Jade asked.

Rachel looked back at the two detectives and laughed harshly. "Jim? An affair? He barely landed Leah, and he didn't even deserve her. No, Jim's not a cheater. That would require effort."

"Was he abusive?" Connor asked.

Another harsh laugh. "No. Jim's not like that. He's a softie. He always did whatever Leah said, and Leah always got whatever she wanted. Jim is . . . he's inattentive, but he's not the kind of guy who would abuse anyone. He would never lay a hand on her or the kids. That was very important to Leah."

"How about Leah?" Connor asked. "Was she having an affair?"

She looked at the floor, shaking her head. "Oh my God, Leah? No. Never. God knows no one would blame her—I mean, Jim forgot their anniversary two years in a row. But no, Leah wasn't like that. Her dad cheated on her mom. She despised cheaters."

"How about her other relationships?" Connor asked. "Extended family? Friends? Work colleagues? Was there anyone she was having issues with?"

Rachel looked back up, meeting Connor's eyes. "Nothing. Leah's parents are dead. Her brother lives in Maryland. They're not close. I can't think of anyone else. Work was work. It could be stressful, but Leah never brought it home with her. She was all about her kids. That was it."

Jade, who had been jotting things down in her notebook, moved on to the next issue. "Did Leah have a drinking problem?"

For a moment, Rachel looked stunned. A small, bewildered smile remained on her face as she looked from Jade to Connor and back again. "What?"

Connor smoothed his beard with one hand. "Did Leah drink? Did she have a drinking problem?"

Rachel burst into laughter. "You're kidding, right?" As her laughter subsided, she stepped back toward the twins' room, glanced at her family, then turned back at the detectives, suddenly looking very weary. "I guess I can see why you would ask that. Why else would a woman drive a bunch of kids into a river? Well, there's no way that was Leah. She never drank."

"Not even socially?" Connor said.

"Especially not socially. Leah was . . . well, she was judgy, okay? There are a few of us moms who get our kids together every week. We like to have some wine when we're together. Not only did Leah not partake, but she walked right out on the group. She refused to join us if any one of us was going to drink with our kids around. I mean she acted like we were leaving our kids out to play on train tracks or something."

Rachel rolled her eyes for good measure. "Look, she never talked much about it, but I think her dad drank. I think . . ." She trailed off, as if searching for the right words. "I think it was very ugly growing up in her household. Leah was very . . . strict about some things. She used to say, 'I had all of my twenties to drink and party. Now I have kids, and I need to be responsible.'"

Jade frowned. "Sounds like she held herself to a pretty high standard."

"An impossibly high standard—at least for the rest of us to live up to. It was . . . it was maddening."

"Do you think the pressure she put on herself was too much?" Connor asked.

Rachel met his eyes. "Like what? Like she snapped? Like a mental breakdown?"

Connor nodded. "Something like that."

Rachel shook her head. Tears welled up in her eyes. "Leah could be rigid and controlling and judgy, but she wasn't the type of person who would have a nervous breakdown. She was . . . she was strong. She was happy. She loved her kids. She loved Jim. She loved her life. She was . . . she would never do something like this."

"How long did you know Leah?" Jade asked.

Rachel wiped at her eyes. "Almost ten years. She and Jim moved in right after Mike and I. We were pregnant with our girls together."

"There was some issue with her dog a few months back," Jade said. "What was that about?"

Rachel's brow furrowed. "Her dog? Well, yeah, it ate something toxic in the yard and died. Leah and the kids were pretty upset about it, but things happen. She wouldn't try to kill our kids over a dog dying."

So Leah had filed a police report about her dog being poisoned but hadn't told her husband or her best friend the truth about how the dog had died. Connor saw Jade make another notation. He asked Rachel, "How about her finances? Did she give you any indication that she and Jim were having financial troubles?"

"They seemed fine. They'd just got his truck paid off. They were talking about putting in a pool for next year. She was happy." She drew out the word *happy*, looking at them meaningfully, like she was trying to convey something in a foreign language.

Connor smiled at her. "Okay. Thank you, Mrs. Irving. Let me ask you: Have the children said anything about today?"

She hugged herself again and looked back at the twins. "Well, Maya said they left soccer. She said Hunter was crying because he wanted to go to McDonald's and Leah said no. She said they stopped at a gas station because Peyton had to pee and couldn't wait until they got home. They said they were at the gas station for a really long time. Leah took

Peyton to the bathroom, brought her back to the car, and then went back into the bathroom for a long time. Then she got back in the car and started driving really fast."

"What time did you expect them back?" Connor asked.

Rachel shrugged. "No time in particular. Sometimes she would take them to eat after soccer. We weren't on any kind of strict schedule or anything."

"We'd like to talk to the girls as soon as possible," Connor said.

"Sure," Rachel said. "But can you come back when they're awake? They're so traumatized. I'd like them to rest for a while."

"Of course," Connor said. He handed Rachel his business card. "We'll be in touch."

CHAPTER ELEVEN

"If I have to hear the word *fine* one more time, somebody is getting punched," Jade groused as she and Connor made their way through the Office of Investigations to Captain Boggs's office. "'We were fine.' 'They were fine.' 'She was fine.' People who are fine don't take out a bunch of motorists and then try to kill themselves and five kids."

"Maybe fine is the new crazy," Connor remarked absently. He looked at his phone again, his heart leaping into his throat every time he read the text. It was from Claire. It had come in while they were interviewing Rachel Irving. All it said was: *Thank you for today. See you soon.*

It was the *"See you soon"* that made him feel like a goddamn teenage girl. He'd forgotten how good she felt in his arms. Had made himself forget. Two years ago, she had shut him down, and he had no reason to believe that she might be willing to give their relationship another try. Today, she had been more vulnerable and afraid than he had seen her in years, which worried him. But she had also been more open and receptive to him than she had been since their first failed attempt at dating. Something had changed between them that morning on the riverbank.

Jade made a *puh* sound, drawing his attention back to the matter at hand. "Please. I bet any amount of money that when the coroner does his exam, she'll come back drunk as fuck. No one is that perfect."

Boggs's door was open, but he wasn't in the room. They went in anyway and sat in the guest chairs in front of his desk. "But she wasn't perfect," Connor pointed out. "Rachel Irving described her as rigid, judgy, and controlling."

"Right," Jade conceded. "You think that's why she didn't tell anyone about the dog? 'Cause she had to be in control?"

Connor shrugged. "Don't know, but that whole dog thing raises red flags."

"So what makes someone that controlling lose their damn mind?"

"I don't know. But she was fine when she got into her vehicle this morning. Somewhere between then and the river, something happened to set her off. We need to get her medical records so we can definitively rule out some kind of medical condition, and then we need to piece together her day, see where things went wrong."

Jade's mouth twisted. "Medical? We have a witness who says she purposely drowned herself. There's no medical event that causes that."

"A brain tumor can make you do crazy shit. Anyway, we need the records to see if she really had a history of mental illness or not."

Connor glanced around the room. Every time he had cause to be in the captain's office, he marveled at the difference in the way Boggs kept it, compared with his predecessor. Their former captain could have been on an episode of hoarders. Boggs kept his office neat and orderly. Nary a stray piece of paper to be found.

"All right," Jade said. "Let's go through it. She took the kids to soccer."

"Right. The Strangler task force will have surveillance of that field, I bet."

Jade grinned at him. "Brilliant!"

"We're going to need her phone too."

"There is no phone," said Danny Boggs as he breezed through the door and around to the chair behind his desk. He looked at the two of them but didn't sit down. "Crime scene techs already faxed over the logs. No phone. Not on the overpass, not in the vehicle. No phone."

"Which means it's in the river," Jade said.

Connor shrugged. "We'll get the records. I'll have someone pick up her PC once the husband gets home, ask someone over in Computer Crimes to take a look at it. I'll see if they can get into her email as well. I'm sure the best friend knows her email address."

Boggs picked up a Styrofoam cup from his desk and sipped from it. "Getting a subpoena won't be a problem. Got the mayor breathing down my neck on this one."

Jade leaned forward in her seat. "Cap, this lady is dead. It's not like charges can be brought."

"No, but there will be civil suits, believe you me. Civil suits out the wazoo. People want to know what the hell happened. How did this happen? Good God. Holy tabloid fodder. Every talk show host and crime reporter in this country just came in their pants. Perfect mom turned mass murderer? This will be on television for months."

Jade stood. "Well, I'm gonna go ask Stryke for the soccer field footage."

Connor nodded at her but made no effort to move. One hand was in his jacket pocket, fingering his phone. "I'll figure out which gas stations were on her route home, and after we watch the soccer video, we'll hit those, see what we can get."

"You got it," Jade called over her shoulder as she left the room.

Boggs came around to the front of his desk and perched on the edge of it. For a moment, they listened to Jade's footsteps fade down the hallway. Then Boggs said, "How is Claire? Is she okay? Stryke told me she was, but I mean really—she okay?"

Connor smiled. Boggs had worked on Claire's original abduction case and then, ten years later, on her cold case with Connor. He had become friends with the Fletcher family. "She's shaken up for sure, but I think she'll be okay." He stood up. "I'm gonna see if Holloway's car had GPS. That may be the quickest way to trace her route from the soccer field to the river."

CHAPTER TWELVE

EARLIER THAT DAY

Leah smelled the alcohol right away. Like a cadaver dog scenting a decomposing body, she could smell it over and above all the other scents surrounding the soccer field: freshly cut grass, sunscreen, concession hot dogs, and cigarette smoke from the parents who had snuck away to have a quick smoke during play.

This booze smell was minty, and at first she wasn't sure if someone had tried to cover the smell with mouthwash or if it was actually some minty-flavored drink. They made all kinds of alcoholic drinks these days: orange cream, fudge brownie, watermelon crush . . . the list was endless. Even under the minty mask, the alcohol stench was every bit as eye watering as gasoline. It took her back to every time her father had gotten drunk and beat the shit out of her mother. It made Leah sick to her stomach.

It was liquor, not beer. Her father had never had a problem with beer. He could pound beer down a case a night and still be the jovial guy all the neighbors knew and liked. It was liquor that turned him. Liquor that made the private man a raging, red-faced monster. And Leah could smell it now, at her six-year-old's morning soccer game. She looked up and down her side of the field. There were two sets of bleachers grouped together near the center part of the field. Those filled early.

Many parents, like Leah herself, brought their own collapsible chairs and planted themselves right at the edge of the field. Hunter was sitting in his own miniature Spider-Man chair, playing on his nabi. Blessedly, Tyler had fallen asleep in his car seat, which Leah had tucked between her and Hunter, with its canopy raised to keep the sun from his eyes. The girls ran up and down the field, their match in full swing. Leah watched Peyton make a pass and clapped, then cupped her hands over her mouth and yelled, "Go, Peyton!"

The girl threw Leah a smile over her shoulder and ran ahead into play.

That *smell*. Leah looked to her right this time, trying to figure out where it might be coming from. Then she saw Alan Wheeler. His daughter was on Peyton's team. He never used to come to the games, but he and his wife were getting a divorce, so every other weekend now he was on soccer detail. Leah studied him. He sat in a fold-up lawn chair. He had on a green windbreaker and jean shorts. His gray hair had gotten long, strands of it lifting in the breeze. He wore sunglasses and a permanent smile. He was facing the green, but Leah noticed that his head never moved to follow play up and down the field. He had a soft cooler beside his chair. In his left hand was a take-out coffee cup with a plastic lid.

It had to be him.

Leah knew "drunk and passed out" when she saw it.

She had taken a step toward him, rage burning inside her, when Hunter's voice stopped her. "Mommy, where are you going?"

She turned to see him squinting up at her, his perfect little brow furrowed. Where her daughter was strong, independent, and stoic, her son was clingy and prone to emotional outbursts, or whining, as Jim would say.

Leah pointed to Alan Wheeler. "I just need to talk to Mr. Wheeler for a minute, okay?"

Hunter's eyes widened. "Mommy, don't get killed by the Strangler!"

For a moment, Leah was paralyzed. It took several seconds to process what her four-year-old son had just said. Seeing her expression, he clarified: "He takes mommies from soccer."

Aware her facial muscles were still frozen in horror, Leah tried to force a smile onto her face, but her lips felt stiff. Her jaw ached. Slowly, as if it hurt to move, she knelt to her son, looking into his cherubic little face. A miniature Jim, he had shaggy hair and cheeks he had yet to grow into. She had kissed them thousands of times.

"Who told you about the Strangler?" she asked softly.

He kept his eyes down and shrugged. "Don't know."

"Was it Daddy?"

Another noncommittal shrug.

Leah leaned forward and kissed his nose. "I won't be mad, Bug. Promise. I just want to know."

She'd been calling him Bug since he was a month old. Unlike Peyton, Hunter had loved being swaddled. She'd carried him around tightly bundled like a little roly-poly bug for months. Hunter looked into her eyes and she forced another soft smile.

"Daddy was watching us when you went to the doctor," Hunter began.

"Did Daddy tell you about this?" Leah asked, unable to say the word *strangler* to her son. She was going to strangle her husband.

"No. He didn't tell me. I saw it on the news. Daddy wouldn't let me watch *Secret Agent Bear*." He sat up straighter and slipped into a whine. "Peyton told him we always watch *Secret Agent Bear*, but Daddy said it was dumb and put the news on."

Leah sighed. *Secret Agent Bear* was a cartoon. Her children were obsessed with it, although Leah had to agree with her husband that it was colossally stupid. It had always bothered her that the cartoon portrayed children relying on an imaginary bear for problem-solving skills instead of going to their parents.

"The news showed the mommies that the Strangler got," Hunter said. He scrunched his face up. "They all had hair like yours."

Leah touched his cheek. "Oh, honey, lots of people have blonde hair."

But the thought had already lodged itself in a corner of her mind—or maybe it had just fought its way to the front. They all looked like her. Or did they? She'd spent hours at her desk at work studying their faces. Wondering. Convincing herself she was wrong.

"The world doesn't revolve around you, sweetheart." Her father's voice. The soul-crushing image of him standing over her—half smirking, half sneering.

Leah stuffed that image back into her mind's Shitty Childhood compartment. She didn't need to think about those things anymore. But her mind had been a frazzled mess lately.

Tyler's hearty wail lifted her out of the quagmire of her thoughts. She squatted, pushing the car seat canopy back, and unbuckled him. She scooped him up, bouncing him in her arms until he quieted and rested his head on her shoulder.

She looked back at Hunter, who stared at her. "You don't need to worry about Stranglers, honey. Let Mommy worry about that. You watch your sister and cheer as loud as you can if she makes a goal, okay?"

Hunter nodded, slumping into his chair and pushing buttons on his nabi again. Leah waited a beat and then made her way over to Alan Wheeler.

She stood directly in front of him for several seconds, but he neither spoke nor moved. She leaned forward, holding Tyler close, and sniffed. The man smelled like a candy cane—an alcohol-soaked candy cane. The soft cooler beside him was unzipped. She shifted Tyler to her right hip and leaned down, flipping the lid open to examine the contents. Two waters crammed between two blue ice packs, a few Capri Suns, a Coke, and a tall, clear bottle of something. Leah lifted it from the cooler and turned it in her hand so she could read the label. Peppermint vodka.

"Son of a bitch," she murmured.

"Hey!" Alan Wheeler's breath was like a thick wave of hot air emerging from an oven, the smell of alcohol making Leah's eyes burn. He gripped her wrist and she quickly pulled it away, maintaining her grip on the bottle. She stood up and tucked the bottle between Tyler and her chest. His chubby little hands wrapped around the neck of it.

Wheeler took off his sunglasses and looked up at her with blood-shot eyes. "What the hell do you think you're doing?"

"You are drunk at your six-year-old's soccer game, Alan. What the hell are *you* doing? I hope you're not getting into the car with her after this game."

"Fuck you," he said. He leaned forward and reached for her, but she stepped back again, out of his reach.

"Watch your language," Leah said. "There are children here. If you don't pull it together, I'm going to call 911. Do you really need that kind of attention while you're going through a divorce? An ugly custody battle? Get your shit together, Alan."

"You meddling bitch," Wheeler spit.

Leah raised a brow. She would probably call 911 anyway before the end of the game. She couldn't let this man drive children around. She pointed down the field toward the concession stand. "They always sell coffee. You should go get some."

Her phone rang, vibrating against her hip. She pulled it out of her pocket and stared at the screen. At first, the number didn't register with her. It was an 855 area code. She didn't get many of those. She was on every "do not call" list there was, and she had no bill collectors chasing after her. But then she remembered that she had been waiting for this call. Dreading it, but waiting for it. Without conscious thought, she pressed "Answer."

"Mrs. Holloway?" an impossibly perky female voice greeted her.

Leah said, "Yes," but the word barely came out. Alan Wheeler was mumbling something at her, reaching for her again. She kicked his hand away with her leg and walked off, away from him, away from the parents crowding the edge of the field. She licked her lips, swallowed, and tried again. "Yes?" she said.

"I'm calling regarding the samples you sent in. I'm calling from—"

Leah cut her off. "I know where you're calling from." She squeezed Tyler tighter to her. He tried to put his little mouth around the cap of the bottle. She pulled it away. "Go on," she told the woman.

"I was just calling to let you know that both of the samples you sent in are a positive match."

Leah pulled the phone away from her ear and stared at it. She knew she should say something. *Thank you. Okay. Goodbye.* Except that she couldn't breathe. She turned back toward Hunter. She ran toward him as if he were the oxygen she so desperately needed. Tyler was crying again. She dropped the peppermint vodka into her purse together with her phone and put Tyler back into his car seat. Then she realized she had at least ten minutes until the end of the game. She couldn't rush the kids off the field. That would arouse too much suspicion. Not that she knew what the hell she was going to do now.

She paced the field, fighting tears, and willing the game to end. "Oh my God," she muttered under her breath. "Dear God."

CHAPTER THIRTEEN

"Am I under arrest or what?" Connor lurched back from Alan Wheeler's breath, which was so laced with alcohol that Connor was getting a contact high. The man sat draped over a table in one of the OOI's interview rooms, which is where they'd dragged him after his six-year-old daughter answered his apartment door and led them to where he was passed out on the living room floor. They had pulled a still of his face from the soccer field footage. A brief text exchange between Jade and Rachel Irving had provided his identity and address.

The man's bloodshot eyes swiveled from Connor to Jade and back. He disregarded Jade and spoke to Connor. "Do I need a lawyer or what?"

"What you need is some mouthwash," Jade told him.

He ignored her. Connor said, "You're not under arrest. We need to ask you some questions about Leah Holloway."

"That bitch," Wheeler muttered. He peeled his upper body off the table and looked around the room, as if seeing it for the first time. "Where's my daughter?"

"Nice of you to remember you have a kid," Jade remarked.

"Jade," Connor cautioned.

She pushed herself off the wall she'd been leaning against and walked over to the table. She folded her arms and looked down at Wheeler. Standing there, she dwarfed him. "She's with her mother."

Wheeler sneered and pointed a finger at Jade. "All of you women are the same—meddling bitches."

Jade snorted. "Oh, really?"

"Fucking right," Wheeler said, erupting into a coughing fit. A mist of what smelled like bourbon sprayed across the table.

"What were you drinking this morning?" Connor asked the man.

"Coffee."

Jade perched on the edge of the table and leaned toward Wheeler. "What type of drinks did you bring in your cooler to your daughter's soccer game?"

He ignored her again and addressed Connor. "Thought you said this was about Leah Holloway."

Connor nodded. "You spoke with her this morning at your daughter's soccer game. She took a bottle from your cooler. What was in the bottle?"

"Water," Wheeler answered quickly.

Connor caught Jade's eye as she turned away from Wheeler. "You watch the news today, Mr. Wheeler?"

Wheeler looked confused. "What the hell for?"

Connor leaned forward, catching the man's gaze. "Leah Holloway drove an SUV filled with kids into the American River today. Killed herself."

Wheeler stared at Connor expectantly, as if waiting for a punch line. When Connor didn't say anything more, Wheeler said, "'Scuse me?"

Connor repeated himself, more slowly. Then he asked, "So what were you drinking that you gave to Leah Holloway this morning at your daughter's soccer match?"

The man's eyes were frozen wide in shock. He licked his lips. "Those kids, in her car. Did they—were they—"

"They all survived," Jade put in. Connor felt her eyes on him as she added, "They were rescued by a bystander. Minor injuries. Mr. Wheeler,

Holloway killed four people in a vehicle traveling southbound on the freeway before she went into the river."

For the first time, Wheeler acknowledged Jade, shooting her a fleeting glance before turning his gaze to his sun-spotted hands, which he placed on the table. "Jesus," he said. He looked up at Connor, worry tightening the lines at the corners of his bloodshot eyes. "I didn't give it to her," he said. "She took it. I was minding my own business. She walked over to me. I don't even know how she knew."

"Knew what?" Connor asked.

Wheeler's head went back and forth like a metronome, his eyes glassy.

"Mr. Wheeler," Jade said.

No response.

Connor pushed back in his chair, eliciting a squeal as the legs scraped over the tile. Wheeler startled, his eyes searching the room until they landed on Connor again. Connor said, "Mr. Wheeler, you're not in any trouble. We're just trying to piece together Leah Holloway's morning. We're trying to figure out why a mother of three with a perfectly normal life would drive a car full of kids into a river. She took something from you. It's important for us to know what it was and whether or not your confrontation had anything to do with what she did."

"I barely knew her. I mean, I always saw her around. She was a real pain in the ass. The bottle she took—my wife said Leah had a thing about drinking. It was this whole thing between her and the other mothers. Leah could be—well, she could be a real bitch. She was like the police. Always worried about what everyone else was doing."

"Like today?" Jade asked. "Did she approach you because you were drinking?"

He hung his head. "I don't know how she knew. Nobody else even noticed. I was—I was—I fell asleep there on the field. I was in my chair. I woke up and she was digging in my goddamn cooler. She found my peppermint vodka and took it. She said she was going to call 911 if I didn't sober up."

Connor and Jade exchanged a look. They'd seen the tape, watched Leah take out her phone, speak on it briefly, and walk briskly away from Wheeler. But no police came. Wheeler never even got out of his chair. Not until the match was over and his daughter ran up to the chair and shook him awake. By that time, they were able to see Leah herding her children, and the Irvings', out of the frame, presumably toward her vehicle.

They could check the 911 logs, but Connor already knew Leah hadn't called the police. "Why didn't she?" he asked Wheeler.

The man shrugged. "No idea. She got a call. She walked away. That was it."

"Did you hear any of her conversation?" Jade asked.

"Nah. I just know she left me alone after that."

"But she kept your bottle of peppermint vodka," Connor pointed out.

Wheeler shrugged. "Well, yeah, but I am telling you, there's no way in hell she drank it. She was a fucking puritan about that shit."

CHAPTER FOURTEEN

Connor and Jade grabbed a late lunch at a fast-food place and then headed over to the soccer field in North Natomas, trying to retrace Leah Holloway's ill-fated ride home. The lab was still working on the GPS system from Holloway's vehicle, and they didn't have time to wait for results. There were three gas stations between the field and the overpass where Holloway had taken so many lives. The surveillance videos from the inside of each one revealed nothing. No sign of Holloway at all, but the third gas station's restrooms were outside, located on the side of the building, well out of the sight of the clerk. Connor asked the guy to pull up the exterior surveillance, and they hit pay dirt.

Connor and Jade crowded together in the minimart's tiny storage room, which doubled as an office, and watched the black-and-white footage on a small television. The disinterested clerk left them alone after queuing up the footage from the time period they'd requested.

"Okay," Connor said, looking at the time stamp on the video as Leah Holloway's SUV pulled up outside the gas station's restrooms. "We know she left the soccer game around ten fifteen."

"She pulls up here at ten twenty-seven, so we know she came right from the game," Jade said. She pulled out her notebook and pen and made a notation.

The camera was affixed to the side of the building, up high near the roof, taking in the doors to both restrooms as well as the four parking spaces in front of them. "Here we go," Connor said as Holloway got out of the vehicle. She slipped the straps of her large purse over her right shoulder, made her way around to the passenger's side, and opened the back door. It was impossible to see inside the vehicle, but of course, they already knew who was inside. Holloway stuck her head into the SUV. Moments passed. Connor imagined she was arguing with her son about McDonald's or perhaps telling the other kids to wait. Finally, she emerged with young Peyton.

Hand in hand, they approached the restroom door. As Leah's hand reached for the door handle, she froze. Peyton turned her face up toward her mother, the look of total trust making Connor's stomach turn. Leah rifled in her purse until she came up with her phone. Pressing it to her ear, she opened the restroom door and shooed Peyton into the bathroom.

Jade paused the video just before they disappeared inside. "There," she said, pointing to Leah's purse. "That's Alan Wheeler's peppermint vodka."

The bottle's neck and cap protruded just enough to be visible from the top of her purse.

"Well," Connor said. "We know what she did with the bottle."

"Why doesn't she throw it away? She doesn't drink. Won't even associate with people who do."

Connor shrugged. "Maybe she forgot it was in there. She seemed pretty frazzled and preoccupied after she got that phone call at the field. Now here's another call."

"You think it's the same person?"

"No idea, but look, we watched the soccer match footage. Almost the entire game she was cheering on her daughter. Then while she's talking to Wheeler she gets a call. After that she was pacing and barely paying attention to the game. Next thing we know she's driving a bunch of kids into a river."

"We need those phone records."

Connor nodded his agreement. "I already put in a request with her phone company. I'll check with them when we get back."

Jade frowned and clicked "Play." Leah disappeared into the rest-room. They waited one minute, then two.

"Fast forward," Connor said.

Jade moved the video ahead until the door opened and Leah poked her head out, the phone still pressed to her ear. She stared at the vehicle for a few seconds before returning to the bathroom again.

"Eleven minutes and twenty-seven seconds," Jade noted. They waited another minute. Then the door opened once more. Leah and Peyton exited. This time, Leah was not on her phone.

"Her purse," Connor said. "She left it in the bathroom."

Leah strapped Peyton into the vehicle and went back into the bath-room. This time she was in there for fourteen minutes, fifty-four sec-onds before there was any sign of her. Finally, the door opened, but all Connor could see inside was blackness, though he assumed it was Leah checking on the kids before closing the door again. Jade fast-forwarded. Twelve minutes, forty-one seconds passed. The door opened again and Leah emerged. No phone, no purse. She went to the SUV, cupped her hands, and peered into the back-seat window like she was a stranger. Turning away, she leaned her back against the vehicle.

"What is she doing?" Jade muttered.

Leah swiped at her cheeks with the heels of her hands. "Crying," Connor answered. "She's crying."

She went back into the bathroom. They waited a minute. When she didn't emerge, Jade fast-forwarded again. "Jesus," she said after over fourteen minutes had elapsed.

"Stop there," Connor said. "Stop, stop. Look."

He pointed to the vehicle door. It pushed open a few inches, closed, pushed open again, and finally opened all the way. Peyton climbed out, pushing the door closed behind her. She went to the door of the restroom, her entire body practically hanging from the knob before it turned. She pushed and pushed until, finally, the door opened a sliver. She slipped a sneakered foot between the door and its frame, then struggled the rest of the way in.

"Smart girl," Jade murmured.

Connor sighed and pushed a hand through his hair. "Yeah, she is. We really need to talk to her."

"We'll do that next."

Jade fast-forwarded again. Eight minutes, thirteen seconds elapsed. Finally, Peyton emerged once more, followed by Leah.

"Jesus," Connor said. "They've been parked there for an hour. How do you get a bunch of young kids to stay calm in a parked car for an hour?"

Jade shrugged. "Don't know. I'm guessing they fell asleep. Or maybe they didn't. Maybe they sat in there and screamed their heads off for an hour. Obviously, this woman was past caring."

"Rewind that," Connor said. "She's stumbling."

Jade rewound the video. They watched Leah follow Peyton out to the vehicle once more. It hadn't been Connor's imagination. As she ushered Peyton back into the car, she fell against the half-open door. She steadied herself, then strapped in her daughter. She held on to the vehicle as she picked her way back to the driver's side. Her purse dangled from her forearm, only one strap over her arm.

"The bottle is gone," Jade pointed out.

"Yeah," Connor said.

Leah fell to the asphalt, her wobbly legs giving out beneath her. Her fingers scrabbled over the surface of the car door, finding the handle. She used it to pull herself up but it opened abruptly, throwing her backward. She landed on her ass, her purse a few feet away, its contents partially spilled onto the asphalt. Connor didn't see a bottle of vodka or a cell phone. Swaying on her knees, Leah crawled and gathered her belongings. She stood on shaking legs and got back into the SUV.

They watched as her SUV pulled out of the frame. Icy fingers scurried down Connor's spine.

Jade said, "Let's check the bathroom."

◆ ◆ ◆

Alan Wheeler's vodka bottle was in the garbage can, about an inch of liquid left in the bottom of it. Its cap peeked out from a small pile of crumpled paper towels. Jade pulled on a pair of latex gloves while Connor snapped some photos of how they'd found it.

"It's almost empty," Jade noted as she held it up, swishing the liquid around.

"So she drank it," Connor said.

"Or poured it out."

Connor shook his head. "No. She drank it. If she was in here pouring it out, she would have emptied the entire thing. You saw her, she was stumbling when she left this bathroom."

Jade looked at the bottle as though she were holding a severed head. "So a woman who never drinks takes this bottle away from another parent who actually was drinking and threatens to call 911 if he doesn't sober up, takes the bottle into a gas station bathroom, leaving five kids parked outside alone for an hour, and drinks the whole damn thing. A woman, by the way, with no stressors in her life. A woman who was just fine. Are you listening to this shit, Parks? 'Cause it doesn't make one bit of sense."

Connor stepped into the first stall and looked around. Toilet paper hung in shreds from an empty roll affixed to the stall's wall. The chrome waste box marked "For feminine waste only" overflowed with bunched-up toilet paper. At his feet, discarded toilet paper formed a wet clump near the front of the toilet. "I'm listening," he told Jade. "Obviously, we're missing a huge piece of the puzzle, Webb."

"You think there was someone in here with her?"

"Nah," Connor said. "What, someone spent an hour in here with her, with her little girl coming in and out?"

The second stall was considerably messier. Wet toilet paper clumped in small mountains on the floor, making a squishing sound as he stepped in it. It looked like someone had had a toilet-paper fight in the place. It hung from the back of the commode and gathered in piles all over the floor.

Connor said, "The phone."

"Yeah," Jade said. "We need to know who called her and why. It all comes down to the phone."

"It's here."

"What?"

He felt Jade at his back. He pointed to the toilet, where a cell phone rested beneath the water in the cradle usually reserved for human waste.

"Fuck me," Jade muttered.

"Doesn't look like anyone used this stall since Holloway was here."

"Who would want to? And who would want to reach in there and pull it out?"

Connor fished his own pair of latex gloves from his pocket and put them on. "We would," he said. "Only we would."

CHAPTER FIFTEEN

Brianna plopped down on the couch next to Claire with a deep sigh. She fussed with her wet curls, her expression pinched. "I took two showers, and I still smell like river."

Claire laughed. "River?"

"You know, like wet, disgusting mud and fish and stuff."

"You don't smell like river. You didn't even get that wet."

Brianna snatched the remote control from the coffee table and hit the power button. "Let's see how wet I was. One of the guys from my bar exam study group texted me and said he saw me on channel three. It was a breaking news alert."

As the big flat-screen television mounted on the wall across from them flicked on, they both put their feet up on their coffee table. It was a large square, uneven thing made from reclaimed wood. Brianna hated it because it looked too unfinished—"Like someone chopped up a tree and threw a slab of it on legs"—but Claire relished its rustic look. She'd paid a local artist way too much for it, but she had loved the idea of reclaimed wood. That was during the peak of her intense Reclaiming My Life period. She would never get rid of the table. Brianna knew that, which was why she tolerated it.

Wilson circled the room and, with a sigh, crawled beneath their legs and went to sleep. Claire dangled one bare foot between the couch and table and used it to massage Wilson's side. She loved the feel of his soft fur. On the television, an old sitcom played.

"I guess it's still a few minutes before the news comes on," Brianna said. She turned her body so that she was facing Claire. "So, how are you feeling? Really. Don't say 'Fine,' because I won't believe you."

Claire reached up behind them and pulled down the afghan they kept folded on the top of the couch. She hadn't been able to get warm since they got home. She could still feel the cold river water enveloping her body. "I don't know," she said. "I don't know how I feel. I'm . . ." She drifted off. An image of wide brown eyes in a pale face framed by blonde hair came unbidden. Not Leah Holloway. It was Miranda Simon. Fourteen years ago, Claire's abductor had killed the girl right in front of her. It was one of the moments she'd worked hardest to bar from her mind. But now, here it was—the terror in Miranda Simon's eyes as clear to her as it had been when she watched the girl die.

"What?" Brianna asked. "What is it?"

Claire could barely get the word out. "Sarah."

"Who?"

"Miranda Simon." The girl would always be Sarah to Claire. Claire had had to give her a name. Reynard Johnson had killed her before Claire could find out anything about her. "They looked the same," Claire tried to explain. She motioned toward the television even though the news was not yet on. "Leah Holloway and Miranda Simon. Blonde hair, brown eyes. That look."

The girl had known it was the end the instant Johnson looped the belt around her neck. There was nothing quite like that kind of stark, putrid fear. Claire had been consumed by it many times when she thought Johnson was going to kill her. Miranda Simon had had no choice. Johnson had overpowered her, kidnapped her, and bound her. She was never in any position to fight back, and Claire, handcuffed to a radiator, hadn't been in a position to save the girl.

But Holloway.

"Why didn't she unlock the doors?" Claire asked.

Brianna frowned. "Wait, are we still talking about Miranda Simon?"

"I'm sorry, no. Leah Holloway. She had a choice. All she had to do was press one button. I could have helped her. I could have saved her."

Claire had spent a great deal of her post-escape therapy trying to assuage her own guilt over Miranda Simon's murder, trying to come to terms with her own powerlessness in the face of her abductor's rage. She thought she had gotten there, but now, she wasn't so sure. Now she felt the same sense of powerlessness. Today, it wasn't a room that had separated her from Leah Holloway. It wasn't a psychopath who had kept Claire from saving the woman. It was a pane of glass, and the woman herself.

Brianna put a hand on Claire's shoulder and squeezed gently. "It's not your fault, Claire. You're right, that woman did have a choice, and she made it when she drove off the overpass. She made her choice before she even made it to the river. Stop beating yourself up. I mean, you got all the kids out!"

Claire tried to tuck the images of both women—Simon and Holloway—away in her mind. She managed a smile for her sister. "No, *you* did. Thank you, by the way, for doing the press interview for me."

"Yeah, well, you owe me one. That Noel Geary is a little vicious, if you ask me."

"What do you mean?"

"Oh, you'll see," Brianna said. "So, where did you and Connor go? How were things between you two? It seemed pretty intense on the riverbank."

Claire told her. Then, because she knew her sister would never let up until she dragged every last detail out of her, she said, "We almost kissed. I mean, I think. I was upset. I—I told him to come by later."

Brianna slapped Claire's knee, drawing a neck-craning look from Wilson. "That's great! So, do you think he'll come by?"

"I don't know. I mean, he's working now and will probably be working pretty much around the clock until the investigation into this accident is over."

"But you want him to come by? You want to see him?"

Claire felt her cheeks pink up. "Yeah. I don't know. I think I want to. I felt so—so jealous when I saw him with that female detective."

Brianna wrinkled her nose. "Yeah. She seemed overly familiar with him, but he only had eyes for you, so I wouldn't worry too much about her."

"It's just that seeing them together made me think of him with other women, you know, in a way I hadn't really thought about it before. I didn't like it. I would love to try again—I just don't know if it's a good idea. I mean, that accident today, it really . . . messed with my head. It brought some stuff back up for me. I don't want to get involved with Connor again as a way of distracting myself from those horrible memories. Nothing has changed from two years ago." She thought of how good and safe it had felt in his arms. That hadn't changed either. She thought of their almost kiss in Dr. Corey's office and the attraction she felt for him, in spite of all of her baggage. That hadn't changed either. And yet, she didn't know if that attraction could carry them into a real relationship. Her fingers worried at the edge of the afghan. "I still may or may not be able to have sex with Connor. It is always going to be an issue between us. I mean how can we have a romantic relationship with no sex?"

Brianna said, "Let me ask you something. Do you enjoy sex at all? Do you feel, you know, attraction toward men in that way?"

It was a subject she'd discussed at length with her therapist over the years. Claire had been fifteen when she was abducted. She'd already developed an attraction to men. She knew what sex was—many of her friends had already been having it. She had, a few times, experienced the breathless excitement of kissing a boy she liked. But then she had been abducted. She'd been raped so many times, she had lost count. Sex began to equal violence.

Sure, since then she had had sex with men who were gentle and caring, but she had never been sure if she'd had sex with them because she was genuinely attracted to them or because she was just determined to be normal. But Connor . . . she had always been attracted to him. He had always made her heart flutter in the way it had when she was fifteen—pre-abduction.

"I'm attracted to Connor," she told her sister.

"Do you like, you know, being with him?"

Claire looked away from her sister, cheeks growing hotter. "I do. I mean, there will just always be certain things I can't do, certain ways I cannot be touched."

Brianna frowned, her expression a mixture of sympathy and anger at the reminder of what Claire had been forced to endure. What had been taken from her. "Well," Brianna said. "Sex is supposed to be pleasurable. It should feel good. That's the whole point—well, I mean other than the whole reproduction thing. Look, if you're not getting any pleasure from it, even with Connor—and I know you two haven't done it yet, but I'm talking even the foreplay, because all of that is sexual—then maybe you're right, and there is no point in going forward. But if being with Connor in a sexual way is pleasurable at all, then I think you owe it to yourself to try."

Pleasure. Of course, who would know better than Claire that sex was about pleasure? Hadn't her abductor raped her for four long years because it felt good to him? Hadn't she had ten years of her life stolen from her because of that very correlation—sex equals pleasure? Her abductor had gotten years of pleasure from her body.

And it pissed her off that now that same body betrayed her. It pissed her off that she should have so much difficulty deriving pleasure from the same act. Why should he have taken all the pleasure out of sex so that now she could have none? It wasn't fair.

But he didn't take it all. "Things do feel good with Connor," she blurted.

Brianna smiled. "Well, there's your answer. Hey, the news is on."

Beneath their feet, Wilson stirred, wriggling out of reach of Claire's foot and standing. He circled the room as Brianna turned the volume up on the television, and sprawled out again on a wider piece of carpet. The news led with the Holloway story. It was the first time in nearly a month that the lead story didn't involve the Soccer Mom Strangler.

Looking as buxom and blonde as ever, Noel Geary stood on the side of the road, the American River and the Jibboom Street Bridge visible behind her. A police crew towed a red SUV out of the water.

"Today, at approximately eleven thirty a.m., a young mother with five children in her vehicle drove her SUV off the I-5 overpass, causing a series of accidents that claimed four lives before crashing through the guardrail and plummeting into the American River. At this hour, it is unclear why the driver would try to take the lives of five precious children."

The screen cut to a man in his forties wearing a Clippers hat and a plain white T-shirt. He stood on the side of the highway, the corners of his eyes pinched. "I saw her coming from the other direction. She was weaving, going way too fast. She was all over the road. I pulled over to call 911, and that's when she hit those other two cars—BAM!"

The screen cut to an image of two badly mangled vehicles, one covered partially with a tarp. The other one had thick black smoke billowing from what was left of its compacted hood. They cut away to a woman this time, standing to the side of the wreckage, her long brown hair blowing in the wind. "Then she went right through the concrete," the woman explained. "It was awful. Just awful."

The broadcast cut back to Noel Geary. "The Dodge Durango plunged into the river where two women were fishing. One of those women, Brianna Fletcher, immediately dove into the water and made it to the car in time to pull the children out."

Claire watched as the camera panned out, revealing Brianna's willowy frame. She looked damp and bedraggled, staring uncertainly at the lens.

"Miss Fletcher, what was going through your mind when you saw the vehicle crash into the water?"

On-screen, Brianna shrugged. "I didn't think," she said into Noel's microphone. "I just went for it. I mean, there wasn't time to think. I just dove into the water."

"What happened when you got to the vehicle?"

Beside Noel, Brianna shifted uncomfortably, wrapping her arms around her middle. "I, uh, I saw that there were people—there were kids in the car and I just—I tried to get them out."

"And you did. You got all the kids out safely. What about the driver? Was she still alive when you got to the car?"

"Oh yeah, she was. She—she was still alive," Brianna stammered. "But, uh, badly hurt. I—I went for the kids first."

"Once the children were rescued, did you go back to car for the mother?"

"Uh, no, I—I didn't," Brianna said. On the television, Brianna shifted from foot to foot, her arms tightening around her middle. She looked away from the camera, opening her mouth to speak but then clamping it shut again.

"You didn't try to rescue the mother?" Noel asked pointedly.

Still, Brianna did not meet the dead eye of the camera. "No, I mean, she was hurt, badly hurt. I didn't think—"

"Did any of the other people who stopped to help get the children out of the river go back to the vehicle for the mother?"

"I don't think so. I don't know."

"Miss Fletcher," Noel went on. "Did the mother speak to you when you swam out there and began rescuing the children? Did she give you any indication as to why she drove into the river?"

Brianna mumbled, "No, no. She didn't say anything."

On-screen, Jade Webb stepped into the frame, using her body to block Brianna almost entirely from view. She said, "We have no additional details to give at this time."

"Detective," Noel said. "Was the mother deceased by the time police arrived?"

Jade ignored her. "This is an ongoing investigation. We will not be releasing any more information at this time."

"Detective," Noel went on as if Jade hadn't spoken. "The driver was left in the vehicle by rescuers. We now know she is deceased. Can you confirm that she drowned while the children were being moved to shore?"

Jade shot Noel a scathing look, but Noel was completely unperturbed. She kept firing off questions as Jade lifted a hand to block the camera. Like a broken record, Jade repeated, "This is an active investigation."

The camera cut back to the anchorman in the television studio, who moved on to other news. Claire let out a breath she didn't realize she was holding and turned to her sister. Brianna's grimace was fixed in place. Claire said, "She basically just accused you—or me, I guess—of leaving Leah Holloway in that car to die."

"I know. It was not good. But what could I say? I didn't want to blurt out that she killed herself. What if her family sees that interview?"

Claire didn't say it, but she imagined it would be worse for Holloway's family to think that Brianna could have rescued the woman and didn't. "I'm sorry," she said. "I should have done the interview. You shouldn't even be in this position."

"Maybe Holloway shouldn't have tried killing everyone she saw today," Brianna replied. "Look, I don't care what anyone says. Those kids are safe. You and I know what really happened. That's all that matters. This will blow over eventually."

CHAPTER SIXTEEN

The Holloway house was a two-story brown-and-white contemporary set back behind a generous, well-kept front yard, ringed by carefully tended flowerbeds. The black-eyed Susans still stood tall, leaning slightly in the direction of the sun, which had started to drop below the horizon. The driveway showed wear, though, the blacktop chipping where it met the sidewalk. Against the garage door leaned a child's bike complete with training wheels, arrayed in pink and yellow flowers, a Hello Kitty bag affixed to its handlebars. Discarded between the driveway and the front door was a child's tricycle, fire-engine red. Connor stepped over a Teenage Mutant Ninja Turtle action figure as he and Jade made their way to the front door. The door itself was white. A wreath made of bright yellow and orange artificial flowers hung from it. A black GMC Sierra sat in the driveway.

Jade rang the doorbell. A moment later, Jim Holloway answered, looking like someone had dragged him ten blocks from the back of a car. He scratched at some dried spit-up on his shirt and stared at them dumbly. "It's you," he said.

Connor managed a tight smile. Behind him he could hear Jade's groan, barely audible but definitely there.

"They're asleep," Jim said.

Connor glanced behind the man into the living room. A periwinkle-blue sectional dominated the room. Along one wall was a white three-tiered particleboard toy organizer, its plastic bins overflowing with toys. Fleece blankets bearing various Disney characters lay atop the sectional. In another corner of the room stood a brown tweed recliner, its frame slightly lopsided. A small table stood beside it, the television remote at its center. The television was easily fifty inches, sitting atop a small entertainment center that held a DVD player and about a hundred children's movies on DVD. Framed photos of the Holloways adorned the cream-colored walls. Quickly, Connor counted the framed photos. From where he stood, he could see at least a dozen. Most were candid shots of the family on vacation: camping, at the beach, what looked like the Sacramento Zoo, Disneyland. A few had been professionally shot, the family dressed in their Sunday best and forced into artificial poses.

On one side of the couch, little Hunter Holloway lay curled up, clutching a Disney *Toy Story* blanket, his thumb firmly in his mouth. His face looked swollen, perhaps from the tantrum he had thrown earlier—or the one Connor had no doubt the child had thrown when they got home, and his mother was still not there. On the other side of the couch lay the baby. He was on his back, his arms spread wide above him like he was raising them to show his muscles. His little face had the blissful look of sleeping with total abandon that only infants and puppies get. Connor felt his heart twinge a little. Across from them on the recliner sat Peyton, her legs thrust out straight, her little feet dangling just over the edge of the chair. She stared straight ahead, unseeing.

"Mr. Holloway," Jade said. "We really need to talk to your daughter about what happened today."

Jim looked over his shoulder at the children. "She, uh, she hasn't talked since I got to the hospital, but you can try. Just don't—don't wake up the other kids. I'm hoping they'll sleep till my mom gets here. She should be here in another hour. Her flight was delayed."

Connor and Jade eased past the man and approached Peyton. She showed no flicker of emotion, no indication that she even noticed they were there. Feeling like the two of them standing over her might over-whelm the girl, Connor hung back and settled gently onto the couch between the two boys. Surreptitiously, he took pillows from behind him and stuffed them beside baby Tyler. If his behavior at the hospital didn't expose Jim Holloway as a rookie right off, the scene at the house certainly did. Connor didn't have children of his own, but in the last few years, his younger brother's wife had given birth to twins, and Connor had learned all kinds of things about babies and toddlers that he never knew before. One of which was that you didn't leave a five-month-old unattended on a couch for fear that he might roll over and fall off.

Jade knelt beside the recliner. "Hi, Peyton," she said. She pulled out her badge. "My name is Jade Webb. I'm with the police. I don't know if you remember me from earlier at the hospital. We didn't really have a chance to talk. I'm trying to find out what happened with your mommy today. Is it okay if we talk?"

Connor noticed that Jade didn't use a syrupy tone. She talked to Peyton as she might to a grown woman—sympathetic, but not pity-ing. It was the same tone she used with domestic violence victims. Peyton's eyes flickered briefly toward Jade's badge and then back to front and center, staring sightlessly at something the rest of them could not see. Connor knew she was suffering from shock and exhaustion. They waited, but the girl didn't speak. Her eyes didn't move. In fact, Connor wasn't sure they would ever find another six-year-old who could stay as perfectly still as Peyton.

Jade gave it another try, after waiting a few more minutes, to no avail. "Okay, Peyton. We don't have to talk right now," she said. "Maybe you can talk to my friend over there. His name is Connor. He's a really nice guy. He's my favorite person to work with."

She stood and switched places with Connor. All the while, Jim stood observing them from the corner of the room, the lines of his face twitching like he was watching a delicate operation of some kind. Like he was actually watching Connor and Jade pull Peyton's teeth rather than just asking her some questions. Connor wasn't sure if Jim was more afraid of the damage it would do to Peyton to dredge everything up, or if he just didn't want to hear what Peyton might have to say.

Connor knelt beside Peyton and smiled, just like Jade had. "Hey, sweetheart," he said. "Do you want to see my badge?" No response. "Listen, Peyton, I know you don't want to talk about what happened today. It was very, very scary, and I know that things are really confusing right now. I'm sorry for what happened today, but it's really important that we find out from you what happened. Anything you can tell us would be a really, really big help."

He waited. Just when he thought that he was going to strike out, as Jade had, Peyton's voice came, small and tremulous. The sound of it alone would've been enough to break Connor's heart. "If I help you, will you bring my mommy home?"

Peyton's words were a knife to his gut. He heard Jim's gasp behind him.

Peyton's little brow furrowed. Just a tiny bit of hope. As though she already knew that her mommy wasn't coming back, but just had to ask.

He hung his head, then looked back up at her. He had never hated his job so much. "No, honey, I'm sorry. I can't bring your mommy home. But what we can do is try to figure out what happened to her, and for that I really need your help. I know that you and your mommy went to a gas station and went into the bathroom. Do you remember that?"

But she had shut down, eyes fixed straight ahead once more as if he didn't exist, as if none of them existed. She was gone. He wanted to scoop her up, cradle her, and whisper soothing things into her ear. He didn't understand why Jim hadn't rushed across the room and done exactly that.

He felt Jade's hand on his shoulder. "Parks," she whispered. "We can come back tomorrow. Maybe after she's had some sleep."

"Okay, okay," he said.

They stood, facing Jim once more. He looked like he might cry.

"Mr. Holloway," Jade said, "you told us Peyton hasn't said anything since she came home today? What about before that? In the hospital?"

Jim shook his head. "No, nothing. She hasn't said a word."

They left the man looking helpless and hopeless. Jade shook her head all the way down the front walk. "Unfuckingbelievable. Nothing from the kid."

"Jade," Connor said. "That child has been traumatized beyond belief."

"Yeah, I know. That's why I want to find out what happened. Why would you do that to your own kid?"

"I don't know," Connor said.

CHAPTER SEVENTEEN

"That bitch in there is totally drunk with power," Jade said as they left a Globocell store in Midtown. Outside, night had fallen over the city.

"Yeah, no shit," Connor said. He swiped a hand through his hair. "She was probably looking at the goddamn numbers while she was telling us to follow proper protocol and contact their corporate office." At the words *follow proper protocol* his tone became high-pitched and mocking.

Jade laughed. "That's Globocell talk for *Go fuck yourself.*"

They had retrieved Leah Holloway's phone from the toilet. Connor thought it had been submerged far too long to salvage, but Jade had insisted on trying. It now sat on her desk in a bowl of dry rice. Earlier that day, Connor had faxed a warrant to the Iowa corporate office of Leah's cell phone provider, Globocell, to the attention of a woman who promised to pass his request along to the legal department, who wouldn't be in until Monday, and would then take five to seven days to process his request. In the meantime, they'd gone to a local Globocell store and taken a stab at getting Leah Holloway's phone records more quickly. Or at least the last two numbers that called her before she drove her car into the river.

"I don't believe I've ever seen a woman turn you down before, Parks."

Connor sighed as Jade started the car. Inside his jacket, he fingered his cell phone. Besides a half-dozen texts from Stryker and one call from Captain Boggs, there was nothing. Nothing more from Claire. Not that he'd been expecting more.

See you soon.

The ball was in his court now. It was up to him to put himself back in her way, take the risk of being rejected again.

"It happens more often than you think," he muttered.

Jade shot him a raised brow. "So," she said. "Claire. She was the one that got away."

Connor didn't comment. He looked out the window, watching the city pass by in a blur of buildings, trees, cars, and pedestrians, lit only by the streetlights and the fluorescent glow of the stores they passed.

"It was nice to finally meet the legendary Claire Fletcher," Jade added. "That was really something, the way she jumped into that river to save all those kids. She's pretty fearless, huh?"

Connor laughed drily. "No," he said. "Not fearless. Just crazy brave. She has no idea what she's made of."

Fear was a second skin for Claire. After ten years in captivity, she had learned to live with it. Connor watched her confront it time and again with courage that was breathtaking to observe, to even be in the presence of. She could save children from a vehicle crashed in a river, yet she couldn't sleep with him. She could risk her life but not her heart. Of course, there was today.

"So what happened with you two?" Jade asked as they pulled into the OOI parking lot.

"I really don't want to talk about it."

"Sure you don't."

"I don't."

"Okay. Talk to me in an hour when we're ass deep in paperwork on this Holloway case."

The paperwork lasted until after midnight. Finally, at half past midnight, Jade yawned and stretched her arms above her head. "I think we should call it a night," she said. "We're not getting anything done on this investigation at least until tomorrow morning."

"Oh, I'll try getting in touch with her doctor in the morning, at his house if I have to," Connor said.

"Yeah, well, that sounds like a good idea, but right now I think we should go home and get some rest."

Reluctantly, Connor called it a night. It was well past the time that would have been appropriate to visit Claire, but he found himself driving to her house anyway. He parked across the street. The living room lights were still on. He pulled out his phone and looked at her text from earlier. He had no idea how to do this. They hadn't been an item, or a couple, or whatever they were to each other, in two years. He didn't know if showing up at her house at one in the morning would look desperate or interested. Or maybe a little bit of both.

He sighed and turned his car back on. This was ridiculous. He was exhausted. Between the Soccer Mom Strangler case and the Holloway crash, he had been awake for almost thirty-six hours. He probably smelled. He had spilled coffee, mayonnaise, and creamer on his suit over the course of the last day. If he was going to try to win Claire back, he should probably be at his best, and this 1:00 a.m. Connor was definitely not his best. He was about to pull away when his phone dinged, indicating a text message. It was Brianna. *Don't be a dumbass,* it said. *She's still awake. Come on in.*

Connor laughed. He rifled through his glove compartment until he came up with some deodorant. Hastily, he slapped it on. He found a couple of mints in his jacket pocket, pushed his hair around on his head a few times, smoothed his beard down, and got out of the car.

He headed for her front door, feeling like a teenage boy picking up his prom date. What if he crashed and burned again? He was starting this all over with her, and to this point it had always ended the same—with her pushing him away. But then he thought of her on the riverbank earlier that day, opening up to him, and knocked. Immediately, Wilson's bark sounded, then whining and frantic scratching at the door. Claire pulled the door open, the smile on her face sending his stomach plummeting. God, he had missed her.

Wilson jumped up, demanding his attention, whimpering, and shaking his furry butt. Claire tried pulling him back. "It's fine," Connor said. "Really."

He got down to Wilson's level and gave him a good scratching behind his ears, his sides, and his back—all of his favorite places. When Wilson was satisfied, they stepped inside, Claire closing and locking the door behind them. She looked beautiful, even in a pair of sweatpants and an oversized UC Davis T-shirt. Her curls, ever unruly, shone in the soft glow of the lamplight coming from the end table. A romantic comedy played muted on the television. Brianna was nowhere to be found.

"You came," Claire said.

CHAPTER EIGHTEEN

SUNDAY

They stood awkwardly in the living room. There hadn't been many awkward moments between the two of them since they'd met. Claire didn't know what to say now that he was here. The whole evening she had paced the living room with Wilson in tow, rehearsing all the things she wanted to say to him—none of which came to mind now that he was standing before her, looking impossibly handsome. Before she could stop herself, she reached out and touched his beard. The hair was softer than she expected. He smiled and stepped closer to her, making her breath catch in her throat. He reached up and pressed her palm harder against his cheek. Closing his eyes, he let out a quiet sigh. Relief.

"Long day?" she managed.

He opened his eyes. She wasn't sure if he said yes. The next thing she knew she was in his arms and they were kissing. Long, soft, slow kisses that sent a delicious thrill of pleasure from her center up to her head with dizzying speed. She shivered as his hands ran up and down her back. She had always loved his hands. Firm but gentle. Always gentle. He was the only man whose touch she had ever enjoyed, even craved. And yet, at a certain point, it ceased to matter. At a certain point past the foreplay, all the horrific things that had been done to her came rushing back, and she couldn't separate her trauma from the moment with Connor. She couldn't get past it.

Beside them, Wilson whined. Claire felt his paw against her leg. She pushed against Connor's chest and he let her go. She felt the air around her like a loss and wanted to be close to him again.

"I'm sorry," he breathed.

She pulled him toward the couch. "I'm not."

There were some frantic breathless moments on the couch, Claire letting herself go, letting herself feel every sensation he evoked in her, reveling in her proximity to him. It was astounding how much she had missed him. He felt—physically and emotionally—like a missing puzzle piece.

"Stop," Connor said. With the utmost care, he slid out from beneath her, disentangling, disconnecting. He stood and walked across the room. His hair was mussed, his clothes in disarray. He smoothed his beard with both hands as he tried to catch his breath.

Claire perched on the edge of the couch. Her fingers fidgeted with the collar of her shirt. The skin of her throat burned where his beard had scraped against it. It was not unpleasant. "Connor?"

He smiled at her. "I just think we should slow down. I don't want to stop, believe me, but I'm not sure we should jump into the one thing we always had . . . issues with."

Claire laughed nervously. "Right."

But she found that she wanted to rush in, now that he was there with her. For once, she wanted to disappear into his arms, into the feel of his skin, into those expert hands, his smell. She wanted to think about nothing but Connor, the one person in the world who made her feel completely safe. She wanted to take that leap. Desperately. But she held herself back, gripping the edges of the couch cushion on either side of her thighs.

"And, Claire," Connor added. "You don't have to do this. I mean, if you're feeling—well, I told you, things with Jade—there's nothing there. I told you before, I'd wait for you."

"Stop," Claire said. "I'm not doing it for that reason. I'm jealous, sure, but I just . . . I want to be close to you right now."

"Okay."

She waited for him to ask what they were doing, to bring up the issue of their relationship, of trying again. But he didn't. He stood, walked over to her, and held out his hand. She took it and led him up to her bedroom. After all these years, she didn't have to tell him what she wanted. He kicked off his shoes and stripped down to his boxer shorts. They climbed beneath the covers together. Grumbling, Wilson took up position in the corner of the room on his bed. Claire and Connor lay down side by side and he wrapped his arms around her, pulling her close, holding her tightly. For a moment, she was taken back to the very first night they met, the very first time they had done this.

"Do you want to talk about today?" he whispered.

She inhaled his scent and closed her eyes. Drowsiness overcame her faster than she expected. "No," she said. "Not now. I just want you to hold me. I just want this."

His lips brushed the top of her head. "Okay," he said. "This it is."

CHAPTER NINETEEN

Claire struggled in his arms that night, nightmares assailing her intermittently. Visions of Leah Holloway—mouth stretched wide in terror, submerged beneath water, sinking—mixed with images from her ten years of captivity. She hadn't had nightmares for a very long time. She had triggers, of course. Some were worse than others, but for the most part, she had that under control. The incident with Holloway had unleashed memories that she hadn't thought of in years. Horrible, terrifying memories. The sound of Miranda Simon's bound body landing on the floor in front of her after Reynard Johnson dragged the girl into the room. The look in Johnson's eye as he stared down at the two of them—two teenage girls at his mercy—like he was about to devour a meal. The way one edge of the duct tape over Simon's mouth peeled away just a little bit, but not enough to allow the girl to speak. Johnson had stuffed a wad of cloth deep into her mouth. Each time Claire woke with a scream lodged in her throat, Connor was there, squeezing her, stroking her hair, whispering in her ear. "You're safe. I'm here. No one's going to hurt you."

Finally, around four, she fell into a deep and mercifully dreamless sleep. She knew when she woke two hours later that she'd been snoring because her throat was dry and scratchy. A crusty line of dried drool went from the corner of her mouth to her cheek. Connor slept, his arms still encasing her, one leg slung over her body. She wriggled in his arms and turned her face toward his so she could see him. Tracing the contours of his face with her fingers, she admired his facial hair. It struck her then that she had never dated a guy with a beard before. Her captor had never had facial hair. For her, to see it on Connor was exhilarating in a way, raising her attraction to him a notch. She stared at him until she fell back to sleep.

When she woke, he was in the shower down the hall. She met him at the breakfast table, where a stack of pancakes and a note from Brianna sat.

Breakfast for you two lovebirds. Don't forget to turn off the coffeemaker.

Connor had put on his suit from the day before. His stained suit jacket hung on the back of his chair. He ate with gusto, hunched over his food, shoveling pancakes into his mouth. Wilson sat beside him, his head perched on Connor's thigh. Claire tried to shoo him away, but he wasn't having it. Every couple of minutes, Connor reached down and scratched the back of the dog's neck.

It was like they'd always been a couple. Eating in contented silence. Maybe they didn't need to talk about their relationship, or trying again, or what last night had meant.

Connor gulped down the rest of his coffee. Then he said her name in a tone that implied that he intended to talk about exactly that.

"Did you get anywhere with the Holloway case?" she asked quickly.

For a moment, he stared at her, as if he were trying to decide on something. Then it all came spilling out, all the details, all the things that they knew so far, which Claire had to agree was not much at all. The only things that Connor really had in terms of the Leah Holloway investigation were questions. Why had she done it? If she really had such a perfect life, what would cause her to snap and drive her children and her best friend's children into a river? Who had called her at the soccer field? At the gas station? Was it the same person both times? What had they said? What could be so bad that it made Holloway do what she did? Why had she drunk Alan Wheeler's vodka? What would make a woman who was dead set against any alcohol consumption suddenly down almost an entire bottle with her children in the car?

"We're going to look at her medical records today," Connor said. "I'll go to her doctor's home if I have to, drag him down to his office, but I don't think we're going to find anything. That's just to rule the medical component out right away and to see if she had any type of mental illness that we don't know about. I think things are exactly the way we saw them on the video. She got a call at the soccer field that freaked her out. She put the kids in the car and drove off. Stopped at the gas station, got a second call, drank the vodka, and ran her car off the road."

Claire put her hands on her lap and stared down at them. She thought about Leah Holloway's eyes. A shiver ran through her body. She knew exactly why Leah Holloway drank that vodka. "She was shoring herself up," she told Connor. "She had to do something, and she didn't have the courage to do it. Maybe if she didn't have that bottle, she wouldn't have driven into the river. But she drank that vodka to work up the nerve to kill herself and those kids."

"You think so?"

"I know so," Claire replied. "You didn't see her. You didn't see her face." She couldn't keep the note of hysteria from rising in her voice.

Connor reached across the table and clamped a hand down over her forearm. "It's okay. I believe you."

"Connor," Claire said. "Whatever was going on with Holloway—and there was something going on—whatever it was was unimaginable. Unimaginably bad."

CHAPTER TWENTY

Connor watched Jade weave her way absently through the bull pen area of the Office of Investigations, a stack of papers in her hands. She flipped through them as she walked, head down, her brow scrunched in concentration. She stopped as she passed his desk, glaring at the large Starbucks cup in Connor's hand as though the cup had personally insulted her. She pointed to it. "What is that?"

Connor smiled and placed the offending cup on his desk. "I didn't go to Starbucks and purposely not get you a cup. Claire stopped by. Brought me a cup of coffee."

Jade continued to her own desk and sat down, looking once again at the pages in her hands. "Must be nice," she mumbled.

A beefy hand clamped down on Connor's shoulder. Stryker's voice was a hot whisper in Connor's ear. "Dude, the profiler is hot."

Connor laughed and swiveled his chair to face him. "You're into men now?"

Stryker rolled his eyes. "Don't be a sexist pig. The profiler's a woman. We were supposed to get a guy named Bennett, but he got stuck in Los Angeles so they sent someone else."

"And she's hot?" Jade asked. "Thought you only had eyes for that obnoxious reporter."

Something dark passed over Stryker's face. He frowned, eyes on the floor. "Yeah, I don't think that's going to work out."

"That's what you always say," Jade said.

Stryker shifted his weight. "No, no," he said. "This time it really doesn't look good."

No one said anything. Silence stretched out until the moment became unbearably heavy. Then Stryker said, "I just came over to let you know the profiler briefing is in fifteen."

"We're on Holloway," Jade said.

"Doesn't matter," Stryker said. "Cap wants everyone in this briefing." He gave her a pointed look as he walked away. "I'll see you there."

Jade tossed her stack of papers onto her desk. They fanned out, sliding almost to the edge. "What've you done today?" she asked Connor. "Besides getting a coffee delivery from your girlfriend?"

"I talked to my guy in computers. He says there was nothing of note on Leah Holloway's PC—she has a PC, by the way, not a laptop. He said it's ancient. Anyway, he said there's nothing on it except thousands of pictures of her kids. He also hacked her email account and the only personal emails that he could even find were from four years ago when she and her brother exchanged pleasantries over the birth of Hunter. I also got a copy of Holloway's medical chart from her family doctor and went through it. What'd you do this morning?"

She bristled but said nothing. "The records were normal, by the way," Connor added. "No major medical problems. A little over a year ago she complained about a lack of concentration and some memory loss, but she had an MRI of her brain and it was normal. Her cholesterol was a bit high. That's about it. No mention of any history of anxiety or depression. No referrals for mental health treatment. No mention of problems with addiction of any kind. She didn't even smoke."

Jade shuffled some papers around on her desk until she found her notepad. She tucked it into her jacket pocket and stood. "I ordered her OB-GYN chart."

"Well, we can cancel that now, right? We know she didn't have any underlying medical condition."

One corner of Jade's mouth lifted in a smile that indicated that Connor was some kind of idiot. "Premenstrual dysphoric disorder," she explained. "Look it up."

Connor leaned back in his chair and folded his arms. "How about you just tell me what it is."

"It's like PMS on LSD. It's a real thing. Lots of women Holloway's age get it. From ovulation to the day you first start bleeding, your pre-menstrual symptoms are worse than normal. It can give you pretty bad mood swings. I'm not saying it could make a woman homicidal or suicidal, but it might make a woman homicidal or suicidal."

"Is that why you're not in a relationship?"

He narrowly avoided a punch to his arm. Jade shook her head. "If you weren't so cute, I'd shoot you in the kneecap."

"So you do have this disorder."

She glowered at him. "The only thing I have is an asshole for a partner."

"Oh, come on, Jade. You like me."

Again, she shook her head. "I like it better when you don't talk. Just stand around and look pretty, and I won't shoot you."

"So you think Holloway had premenstrual dysphoric disorder?" Connor said.

"No, but I think we should check."

Connor stood and they started in the direction of the conference rooms. He said, "The coroner is moving her autopsy up at the request of the mayor. The only thing people are hotter about than Holloway is the Soccer Mom Strangler."

"Speaking of which, do we really need to go to the stupid briefing?"

Jade took a few more steps before she realized he'd stopped. She turned, hands on her hips. "What?"

"What's your problem, Jade? It's what—maybe an hour out of our day? Holloway can wait. She's already killed all the people she's going to kill. This guy—he could be out there murdering someone right now."

She made a noise of exasperation. "Calm down, Mr. Superhero. I'm just saying it's not even our case."

"It's all hands on deck, Jade. If we wrap up Holloway today, we're getting put back on the Strangler tomorrow."

She raised a skeptical brow. "Holloway won't get wrapped up today. Tox screens take at least six weeks."

"You know what I mean."

"Why don't you go and you can tell me what this profiler person says?" she said, the words *profiler person* laced with disdain, as though Stryker had invited a snake charmer to come and speak about the case. So that was it.

Connor smiled and got closer to her. "It's because she's hot, isn't it?"

Jade swatted his shoulder. "Oh please. I don't give a rat's ass if she's hot. I don't care if she gives the briefing in a *Sports Illustrated* swimsuit. It's a waste of time."

"What's that?"

"Profiling. Let me guess what your bad guy is like: He's bad. He likes to rape and murder moms. What more do you need to know? There's your profile. I just saved us all an assload of time."

Connor laughed. He put both hands on her shoulders and steered her into the packed briefing room. "I'm pretty sure there's more to it than that."

CHAPTER
TWENTY-ONE

The profiler was attractive, Connor had to agree. She was slender with delicate features and long, flowing dark hair. But her electric-blue eyes and well-defined legs, shown off by her light-gray skirt suit, no doubt went a long way toward the relative hush that had fallen over the room. There was none of the talking or rustling that had gone on in Stryker's briefing the day before. Connor hoped the straight male officers in the room would actually hear what she had to say.

"Good morning," she began, her voice clear and confident. No smiling. All business. "My name is Special Agent Kassidy Bishop. I'm with the FBI's Behavioral Analysis Unit. I was asked to lend support to the investigation." She went on to talk briefly about the BAU and what they did. Connor had already known that they would only assist on a case if they were invited to do so. Their primary role was to review all the evidence and then come up with a profile, a description of the sort of person the local police should be looking for.

"This is especially useful in narrowing a pool of suspects," Bishop said. "Now, I understand you do not have any suspects in this case at this time, but that's okay. The profile I am going to give you today will still be useful in your investigation, although I caution you not to try to fit any potential suspects to this profile. Remember that any aspect of this profile could be wrong. We are usually pretty accurate, but don't get too caught up in getting everything to match up with the profile. Let the evidence be your guide."

She turned to the dry-erase board and began writing, talking as she went.

"You're looking for a Caucasian male. Serial killers rarely murder outside of their race, and the majority of true serial killers are Caucasian males. This UNSUB—Unknown Subject—is what we call a disorganized offender. These are crimes of opportunity. No planning went into them, at least not the first one. The three murders after that only show that he has chosen a hunting ground for his victims. He hasn't refined his approach. He isn't expanding on some elaborate fantasy. He is still acting spontaneously. He doesn't bring anything with him to the crime scenes. He doesn't stalk these women beforehand for any length of time. The first time he sees them is when he decides he is going to rape and kill them. He has a type. If he finds his type and thinks that he can get away with it, he's going to do it.

"So your UNSUB is in the area, sees the opportunity to carry out his crime, and goes for it. It is impulsive and poorly thought out. He takes huge risks committing these crimes in broad daylight in areas where anyone might see him, and he leaves evidence behind. He started to wipe the vehicles down for prints, yet he leaves his DNA at the scene. Given this lack of sophistication, I believe you are looking for a young man between the ages of eighteen and twenty-six, more likely on the lower end of that range. I would say that he has some high school education. Given the impulsivity, he probably uses drugs or alcohol or both, and was likely under the influence of one or both at the time of some, if not all, of these murders."

Beside Connor, Jade whispered, "Holy shit, this is boring."

Without looking at her, Connor nudged her with an elbow. "Shhh."

"Now, there is the matter of his ability to easily approach these women. They were all outdoors, all within shouting distance of other people. There is no evidence that he brought a weapon to the scenes. It is certainly possible that he has a knife or a gun, but doubtful. A man with a knife or a gun would stand out in these areas. I do not believe that he is armed when he approaches his victims. So how does he walk up to these women and engage them without setting off their internal alarms?"

"He knocks them over the head and forces them into their vehicles?" O'Handley offered.

"It is certainly a possibility that he simply overpowers them, but there's no evidence of blunt force trauma to any of their heads," Agent Bishop countered. "Two things: he looks like he belongs there. He is known to many of them or he is of an age where his presence would not be unusual, which is another reason why I think he is young. A young man—even a teenager or college-aged male—at a youth soccer match is not going to raise alarm bells. Two of the crimes occurred in the Pocket area, one of which was the first murder. He either lives or works in that area. Serial killers usually start out in what we consider their comfort zone. The first murder is especially likely to take place near their home. Although he is young with average intelligence, he is likely either charming or attractive, or both. Average intelligence does not preclude charm. He will know what to say to these women to get them to let their guards down. The use of drugs or alcohol will lower his inhibitions and make him bolder.

"Let's also consider the victims. They're all mothers. What do all mothers want?"

"Sleep," one of the female officers shouted from the back, drawing laughter from around the room.

"Time," another woman put in. "And a clean house."

Agent Bishop smiled. "Yes. Sleep, time, a clean house. All of these things require help from someone else. Moms need someone to watch their kids so they can sleep. They want a few quiet hours away from their duties, for which they need help. They want their partner to pick up the slack and clean the house. Help. Assistance. Your UNSUB knows this. He sees a harried mother sneaking a smoke or trying to get a stroller out of her vehicle, he will be there, as sweet and solicitous as can be. If he is attractive to boot, they will be more likely to let their guards down. They won't see him as a threat. In fact, I believe he is likely extremely attractive. His attractiveness and charm will make it more likely that women will let their guards down. This case has been pretty well publicized for the last several weeks. These mothers should be well aware that a killer is targeting soccer moms. Still, they will not see this UNSUB as a threat because of the way he looks and the way he acts. But his charming demeanor won't last long. Once he is close enough to strike, it will be a blitz attack. Quick and dirty."

The sound of Jade's foot tapping against the tile floor drew Connor's attention. He caught her gaze. "Do you mind?" he asked as quietly as he could. She rolled her eyes but stopped tapping.

Agent Bishop continued. "He has an intense hatred of women. As I mentioned before, he has a type. He is looking for women of a certain body shape. Women who are mothers. The victims are surrogates, or stand-ins, for a mother figure. They represent someone to him. He has a great deal of rage toward mother figures. As a child, he may have been adopted or more likely abandoned. The first thing a mother would do is plead for her life based on the lives of her children. She'll say something like, 'Please, I have children,' which will only enrage him more. This is about punishing them. His intense rage is evident in the crime scene photos. These assaults are savage, yet they are intimate in the sense that he is killing them with his hands. There is no weapon between him and the victim. He even bites them, which is something a toddler does in a fit of anger. Small children don't yet understand that biting as an expression of anger is not acceptable. Most children outgrow it or are taught that it is not acceptable behavior. Again, we see a regression to a childlike state. The child taking out his anger on his mother.

"The UNSUB has absolutely no remorse for what he has done. Clinically, he probably has some sort of antisocial personality disorder. He doesn't care about these women or their children. They are not human to him. He will have difficulty maintaining relationships, so he will likely be single, although a breakup with a girlfriend or lover may have been the precipitating event in all of this. It is possible that the end of a romantic relationship re-created the abandonment he felt as a child and triggered these homicidal episodes. He did it the first time. It felt good. He got away with it. He will keep going until he is caught."

"No shit," Jade grumbled.

"Shhh," Connor said.

"You're looking for a loner who has some superficial friendships that are in place mostly to provide for any needs he might have. He will use his charm to get what he needs, but his relationships will have little depth other than that. He may be marginally employed, in some kind of unskilled job, but his sense of entitlement will prevent him from keeping a job for very long, and his ability to manipulate others will allow him to get by during periods when he is unemployed. He may have had some run-ins with the law as a juvenile. You're likely to see one or all of the elements many consider the trifecta of serial killers: bed-wetting, cruelty to animals, and arson. But he is too young to have gotten into much trouble before this, so he doesn't have a record. That's why his prints aren't coming up—assuming that the unidentified prints recovered from the first victim's vehicle are his. He does not drive. He moves around by foot or uses public transportation. By virtue of his age and lack of assets, he has no transportation of his own, but this works to his advantage in committing these crimes. As I said, he'll blend in easily in these areas. An attractive young male walking around a soccer field is not going to draw attention, and he can easily hop on a bus and be quickly out of the area after the crimes."

Connor studied her list:

Male
Caucasian
Disorganized, impulsive
Age: 18–26
High school education
Drug/alcohol use
Likely not armed
Attractive, superficial charm
Hatred of women (mother figure)
Will blend in
Lives/works in Pocket
Single/recent breakup (triggering event)
On foot/public transportation
Unskilled job/possibly unemployed

He turned to Stryker, who stood on his other side. "You should get a few people to review all the footage you have so far. See if we can see this guy trolling for victims."

Stryker nodded. "Yeah. I'm gonna put some more people in Pocket. We'll go door to door if we have to. Hey, you live in Pocket. You haven't seen anyone suspicious?"

"You're funny," Connor said. "You know I'm never home. I'm always here."

Agent Bishop answered a few questions and concluded the briefing. "I'll be in town until tomorrow if you have any additional questions or if anything comes up. Detective Stryker has my contact information." She gave them a grim smile. "Good luck out there."

CHAPTER

TWENTY-TWO

"Now come on," Jade scoffed when they were back at their desks. "Do you really believe all that bullshit about the Strangler killing mommies because he was adopted?"

A large manila envelope sat atop the mess of paperwork on Connor's desk, its contents so thick that the folds holding it together threatened to burst. In thick black marker, someone had scrawled "Webb/Parks" across the front. It had some heft. In the return address corner, tiny block print announced: "Tasker Greaves, OB-GYN."

"Leah Holloway's OB-GYN records," Connor said. "Looks like someone put them on the wrong desk. How come these doctor's offices will respond to a warrant within twenty-four hours on a weekend, but the chick at Globocell won't tell me the last two numbers that called Holloway's phone?"

Jade plopped into her chair. "Because the chick at the Globocell store is an asshole," she said. "Open 'em up. We'll split up the chart."

Connor slipped a finger under the flap of the envelope and tore it open. "Why so thick?" he asked. "Her primary doctor's chart wasn't this thick."

"She was healthy. No reason to see her family doctor, but she had three kids. Lots of visits to her OB."

Connor handed her the bottom half of the chart.

"Speaking of the kids, I guess we can assume that both her boys will grow up to be serial killers, huh? I mean, since Mommy abandoned them when she killed herself. According to the profiler, right?"

Connor froze, Leah Holloway's OB-GYN records in his hands. He stared at Jade, but she had already pulled her chair up to her desk, head bent to the pages in front of her.

"Jade," he said. "I think you're taking this a little too personally."

She glanced up at him, a sardonic smile twisting her lips. "Personally? Please. I'm not taking anything personally. I—" She stopped, and her smile flattened out.

"Forgot you told me, didn't you?"

Her cheeks colored. She looked away, flustered, riffling through the pages before her with sudden vigor. Connor sat down in his chair and wheeled it over next to hers, so close their legs were almost touching. Jade stopped riffling and hung her head. "It was the Baker case, wasn't it?"

"Those were long, boring hours on stakeout," Connor said.

"Fuck."

"Agent Bishop wasn't making a commentary on women who give their kids up for adoption, you know that, right? She's just throwing out theories about what kind of person might be committing these crimes. You know as well as I do that not all adopted or abandoned kids grow up to be killers. Whoever this guy is, he already has issues. Shit, what might not even faze a regular kid is going to be totally different for this guy. Jesus, Jade. Some serial killers grow up in perfectly normal two-parent households. It's not a predictor. This is not about you."

She squeezed the bridge of her nose. "You're right. Of course, you're right. I'm sorry. I just . . ." She lowered her voice even more. "He'd be about the same age as the UNSUB right now."

"So what? You think it's him?"

Jade laughed. "Of course not. Don't be ridiculous. It's just—it just brings it all up again, you know? This time of year always reminds me. It messes me up."

Connor patted her shoulder. "I'm sorry," he said.

She shook her head, shrugged his hand away, and forced a smile. "I'm fine. It's fine. Thanks for not being a prick."

Connor winked and wheeled off to his own desk. "Not being a prick is my specialty."

Silently, they paged through their respective halves of Leah Holloway's OB-GYN chart. "I can't even read this chicken scratch," Jade remarked. "Seriously, you don't need to know how to write to get in to medical school?"

"The nurses' notes are better," Connor said. He too could not make out anything the doctor had written. Hieroglyphs. But the nurses' handwritten notes were excellent. They were mostly unremarkable. Yearly visits, all with normal findings except for her pregnancies, but even those were without complication.

Jade said, "There's nothing here."

Then Connor saw it. He had to read it three times to make sure he was getting it right. He wheeled over to Jade and handed her the nurses' notes for the visit.

"Parks, this is from over a year ago."

He pointed to the section that had caught his eye. "Yeah, but it is a pretty good indicator that things weren't 'fine' in the Holloway household."

Jade read it quickly. "I would not have pegged her schlub of a husband for a cheater."

"Me either," Connor agreed.

Leah had asked to be tested for every STD known to man. *Husband had unprotected sex with unknown partner.*

"All her tests came back negative," Connor said. "So he didn't give her anything."

"Because he wasn't the one having an affair," Jade said.

"That's what I'm thinking," Connor said. "I can't see Jim Holloway carrying on an affair. I can see Leah throwing him under the bus, though. Image was everything to her. No way would she want to admit that she was the one cheating."

"Still," Jade said, chewing the tip of her pen. "Imagine what it would have taken for someone so worried about projecting the perfect image to have to tell a lie like that, then undergo all those invasive tests. It must have been so humiliating."

"A month later, she's pregnant."

"Let me see the rest of the notes," Jade said.

Connor retrieved the stack from his desk, and together they read the rest of the records from that visit. "This is when she found out she was pregnant," Jade said. "At this visit. The same visit."

"You think that's why she didn't leave him?"

"I think appearances were really important to her. She probably stayed so she wouldn't break up her family."

"Neither the husband nor the best friend mentioned this cheating stuff, the STD scare," Connor pointed out.

"Hardly surprising she wouldn't tell anyone. This is not something you want people knowing about, especially if you're going to stay in your marriage."

"Well," Connor said. "We need to have another talk with Jim Holloway. He said everything was fine."

Jade shrugged. "Maybe it is now. Maybe they worked it out. This record is over a year old. Maybe things got better after this."

"Maybe. I mean we don't even know if she was having an ongoing affair or if it was a one-time thing. Maybe the STD scare helped her get her head back on straight."

The phone on Connor's desk rang, and he wheeled back over and snatched it up. "Parks."

"You gotta get over here now," said Davey Richards of the Sacramento County Coroner's Office.

"You got something on Holloway?"

Davey let out a low whistle. "Do I ever. Is Stryker there?"

Connor looked around and spotted Stryker across the room, talking on the phone. "I'm looking at him."

"Bring him too."

CHAPTER

TWENTY-THREE

"Davey fucking Richards," Jade grumbled as she, Connor, and Stryker made their way into the coroner's office. The coroner was housed in a large tan two-story building on Broadway with a rounded portico entrance. Meticulously kept foliage and greenery surrounded the building, its beauty in stark contrast to the death investigations that went on behind its walls.

Stryker hooked a thumb in Jade's direction. "She sure complains a lot."

Jade glared but Connor laughed. "She and Davey were involved for a while. It didn't work out."

Stryker shrugged. "Maybe it was for the best. Do you really want those hands on you after they've been cutting up bodies all day?"

Jade considered this. "Maybe that's why he didn't know what the hell to do with a real live woman."

Stryker roared with laughter. "I'm telling him you said that."

Jade raised a brow. "What's that? Did you just say you want me to shoot you in the kneecap?"

That only made Stryker laugh harder.

"She's running a special on kneecaps today," Connor told his friend.

They all fell silent once they entered the autopsy area. It was a large, sterile, well-lit room with tan tiled floor and taupe walls. In spite of the sunlight streaming through the high windows, it felt cheerless and gloomy. Someone had brought in a handful of lush green houseplants and placed them throughout the room, but for Connor, they only made the space creepier. Especially hanging across from the scale he knew they used to weigh internal organs.

Then there was the smell. Not the coppery scent of blood like one might expect, but a combination of a fetid earthy odor and a chemical smell. It was enough to make Connor puke, and they hadn't even seen anything yet. Lucky for all of them, Leah Holloway's actual autopsy had already been performed.

"I called you after the exam was finished, you know, so you guys don't actually have to watch," Davey explained, with a wink at Jade. Connor wasn't sure if the wink was meant to be some kind of flirtation or what, but he could tell by the disgusted look on Jade's face that she too found it creepy as hell. Maybe Davey really was as inept around the living as Jade had intimated. With his long black hair pulled back in a ponytail and his thick glasses, Connor still didn't get what Jade had seen in the guy in the first place. He didn't know Davey that well. They had only met a handful of times—all under these types of circumstances.

Leah Holloway's body lay covered on the nearest slab. Connor could only see a tuft of blonde hair peeking out from the top of the sheet. The other stainless steel tables lining the room stood empty.

"You got something for me?" Stryker asked. "Or you just wanted to see my smiling face?"

Davey smiled. "You need to see this."

Stryker and Connor exchanged a look but kept silent.

"First of all," Davey said, "this lady is as healthy as can be. I mean, she's a little overweight. She's got a little bit of erosion to her esophagus, so she probably had chronic acid reflux that wasn't being treated effectively. Because of the circumstances, we had a blood sample taken as soon as she came in yesterday to check her blood alcohol level."

"Thought you couldn't do that to a corpse," Stryker said.

Davey shrugged. "Well, they're not totally reliable. The body produces all kinds of alcohol byproducts during the process of decomposition. Plus, a body that's been submerged usually shows a spike in its blood alcohol levels. But she wasn't in the water long enough for that to be a factor. Wasn't dead that long. I'd say the number we came up with is fairly reliable. In actuality, her level might have been slightly lower, but I don't think there's any question that this lady was drunk when she went into the water."

"So she did drink the vodka," Jade said.

"Well, yeah, she drank something," Davey said. "That's not what killed her, though. She died from asphyxia due to aspiration of fluids."

"In English, please," Jade snapped.

Davey smiled. "Drowning. She died from drowning."

"What was her blood alcohol level?" Jade asked.

"Point one zero."

"That fits," Connor said. "She was stumbling around when she left the bathroom."

"So there's your answer," Jade said. "Simple. She cracked under the strain of her perfect life, got drunk, and killed herself. Case closed."

"But that doesn't explain these," Davey said.

Gently, he pulled the cover away from Leah's body, folding it down, stopping just above her pubic mound. Her eyes were closed, her mouth slightly open. Aside from the coroner's massive Y-shaped incision on her torso and the waxy paleness of her skin, she might only have been sleeping. Her large breasts fell to each side. Connor saw immediately what Davey wanted them to see. It sent an electric jolt through his body.

"Three bite marks," Davey said, pointing to each one with a gloved finger. "One on the anterior aspect of the left shoulder, one on the lower, outer quadrant of the right breast, and one to the anterior of the right hip. From what I can tell, they are about three to four days old. I've already done the comparison to the four Soccer Mom Strangler victims. They are the same."

Connor had never known his colleagues to be rendered speechless, but even he could think of nothing to say. Davey clapped his hands in the air, then waved in each one of their faces. "Did you hear me, Detectives? Leah Holloway has bite marks on her body that match those of the Soccer Mom Strangler."

CHAPTER

TWENTY-FOUR

Jade found her voice. She pointed a finger at Davey, as though he were trying to sell them something. "You're saying that in the last three or four days, Leah Holloway was attacked by the Soccer Mom Strangler and she survived?"

With gentle, loving care, Davey covered Leah back up. He shook his head. "No. I'm saying sometime in the last three to four days she had an encounter with the Soccer Mom Strangler, and he bit her multiple times."

"An encounter?" Stryker said.

"You're saying you don't think she was raped?" Connor said.

"The findings are inconclusive in that respect. She has a couple of old rectal tears and some vaginal bruising that are consistent with rape, but could also just be from rough sex. The bites themselves aren't as deep as the ones on the Soccer Mom Strangler victims."

"You think the encounter was consensual," Connor said.

Davey pursed his lips. Connor could tell he was struggling. "No," he said. "I personally don't think it was consensual, but if I were called to testify in court, I couldn't say with one hundred percent certainty that she'd been raped. She certainly does not have the type of bruising elsewhere on her body that I would expect to see in a woman raped by the Soccer Mom Strangler. That guy is angry as hell."

"Agent Bishop, the profiler," Connor explained for Davey's benefit, "said that victimology is really important in cases like these. She said without realizing it, the victims may have escalated him by pleading for their lives for the sake of their children. Maybe Holloway didn't fight back. Maybe she didn't say a damn thing, just let him rape her, in hopes that submitting would save her."

Jade's brow furrowed. "That's a stretch. She's raped by the Soccer Mom Strangler and doesn't report it? Doesn't tell anyone?"

"It's not that easy, Jade," Connor said quietly, thinking about Claire. "It's not that easy to report it."

"Or her husband is the Strangler," Stryker said. "Claire said this lady killed herself. She tried killing her own kids. If you found out your husband, the father of your children, was a serial killer, that would give you a pretty good reason to off yourself."

They stared at one another. Connor exchanged a glance with Jade. They'd both gotten the same impression of Jim Holloway: at worst, he was simply useless.

"Hard to see the husband as the Strangler," Jade said.

"He doesn't fit the profile," Connor agreed. "Too old, steadily employed, has a family."

Stryker shrugged. "She said to let the evidence be our guide. Hell, she said any aspect of the profile could be wrong."

"Well, he does work evenings," Jade said. "Sleeps during the day."

"I don't think it's him," Connor said.

"Agent Bishop is still here. We can run it by her," Stryker said. "But I think we should at least check the husband out. We can't take any chances. It could be him."

"There's one way to find out for sure," Davey said.

"Bring him in," Stryker said. "We'll get a DNA sample and dental impression."

CHAPTER

TWENTY-FIVE

For the second time that day, Claire found herself at police headquarters, lingering outside a conference room in the Office of Investigations. Connor had called her and asked her to meet with the FBI profiler. She was more than a little intimidated, especially standing outside the room listening to the woman give the group of seasoned investigators instructions like she was about to lead the charge in a battle.

"It's very unusual for a victim to survive, given the level of rage we saw in this killer's previous crimes. I think that Detective Parks is correct. Holloway likely reacted differently to the UNSUB than the other victims and de-escalated the assault. You need to take a very careful look at her life. She was the last person known to be in contact with him. You need to find out every single detail about her life for the last week. Try to pinpoint the date of the assault, if you can, and then figure out every place she went that day."

"What about the husband?" Claire recognized Stryker's voice. "He doesn't fit the profile, but do you think he could have done it?"

"Profiles aren't ironclad. We hope to be as accurate as we can. He fits certain aspects of the profile—he is Caucasian, an unskilled laborer, and although he's not a teenager, as the father of a youth soccer player, he would likely not be out of place at a soccer match. But I still maintain you're looking for a younger male. That said, you should rule out the husband before you go any further. That should be easy enough to do. Run his prints against the unidentified prints from the first victim, get a DNA sample and a bite impression. Did she find out that her husband was the Soccer Mom Strangler and decide to do a murder-suicide? It wouldn't be the first time a wife was shocked to find out her husband was a serial killer. Dennis Rader managed to fool his wife for decades."

"Who's Dennis Rader?" Jade asked.

"BTK Killer," Connor put in.

"That's correct," Agent Bishop said in an appreciative tone.

Claire edged around the doorway, trying to peek inside. Just what she needed, a hot FBI profiler in the mix. A woman who could talk shop with Connor and who was infinitely more impressive and interesting than she was. The woman's back was to her, but Claire felt a sigh escape her at the sight of the woman's long, shiny brown locks and well-muscled calves. To the woman's left stood Jade Webb, silent, arms crossed over her chest, a sullen look of disgust on her face. Apparently, Jade was not as enamored of the FBI agent as her colleagues.

"Now Rader's wife maintains she had no idea he was a killer. We had a case once near Seattle, the Traveling Salesman. He killed five women before he started sending the police notes. The murders were so spread out up and down the Washington coast that law enforcement didn't make the connection until he started sending letters. We theorized that his first kill was closest to where he lived, so we took out a billboard and put a handwriting sample on it with the tip-line number. Guess who drove down the interstate and saw it?"

"His wife," Connor guessed.

"What did she do?" Stryker asked.

"She went home and slit her wrists."

"How do you know she saw the billboard?" Stryker asked.

"She called and left a voice mail for her sister before she did it," Agent Bishop said. "She said she had seen the billboard, she knew her husband was the Traveling Salesman, and to tell the police to search his hunting cabin, which of course turned up all the trophies he had collected from his victims."

"Holloway didn't make any attempts to give up her husband as a killer, though," Connor pointed out.

"No, but it is interesting to note that your department leaked the detail about the bite marks only a few days before Holloway went into the river."

Claire knew from Connor that the bite mark leak had been a mistake, but none of the detectives in the room mentioned this.

"So you're saying it was something her husband had done to her, and when she heard about the Soccer Mom Strangler doing it to his victims, she made the connection?" Stryker asked.

Agent Bishop shrugged. "Perhaps. We'll know soon enough. Right now I'd like to see Ms. Fletcher, if that's possible."

Quickly, Claire slipped out of sight.

"She's in the hall," Connor said. "I'll go get her."

"No," Agent Bishop said. "Not here. I don't want her to feel as though she's being interrogated. Is there a coffee shop nearby we could use?"

CHAPTER

TWENTY-SIX

Fifteen minutes later, Claire was sitting across from Agent Kassidy Bishop in a small coffee shop a few minutes from police headquarters. Claire had never been there, but she could see why Connor and Stryker had recommended it. It was roughly the size of a walk-in closet and completely empty except for the two of them.

"Ms. Fletcher," Bishop said. "It's a pleasure to meet you."

Claire nodded.

"Thank you for meeting with me," Bishop added. Up close, the woman looked familiar somehow. Her blue eyes were penetrating. If she weren't smiling, Claire would have felt like prey. As it was, she already felt like the woman already knew everything Claire was thinking. She exuded intelligence, like perfume wafting across the table. Claire reached up and tugged at an unruly curl, reminding herself that she wasn't an idiot. She was, after all, a college graduate now. She'd gotten into veterinary school, which was harder to get into than medical school.

A smile fought its way onto Claire's face. "I'm not sure what I can offer you, Agent Bishop."

"Call me Kassidy. In the interest of full disclosure, I've read your file."

"My file? Oh, right."

Claire had nearly forgotten that she had an FBI file. Of course Kassidy had read it.

"You're quite exceptional," Kassidy said.

"Because I survived?"

"You must know that while stranger abduction is rare, the survival rate among victims is very low."

"Yes, I'm aware."

"We're seeing more cases of children recovered alive after stranger abductions, but it is extremely uncommon."

Claire shifted uncomfortably in her chair. "I thought we were here to talk about Leah Holloway. Although I'm not sure what I can tell you. I never met the woman before yesterday."

"Fair enough," Kassidy said. She took a sip of her coffee and set her cup back down on the table. Claire noticed how still the woman kept her body. No fidgeting, no shifting in her chair, no fingers sifting through her brown locks. She didn't even seem to blink. It was unnerving. "You were the last person to see Mrs. Holloway alive. Have you ever heard of victimology?"

"Is that where police—uh, law enforcement—study the victim of a crime?"

Kassidy's smile widened. "Yes, exactly. We study the victim closely, in the same way we would study a perpetrator. We find out everything we can about them, try to figure out what makes them tick, then we take that information and combine it with everything we know about the perpetrator, so that we have an idea of how the crime may have played out between them. Not all victims react exactly the same way. Sometimes, the way a perpetrator and victim interact tells us things about the crime and about the perpetrator. Now, I have spoken with Detective Parks at length about what you told him, but I'd like you to take me through the events of yesterday morning."

Feeling better talking about Holloway instead of her own case, Claire started with hearing the sounds of the impacts on the overpass and ended with speaking to the group of detectives on the bank of the river. She didn't talk about how her consciousness had separated from her body for the first time in years. She didn't talk about the memories that the entire experience had dredged up or about the nightmares it had given her.

Kassidy asked, "Did Mrs. Holloway appear intoxicated to you?"

Claire shrugged. "I hadn't thought about it. I don't know. Like I said, I had never met the woman before, so I don't know what she looked like when she wasn't drunk. I just know that she was terrorized."

"You mean terrified?"

"No, I mean terrorized. She wasn't afraid to die. She was afraid to live. She was committed to dying in that river. You don't—" Her voice cracked. Emotion hit her like a lightning strike. The sounds of Miranda Simon's muffled screams rushed back at her. Pushing the memory aside, she gathered herself back up. "You don't forget that feeling. You recognize it in someone else when you see it."

Kassidy leaned forward and rested her elbows on the table, her hands folded beneath her chin. She lowered her voice even though they were the only two in the place. "I know what it's like to be terrorized, Miss Fletcher."

And just like that, Claire knew why she was familiar. "You were attacked."

Kassidy grimaced. "Yes. In my home. By a serial rapist who should have been in prison."

It had been national news two years earlier. Claire couldn't help but pay special attention to assaults and rapes that made their way into the news. Sometimes she had to stop watching the news. It was all too much—the damage human beings did to one another. But she remembered it now. The East Coast, a rapist on the loose, the FBI called in. A hard-won arrest. Then the rapist got off on a technicality and came after one of the female FBI agents. Kassidy Bishop. A shiver worked its way down Claire's spine. She said, "I'm sorry."

"Don't be," Kassidy told her. "It's given me . . . perspective. As an investigator. I also have a gun and a large dog."

Claire smiled, a genuine smile this time. "Me too."

"What would you say if I told you that Leah Holloway had been raped a few days before she went into the river?"

"Is that the theory now? She was raped and then tried to kill herself, her kids, and her neighbor's kids?"

"I don't know. What made you think she was committed to dying in that river?"

Claire shook her head, but it was more to shake the horrible memory from her mind than because she didn't know. "She pushed her daughter."

"What do you mean?"

"Her daughter, Peyton, she was trying to wake her. She had climbed into the front seat with her mother. The car was filling up fast. The entire front seat was almost under. When Leah came to, she pushed Peyton—not to safety. She pushed her into the water. A mother's instinct would be to save her child."

Kassidy was nodding as she spoke. Her tone was conversational when she said, "Yes, but she drove her children off an overpass into a river."

"I know. I get that. But you weren't there. She looked into that little girl's eyes, and then she pushed her deeper into the water."

"Do you think the rape would be enough to send her over the edge?"

"Do you?"

Kassidy shrugged, a pained look crossing her face. It was the first sign of true emotion Claire had seen in the woman. A ripple in her otherwise pleasant demeanor. She said, "Rape would certainly be enough to terrorize someone. It would be enough to make someone want to die."

Claire remembered how slowly her abductor had undressed the first time he raped her. The way the squeaking bed sounded like a sonic boom in the hushed room. It was hard to get the word out. "Yes."

Abruptly, Kassidy said, "Does it get easier? With time?"

Her mask of cool efficiency was gone. Beautifully manicured fingernails tapped against the side of her coffee cup. She was just a woman. A survivor asking another survivor a question. *Will I be able to do this?*

Claire blew out a breath, not even realizing she'd been holding it. "Yes. It gets easier. With time, with therapy, with love." She sought out a soothing memory to combat the horrific memories the conversation had brought to the fore. She thought about Connor. His kind eyes, the way she felt in his arms. "But you have to let people in. I mean, I think. I'm not that great at it."

Kassidy laughed. "Neither am I." A moment passed in easy silence. Then Kassidy added, "What happened to me—it wasn't . . . sustained, like what happened to you, and yet, sometimes I can see how doing what she did might have seemed like a good option to Leah Holloway."

Claire lifted her own cup to her lips. It was lukewarm but creamy and delicious nonetheless. There was a time, early on in her captivity, that sitting in a coffee shop, talking with another person, enjoying a latte would have seemed utterly impossible. Completely out of the realm of her reality. There was a time when she had considered going to the bathroom alone to be a luxury. For months during her captivity, she had had to relieve herself in a bucket in the corner of a cold, dim room, under the watchful eye of Reynard Johnson. She remembered being bound so that she couldn't even reach her face to wipe away her tears. Being so starved and thirsty that she'd had to drink her own cold, dirty bathwater. The bad things, the truly horrific experiences in life, did give one perspective.

"There's a secret," Claire confessed. "To surviving. To living after."

Kassidy leaned in closer. "Care to share it?"

"Ordinary moments are the miracles in life."

"Go on."

"There is so much evil in the world. People do horrible, horrible things to one another constantly, and when we're not killing, maiming, raping, and betraying one another, we get to worry about accidents, mistakes, diseases, and acts of God—floods, fires, car accidents, plane crashes, cancer, doctors operating on the wrong body part. You name it. Turn on the news for five seconds. You'll want to off yourself in no time at all."

"I get a front-row seat to the really depraved stuff," Kassidy admitted.

Claire shivered involuntarily, thinking of all the stories Connor had told her over the years about his own job. "In your line of work, you certainly do. It's easy to catalog the bad things. There are so many. Your work is never done, and next to such a stunningly large and endless supply of horror, the good in the world can seem small and silly and pointless by comparison. People are always looking for something really huge to rival all the bad. They want supernatural things that defy all reason. Impossible feats. The truth is that every second of your day that you are healthy and unharmed is a miracle. Given all the things that can go wrong at any time, the idea that we should get any pleasure out of life at all, get through an entire day without anything truly terrible happening, is a miracle to me."

"Perspective."

Claire's gaze dropped to the table. Her cheeks flushed. "I'm sorry. I probably sound hokey."

"Not at all," Kassidy said. "I appreciate your sharing that with me."

The digitized beat of a cell phone ringtone filled the air. Kassidy fished in the purse she had slung over the back of her chair and came up with her phone. She silenced the ring and smiled at Claire. "Duty calls," she said. "More horror. Looks like I'm off to Portland after this case."

CHAPTER
TWENTY-SEVEN

Jim Holloway's mother was a chain-smoking waif of a woman whose voice sounded like tires on gravel. She answered the Holloways' door wearing a sleeveless pink blouse and denim miniskirt, the colors doing nothing for her leathery skin and thin strawberry-blonde hair. Baby Tyler sat on her hip, and little Hunter clung to one of her freckled legs. She asked questions that she then immediately answered: "Who're you? The police? Whattaya want? You wanna talk to my Jimmy? Wait here. Jimmy!"

The last word was a shrill bark that made both Holloway boys jump. The baby started wailing, and Jim's mother patted his back, shushing him in her low, gravelly tone. He stopped crying and turned his head to regard Connor and Jade. His wide brown eyes were wet and wary, as if it were the detectives who'd just made such a loud, startling noise. He grabbed a strand of the woman's hair and stuffed it into his mouth. Mrs. Holloway sighed noisily. "Wait here," she instructed and disappeared into the house. They heard banging and some indistinct arguing. Then Jim Holloway appeared in the doorway. His freshly washed hair was combed neatly to one side, and Connor couldn't help but wonder if his mother had combed it for him. He wore clean gray sweatpants and a red T-shirt that bore an old, set-in stain of some kind down the right breast side. His mouth worked, obviously chewing something. Connor was certain that his mother had prepared the meal.

Jim opened the screen door to let them in. Connor's eyes were drawn to the couch where young Peyton slept, sprawled and sweaty, her little mouth partially open. "Catching flies," Connor's brother always said when his kids fell asleep like that. Connor could hear the girl's light snores from where he stood.

"Did you guys find something out?" Jim asked, his expression earnest. "About Leah?"

"Mr. Holloway, we need to talk," Connor said. "We'd like you to come down to the division."

"Okay. Let me tell my mom."

As he went toward the back of the house where Connor presumed the kitchen was, Jade said, "Well, that was easy."

Connor shook his head. "This guy is not the Strangler."

"And if he's not, the dental impression and DNA will rule him out," Jade said. "Assuming he'll give it to us."

"He will," Connor said. "'Cause he's not the Strangler."

◆ ◆ ◆

Jim Holloway was used to being told what to do. He sat in the back of Connor's police-issue vehicle in complete silence the entire ride to the division. No questions, no protests. The only hint of nervousness was the constant drumming of his fingers atop his knees. He stared out the window the whole time. Like a well-trained dog, Connor thought.

At the division, they ushered him into an interview room and offered him some water, and then Jade read him his Miranda rights. When she asked if he understood the rights as she had read them, he laughed nervously. "Am I under arrest for something?" He said it as if it were a joke, like the idea was so absurd, it was humorous.

"No, you're not under arrest at this time, Mr. Holloway, but I have just advised you of your rights. Do you understand them?"

He looked from her to Connor uncertainly. "Uh, sure, yeah. Okay. Did you find out something about Leah? Did you find out why she—I mean, what happened? Like, did she have a heart attack or something?"

Connor could hear the man's fingers drumming once more against his knees. "Mr. Holloway," Connor said, taking the chair across from the man, "before she went into the river, your wife drank a large amount of vodka."

Holloway stared dumbly at him. A few times, the corners of his mouth lifted, forming a small smile that was at first uncertain and then incredulous. "What?"

Connor repeated himself. Jade said, "She was drunk. Your wife was drunk."

Holloway's face darkened. "What? No. That's impossible. Leah never drank. Never. You couldn't pay her to drink. I told you yesterday. You gotta do one of those—what're they called, when they cut up a body to find out why the person died."

"An autopsy?" Connor said.

"Already did one," Jade said. "Your wife's blood alcohol level was point one zero. The legal limit in the State of California is point zero eight. She left the soccer field, stopped at a gas station, drank almost an entire bottle of peppermint vodka, and got back into the car. She left the bottle in the bathroom. She was so drunk she was stumbling when she walked back to the car."

Holloway stared up at Jade with a look so uncomprehending, Jade might as well have told him that aliens had abducted his wife. His eyes grew slowly moist, disbelief and confusion blanketing his jowly face. "No," Holloway said. "No, no. That's wrong. You're wrong. You've got the wrong person." His hands came up to the table and he fanned his palms out, beseeching. "You got the wrong body. Leah didn't—she wouldn't—" His voice cracked and again, Connor was struck by the very real, bone-deep disbelief on the man's face. He remembered seeing a similar look on his father's face when the doctors told them Connor's mother was dying of cancer. It was so big, so awful, so unexpected, and so entirely foreign to everything he knew to be true about his life that he simply could not process it.

Connor remembered his father's words in that doctor's office, stilted, awkward, and delivered in the same cracked tone as Jim Holloway: "Wives don't die."

Wives don't die. They don't leave their husbands and children behind to fumble through the pieces left of their lives. Wives live. They stay. They run things. They hold the world together. Connor had no doubt Leah Holloway had been holding her husband's very existence together for as long as they'd known one another.

"Mr. Holloway," Connor said calmly, a pained smile on his face, "I'm very sorry. I know that this is difficult to hear, but Detective Webb is correct, we are absolutely certain that your wife was drinking vodka before she crashed her vehicle into the river."

Tears welled in Holloway's eyes. He looked down at his outstretched palms. "But I—I don't—where did she get vodka?"

"Alan Wheeler," Jade supplied.

"Alan Wheeler? What the—?"

"Wheeler was drinking at Peyton's soccer game," Connor cut in. "Leah caught him. She confiscated the bottle."

Holloway's features lifted and brightened at the word *confiscated*. That must have sounded like his wife.

"She took it with her and, when she stopped at the gas station, she drank it," Connor finished.

Holloway's features fell again. He shook his head, as if this entire thing were just nonsense. Connor wished it was. He kept picturing little Peyton in his mind, hearing her small voice. *"Will you bring my mommy home?"* He wished the whole thing were just a nightmare they'd all wake

132

up from. Peyton could have her mother back. Jim could go back to doing whatever his wife told him to do.

Unless, of course, he was a serial killer.

"Mr. Holloway," Jade said, "your wife received two phone calls before she died." She flipped open her notebook. "One at nine fifty-two a.m. and another at ten twenty-eight a.m. It was after she received those calls that she decided to drink herself stupid and kill a bunch of people, including your kids."

Horror stretched Holloway's eyes wide. His head reared back like he was trying to get away from her.

"Jade," Connor cautioned. He caught Holloway's gaze. "Do you have any idea who might have called Leah?"

Holloway shook his head. "No, I don't. I don't know. Maybe Rachel?"

"What about you?" Jade asked. "Did you call your wife yesterday morning?"

"No, I was asleep most of the morning, like I told you yesterday."

They'd have the phone records soon enough. Jade asked Holloway for his cell phone, and he relinquished it instantly, another indication to Connor that Jim Holloway wasn't hiding a damn thing. Jade took the phone out to Stryker, who would go through it thoroughly. When she returned, she slid a piece of paper in front of Connor. On it, Stryker had written the dates and times of the Soccer Mom Strangler murders.

Jade leaned back over the table. "When's the last time you had sex with your wife, Mr. Holloway?"

Holloway's face colored. "Wh—what? Why would you ask something like that? That—that's none of your business."

"How was your sex life? Did the two of you like to experiment? Maybe you liked it a little rough?"

Holloway's cheeks flashed from hot pink to fire-engine red. "Hey," he shouted. "That's private stuff."

"Mr. Holloway," Connor cut in, "where were you on April nineteenth at eleven a.m.?" He chose the date of Hope Strauss's murder, the first victim.

Bewilderment. "What? I don't know."

"You don't know?"

"I don't remember. That was months ago."

Connor went to the most recent victim, Ellen Fair. "How about October fifteenth at noon?"

"How the hell should I know? I work nights so I was probably sleeping or—or getting ready for work. Jesus. Why are you asking me this shit? What's this got to do with my wife?"

Jade pulled the paper over to her and rattled off the other two dates. "Do you remember where you were on September eighteenth at one p.m. and October second at nine thirty in the morning?"

He threw his arms in the air. "I have no idea. I don't keep a calendar. During the week I go to work from four to midnight. I come home, I go to bed, I sleep until ten or eleven. Then I get the kids at three. Leah gets home at three thirty, and I go back to work. On weekends, I fish."

"So you can't account for your whereabouts on those dates?" Jade said.

Holloway shrugged helplessly. "I don't know. I guess not. I don't keep track of my whereabouts every second of every day. You want to know where I was every second of my life, ask my wife."

The joke died on his lips almost before it was finished coming out of his mouth. His face paled instantly. "Oh God," he said. For a moment, Connor thought the man was going to be sick.

Jade said, "Mr. Holloway, have you ever cheated on your wife?"

Still chalk white, Holloway's eyes snapped toward Jade. "What? What the hell kind of question is that? Of course not. I love my wife. I don't—I don't know why this is happening."

Jade placed a hand on her hip and narrowed her eyes at Holloway. "So you've never cheated on your wife?"

Holloway shook his head. "No. Never."

"How about your wife?" Jade asked. "Are you aware that she was having sex with someone else last year?"

Holloway stared at Jade, unblinking, a blank look on his face. "N-no," he stammered. "Leah didn't—she wouldn't—"

"Last year your wife went to her gynecologist and asked to be tested for every STD under the sun. Do you know why she would do that? Why a presumably faithful married woman with a great marriage would do such a thing?"

Holloway didn't answer. Connor could see the man slipping away. It wasn't that he was tuning Jade out, it was that the situation was becoming too overwhelming for him to comprehend. He was shutting down. He couldn't process the things Jade was telling him about his wife.

Connor tapped his palm lightly against the table, drawing Holloway's eyes to him. He smiled sympathetically. Good cop. "Mr. Holloway, your wife told her doctor that you were having an affair. That was why she needed to be tested for STDs. We believe that Leah was the one having an affair. Do you have any idea who she might have slept with?"

"Wh—what?" Holloway spluttered, spittle flying across the table. "Leah didn't cheat. She wouldn't. This is a mistake. This is all a big mistake. She was—she was lying. She lied."

Jade said, "How long did you know your wife?"

Holloway shrugged, the movement jerky and spastic. "I don't know. Ten, eleven years."

"Did you know her to lie regularly?"

He slumped. "No. Leah didn't lie about anything. Leah is good. She was good. She was a good person."

"Then why would she lie about needing to be tested for STDs? Why would she put herself through all that invasive testing?" Jade asked. "Why would a good person, an upstanding person like your wife, just start lying about things?"

"Jade," Connor said.

Jade went on as if he hadn't spoken. "Why would a woman who didn't drink gulp down a bottle of vodka before getting behind the wheel and driving a bunch of kids around?"

Connor stood and stepped toward her. He spoke in a low voice so that Holloway wouldn't hear him. "Jade, you're not going to get anything out of him by bullying him."

Jade stepped around Connor, her eyes locked on Holloway. "Why would a woman who, as you told us yesterday, had no stress in her life try to kill herself and her kids? Why, Mr. Holloway? What are you not telling us?"

"That's enough," Connor said. He took Jade's elbow and ushered her out of the room. Jade's bad-cop routine worked on some suspects, but it was clear that Holloway had nothing to confess to them. As Connor turned back toward him, the man put his face in his hands. His voice was a muffled wail. "I don't know. I don't know what you want from me."

"I'm sorry, Mr. Holloway," Connor said, resuming his seat across from the man. "Can you just tell me if your wife ever talked to you about having had an affair?"

Holloway shook his head no.

"Can you think of anyone she might have had an affair with?"

Holloway's "no" came on the end of a long sob. As he dissolved into tears, shoulders heaving, a knock sounded at the door. Connor stood and answered it. Stryker beckoned him into the hallway. "Nothing on his phone. I need his prints, DNA, and a dental impression."

"Now's the time to ask," Connor said. "He's pretty beaten down. But I think we should keep digging into Leah Holloway's life, like Agent Bishop said."

Stryker nodded. "Let's explore every avenue. The prints will come up pretty fast. If he's not a match to the unidentified prints we have on file, then we'll get DNA and a dental impression from this guy and turn him loose. I'll put someone on him. We'll see what he does. Cap said I could call in the forensic dentist to compare the impression to the Strangler bite marks. She'll be here by the morning. In the meantime, why don't you guys talk to everyone Leah Holloway knew."

"We should take another crack at the little girl," Jade said.

"And the best friend," Connor agreed. "Coworkers too."

CHAPTER

TWENTY-EIGHT

Jim Holloway consented to fingerprinting, a dental impression, and DNA sample without question, if it meant he could go home. His prints didn't match the unidentified prints from Hope Strauss's vehicle, but that didn't eliminate him as a suspect since they had no idea whether or not the mystery prints had been left by the Strangler. For all they knew, the prints belonged to someone in Strauss's book club. Jim also gave consent for Connor and Jade to speak with Peyton again, under his mother's supervision. Mother Holloway wasn't too happy about it, but she let Connor and Jade try to question the girl again. This time, they got nothing at all. Not one word.

They went next door to the Irving household, which was nearly identical to the Holloway house except that it was painted a muted periwinkle with dark-brown accents. The flowerbeds around the perimeter of the house looked more like they'd been planted by professional landscapers, but the trail of discarded toys, bikes, and scooters leading from the edge of the driveway to the front door was equal to that of the Holloway household's.

Rachel Irving answered her door wearing exactly the same outfit as she'd worn the day before, only her yoga pants were purple instead of black. This time her face was flushed, and a light-blue dish towel was thrown over one shoulder. Wisps of hair escaped from her ponytail and floated around her face. She frowned when she saw them, and Connor wondered if they'd interrupted a workout.

"Mrs. Irving," he said. "We met yesterday. I'm Detective Connor Parks. This is Detective Jade Webb."

She rearranged her face into something closer to a smile. "I remember," she said. "Can I help you?"

"We need to talk to you about Leah," Connor said.

Her brow furrowed. "What do you need to know? I mean, I told you everything I know already, which isn't much. I have no idea why she did what she did."

"You were very helpful," Connor replied. "We have some questions about the last week of Leah's life. Was she acting any differently in the days before her death?"

"Scared, fearful, anxious?" Jade added.

Rachel stared at them for a long moment, as though waiting for more. When neither of them spoke, she said, "No. She wasn't acting differently. Leah was Leah. She was fine."

"Did you notice anything off about her?" Jade asked. "Physically? Did she seem like she was in pain?"

"No. Why? Did you find something? I assume the autopsy is finished."

Connor and Jade looked at one another. Jade nodded at him to take the lead. "We believe that Leah was sexually assaulted a few days before her death. We were wondering if she had confided in you about any sort of attack."

Rachel looked incredulous. Nervous laughter erupted from her diaphragm. "Leah? You think Leah was raped? That's absurd."

Connor could practically feel Jade's annoyance. He looked over and saw her brow severely arched. "Absurd? Why is it absurd?"

More laughter. "Well, no one would want to—I mean Leah wasn't the kind of woman who—I just can't see it. Where would that have happened? She's only ever at work or at home."

"Surely she went other places," Connor said. "Grocery shopping, out to eat, soccer practice."

Rachel made a *puh* sound. "I was with her during the soccer practices this week, and she only goes grocery shopping on Sundays. I don't see when she possibly could have been attacked. If someone came into the house, the whole street would know about it."

"What about her sex life with her husband?" Connor said. "Did she ever talk about it? Were they into anything unusual?"

Rachel shook her head. "Leah was very private. She didn't talk about that stuff. She was good at putting on a brave face. Half the time she was fighting with Jim I didn't even know about it until later."

Jade said, "So she did fight with her husband? About what?"

Rachel waved a hand in the air. "You know, the stuff every married couple fights about. Schedules, day care, who's going to pick up the kids. Jim wasn't much help. She was always on him about taking on more responsibility with the kids. Really, I shouldn't even call them fights. They had spats now and then, nothing out of the ordinary. Is that all?"

"Did Leah ever tell you about her affair?" Connor asked.

Rachel's right hand grabbed at her "#1 Mom" charm. She looked uncertain, then slowly her expression morphed into a quizzical smile. "What are you talking about?"

Connor said, "We have reason to believe that Leah was having an affair, possibly as far back as before she got pregnant with Tyler."

"That's absurd. Leah never had an affair."

"You mean she never told you she was having an affair," Jade said.

Rachel met Jade's eyes. "No, I mean she never had one. I've already told you: Leah would never cheat."

Connor sighed. "You also said Leah never drank, but the coroner found that she was legally drunk when she went into the river. You said she'd never hurt her kids, but she tried to kill them. So, I'll ask again, did she ever talk to you about her affair?"

Rachel crossed her arms over her chest. "She never talked about having an affair. I know you don't believe me, but I am telling you, Leah never had one. I mean, I know what you're saying, like, if she didn't drink or whatever. Look, I don't know what happened yesterday." Her eyes shone with unshed tears. "It was crazy, right? But maybe that's just it—maybe she just snapped and went crazy. Like when people go postal. What other explanation could there be? It happens. People with good lives, happy lives, they just lose it. There's no reason. Or maybe they weren't that put together to begin with. I mean, I told you Leah had a bad childhood, right?"

"You alluded to it," Connor said.

Rachel was pacing now, this explanation, this theory, which she'd obviously given a lot of thought, propelling her back and forth across the small foyer. "She never gave me details, but I know it was bad. So maybe she was, you know, predisposed to depression. Her mom killed herself—I don't think I told you that before. Maybe it's something that runs in the family."

"What makes you so sure that Leah wasn't having an affair?" Connor asked.

"I told you at the hospital, she totally hated cheaters." She looked at Connor. "I told you how judgy she was. How her dad ran around on her mom. She just wouldn't. I mean, it's one thing to go postal and kill a bunch of people, but having an affair? Doesn't that take planning? Calculation? She just wouldn't."

"You think she was incapable of being seduced?" Connor asked. He had seen time and again on the job the way that people could be manipulated, especially by someone very skilled and given the right circumstances. People could be charmed and seduced and made to do things they might not normally do. No matter how rigid or controlling Leah Holloway had been, they knew for a fact that she had deviated from her normal behavior. Otherwise, she wouldn't have needed to be tested for STDs.

Rachel laughed. "Seduced? Leah? Now I know you're not serious."

Jade put her hands on her hips. "What makes you think we're not serious?"

Rachel's posture relaxed, her arms uncrossed. She looked at them like they were missing something glaringly obvious. Then she dropped her gaze to the floor. "I forgot, you never met her. But you saw her, um, body, right?"

Jade and Connor looked at one another. Rachel gave an exasperated sigh. She pulled her cell phone from her pocket and swiped several times until she found what she was looking for, which turned out to be an unflattering photo of Leah lying in a large inner tube with Hunter in her lap at what appeared to be a water park. The two of them were completely soaked. Leah's dark one-piece bathing suit showed little, but lying on her back, all of her excess weight fell to the sides, making her look much larger than she must have been. Connor had seen countless photos of Leah in her home. Certainly, she had been no size zero, but she hadn't been unattractive. She'd been curvy in all the places that many men enjoyed curves, and she had had a beautiful smile.

"Look," Rachel said. She swiped a few more times until she came to a photo of Leah, Peyton, and the Irving twins gathered round a picnic table with ice cream cones in hand. Smiles split their faces. Leah's hair was windblown, sticking up in several directions. Her face was badly sunburned, and a drip of chocolate ice cream stained her shirt. "Do you really think a man would try to seduce . . . that?"

From the corner of his eye, Connor caught Jade's raised brow. He hoped she wouldn't blurt out what he knew she was thinking: *Is this bitch serious right now?*

They stared at Rachel until she put away her phone and crossed her arms again. "Okay, I get it," she said. "You think I'm being mean. Leah was my friend. She was a good friend, and I loved her. Believe me, I still can't believe this is happening. But I am just being realistic. Leah wasn't . . . unattractive, but she was not the type of woman that men—that men were . . . interested in."

"Jim Holloway was interested in her," Connor pointed out.

Rachel gave him an *oh-please* look. "Jim just needed someone to feed and clothe him. He would have married a woman with two heads if she said she'd take care of him."

"So you don't think their relationship was genuine?" Connor asked.

"No. I didn't say that. God knows why, but I think they loved one another in their own odd ways. I'm just saying it wasn't hard for Leah to get Jim. But the men don't line up for women like Leah. Besides that, even if Leah could get a guy to carry on an affair with her, she didn't even like sex that much."

"What makes you say that?" Jade asked. "I thought you said she didn't talk about sex."

Rachel shrugged. "Well, I mean not *never*. She just didn't go into detail. She always talked about it like it was a chore. She used to say, 'Thank God Jim is more interested in fishing than sex.' She used to joke about it. You know, she never said, but I think when she was young, she had some bad experiences, like maybe she was abused."

None of those things precluded Leah from having an affair. Connor knew this. But there was no telling Rachel. Then again, they didn't need to convince her to get the information they needed.

"Mrs. Irving," Connor said. "Can you think of any men that Leah might have come into contact with in the last couple of years besides her husband? Anyone she talked to or saw at events for her children? Did she talk about any of the men at work?"

"No," Rachel said. "No one. Really."

"Okay, how about anyone here in the neighborhood? Any male neighbors she was particularly friendly with? Any men living around here that she had a lot of contact with? Men who visited the neighborhood regularly—maybe someone who was visiting relatives or doing work on neighbors' houses or anything like that?"

She started frowning as he spoke. "I really don't know," she said. "Most of the men around here are married—although I guess that doesn't mean anything. You're saying you think Leah had an affair, and she was married. But I can't think of anyone. A lot of husbands travel. Leah didn't talk to any of them. She barely even talked to their wives. There are contractors who come through occasionally and work on people's houses, but no one regular. Well, except landscapers. But they have a lot of turnover, so it's rarely the same group of men coming through. The only regular was a guy who used to do Glory Rohrbach's landscaping, but he doesn't come around anymore."

"Who is Glory Rohrbach?" Jade asked.

"She used to live a few doors down. A few months before Leah got pregnant, Glory got caught having an affair with her landscaper. It was quite the scandal. He was way younger than her. Like, in his early twenties."

Connor caught Jade's look. A young man in his early twenties. The first Strangler victim had lived in Pocket, as had the fourth victim, Ellen Fair. Agent Bishop had theorized that the Strangler likely lived or worked in the neighborhood, as serial killers often carried out their first killing in their comfort zone. A landscaper would be out working during the day and would not be out of place in a residential neighborhood.

"You remember his name?" Connor asked. "Or the name of the landscaping company he worked for?"

"No, I'm sorry, but her husband would. He still lives in the house with their kids. Glory moved in with the landscaper, I think, in some studio apartment in South Sacramento. It doesn't matter, though. He was sleeping with Glory. I don't think Leah ever even met him, and like I said, she wouldn't give another man the time of day."

"Well," Connor said, "if you think of anyone that Leah might have been having an affair with, please give us a call. We need to talk to him. It's important."

"Why? Why is it important?" Rachel asked. "Leah is dead. Why does it even matter if she had an affair or not?"

Connor said, "She killed four people on the overpass, Mrs. Irving. We are trying to figure out what was going on in Leah's life that would make her desperate enough to do what she did. Unfortunately for us, 'she just snapped' isn't going to satisfy our supervisors."

Jade mustered a tight smile for the woman, even though Connor could tell by her rigid stance that she did not particularly like Rachel Irving. "We're just doing our job, ma'am. We were hoping we could talk to your children as well."

Rachel looked over her shoulder. For the first time, Connor could hear a television playing in the background. "Now's not the best time to disturb the girls."

Connor tried his best sympathetic smile. "I understand," he said. "I know we've taken up a lot of your time already today. We hate to intrude, and we wouldn't, except, like I said, it's really important."

At the end of the long hallway behind Rachel, Connor could see white kitchen tile and a counter with a toaster atop it. Rachel bit her lip. Then she said, "Haven't you talked to Peyton? Molly said Peyton went into the bathroom with Leah when they stopped."

"We still need to speak with your girls," Jade insisted. "They might know something and not even realize it."

"Can you come back tomorrow?"

"No, Mrs. Irving, we can't," Connor said, making his voice a little firmer. He had a feeling that if they returned tomorrow just as she asked, that too would be a bad time. Most people didn't want the police to talk to their children. Connor understood that. But Rachel's best friend had tried to kill her children. Connor would have expected her to show more interest in finding out why.

"Okay," she sighed. "Come in."

CHAPTER

TWENTY-NINE

The Irving house was laid out in the same way as the Holloway home. The living room to the right, behind that a dining room, and then a small, narrow hall leading to the kitchen. Off the side of the kitchen was the garage. The hallway walls were dotted with framed family photos. Rachel, her husband, and their twin girls in Disneyland, in front of the Washington Monument in Washington, DC, on a beach somewhere, at the Grand Canyon. Obviously, they traveled often. Connor was nearly forty and hadn't been to half the places he saw on the Irving family photo wall of fame. Interspersed with vacation photos were the girls' school photos, showing the progression from chubby-cheeked preschoolers to thinner, more mature-looking first graders. Candid shots hung on the fridge. Connor saw Peyton and Hunter Holloway in several of those photos. He saw at least two photos of Leah and Rachel together, both of which looked to be from school events. The Irvings had many family photos decorating their house, but not nearly as many as the Holloway home boasted.

Off the other side of the kitchen, where the Holloways had built a deck, the Irvings had added a family room, complete with a fireplace and three large brown leather couches that circled around the biggest flat-screen television Connor had ever seen. There were two floor-to-ceiling windows, which were covered by heavy drapes, obscuring the view of the backyard. Along one wall Connor saw two matching wooden toy boxes painted white with pink princess crowns emblazoned across their front. One said "Molly," the other "Maya." It had the feel of a man cave that had been interrupted by the arrival of children.

Those children lay sprawled each on their own couch, staring sightlessly at the television, which played an episode of *My Little Pony*. They didn't even look up as the adults entered the room. One of them lay with her casted foot atop a pile of pillows. Rachel turned the television off and gestured for Connor and Jade to sit on the empty couch. Jade took a seat. Connor remained standing. From his position, he could see into the kitchen, to where the door to the garage hung open. Two large plastic storage bins stood stacked on top of one another near the door. Rachel saw him register the bins and smiled tightly. "I was just getting rid of some old things in the garage," she explained.

"Mrs. Irving, did you happen to call Leah Holloway yesterday morning?" Jade asked.

Rachel's brow knitted. "No," she said. "No, I didn't." She turned to the nearest twin, the one without the cast, and nudged her shoulder gently. "Molly and Maya. These are police detectives. They need to ask you some questions about what happened yesterday."

The girl without the cast on her leg sat up. "I'm Maya," she said.

"She's my shy one," Rachel joked.

"I was in the car crash," she told them.

"So was I," the other twin said flatly. She continued to look at the television even though Rachel had turned it off.

"Molly broke her ankle," Maya informed them. She touched the back of her head. "I hit my head."

"I'm very sorry to hear that," Jade said. "Maya, can you tell me, was Mrs. Holloway acting any different yesterday after your soccer game?"

The girl thought about it, bringing her hand to her chin. While she thought about it, Molly said, "She was kinda mad."

"What makes you say that?" Connor asked.

Molly shrugged. "Like, she kept yelling at us to hurry up. When we were all getting in the car. Also, she said a bad word."

Rachel's frown returned. "What word was that, honey?"

"We can't say it, Mom," Maya said in a tone that implied that Rachel had asked a very silly question.

"She said 'hell,'" Molly told them matter-of-factly. Connor instantly liked the girl and her no-nonsense attitude. She seemed older than six. Not as old as Peyton Holloway, but older than her wide-eyed, earnest sister. "She told us to hurry the hell up."

Rachel put a hand to her chest. A line of dismay creased her forehead. "Leah said that?"

Both girls nodded.

"So," Connor said. "She told you to hurry the hell up and get into the car. Then what happened?"

Maya shrugged, picking up the tale. "We drove in the car. Then Hunter said he was hungry and could we go to McDonald's. I was kind of hungry too and we all wanted to go, but Miss Leah said no."

"Was Mrs. Hollo—Miss Leah talking on her phone in the car?"

"No, she was just yelling at Hunter."

Rachel took a step toward Maya. "Leah yelled? You didn't tell me that yesterday, Maya. Was she really yelling? Did her voice get loud or was she just being very serious?"

"She yelled," Molly put in. "She told Hunter to shut up 'cause she had to think."

"Oh my God," Rachel said. She looked helplessly at the two detectives. "That doesn't sound like Leah at all. She never talked to the kids that way. Sure, she would get frustrated sometimes, but she never raised her voice or swore in front of them. She was always patient and kind."

Connor looked at Molly. "Did she say what she needed to think about?"

"No."

"Then what happened?"

"Peyton had to pee," Maya said. "Miss Leah asked if she could hold it, but Peyton said no, so we went to a gas station, and they went to the bathroom for a real long time."

"Like forever," Molly said. "Like ten hours."

Connor smiled. "Ten hours, huh?"

"I think it was more like eight," Maya said seriously.

"Girls," Rachel admonished.

"What?" they said in unison.

Connor held up a hand. "It's fine," he said. "We've got video surveillance. We know exactly how long it was, but it probably felt like hours to them."

"It was sixty-two minutes and forty-seven seconds," Jade said.

"Oh, wow," Rachel said. "That is a long time."

"Mrs. Irving, you didn't call Leah during that time to see where she was?"

"No, I didn't. Sometimes games go long. Sometimes Leah takes—took the kids out to eat after." Tears filled her eyes. "I never had to worry with Leah. She always treated my girls like they were her own. She was responsible, dependable. I knew my kids were safe with her. Oh my God."

She walked briskly into the kitchen where Connor heard the sound of water running and then Rachel blowing her nose. He turned back to the twins. "Girls," he said, "before the crash, did Miss Leah say anything?"

They spoke at the same time.

Maya said, "No."

Molly said, "Yes."

Connor and Jade looked at Molly. The girl's voice took on its first hint of emotion, sadness, and a little bit of confusion. "She said, 'God help me.'"

Rachel stepped back into the room. Tears streaked her face. Her hand clutched a balled-up tissue. She said, "I think you should leave."

Jade put her notebook away and stood up. Connor thanked the girls and followed Rachel to the front door. Before he stepped over the threshold, Connor turned toward Rachel and asked her, "Would you mind if we had a quick glance at your cell phone? I know you said you didn't call Leah yesterday, but our captain really isn't going to let us rule that out unless we actually see your phone."

Rachel used her thumbs to wipe the tears from her eyes. She smiled uncertainly. "Don't you guys need a warrant or something for that?"

Connor smiled. "If it would make you feel better."

She nodded and shooed them out the door.

In the car, Jade said, "What the hell was that about?"

"I just wanted to see if she'd refuse," Connor explained.

CHAPTER THIRTY

Even late in the day on a Sunday, the division was all hustle and bustle. Connor and Jade squeezed past a bench full of witnesses sitting just inside the doors. Detectives rushed around. The department was stretched thin trying to run down all the Soccer Mom Strangler leads and deal with its normal volume. Captain Boggs appeared in the doorway to his office and beckoned them over. They sat in front of his desk. Jade crossed her legs and pulled her notebook out of her pocket, leaving it in her lap.

"You got anything new on Holloway?" Boggs asked.

"We have a lead on a twenty-something landscaper who was having an affair with one of Leah's neighbors," Connor said. "Apparently, the neighbor, Glory Rohrbach, moved in with the landscaper. Her husband and kids still live a few doors down from the Holloways. We stopped at the house, but no one was home. One of the other neighbors said they're away on vacation. A Disney cruise or something. We'll keep trying."

"Guy's in his twenties," Jade added. "Used to work in Pocket. Could be a Strangler connection too."

"I'll put O'Handley on it for now. He's been working the Strangler case. Maybe he can track down this Glory person and her landscaper friend without her husband's help," Boggs said. He stood up from behind his desk and paced. "I've got to release Leah Holloway's name to the press."

Jade groaned.

Boggs stopped pacing and stared at her. "It's a goddamn feeding frenzy out there. Fucking press. I gotta give them something. The Holloway story is big. Big enough to get them to shut up about the Soccer Mom Strangler for a while. We'll need to do a press conference this evening. Obviously, we're holding back the bite marks on Holloway's body. Jade, you want to get something ready?"

She smirked. "I thought Parks might like to do it."

"You're the lead," Boggs said.

Jade nudged Connor's leg with her foot. "Come on, Parks. You've got the face. All handsome and rugged. The cameras love you."

There was nothing Connor detested more about his job than leading press conferences, and not just because of the pressure or scrutiny. He would never live down the aftermath of his last press conference on a string of burglaries plaguing the upscale homes of the Sierra Oaks neighborhood in Sacramento. Even the expensive and elaborate security systems in some of the houses were no match for the thieves, but Connor had caught them eventually and had been hailed a hero by a number of female viewers.

"What color were those lacy panties you got in the mail?" Jade goaded.

"Piss off," Connor muttered.

Jade feigned offense, placing a hand on her chest and batting her eyes. "Now really, Detective Parks. Is that any way to talk to a lady?"

"Piss off, *please.*"

"Okay, you two," Boggs cut in. "Just have something ready. You can release everything but the information about the bite marks."

"Any news on that?" Connor asked.

Boggs shook his head. "We sent Jim Holloway's impression to the coroner's office, but they're saying it's inconclusive."

"What?" Jade said. "What the hell does that mean?"

"It means the coroner doesn't think Holloway is our guy, but he won't stake his career on it. We have to wait for the forensic dentist."

◆ ◆ ◆

While Jade gave the press conference, Connor went back to work on Leah Holloway's phone records. He lifted the phone from its bed of rice and tried to power it up, but it was no use. He tried calling Globocell again. He was on the phone for an hour, being transferred from one clueless representative to the next before he found one who could speak intelligently without their Globocell script. Now that the Holloway case had been linked to the Soccer Mom Strangler case, he could at least use that connection to lend more urgency to his request. He explained to the woman that a serial killer was on the loose in the Sacramento area and was believed to be responsible for the deaths of four mothers.

"The press is calling him the Soccer Mom Strangler. We have reason to believe that Leah Holloway had some connection to him. It is extremely important that we get Mrs. Holloway's phone records as soon as possible. We believe they might be helpful in moving the Soccer Mom Strangler case forward. I've already faxed the warrant multiple times. I'm not asking for any favors. I'm just asking you to speed up the process you already have in place."

The woman on the other end, whom Connor couldn't help but imagine as a perky blonde, said, "Sure. What's the phone number associated with Mrs. Holloway's account?"

For a moment, Connor was so stunned he couldn't speak.

The woman said, "Sir?"

Papers flew across his desk, fluttering to the floor as he searched frantically for Leah Holloway's cell phone number. He found it and rattled it off. The woman put him on hold for twenty minutes.

Finally, she came back on the line. "Detective? I think I can get you the last twenty-four hours of calls within the next two to three hours. What's your fax number?"

Connor gave it to her. He still didn't understand what could possibly take them so long to print out a list of phone numbers and fax it, but that didn't stop him from leaping to his feet and pumping a fist high in the air. He drew some looks from the other detectives in the room, but he didn't care.

"Thank you," he told the woman. Moments later, Jade returned, looking sweaty and exhausted. She pulled off her tailored black suit jacket, tossed it across her desk, and lifted her arms in a chicken dance motion. Connor could see the large circular sweat stains darkening her armpits.

"I hate the press," she said. "Did I mention that before?"

"You might have," Connor said.

She plopped into her chair and wiped her brow with the back of her forearm. "So many fucking questions."

Connor grinned. "The press? Asking questions? I don't believe that for a second."

She narrowed her eyes at him. "Why are you so happy? Did your girlfriend come by while I was downstairs?"

He told her about the phone records, which garnered him two high fives. "So what now?" she asked.

"They're cutting Holloway loose," Connor said. "They can't hold him, and the press is going to be all over him. Stryke wants us on Holloway until the morning."

Jade frowned. "On Holloway? What—like a stakeout?"

Connor nodded.

"Can't patrol do it?"

"Patrol is already over there. We can relieve them in two hours."

"You volunteered us for this, didn't you?"

Connor said nothing, trying not to look sheepish.

"You're a bastard," Jade told him.

CHAPTER

THIRTY-ONE

"Look at this fucking circus," Jade said. She uncapped her coffee, and the smell wafted over to Connor, who sat in the passenger's seat of the department-issue Chevrolet Malibu they'd taken out so they could keep tabs on Jim Holloway for the next four hours. They'd parked four houses away, in front of the empty Rohrbach home. Evidently, Mr. Rohrbach and his children were not coming home from their cruise that evening.

"If you drink that, you're going to have to pee," Connor said.

Jade sighed and put the cap back on. She gestured to the myriad of news vans parked outside of the Holloway home. Some had even edged onto the driveway. "You think these vans have shitters? Wait a minute, don't you live a few blocks from here?"

"Yeah."

She took the cap off her coffee cup and took a long sip. "I can just go at your place."

The press had laid siege to Jim Holloway's home, even before Jade had finished giving her press conference. Most of them had broadcast live for the eleven o'clock news right from the Holloways' front lawn. Holloway's mother had come out to yell at them until she became overwhelmed by the lights of the cameras and the shouted questions and fled back inside.

It was only for one night. By the next evening, they'd know whether or not the impression matched. If it did, Holloway would be taken into custody immediately.

Connor pulled out his cell phone and dialed the division. He asked for O'Handley. "Matt," Connor said when the young detective came on the line. "You get that fax yet?"

A sigh. "No, nothing. I've been babysitting this fax machine for two hours, Parks, all while trying to find Glory Rohrbach's new address. She's not in any database. I got nothing."

"In the morning, we can canvass and see if anyone remembers the name of the landscaping company her lover works for. Keep up the good work, and call me when you get that fax."

O'Handley hung up without another word.

"You put O'Handley on the Globocell fax?" Jade said.

Connor nodded.

"You work that kid like a fraternity pledge."

"Please. He's earning his stripes like everyone else."

"You could give him something more important to do," Jade said.

"He's trying to find Glory Rohrbach and her landscaper lover," Connor said. "That's important, and so is this fax. I don't want it getting lost."

"'Cause we lose so many faxes."

"You got a thing for O'Handley or what?" Connor teased.

Jade's smile was wicked. "He could use my fax machine anytime, I won't lie."

Connor howled with laughter. "Oh, is that the 'more important' thing he could be doing?"

Jade shrugged and looked away. "I don't dole out the assignments, I just take them."

Connor's sides ached with laughter. He slid down in his seat and stared straight ahead, watching the news vans come and go from the front of the Holloway home. As the night wore on, many of the reporters departed. By midnight, there were only two vans left.

Jade snored softly in the driver's seat while Connor texted back and forth with Claire. She couldn't sleep. Not without him, she said. Again, there was the giddy teenage girl who suddenly lived inside Connor. His mind kept drifting back to the night before, holding Claire again. He could feel her skin beneath his palms, smell her faint lavender scent, feel her brown curls tickling his face.

Damn this job, he texted her.

Your job is important, she responded. *I'll be here when you're finished.* Then, what had become their own little catchphrase: *We have time.*

Connor grinned. He was trying to think of something to write back when his phone rang, the noise startling Jade awake.

"It's Matt," Connor said, pressing the "Answer" button.

"I've got your fax," Matt told him.

Connor flashed Jade a thumbs-up. "Put him on speaker," she said.

Connor held the phone out and looked at the glowing screen. "I don't know how."

Jade reached over and hit a button. Then, she said, "Hi, Matt."

Matt's voice was slightly grainy. "Detective Webb."

Connor noted Jade's frown at Matt's formal greeting. He rolled his eyes.

"There are two numbers that match up with what we've got on video. The last call Leah Holloway received while she was at the gas station lasted eleven minutes and fifty-eight seconds. It was a cellular phone, but a burner. Could be anyone, anywhere."

"You try calling it?" Connor asked.

"From the restricted line, yeah. It just rings. No answer, no voice mail. The second number—the call she took earlier, at nine fifty-two—"

"At the soccer field."

"Yeah," Matt said. "It's an 855 number. Toll-free, private. Took some digging but I found out it belongs to an outfit called Genechek."

"Genechek?" Jade said. She and Connor exchanged a raised-brow look.

"Yeah," Matt said. "One of those places that do DNA tests through the mail."

"Like paternity tests?" Jade asked.

"Yeah, exactly."

"Did you—" Connor began.

Matt cut him off. "I called. They don't open till eight thirty in the morning. They're based in Portland, Oregon, so we don't get the benefit of the time difference."

Connor ran a hand downward over his face, smoothing his beard. "How long was the call?"

"About a minute."

"Long enough to say he's not the father," Jade remarked.

"So Genechek calls her at the soccer field. She gets to the gas station, and whoever is on the other end of the burner calls her, and she starts drinking the vodka," Connor said.

"Matt," Jade said. "I'm sending Parks back to the division to write the warrants."

"Sounds good."

They ended the call. They sat in silence for a moment, watching the darkened Holloway house in the distance. Connor said, "My money's on the five-month-old."

"You mean for the DNA test?" Jade asked. "The math works out from what we got from her OB-GYN records."

"She has unprotected sex with someone outside of her marriage, asks for a bunch of STD tests, finds out she's pregnant instead. Stays with her husband, has the baby, and then starts having doubts about the baby's true paternity. Maybe she finds out the baby's not his, and it drives her over the edge? But why now? The kid is five months old. What happened to suddenly make her want to test paternity?"

"I have no idea," Jade replied, "but even if that's what drove her over the edge, why kill all of her kids? Why kill her best friend's kids?"

Connor sighed. "I don't know. It doesn't make any sense."

"Her best friend is a bitch, no doubt, but that doesn't warrant killing her kids. Holloway didn't start drinking until she got the second call at the gas station," Jade pointed out. "Before that, she told the kids she just needed time to think. I don't think she started thinking about ending it all until the second phone call. Are the two calls even related?"

"They have to be," Connor said. "I'll see what I can find out about the burner. Maybe we can triangulate it and find out the last place it pinged. I'll get the warrant out to Genechek so it's there by the time they get in at eight thirty. We need those DNA results. You'll be okay here by yourself?"

"Oh please," Jade replied. "I just have to stay awake. You write the warrants, get them signed, and fax them now. That way in the morning we can get right on it. Now go get started on those warrants and send Matt back over with some food."

"You just want to be alone in a confined space with Matt."

Jade winked. "Only because you're off the market, Parks."

Connor laughed and got out of the car. He jogged the block back to his own vehicle and made it back to the division in less than fifteen minutes. Matt was thrilled to be relieved.

"Just pick up a cheeseburger from that all-night place on R Street and drop it off to Jade on your way home. Onions, no pickles. And a Coke."

Matt only looked half-annoyed. "She want fries with that?"

"Nah," Connor said over his shoulder, heading toward his desk. "Just the burger."

The division was fairly quiet. It didn't take long to get the warrants ready. The burner's user hadn't been required to register online or with the retailer it was purchased from, but Connor might be able to triangulate the phone's signal to within a couple of miles. The phone was manufactured by a company called Spur Mobile, which was an MVNO, mobile virtual network operator. Connor knew from a previous case that Spur leased space on Globocell's network. He also knew that Globocell kept its data on subscribers and nonsubscribers separate. If he could get in touch with Globocell's legal department in the morning, he should be able to get them to triangulate the phone's signal. He was in the process of preparing another warrant for Globocell when one of the night-shift detectives called his name from across the room.

"Yeah," Connor said.

"Webb just radioed for backup. Saw a man in a dark hoodie walking between the houses on Holloway's street. She was going to check it out. Thought you'd want to know."

Connor jumped up and glanced at the clock on the wall. "Thanks," he said. "I'm on my way. O'Handley should be getting there any minute. He's probably closer than the marked units."

Connor was only a few minutes away from Holloway's street when his cell phone rang. He used one hand to swipe "Answer" and pressed the phone to his ear. "Parks."

Matt's voice was high-pitched. "It's Jade," he said without preamble. "Something happened. I got here—I—I pulled up—I—couldn't find her. The marked units weren't here yet. I went looking for her. I—I—"

"Matt," Connor said, fear tickling the back of his neck. "Slow down. Is Jade there? Put her on."

The young man's voice cracked. Connor heard a screechy sob. "I can't," he said. "She's dead."

CHAPTER

THIRTY-TWO

By the time Connor arrived, marked units had pulled up behind the vehicle Jade had been sitting in. Their red-and-blue flashing lights had drawn the few press members left in front of the Holloway house. Connor watched as a uniformed officer pushed a cameraman away from Jade's vehicle. Another uniformed officer was cordoning off the front of the Rohrbach house with yellow crime scene tape.

Matt stood on the sidewalk, typing something into his phone. As Connor got closer, he could see tears streaking the younger detective's face. Matt wiped them away with the sleeve of his suit jacket, pocketed his phone, and sucked in a deep breath. "I had to stay here to preserve the scene," he told Connor. "I have one unit driving around to see if they can see this guy on foot and another unit knocking on doors to see if anyone saw or heard anything."

Connor looked up and down the street. The windows of nearly every house on the block were squares of yellow light in the darkness. Some neighbors had wandered out to their front yards in pajamas and slippers, watching the police closely. He noticed that both the Irving and the Holloway households had been wakened.

"Where is she?" Connor asked.

Matt used his sleeve again to swipe beneath his nose. He looked over his shoulder at the Rohrbach house. "She's in the backyard."

"What happened? Was she shot?"

Matt shook his head. "No. I don't think so. Looks like she was beaten. Her face looks pretty bad. I checked on her first. No pulse. I did a quick sweep of the surrounding yards but didn't find anyone. No idea where this fucker went. By that time, the marked units were arriving. Like I said, I sent one of them to see if they can find a male wearing a hoodie skulking around here. Then I called you."

"I want to see her," Connor said.

"You can't go back there, not yet. We have to wait for the crime scene unit and the coroner." Matt waved his phone in the air. "They're on the way."

The rational part of Connor's mind knew this, of course. But he wasn't feeling particularly rational at that moment. Jade had been his partner on this case. He had volunteered her for this assignment, then left her there alone, and something terrible had happened. He started walking toward the side of the Rohrbach house. Matt reached him before he made it under the crime scene tape, putting his body between Connor and the tape. "Parks," Matt said. "Stop."

Connor motioned toward the grassy path that ran between the Rohrbach house and the house next to it. "What if she's still alive?" he said. "Are you sure? You're sure she had no pulse? Did you try to resuscitate her?"

Matt squeezed Connor's shoulder. "She's gone, man. Believe me. She was already gone when I got here."

"You're sure?"

"Of course I'm sure. Parks, we gotta wait. You know this."

Acid burned Connor's throat. His stomach felt like it was somewhere around his feet. "What's the ETA on the crime scene unit and the coroner?"

"Half hour for the crime scene unit. Maybe a little longer for the coroner."

Connor couldn't stand there on the sidewalk for a half hour or longer, trying to tamp down his shock and grief while the press and the neighbors gawked, thinking about Jade alone in the Rohrbach yard. He cleared his throat, though it did nothing to dislodge the lump that had formed there. "Let's get to work," he said.

Matt stood guard at the front of the house to ensure that no one but the crime scene unit and the coroner were let inside the perimeter that the uniformed officers had secured. Connor joined the uniforms canvassing the neighboring houses. They checked yards, sheds, and garages to make sure the perpetrator wasn't hiding out right under their noses. Two hours later, they'd turned up nothing. No bad guys hiding in bushes. No witnesses. A few of the neighbors closest to the Rohrbach household had heard some noises but hadn't actually seen anything.

By the time Stryker arrived, the coroner was ready to walk them through the scene. Connor, Matt, and Stryker donned protective Tyvek suits, complete with shoe coverings, and followed coroner Roger Zeliff along the side of the Rohrbach home. The backyard, lit by the crime scene unit's portable lights, was large, with a jumbo trampoline in one corner and a blue garden shed in the other corner. It was separated from the properties flanking it by flower beds, and from the property behind it by a row of Japanese boxwood shrubs. The shed doors hung open. A white tent had been erected just outside of the doors. Connor looked around, noticing for the first time all the neighbors watching from the windows at the backs of their houses.

Zeliff walked over and waited at the entrance to the tent. Matt pointed toward the house behind the Rohrbachs', on the other side of the boxwood shrubs. "There's a decent-sized opening between two of those shrubs. I think the perp came through there. From where Jade was parked, she would have had a direct sight line from her car, down the side of the house to that point."

"At which point she got out to pursue him," Stryker said.

Matt nodded and walked across the yard, past Zeliff and the tent, to the flower bed that separated the Rohrbach yard from the yard of the next house over. The mulch was disturbed, the brown mud beneath it tracked into the next yard. The begonias had been trampled, their white petals crushed into the ground. "I think she pursued him into the next yard and the yard after that."

"They stopped right before she got to the Irving house?" Connor asked.

"I think so," Matt said. "Nothing in the Irving yard is disturbed. It doesn't look like anyone tried climbing the fence."

"Rachel Irving said they didn't hear anything," Connor said.

"I think Jade turned back before she got there," Matt said. "Like I said, it doesn't look like they went through the Irving yard, but there are some trampled flower beds and overturned lawn furniture in the other two yards. I think the perpetrator must have circled back and hid in the shed. You can't tell with all these lights, but it was pretty fucking dark back here when I got here. It would have been easy for the perpetrator to lose Jade—or make her think he did. I think he knew his way around. She probably just turned around to head back to the car."

They followed Matt to the mouth of the tent, where Zeliff waved them in. Jade lay in the grass, face up. Her eyes were open and fixed upward. All the things that made Jade Jade were gone from her face. Her eyes were just vacant glassy bulbs. Her lips were parted, her skin a pale, waxy color. There was a purple bruise beneath her left eye. Above that eye, a laceration gaped open, extending from her left eyebrow into her hairline. Dried blood crusted on the side of her face and in her hair.

"Jesus," Connor said.

"It's from a shovel," Zeliff said. He motioned toward the corner of the tent, near the open doors of the shed. Connor saw a yellow evidence marker. Beside it, discarded a few feet from Jade's head, was a steel shovel with a wooden handle at least two feet long. It had an open back and a round point at its edge. In the hands of a bigger opponent, with the element of surprise, it would cause a lot of damage.

Connor heard Stryker's voice from beside him, low and calm, like this nightmare was happening to someone else. Stryke had always been good like that. "He hid in the shed? Popped out and hit her with the shovel? Was there a lock on the shed?"

Zeliff squatted next to Jade's right hand. "No lock. I believe he knocked the gun out of her hand. I can't be sure if he did it before or after he hit her in the head, but he broke her radius just below the wrist." Gingerly, he pushed her sleeve upward, revealing an unnatural curve in Jade's forearm. "I'd need an X-ray to confirm it, but I think it's pretty obvious."

Connor's stomach churned. Stryker said, "We'll need to see if we can get prints from that shovel. So he used the shovel to knock the gun out of her hand. Hit her over the head. Is that what killed her?"

Zeliff stood and walked away from Jade's body to where a yellow plastic evidence marker stood beside Jade's gun. "You're right, Detective. Her gun went this way, her flashlight went that way." He pointed across the tent where another evidence marker stood beside her flashlight. It still emitted a dim glow, running off the last of its battery strength. "Like I said, it's hard to say which body part he struck first, but she sustained substantial injuries to her arm and her head. I'm not sure that's what killed her, though."

Zeliff walked back toward Jade's body and squatted again, this time near her head. Her left arm was extended upward, almost over her shoulder. He didn't want to do it, but Connor looked again at Jade's face. He felt the hot sting of tears behind his eyes and blinked them back. His gaze trailed downward, searching for additional injuries. Her clothes were still on. It didn't look like she'd been raped. Her blouse was torn, her white camisole showing a sliver of cleavage.

"Here," Zeliff said. "This is what you need to see." He pointed to her neck. Both Connor and Stryker stepped closer and leaned over to get a better look. Then Connor saw it, showing from beneath the edge of the collar of her shirt, where her throat met her collarbone.

A bite mark.

Bile rose in the back of Connor's throat. "Fuck."

Beside him, Stryker's voice sounded, emotion breaking through for the first time since he had arrived on scene. "That motherfucker."

CHAPTER THIRTY-THREE

"Talk to me," Claire said.

Connor sat on the edge of her bed, shirtless, his head in his hands. He'd been that way for so long, she was starting to wonder if he'd fallen asleep. He'd come to her like this at 5:00 a.m. Numb, silent, on some kind of automatic pilot. He was in shock. She recognized it well. He had told her some basic facts in a voice that didn't sound like his at all. Jade was dead. She'd been beaten and strangled. They suspected the Soccer Mom Strangler. Once her body was removed from the scene, Boggs had sent the detectives home to get a few hours of rest while the coroner performed her autopsy. He needed them rested for the day to come.

Wilson had initially tried to comfort him, but had finally given up and now lay snoring heavily from his bed in the corner of the room. Claire sat on the bed behind Connor. His back was a wall radiating heat. Tentatively, she reached up and traced the hard planes of muscle cut into his back.

"Connor, please. Talk to me."

"I can't believe she's gone," he said finally.

It was so hard to believe, Claire almost hadn't. For a split second, she had wondered if it was some kind of joke. But of course Connor would never joke about something like that, and she had never seen him so broken. She'd been trying to process the news since he showed up, and she still couldn't wrap her mind around it.

He'd asked if he could stay, and she'd said yes. He'd asked if he could take a shower. She had said yes. He'd gotten his shirt off and one shoe, and then he'd frozen just like this on the edge of her bed. She drew closer to him, pressed her lips to the back of his neck. His skin was warm and salty. She felt him relax just slightly, felt the wall give way just a little.

"I'm sorry," she whispered.

"We woke up Holloway while we were canvassing," he said finally. "His mom was already up. She heard all the activity going on outside. She got Holloway out of bed. He seemed like he'd genuinely been sleeping. Had indents on his face. We don't think it was him. I guess he could have snuck out of his house, killed her, and gone back to bed, but God, that's so ballsy."

It wasn't what Claire had meant when she'd asked him to talk to her, but this was where he needed to start—with facts and evidence and theories. "Even if it wasn't Holloway, it was ballsy," she said. "Why was the Strangler there prowling anyway? He had to have seen the news vans and Jade sitting outside."

Connor shrugged. He still didn't look at her. "I don't know. No one saw or heard anything. No one reported any attempted break-ins. I'm not sure why he was there. I don't get it. And Jade. I don't—I don't—why didn't she wait for backup?"

Claire's fingers left his back. She put her hands in her lap and stared down at them. Tears threatened to burn her eyes. "She must have thought she could handle it. She was armed. She knew backup wouldn't be too far behind. Maybe she was afraid she'd lose him completely if she waited."

"But I've seen her take down guys twice her size," Connor said.

"But, Connor," Claire replied, "you said yourself he hid and snuck up on her." She had a sudden flash of one of the first times Reynard Johnson had beaten her. He had stridden across the room, fists flying before he even reached her, his punches raining down on her in rapid-fire fashion. Her body had been like a snare drum. She'd hardly had time to suck in a breath in the time it took him to beat her to the edge of consciousness. "A blitz attack can be hard to fight," she added. "Even with quick reflexes and fighting experience, there are no guarantees in a fight, especially when the other person fights dirty."

Another flash. Claire at nineteen, doing dishes, her back to the kitchen. Johnson had snuck up behind her and smashed her head into the windowsill above the sink. The gash had bled something awful. Fighting dizziness from the blow to her head, she hadn't had the time or wherewithal to do anything except brace herself against the sink while he tried to rape her. But she'd been too old for him by then, and he had given up. Still, by that time, she had become attuned to the sounds of his movements, always on edge and ready for the next beating or rape. She had never stopped fighting. That was the fourth year of her captivity, and he had still been able to sneak up on her.

Connor's words broke through her thoughts. "It must have happened so fast. It didn't take long for Matt to get there. He had already left. I told him to stop and get her food, but still, he was close by. The coroner thinks the cause of death will be strangulation."

Again the unwanted images swept past her defenses. The memory played like snapshots flashing in machine-gun bursts across her mind. Miranda Simon again, Johnson's old brown belt looped around her neck, sinking into her flesh. The girl's eyelashes wet with tears. The life receding from her eyes. "It doesn't take that long," Claire croaked because her throat had constricted, her voice weakened. "To strangle someone. It takes no time at all, really. Unless you have to watch."

Slowly, Connor turned, lifting his legs onto the bed and sitting cross-legged so he could face her. He rubbed her arm. "You're shivering."

"I'm sorry," she said.

"Don't be."

"No," she said. "About Jade. I'm so sorry. It's—" *A horrible way to die.* She swallowed the words. He already knew how horrible Jade's death was; he had seen her body. His colleague. His friend. "It's very sad," Claire said instead. "Is there anything I can do?"

He smiled and touched her hair, her cheek, wrapped a hand around her neck and pulled her toward him. "You're doing it," he murmured.

Their lips met slowly. She felt his pain in every small movement of the kiss. When she touched him, she felt his pain in every tensed muscle of his body. His hands caressed her as gently as ever, roving over her like he was blindly searching for something. In his touch, she felt something new, something different. His need to forget. His need to be so close to her that she would displace his grief, if only for a few moments.

They lay back on the bed, side by side, limbs tangling, still moving with slow, purposeful movements. She felt his need to bury himself so deep inside her that he would remember nothing. It was a need for absolute and utter oblivion. The blessed absence of pain.

This, Claire could relate to. For ten years of her life she'd been achingly desperate to forget the bad things, to be free from such pain. She had just never imagined that physical sensation, that release, could get her there. But now she felt every light press of Connor's fingers, every heated probe of his mouth like a tiny prayer on her skin. She felt him and nothing else. She inhaled his scent, ran her fingers through his hair and down to his shoulders. She pushed him away from her and stood up long enough to pull her clothes off. Connor moved to the edge of the bed, sitting up and watching her, his eyes wide, and his expression filled with panic and hope, fear and elation.

"Claire," he said, and the sound of her real name whispered by the man she loved was like a stitch in the wounds left behind. Inflicted by someone else. Someone cruel and inhuman and gone. Someone who could never hurt her again.

"Say it again," she told Connor.

"Claire."

She smiled and stepped toward him, standing between his legs. She took his hands, placing them on her breasts, her skin hot and tingly beneath his touch. "I want this," she said.

He didn't pull her down onto the bed, as she expected, so he could roll on top of her and fit his body over hers. Instead, he slid his palms around her body, cupping her bottom and pulling her into him. His hands ran down the backs of her thighs, urging her to wrap her legs around him and fit herself into his lap. He raised his face to hers, and she felt like she was falling into his eyes. She kissed him. One of his hands stayed splayed across her back, holding her gently while the other explored her. She could feel his hardness beneath the pants he wore, and she found herself rocking against it until she began to feel an alien sensation between her legs.

Pleasure.

She broke from the kiss. "It feels good," she gasped.

His mouth was already at her throat, his tongue flicking along each collarbone, one at a time. "You feel good," he said into her skin. "Claire."

She threw her head back, reveling in the sensation, enjoying his mouth on her body as it worked its way to her breasts. She focused hard on it. She wanted to remember it. His beard tickled her skin, rough but soft at the same time. The sensation woke every cell in her body. More, she wanted more. That feeling inside her—it was building, working toward something. It was an exquisite fullness like she had never, ever felt, and she wanted release.

It didn't take much negotiating to free Connor from his pants. He was quite ready for her. Once he was naked, she pushed him back into a sitting position on the edge of the bed. There was some awkwardness, especially when she pulled a box of condoms from her nightstand—a relic of her ill-fated time with Too-Concerned Todd. She'd only used one from the box. She'd often thought she should throw the box away, but that had felt like throwing away all hope of a normal relationship. Now she was glad she'd clung to that hope. The mechanics of getting the condom on gave her the giggles momentarily, but then her nervousness gave way to pregnant silence as she sat astride Connor once more, shifting on his lap until he was poised to enter her.

He said, "Claire, maybe we shouldn't do this right now," and then she seated herself on him. She was shockingly ready for him—her body had never been so welcoming of a man. A soft, shivering sigh pushed its way from between her lips. Connor made a noise in his throat, and then he was very still, his forehead resting on her sternum, his hands at the small of her back, gathering her into him.

The intense feeling of pleasure was still there. But Connor wasn't moving, wasn't even breathing. She rested her elbows on his shoulders, pulled at his brown hair. "Stop holding your breath," she said into his ear.

He let out a shaky breath. "Oh my God, Claire."

She moved, just a fraction, using his shoulders for leverage, tightening her thighs around him. The feeling was still there. It felt even more intense when she moved. Friction, she needed friction. So she moved. She moved and shifted and wiggled until she worked herself into a rhythm that sent that pleasurable feeling into a frenzy. Connor let her, moving only to caress or kiss her skin, to look up and watch her face. He rubbed his beard against her tender skin and whispered her name until the explosion inside took her, sending her over an edge into a chasm of such exquisite forgetfulness, she cried out and seized in Connor's arms.

Afterward, they sat fused together for a long time, their chests heaving. Connor's skin was sticky against hers, a fine sheen of sweat enveloping them both. The room suddenly felt close and hot. Claire didn't want to separate, didn't want to remember again. She wanted to stay in his arms, hot and content, the aftershocks of their lovemaking shuddering through her body every now and then. She wanted this moment to last forever. She wanted to remember every last detail. Every sensation, every touch, every smell.

Connor reached up, smoothed her hair away from the side of her face, and kissed below her ear. "I love you," he said.

She smiled and moved her head so she could capture his mouth. Then she said, "I love you too."

They showered together. This too was something new for Claire. She felt like she had won a war. On the other side of the battle was uncharted territory, and it was hers for the taking. She knew that many rape survivors were unable to orgasm after being attacked. She had never come close before, even with Connor. She had talked with her therapist at length about whether she would ever be able to have a normal sexual experience with a man. She had known that the odds were not in her favor. She also knew that this single experience didn't erase the years of trauma she had endured. But here she was—she had had a pleasurable sexual experience with a man she loved. She wanted to revel in it, to drink in every crazy, new second of it, but Connor needed her. The lovely forgetting that the act had brought them was already receding. Claire felt the heavy grief of Jade's death like a specter looming over them. Beside it was her own guilt. She had disliked Jade on sight, based on nothing more than the woman's relationship with Connor. Claire had never given her a chance. Now she was dead. Claire knew that her private jealousy had had nothing to do with the woman's murder, but that didn't stop her from feeling guilty. Connor had obviously cared for her.

Back in her bed, Connor lay with his eyes open, staring at the ceiling. Claire laid her head on his chest, and he wrapped an arm around her, planting a kiss on the top of her head. "You're amazing," he whispered.

She said, "You should sleep."

He turned his head and looked at her bedside clock. "I have to be back at the division in an hour. Genechek will be open by then. I have to make some calls, then meet Stryker and Boggs at the coroner's office."

She put a finger to his lips. "Stop," she said. "You need to sleep for at least a little bit or you'll be no good to Jade. Captain Boggs told you to get some rest, right? Take two hours, at least. Genechek isn't going anywhere. I'll wake you up, I promise."

She leaned across his body and pushed several buttons on her clock before setting the alarm. "See?" she said.

He managed a smile. "Okay," he said. "Just don't leave."

CHAPTER
THIRTY-FOUR

True to her word, Claire woke him two hours later. She made him eggs and toast and sent him on his way with a travel mug of coffee in one hand—an excessive amount of cream and two sugars, just the way he liked it—and a fully charged cell phone in the other. He kissed her on the porch while Wilson whined beside them. Connor felt like whining too. He wanted to stay there with Claire, in her house where nothing bad happened, where he didn't have to think about Jade and her brutal murder.

His heart ached as he got in the car and looked back to see Claire and Wilson standing side by side, watching him go. Guilt assailed him. Hours ago, his friend was murdered. She had died alone. He should have been there. The Genechek lead could have waited until the morning. But then he never would have gone to Claire's in the state he'd been in. They might never have finally come together. They hadn't discussed it, and Connor hadn't wanted to jinx it by saying it out loud, but they had reached a huge milestone in their relationship. In fact, they'd gotten past the one thing that had always kept them from having a relationship. He knew it didn't mean smooth sailing from here on out, but it was a pretty big deal for them. His thoughts of Claire got him to the parking lot. They helped keep the sight of Jade's face at the periphery of his mind. Then he was at the division, and he had no choice but to think about Jade.

The mood was somber and subdued. No one spoke. They just went about their work in absolute quiet, faces drawn, visages dark. Connor spotted Matt hunched in front of a computer in his shirtsleeves, three empty Styrofoam cups beside him. His knee bounced up and down rhythmically.

"Did you even go home?" Connor asked.

Matt shook his head without looking up. "No. Stryke did. He should be back in soon. I'm working on the reports."

Connor clapped the man on the shoulder. "Go home, Matt."

Connor was almost to his desk when Matt said, "I can't. I keep seeing her. In my head, you know?"

"I know. But, Matt, you did good work out there. We need you on this. Go home. Do whatever you have to do to get some sleep."

"In a few minutes, I will," Matt promised.

Jade's empty desk stopped Connor in his tracks. A lump formed in his throat, and unshed tears stung the backs of his eyes. *Don't lose it,* he told himself. *Not here.* Her chair sat a couple of feet away from the desk, its back turned slightly so the chair itself faced his desk. As if she had turned toward him and then stood without pushing the chair back in. Files were stacked on the desktop, some partially covered by random paperwork. A stack of Leah Holloway's medical records threatened to tip over. A half-finished bottle of Coke Zero stood beside the plastic bowl of rice that couched Holloway's defunct cell phone. Connor took a couple of steps, pushed Jade's chair in, and returned to his own desk, determined not to look to his left the entire morning.

Compared to his Globocell experience, dealing with Genechek was an absolute dream. The third person he spoke to was able to locate both the warrant he had faxed and Leah Holloway's file.

"Would you like me to mail this? Or if you're in a hurry, I can email it."

God bless her.

"Emailing it would be great," Connor told the woman. He rattled off his department email address and thanked her profusely. The click-clack of her fingers moving over a keyboard filtered through the receiver.

"Now, there are two separate tests," the woman said. "Do you want me to scan both files into one PDF or just send them in two separate files like they are right now?"

"Whatever is fastest," Connor said. Then: "Wait, what do you mean there are two separate tests?"

"Mrs. Holloway paid for both a paternity test and a maternity test. Both were positive matches. She was notified by phone on Saturday."

"Right," Connor said as though he had known this all along and just forgotten.

"I'm sending them over now," the woman said. "Will there be anything else, Detective?"

His mind was still a little punch-drunk from everything that had happened in the last twelve hours, but he remembered to ask, "Do you still have the samples that Mrs. Holloway sent in?"

"Oh no, I'm sorry. We don't retain the samples once they are analyzed. But the DNA profiles for each person will be in the PDFs I am emailing you."

Given that he and Jade had theorized that Leah had been having an affair nearly two years ago, it made sense for her to have sent in for a paternity test. But the *maternity* test? What was that about?

At least Connor had the DNA profiles coming. That could be helpful in locating the person she'd been having an affair with. But that hope was shot all to hell once Connor downloaded the file and printed it out. Genechek required customers to fill out detailed forms with the name and biographical information for the owner of each sample, together with signed consent forms. He studied the forms for the maternity testing first. The test positively matched Leah to her son Tyler. Proof of something everyone already knew. It was useless and bizarre. Why would she need a maternity test? Surely she remembered giving birth. Connor had records proving that she had given birth to baby Tyler. He studied the application, the profiles, and the maternity test results but found nothing that might explain why she had felt compelled to test her own maternity. Frustrated, he turned to the paternity test. The paternity test wasn't to match some other man to baby Tyler, it was to match Jim Holloway to the child, and he was a positive match.

"Shit," Connor muttered, more loudly than intended. He drew a few stares from other detectives seated at their desks, all of whom quickly returned to their own work.

Stryker appeared behind him. He gestured to the papers in Connor's hands as he came around and perched on the edge of Connor's desk. "What've you got?"

Connor looked at his friend and bit back a *Holy shit*. Stryker had done as Boggs instructed and gone home, but he obviously had not slept. Huge bags hung beneath Stryker's eyes. Stubble grew over his cheeks and chin in uneven patches. Connor could see why he never grew facial hair. A ghost of a moustache shadowed his upper lip. His scalp, normally close shaved and shiny as chrome, was stippled with black hair. He seemed to have lost twenty pounds overnight, his suit hanging on him a little, his cheeks sunken. His normal olive complexion had taken on a sickly gray hue.

Connor got it. It was even more personal for Stryker than the rest of them. Stryker was in charge of catching the Soccer Mom Strangler. Not only had the guy killed someone on Stryker's watch, he'd taken one of their own.

Reminding Stryker of this would not help, so Connor said, "Leah Holloway sent in a request to test her own maternity. She's

Tyler Holloway's mother, by the way. Oh, and Jim Holloway is Tyler Holloway's dad." He shoved the DNA profiles and paternity test application at Stryker.

Stryker flipped through the pages until he came to the application forms that had accompanied Leah's request. "Why the hell did she need a maternity test?"

"That's what I can't figure out," Connor said.

Stryker pointed to the bottom of one of the pages. "Jim Holloway signed this a few days ago. He never mentioned this to you or Jade?"

"No. They had no problems in their marriage. His wife was a saint. Everything was fine." Connor could practically hear Jade's voice, as though she were standing over his shoulder, whispering some snide remark, like, *He's a dumbass.*

"I think we need to ask him about this," Stryker said. "He's here."

"You brought him in?"

"We asked him if he would come in this morning to answer some more questions. If he's the Strangler, I don't want him at large. Until we clear him for good, I need eyes on him. With Jade's murder, we're running out of manpower. I've got someone trying to track down Mr. Rohrbach to let him know there was a murder in his backyard and to find out the name of the landscaper that stole his wife. There are still other Strangler leads to follow up on. Everyone is exhausted and sick over Jade. It was easier to get Holloway to come in. He seemed happy to get away from his mother or maybe his kids. Or both."

"Well, let's go talk to him, then," Connor said.

Jim Holloway sat in an interview room much the same as the one he'd occupied the day before. He still hadn't demanded a lawyer. Connor couldn't figure out if he was just that stupid or if he was just that innocent, although it seemed to Connor that even an innocent man would have asked for an attorney by now, given how many questions he was being asked. Maybe the man was just so relieved to be away from his kids that he welcomed the long, silent hours in the interview room.

He sat slumped at the table, one hand wrapped around a Styrofoam cup. It was empty, but Connor could see the remnants of coffee beading the inside of it. Holloway sat up straight when they entered, his face searching and earnest. "What's going on?" he asked. "How'd that cop get killed by my house? Why was she sitting on my street, and what the hell is going on with my wife's case? You guys don't tell me nothing. You ask a whole lot of questions, but no one tells me jack shit. You ask me to come in here, and then you leave me in this room. What the hell are you guys doing?"

It was the most Connor had ever heard the man say. It was also the most animated Holloway had been since his wife's death. Maybe the shock was wearing off. He was coming out of the mental fog he'd been plunged into when Leah went into the river with the children.

Connor pulled out the chair across from him and sat. Stryker remained standing. It was nearly identical to the scene that had played out the day before, except Stryker took Jade's place. Connor swallowed over the renewed lump in his throat and smiled at Holloway. "I'm Detective Parks."

"I remember you."

"That's Detective Stryker."

Holloway looked at Stryker but said nothing.

"Mr. Holloway," Connor said. "We told you everything we know about your wife's death already."

"She wasn't drinking," Holloway insisted. "You need to check for a heart attack or—or my mom said she could have had a brain aneurysm."

Stryker met Connor's eyes. Connor could see from the muscle pulsing in Stryker's jaw that he was losing patience with Holloway, and they hadn't even started yet.

Connor stood and put both hands on the table, leaning forward. His tone was firm and commanding, leaving no room for questions.

"Mr. Holloway, I know this is difficult to hear and to accept, but your wife did not have a heart attack. She did not have a brain aneurysm. There was no sudden medical event that caused her to do what she did on Saturday. Your wife purposely got drunk. She killed four people on the overpass. She purposely tried to kill herself, your kids, and the Irving children. We are trying to figure out why. The sooner you accept the coroner's findings, the sooner you can help us find out why your wife went from being 'fine' to being suicidal and homicidal."

Holloway said nothing, his gaze dropping to the table. They waited for further protest, but none came.

Connor slid the Genechek form across the table. "Mr. Holloway, is this your signature?"

He glanced at it and shrugged. "Yeah, I guess."

Stryker moved closer to the table. "Do you remember signing that form?"

Holloway looked more closely at it, his brow furrowed. "What is it?"

Connor tapped the top of the page, where the title of the form was clearly stated in bold. "It's an authorization for a paternity test."

Holloway's eyes jumped to Connor's face. "A paternity test? I never signed no paternity test. A test for who?"

"Mr. Holloway," Stryker said, "did you give your wife a DNA sample to use for this paternity test? They're usually done by buccal swab—meaning a swab from the inside of your cheek."

Holloway looked like someone had hit him over the head with something large and heavy. "The inside of my—what? What? No. What the hell are you guys talking about?"

"Your wife used a mail-order DNA testing outfit called Genechek to get a paternity test for your son Tyler."

Holloway's expression slackened. "Tyler?"

Connor nodded.

"That's impossible. You have the wrong person. My wife wouldn't do this. I mean, why would she? I'm telling you—you've got all of this wrong."

Connor said, "Mr. Holloway, your wife did this. I know it's hard to believe, but your wife apparently did a lot of things that you didn't know about, including ordering a paternity test."

"No, no she didn't. She couldn't have."

Stryker pointed to the paper. "Did you sign this?"

Holloway held out his hands helplessly. "I don't know. Leah's always asking me to sign stuff—for the kids, for school, for our finances and stuff. I usually just sign."

"This would have been about three or four days ago," Connor said.

Again Holloway shrugged. "I don't know. I don't remember. I guess so."

"So you signed this?" Stryker asked. "You didn't find it odd that your wife was asking you to sign an authorization for a paternity test?"

Holloway's cheeks colored. "No, I—I mean I didn't read it. I don't read everything she asks me to sign."

"So you have no memory of having seen this form before?" Connor asked.

"No, of course not."

"But you're saying that your wife could have put it in front of you, and you would have signed it without reading it?"

"Yeah, I guess. I mean, like I said, she's always asking me to sign stuff. She takes care of everything. I just—I just—" Holloway choked on a new onslaught of tears.

A figurehead husband. Connor heard Jade's voice in his head.

"You just hand over your paycheck," Connor said softly, without malice.

Holloway nodded, his lips pressed together hard, like he was trying to hold something back. Sobs, Connor imagined.

Connor stood to leave. When they were halfway out the door, Jim's voice stopped them. "Tyler," he said. "Is he—is he mine?"

Connor gave him a grim smile. In spite of Jim Holloway's utter incompetence as a parent, the hopeful look in his eyes told Connor that he really wanted to be Tyler's dad. Perhaps that made it easier on him. At least what was left of his family was still intact. He could go on more easily with the illusion that his wife had been a wonderful, honest woman, and that their lives were completely fine.

"Yeah," Connor said. "He's yours."

CHAPTER

THIRTY-FIVE

"It's a match," said coroner Roger Zeliff.

He stood beside Jade's lifeless body, which mercifully he had covered up for the benefit of Connor, Stryker, and Boggs. He used his index finger to push his glasses higher on the bridge of his nose and regarded the three of them like a teacher looking at students. "Did you hear me?" he said.

Maybe it was the proximity to their fallen colleague, the images of her murdered body still playing in their heads, or just sleep deprivation, shock, or the three of them, but they all stared at the man without speaking.

Roger waved a hand. "Gentlemen, it's customary to speak in these situations."

Connor noticed that beneath his white Tyvek suit, he was wearing expensive cufflinks. He hadn't picked up on them at the crime scene. The man had gotten up in the middle of the night and put on a suit before coming to examine Jade's body on scene and perform her autopsy.

Boggs said, "The bite mark?"

Roger nodded. "Was there ever any doubt? The bite mark on Detective Webb's neck matches those found on the Soccer Mom Strangler victims. The man who killed those women killed Jade. Cause of death was manual strangulation, same as the other women. He broke her hyoid bone, so the degree of force was considerable. She sustained a fracture of her right radius, as I suspected, as well as a skull fracture. No sexual assault. It doesn't even look like he tried. She struggled but likely not for long. Her injuries would have made it difficult for her to fend him off. She got some of his skin under her nails, so we are running the DNA, but I can already tell you that it was the Strangler."

Silence descended on them again. No one so much as fidgeted. Connor found some small relief in knowing Jade hadn't been raped before she was killed. She'd gone out fighting. It was still difficult for Connor to accept that she'd been bested by the Strangler, but he realized they'd been underestimating the killer. The Strangler was stronger, more ruthless, and more filled with rage than they initially thought. He glanced at Boggs, who kept one hand over the lower part of his face. Stryker's eyes were wide, as if he were forcing his eyelids apart.

Finally, Stryker cleared his throat. "The Jim Holloway impression? Does it match the bite marks? In your opinion?"

Roger frowned. "No, and we had your forensic dentist give it an initial look, and she agrees. Holloway is not your guy, at least based on the dental impression. We're still waiting on the DNA results."

"The forensic dentist?" Connor asked. "Didn't you just call her yesterday?"

"She flew right up," Boggs said. "Got a hotel room last night."

"We woke her up at her hotel," Roger added. "Asked her to come in early. She will do a more thorough examination later today and prepare a report."

The men looked at one another again. Connor couldn't shake the utter creepiness of the whole thing. A day ago, Holloway had been a suspect. Twelve hours earlier, Jade had been sitting outside of his house.

Now she was dead. Yet, Holloway was not their man. Connor had never bought Holloway as the Soccer Mom Strangler, but now with objective proof he felt more unsettled than ever.

The three detectives left the examination room like zombies. Finally, Boggs said, "So Holloway is out. Where does that leave us?"

"Jim Holloway may be out," Stryker said, "but Leah Holloway is still the closest connection we have to finding this guy. They were practically in Holloway's backyard when he killed Jade."

Boggs said, "Follow the Holloway leads. See if you can track this guy down that way. We're back to the profile. A young white male. Try to find out if there was anyone in her life who is close to the description that Agent Bishop gave us—maybe this landscaper we're trying to track down or someone Leah worked with."

"We're heading over to Leah Holloway's employer now," Stryker said.

"I just need to do one thing," Connor said. "Who's on the DNA samples?"

"Stark," Stryker said.

Connor said, "Meet you at the car in fifteen, okay?"

Boggs and Stryker left, their strides more purposeful now that the investigation had a direction to go in. It was then that Connor noticed Davey Richards slumped on the hallway bench. He wore a rumpled suit. A five-o'clock shadow covered his cheeks. His hands rested on his thighs. For a moment, Connor thought he was sleeping, but as he drew closer, he realized he was just in a state of disbelief. Red-rimmed eyes looked up from beneath a shock of black hair. "Roger won't let me see her," Davey said hoarsely.

Connor tried to remember how long ago Jade had broken up with Davey. It had been at least a year.

"I just want to see her," Davey said, his gaze dropping to his feet.

"You don't want to see her like that."

"I saw her yesterday," Davey whined.

Connor swallowed his annoyance. He'd worked with Jade on a daily basis. They'd been good friends. He'd been with her less than an hour before she was murdered. He had left her, and she was dead. He had little patience for Davey's grief, palpable though it was.

"I didn't realize you two were so serious," Connor said.

"We were together for two years," Davey said.

Connor tried to keep the surprise from his face. He hadn't realized that they'd dated that long, mostly because he knew for a fact that Jade hadn't been with only Davey during the last few years. She hadn't been the monogamous type.

"On and off," Davey added, as if sensing Connor's discomfort. "You know she didn't want kids?"

"Yeah," Connor said. "She mentioned that."

"That was what did us in. I wanted kids, and she didn't."

"Hard to get around that," Connor agreed. He looked up and down the empty hallway. The place was unusually quiet for a Monday morning.

"I still loved her."

"I know."

A female voice shattered the stillness of the moment. "Parks, is that you?"

Lena Stark worked in the Sacramento County crime lab. She and Connor had always had a good rapport. They'd dated briefly after Connor's divorce, but his heart hadn't been in it. Then he'd met Claire. Lena had actually helped him with her cold case. Now, she waddled down the hall toward him in a white lab coat that barely reached around her swollen midsection. He hadn't seen her in a few months. It had slipped his mind that she was pregnant.

He motioned to her belly. "How are you feeling?"

She blew out a breath, sending her blonde bangs up in the air. The rest of her hair was tied back in a ponytail. "I feel like I'm about to give birth." She rested both hands on the top of her belly and looked down at Davey. "Jesus, Davey," she said. "Go home and get some sleep. You know what Jade would say if she saw you here, right?"

A smile pinched Davey's lips. "To stop stalking her."

"Yeah," Lena answered. "And to get a grip." She reached out and squeezed his shoulder. "This is hard on everyone. There's a lot of work to be done on Jade's case. We need all hands on deck. Go home and get some sleep."

Wordlessly, he stood and nodded at Connor before shuffling off down the hall. Lena let out a low whistle once he was out of sight. "He's taking it hard."

Connor swiped a hand through his hair. "No shit."

Lena winced and rubbed the side of her belly. "What's going on?"

Connor was glad she didn't ask him how he was holding up. It was a conversation he wasn't ready to have. Not while he was trying to find Jade's killer. He needed to stay focused.

He pulled a folded copy of the Genechek file from his jacket pocket. "I have this maternity test," he began. He explained what he was trying to figure out and left the file with her. She promised to review it as soon as she finished processing the evidence from Jade's case.

CHAPTER
THIRTY-SIX

KZLM Radio was located in an industrial complex in the Southport Parkway in West Sacramento. The office suite was housed in a converted warehouse with high ceilings and huge windows. The place was bright and airy, glass partitions dividing up the offices in the open floor area.

Connor was thinking about Leah and how her life seemed so normal and transparent, and yet she'd obviously been hiding some large and terrible things—an affair and possibly a sexual assault. He was no stranger to people's capacity to hide scandalous secrets, but he wondered how she had done it. From all accounts, all she did was work and come home to her kids. Sure, her husband was oblivious. Connor wasn't at all surprised by Holloway's lack of knowledge of his wife's life. But her best friend lived right next door, and the two seemed very involved in one another's lives. How had Leah hidden things from Rachel? How had she surreptitiously gathered enough secrets behind her glass partition to make her want to kill herself, her kids, and her best friend's kids?

Stryker elbowed him sharply. Out of the side of his mouth, he said, "I feel like we just crashed a funeral."

"Bad choice of words."

Everyone in the place had stopped what they were doing to stare at the two men. In their suits, they stood out. Connor didn't even think it was necessary, but he pulled out his credentials and handed them to the woman at the reception desk, explaining that they needed to talk to people who had worked closely with Leah Holloway.

"Her assistant?" the woman asked.

"Sure," Connor said. "Let's start there."

Silently, the receptionist led them through a maze of desks, each one with a new, gawking face behind it. Connor felt like he was the star attraction in some kind of freak-show parade. The silence in the place was a cacophony. Stryker whispered, "Any chance her assistant is a white male between the ages of eighteen and twenty-six whose mother abandoned him?"

The receptionist stopped abruptly and the two men nearly bowled her over. She turned to face them and waved her arm to her left with a flourish, like Vanna White presenting the answer to a puzzle. "Mrs. Holloway's office."

Outside of Leah's glass-enclosed office they were greeted by a tiny brunette with ruddy cheeks and four-inch heels that still didn't make her very tall. Her hair was thrown up in a messy bun. She wore a white wrap dress over black leggings. Everything about her looked thrown together. She stood up from her desk like they'd pulled their guns on her. Hands raised, eyes wide, back searching for a wall.

"You're here about Leah," she said.

They handed her their credentials, and she studied each one like she was looking for something counterfeit. The nameplate on her desk read: "Ashley Copestick."

Connor said, "Ashley, we just have a few questions."

She folded her hands and hung them over her midsection. "Is it true?"

"Is what true?" Stryker asked.

"She killed all those people?"

Stryker nodded. "She killed four people and herself."

"Oh my God."

"Ashley," Connor said. "How well did you know Leah?"

She shrugged. "Pretty well. Better than anyone else here. I mean I am—I was her assistant." Her eyes closed and sprang open on the exhale of a long sigh. "Guess I'm out of a job. God, no, that sounds terrible. How are her kids?"

"Traumatized," Connor said. "Ashley, can you tell us if anything unusual happened in the last week? We believe that Leah may have been attacked by someone in the days before her death. Did she say anything to you? Start acting odd?"

Two pink circles appeared on her cheeks. "Well, I don't even know if this counts. I mean, I don't actually know if anything happened, but last week, Wednesday, I think it was, she went out to lunch, which she never does. She was gone almost two hours. When she came back, she looked . . ."

"How did she look, Ashley?" Connor coaxed.

"She looked . . . in disarray. Pale. Like something bad had happened. Her blouse, it was missing its top three buttons. She was walking funny, like it hurt her to walk."

"Did she have any marks on her?" Stryker asked. "Bruises? Abrasions?"

Ashley shook her head. "No, none at all. That's why I wasn't sure if something had happened or not. Like maybe it was my imagination or something. I asked her if she was okay, and she said she was fine. She said she had fallen in the parking lot. I asked her if that was what really happened or did she want me to call the police, but she insisted everything was fine. She had fallen, and she was already embarrassed enough, could we just stop talking about it? So we did."

Tears filled Ashley's eyes. "Oh my God. I should have called the police, shouldn't I?"

"If she was sticking to the story about falling, there's little even the police could have done," Stryker assured her.

"Do you know where she went to lunch?" Connor asked. "Was she meeting anyone?"

Ashley shook her head. "She never said. It was weird. She was in her office, working, and then she just came out with her purse and said, 'I'm going to lunch,' and before I could even ask where or with whom, she was gone. It was weird, though. Like I said, she never went out for lunch. She always ate at her desk."

"She never went home for lunch to meet her husband or out with a friend?" Stryker said.

"No, no. She always ate here. She worked through lunch. Not that she would have told me where she was going anyway. Leah was very private. I mean, I know a lot of stuff that happened to her, but not really because she wanted me to or because we were friends, just because I'm her assistant."

"What kind of stuff?" Connor asked.

She looked at them meaningfully. "You know about Lucky, her dog?"

"That he ingested something that killed him?" Connor said.

"That someone poisoned him with Xanax," Ashley said.

"So she told you."

"Yeah. Well, I took a message from the vet. She was so upset. She asked me not to tell anyone, at least until she had a better handle on things."

"What things?" Stryker asked.

Ashley's shoulders sagged. She put a hand on the back of her chair. "Well, I think maybe someone was messing with her. She never said, but there was the thing with her dog and right after that, the thing with the car seats."

Connor flipped open his notepad. "The thing with the car seats?"

She nodded. "She put the kids into her car one morning to take them to day care, and all their car seat straps had been slashed."

"When was this?" Stryker asked.

"Two months ago."

"She told you this?" Connor asked.

"She was late for work. She called and asked me to meet her down the street from her house. She had me sit with the kids while she went to the store and bought new car seats. She used her credit card. Cost her a fortune too. She asked me not to tell anyone."

"Did you?"

"No, of course not. When people ask me to keep something a secret, I do. I'm telling you guys now 'cause Leah's dead, and I guess it doesn't matter now."

"Why didn't she just get her husband to help her?" Connor asked.

Ashley shrugged again. "I don't know. She said she didn't call Rachel—that's her best friend—because she would be too gossipy about it. She really didn't want anyone to know. She was pretty embarrassed."

"What did she do with the old car seats?" Connor asked.

"She brought them here and threw them into the dumpster. I thought she should call the police, but she wouldn't. She said she couldn't get them involved."

"Did you ask her what was going on?" Connor said.

"Of course. I was concerned. For someone to target her kids is pretty messed up. Right before that, Hunter sliced his palm on glass in the sandbox."

Connor and Stryker looked at one another. "What sandbox?" Stryker asked.

"The one in their backyard. Jim called here one day. He had the kids after school and day care before Leah got home. I guess he had them in the yard playing. They have a sandbox. Hunter and Peyton were playing in it, and Hunter sliced his hand pretty good. Jim called here furious—said there was all kinds of broken glass in the sand and basically blamed Leah. Like she would put glass in her own kids' sandbox. Her husband is kind of an ass."

Connor immediately imagined Jade's response to that. *You think?* It was like a punch to the gut. But it would be like that now. She was gone. Her scathing commentary would live on in his head.

Ashley continued. "Anyway, naturally, I heard them on the phone arguing about where it came from. Then she flew out of here to meet them at the ER."

"Which ER?" Stryker asked.

"Sutter Children's, I think. I'm not sure. She acted like it didn't even happen the next day. But I knew something was wrong. She was rattled."

"In what way?" Connor asked.

"She just seemed like scared, you know? Distracted. She wasn't worried about every little thing anymore. Her hair was always a mess, like she didn't even care how she looked anymore. She started walking out with me at the end of the day."

"You two didn't walk out together normally?" Stryker asked.

Ashley gave them a wry smile. "I'm the assistant, remember? I always got here before her and left after her. I'd be here for an hour after she left, finishing up work. But then it was like she didn't care whether or not I got things finished before the end of the day. At three she would say 'Stop whatever you're doing, let's get out of here.' At first I thought she was grateful for me helping her out with the car seats, but then I started thinking she was just scared to walk to her car alone. I could tell 'cause she was always looking around the parking lot like someone might jump out at her."

Connor said, "And these things, they started a few months ago?"

Ashley nodded. "Like right after she came back from maternity leave."

"She never gave you any indication that she knew who was doing these things?" Connor asked.

"No. Well, I only asked her about it that one time, and she really wouldn't talk about it. At that point, I already knew way more than she would want anyone to know about her life. Like I said, Leah is—was very private."

"And there were no strange incidents during her pregnancy with Tyler or before that?" Connor asked.

Ashley took a moment to consider this. Then she said, "No. It started after Tyler was born. She took six weeks of maternity leave. The glass in the sandbox, the car seats, the dog—those all happened in the last few months. I mean that's just the stuff I know about. I couldn't tell you if anything happened while she was home."

"And you're not aware of any other unusual incidents?" Connor asked.

"No, nothing."

"How long were you Leah's assistant?" Stryker asked.

"Almost five years."

"Ashley, we have reason to believe that Leah may have been . . . involved with someone other than her husband within the last couple of years. Are you aware of anyone in her life she might have been seeing?"

Nervous laughter bubbled up from her diaphragm. "You're joking, right? You think Leah was having an affair?"

"Something like that," Stryker said.

Ashley shook her head. "No way. I mean, no one would have blamed her—her husband was a big, dumb douche—but for some strange reason, Leah loved him. She never cheated. She wouldn't."

"What makes you say that?" Connor asked.

She shrugged. "She told me her dad ran around on her mom her whole life, and then her mom killed herself. Leah said she would never do that to her kids. That's why she married Jim. She knew he wouldn't cheat."

"Who else was she friendly with here?" Connor asked.

Ashley laughed. "No one. Like I said, Leah was private. She was nice to everyone, but there wasn't anyone she really confided in. I can give you a list of names of people she works—worked with the most, if you think it will help."

"That would be great," Connor said.

"How about men?" Stryker asked. "Anyone here Leah might have been involved with or who might have been interested in her?"

"She probably had the most contact with Kyle in accounting, but he's gay."

"What about young men?" Stryker continued. "Do you have any male staff members—say, under the age of twenty-six, twenty-seven—who might have taken a recent interest in her?"

"Leah and a young guy?" She gave her head a sharp little shake. "Listen, the Leah you're talking about, I just can't—Leah was all about her kids. She had her hands full with that idiot husband of hers. Even if we did have a hot, young guy working here, she wouldn't give him the time of day." She seemed to notice Stryker's withering glance and added, "But we do have a male intern. He's about twenty-six, good-looking. He gets a lot of female attention. I'm sure HR can give you a complete list of employees."

"Can you look it over for us and tell us everyone Leah might have had regular contact with? We'll need to talk to everyone. We'll also need to take a look at her computer."

Ashley smiled wanly. "I'll talk to Leah's supervisor."

CHAPTER

THIRTY-SEVEN

Sammy's was a small bagel shop not far from Claire and Brianna's house. It was nestled in the middle of a strip of stores amid otherwise tree-lined residential streets. Parking was impossible, as the two spots out front that were allocated to Sammy's were usually taken by people picking up their clothes at the dry cleaner next door. The inside was decorated in black and chrome with three rows of metal tables and chairs, each set made to seat only two people. A long counter at the back sat next to a large glass case displaying the various types of bagels they offered. Behind that hung a large chalkboard that the staff updated daily depending on what was available. Claire and Brianna had become regulars shortly after moving into their house. The owner, Sammy, had become a good friend. The first time Claire met him, he had wept at the sight of her. "It's so good to see you alive," he had told her.

It wasn't until she saw the many yellowed missing-persons fliers taped in his window, behind his register, in the bathroom, and on the community corkboard that she understood. He had been captivated by her case since she'd disappeared, had helped with various community searches, attended vigils, kept her face in front of his customers for ten long years. He was a stranger to her, and yet he had held out hope for her safe return for a decade. Held it out for others to see in the hopes that one day someone would see something and say something. Most of the time, the attention that her ordeal brought her made her uncomfortable. She felt like a spectacle, a circus act, a curiosity. But Sammy made her feel like an old friend returning from a long, arduous journey. For a long time, Sammy's was the only place she could go.

The staff there had gotten to know both Claire and Brianna over the years, so when they walked in on Monday morning for their usual bagels and coffee to start the week, a small cheer erupted from behind the counter. Three staff members were on—two women and a man, all college aged. All the workers wore baseball caps declaring "Sammy's" and beneath that: "Sacramento's Best Bagels." Claire knew them all. One of the young women, Nancy Thompson, hurried around the counter, smiling broadly beneath her cap, and hugged Brianna tightly to her. Claire smiled to herself, watching Brianna stiffen in the embrace. Although Brianna was very affectionate with Claire and the rest of their immediate family, she hated casual affection. You had to earn Brianna's desire for affection with time, loyalty, and proximity. Nancy's unexpected hug caught her off guard, particularly when she realized the dozen or so customers in the shop were now staring at her, wide-eyed.

"You're a hero!" Nancy said, releasing Brianna from the hug but holding on to her shoulders and looking her up and down, an expression of wonder on her pale pixie face. "Your breakfast is on the house," she told them. "Sammy's orders. For every kid you pulled out of that car, you eat here free for a week."

"Wow," Claire said. "That's great. Does she get a plus one with that?"

Brianna turned to Claire and rolled her eyes. "Like you've ever paid for a bagel in this place."

Claire moved past her to get in line. "Once, when Buddy first started, I did."

From behind the counter, Buddy hollered, "It was my first day! I didn't know!"

Claire winked and smiled at him. She always made sure to leave a decent amount of money in the tip jar in spite of Sammy's insistence that she eat for free.

A young man in a River Cats hat came up behind them. He gestured to the counter. "Do you mind if I go?" he asked.

"Not at all," Claire told him.

He smiled his thanks and moved to the counter to place his order.

"So what was it like?" Nancy asked Brianna.

One of the rapt customers pointed and said, "Are you the chick who saved those kids from the river on Saturday?"

A woman who had just gotten in line touched Brianna's shoulder and said, "God bless you. It's terrible what happened to those kids. The poor families."

A half-dozen conversations about the Holloway crash erupted all over the room like tiny geysers of morbid curiosity. Claire heard snippets rising from the cacophony.

"Can you believe she was drunk at ten in the morning?"

"I heard they weren't even her kids."

"Killed four people on the overpass."

"What kind of person would do something like that?"

Claire glanced around, beginning to feel some of Brianna's discomfort. It was crowded, as it was most weekday mornings. Their preferred table near the front window was taken, but that wouldn't have afforded much privacy anyway. Sammy's only had one semiprivate table—the one that sat at the mouth of the small hallway leading to the restrooms. But the man in the River Cats hat had taken it, a bagel and steaming cup of coffee in front of him, as yet untouched. He was engrossed in something on his phone. Claire was thinking about how she might go about asking him for the table when Brianna dug an elbow into her side.

Buddy had slid a tray across the counter with their usual on it. Brianna moved past Claire and scooped it up. "Let's go," she said.

"You sure you want to eat here?" Claire said.

Brianna rolled her eyes. "We eat here all the time. I'm not leaving. Just grab a table."

They found one along the wall. Claire was acutely aware of the patrons staring in their direction. Brianna kept her eyes on Claire and picked up the conversation they'd been having before they left the house. "I just can't believe that detective is dead. They said on the news it was under 'suspicious circumstances.' Is that cop talk for murdered?"

Claire shrugged. She couldn't bring herself to meet Brianna's eyes. Talking about Jade Webb made her uncomfortable, and not just because Connor had told her things about the case that she could not repeat, even to her sister. "I don't know. I know they're investigating."

"I can't believe we just saw her. How is Connor?"

"He's completely broken," Claire said. "I don't think I've ever seen him so down."

"And you?"

Finally, Claire looked at her sister. "You can tell?"

Brianna smiled. "You know what you look like when you feel guilty? Remember when we were little and you cut off your hair and stuffed it into your footie pajamas and then the zipper got stuck?"

Claire laughed. "God, what was I? Five?"

"Four," Brianna corrected. "Dad had to use pliers to get the zipper open. You had stuffed so much hair in there, it got caught in the zipper and broke the damn thing. You were so squirmy and uncomfortable. That's how you look whenever I mention this woman. As your big sister, let me start off by saying that what happened to her is not your fault."

Claire put her bagel down, placed her hands in her lap, and stared at them. "I disliked her on sight."

"So? You don't have to like everyone you meet."

"I didn't like her because she seemed so familiar with Connor. I was worried that they had been—that they had had a relationship, you know, a romantic relationship. I never even gave her a chance."

"It's called jealousy. We all feel it from time to time. Even if you had loved the woman from the instant you saw her, it would change nothing. She would still have died."

Claire knew that Brianna was trying to make her feel better. She couldn't say the one thing that she kept coming back to because it was just too shameful: she had wanted Jade gone. Not dead or harmed in any way. More like transferred to another department or another city. Just gone in a way that she wouldn't get to see Connor every day, laugh at his jokes, playfully touch his arm, wink at him, and generally flirt with him. This was unfamiliar territory for her. Guilt was a heavy stone in her stomach, lightened only by the memory of the night she had spent with Connor, even though he was inextricably bound up in her conflicted feelings about Jade's death.

"Well," Brianna said. "I don't think you should spend too much time on it. Connor needs you right now. I mean, his colleague dies, and he comes directly to you."

"Excuse me." An elderly woman with short gray hair and a thick middle approached the table. She smiled kindly at Brianna. "I don't mean to bother you. I just wanted to say God bless you for what you did, saving all those kids."

Brianna swallowed the food she'd been chewing and returned the woman's smile. Only Claire could see the waver of her lips, her awkwardness, the struggle to remember that she had a good reason to lie to people, which was to protect her sister.

"Thank you," Brianna said. "I appreciate that."

The woman patted Brianna's shoulder and walked off. Claire and Brianna hunched closer together. "I gotta say, I'm relieved no one here is crucifying me after that horrible newscast."

"Me too," Claire said. "Seems like people are just happy you saved all the kids. Plus, the news that Holloway was drunk probably deflects a lot of attention away from why you didn't try to get her out of the car."

"Maybe," Brianna said. "So, what I was trying to say before was that Connor needs you right now. I think it's a good sign that he came to you."

"Excuse me," a man said, appearing next to their table. He looked to be in his forties, with deeply tanned skin and a tattoo sleeve on his right arm. "You're on TV," he said. He pointed over his shoulder where the large flat-screen TV Sammy had mounted on the wall showed clips from the original newscast in which Brianna had given her interview. Sure enough, there she was, soaked and bedraggled, talking in stilted sentences about a rescue she didn't make.

"Yeah, that's me," Brianna said to the man, smiling tightly.

"Well," he said. "That's pretty badass, what you did."

"Thank you," Brianna said, the tight smile frozen on her face.

That man chatted with them for a few minutes and went on his way only to be followed immediately by the young guy in the River Cats hat from earlier. "Ladies," he said. He held his hat in his hands and smiled, showing off beautifully straight white teeth. Thick golden-brown hair fell into his blue eyes. Claire knew Brianna had been about to say something borderline rude, this being the third interruption in less than ten minutes, but after she got a good look at him, she clamped her mouth shut. The man pointed toward the table he had just vacated.

"You can have my table if you want," he said. "I'm leaving. It's more private back there."

Brianna smiled. "Thank you so much." She stood and shook his hand. "My name is Brianna."

He winked at her. "I know. I saw you on TV. It was pretty brave, what you did, by the way."

"Thanks," Brianna acknowledged.

"Guess you're famous now."

"Only in here," Brianna replied.

"Well, in that case, take my hat too. Between that and the table, you should be able to eat the rest of your meal without anyone bothering you."

Without another word, he fitted the cap onto Brianna's head, and she let him. His smile was captivating. Brianna touched the brim of the cap lightly. "I can't take your hat."

"Please. I have ten of them at home. It's my pleasure. For the hometown hero and all that."

Brianna returned his smile. "That's so sweet."

Claire felt like she was intruding on the moment. She cleared her throat, but neither one of them acknowledged her.

"What was it like?" he asked. "In the river?"

"Wet," Brianna said.

The man laughed softly. "I guess it was," he agreed. "So, that lady, the driver, you couldn't get her out of the car?"

The flirty moment came screeching to a halt. Brianna's body went still. She had that awkward, deer-in-the-headlights expression she'd worn when Noel Geary had asked her the same question. She adjusted the cap on her head. "Uh, no. I had to get the kids out first. By the time they were all out of the car, she was . . . she was gone."

"Why didn't you just get her out first?"

Brianna's smile began to fail. "I couldn't. She was—there was something wrong with her door. It was . . . chaotic. I was just trying to get the kids out."

"You said on the news that she was hurt. If she was hurt, wouldn't you want to get her out first, so you could get her help?"

"I couldn't get her out," Brianna said. "The door was lo—jammed. She was—I'm sorry. I'm really not comfortable talking about this anymore."

The moment stretched out. He stared at Brianna's face. Claire was suddenly hyperaware of the ambient noise—the hushed conversations of other patrons, the staff behind the counter shouting out orders, the gurgle of the coffeemakers, the *thwap* of the bagels falling from the toaster onto the cooling tray. The man glanced at Claire briefly, then toward the front door. When he turned back, a smile was pasted on his face. "I'm sorry," he said. "I'm being a douche, aren't I? Too many questions. I'll go. Maybe I'll see you around."

He didn't wait for a response, instead turning and walking briskly toward the front door. Brianna watched him leave. Even Claire couldn't help watching him walk away. He looked as though he should be modeling men's underwear.

They moved quickly to his table. Brianna left the hat on. "Strangeness aside, he was pretty hot," she said.

Claire laughed. "I think he's a little too young for you."

"Oh please. I don't want to marry him, I just want to have a sleepover." She lowered her voice, hunching forward over her bagel. "Speaking of sleepovers, can we please talk about last night?"

Claire blushed instantly. Had Brianna heard her and Connor making love? She hadn't thought they were loud. They hadn't even woken Wilson. Claire took a gulp of coffee. "Last night?"

"I know something happened. I don't know what, but something happened. You're different today. Besides, I saw the two of you saying goodbye. It was like no one else in the world existed, and you were leaving each other for all of eternity, which would be absolutely sickening if it weren't you and Connor. I mean, a marching band could have shown up in the street at that moment, and you two would have been oblivious."

The memory pushed all lingering thoughts of Jade out of Claire's head, at least for the moment. She suppressed a giddy smile. She felt like a teenager again—like the teenager she had been before a raging sicko of a pedophile took ten years of her life. Even though she was sad and distressed about Jade's death and very worried for Connor, she also felt light-headed, slightly drunk with the thought of what had happened between them. She had resigned herself to the fact that sex was perhaps a part of her life that her captor had permanently taken from her. She had done it with other men, as a sort of *fuck you* to her abuser and to those ten years of hell, but had doubted she would ever derive any real pleasure from it. It would always be something she did with tensed muscles and gritted teeth, gripping bed sheets and wishing it over quickly, like getting a tetanus shot. But she had been wrong.

She was never so happy to be wrong.

"Oh my God, you did it," Brianna said. "I can tell by your face. You did it."

Claire's cheeks flamed. "Shh! Keep your voice down, would you? Your fans might hear!"

Brianna shook her head. "Please. They should be your fans, and they won't hear us back here. So, tell me!"

Claire smiled. She picked up her bagel and put it back down. Where to start?

"We did it," Claire whispered.

Brianna squealed with delight, clapping her hands together. "I knew it."

The words seemed so inadequate to describe what had happened. Sure, they'd had sex, but it had felt like so much more. It was still so hard to believe. She had always wanted this but never thought it would happen. In the past, acting on any attraction she felt would inevitably cause her trauma to rise quickly to the surface. The flood of memories made her shut down. A trigger, her therapist called it. It would be a certain level of pressure in a man's touch, a certain way of breathing, certain acts. Most of it was so subtle, even Claire had trouble pinpointing the triggers.

Early on in their relationship, before they'd broken up, Connor had tried to avoid every trigger she had, but it was an impossible feat. Maybe she hadn't been ready then. Maybe she still wasn't. As elated as she was, she was already nervous for the next time. There would be a next time. That's how romantic relationships worked. She remembered how he felt quivering beneath her, his skin hot and damp against hers, his smell, his beard scraping over her skin, and some of her nervousness gave way to excitement.

"So?" Brianna asked. "How was it? Did you cry this time? I mean, you were okay with it?"

"Better than okay. It was amazing. I think I—I know I had my first, you know . . ."

"Orgasm?" Brianna blurted.

Claire glanced out into the main dining area, but no one appeared to be listening. Her cheeks felt like she'd tried to iron them. "Uh, yeah."

Brianna grinned. "Well, that changes things, doesn't it?"

Claire could not contain her own smile. "Yeah," she said. "I think it does."

She didn't talk about Connor's grief or the blissful forgetting they had found in one another. She'd finally had sex, real sex, with someone she loved. It was nothing at all like a tetanus shot.

"I'm happy for you," Brianna said. "You deserve amazing."

The scorching feeling crept down her neck. "It was better than amazing. I had no idea."

Brianna's ear-to-ear grin was only dimmed by the sound of her phone dinging. She fished it out of her purse and glanced at the screen. "I'm sorry. I really need to get to this study group, and I've been charged with picking up pastries. Can you drive me back to the house to get my car?"

Claire stood and cleared the table. "Sure."

They had parked around the corner from Sammy's, a couple of blocks away. Brianna trailed behind Claire, riffling through her purse and talking at the same time. "Oh my God. I'm so happy for you. This is huge. I mean, this changes things in a big way. I think it's so awesome. I knew you two were meant to be."

"Don't start planning our wedding," Claire warned, a wry smile twisting her lips.

"Too late!" Brianna joked. She had stopped walking, her head still down as she searched her purse, her movements more frantic now.

"What are you looking for?" Claire asked.

"My wallet. I can't find it. I need it to get the pastries." She groaned. "I must have left it at Sammy's."

"We didn't pay at Sammy's," Claire reminded her.

"I know, but I took it out of my purse to put money into the tip jar. I must have dropped it or left it there. Let me run back, and I'll meet you back at the car in a minute."

Brianna turned back toward Sammy's, and Claire continued in the direction of her Jeep.

"I'm going to be your maid of honor," Brianna called over her shoulder, her tone teasing.

CHAPTER
THIRTY-EIGHT

Leah's work computer revealed almost nothing personal. The most damning thing on it was the amount of Internet shopping she had done while at work, and even that had been almost exclusively for her children. Diapers, onesies, rain boots, Halloween costumes, and books. She had never even used her work email to send a personal message to anyone. It was a dead end.

The intern that Ashley Copestick had mentioned checked out. He worked days and had alibis for every one of the Soccer Mom Strangler murders, even Jade's. He'd spent that night at his girlfriend's house. Stryker put a couple of other detectives on the list of KZLM's male employees even though none of them were under thirty-five and nearly all of them worked during the day. They interviewed the handful of coworkers Ashley had said Leah had the most contact with but turned up nothing new or helpful. Leah had chatted with them often about their own lives—evidently, she was a great listener—but had never talked about her life other than in very broad strokes.

It seemed that Ashley Copestick had the clearest picture of Leah's life in the months before her death. Ashley had been privy to things Leah had chosen not to tell her husband or her best friend, and not just because Leah had had little choice over Ashley finding out. It made sense to Connor that she might choose to let down her guard with her assistant. Leah didn't see Ashley socially, and they didn't travel in the same circles outside of work. Ashley had little cause to come into contact even with Jim Holloway. Allowing Ashley a glimpse into whatever Leah had been dealing with posed little risk to Leah's carefully constructed world. Ashley was obviously loyal and, as she had told them, discreet. She'd told them a lot, confirmed a lot of suspicions, but brought them no closer to finding the Soccer Mom Strangler.

"So," Stryker said as they drove back to headquarters. "She catches this guy's eye a few months ago. He stalks her, eventually rapes her, but doesn't kill her."

Connor pulled his notebook out and flipped back through the notes he had taken in the last several days both on the Holloway crash and the Strangler case. "But the Strangler's not really a stalker. He's an opportunist. It doesn't fit. None of his other victims had stalking incidents in the months or weeks before their murders, right?"

Stryker frowned. "Right. That's true. So, who's the stalker?"

"I think the stalker was her lover."

"The guy she had an affair with?"

"That makes the most sense, don't you think? It started after Tyler was born. She just took a paternity test. Maybe this all had to do with the baby, and she thought she could get him to back off if she could prove that the baby was Jim's."

Stryker said, "But why did the stalker focus on her kids—the glass in the sandbox, the severed car seat straps? And you're saying she was being stalked for months by someone who clearly had no problem harming her kids, even killing her dog, and then just by coincidence she gets raped by the Soccer Mom Strangler. Do people really have luck that bad?"

"Let's run it down," Connor said. "Roughly fourteen, fifteen months ago, she's having an affair. According to the OB-GYN records, she asks to be tested for STDs. That's when she finds out she's pregnant with Tyler, the baby."

Stryker was nodding as Connor spoke. He said, "She obviously had concerns about Tyler's paternity. If she needed to be tested for STDs, it's not a stretch that she would have had questions about the baby's paternity back then. So now she's pregnant and not sure whose baby it is, and she just stays with her husband?"

"Well, it was easier for her to do that. From everything we know about her now, it seems as though the appearance of a happy family life was very important to her. But I don't think she ever confessed her affair to her husband. Jim Holloway was genuinely shocked by the affair and the paternity test."

"I agree. I don't think he had any idea. Okay, so she stays with her husband. We have no way of knowing whether she broke off the affair or not. Fast forward to after the baby is born. Someone begins stalking her. Kills her dog, slashes her kids' car seat straps, puts glass in her kids' sandbox."

Connor said, "But she doesn't tell a soul."

"And the only reason that Ashley knows is because Leah couldn't avoid telling her."

"That's the other thing. This woman was having an affair, and yet there is no evidence of it anywhere. Not on her computers at home or at work, not in her email."

"Yeah, but you only have her phone records going back twenty-four hours before the accident, right? There could be something there. What if the person on the burner phone is the person she was having the affair with? What if he's been calling her for years? I can get her records going back three years. That should be long enough to turn something up if she was communicating with her lover by phone." As they pulled up to a red light, Stryker whipped out his phone and fired off a text. "Done," he said, like a true task force leader.

Connor laughed. He made his voice higher, imitating a woman's voice, her tone bland and almost robotic. "You can expect those records in five to seven business days."

"Nah. You've got the warrant out already, right? That lady you talked to last night sent you the last twenty-four hours of calls as a favor. I'll have someone harass Globocell all day until we get the rest of them. It's a weekday. They have no excuses. So, back to Leah. Last week, she goes out to meet someone for lunch—presumably her ex-lover who is now her stalker, because where else would she be going?—and just happens to get raped by the Soccer Mom Strangler? Where was the stalker during all this?"

Connor said, "They're the same guy."

"What?"

"It's all the same guy. The ex-lover turned stalker and the Strangler. She was seeing this guy a couple of years ago, right? She gets pregnant, breaks off the relationship. Or maybe she keeps seeing him through the pregnancy. We have no way of knowing at this point. Once the baby comes, he starts stalking her."

For the first time that day, Stryker's face had color again. "Ashley said the stalking started after she came back to work."

"True," Connor said. "But Ashley also said she had no way of knowing whether there were any incidents before Leah came back from maternity leave."

"But she didn't know of any before that, so we can safely say the stalking started when baby Tyler was born," Stryker said. "And he's five months old, which means he was born in May."

Connor saw where Stryker was going. He flipped through his notebook. "The first Strangler murder took place in April, just a few weeks before his birth. Maybe she was seeing him through the pregnancy and broke it off the closer she got to having the baby."

"Holy shit," Stryker said. "That could be the trigger."

Silence filled the car as this realization sank in. Then Stryker asked, "Do you think he knew Tyler's paternity was in doubt?"

"I don't know. I don't think the baby mattered to him all that much. Remember, Agent Bishop said that the Strangler victims were surrogates for a mother figure. Maybe Holloway was a surrogate too. A mother figure."

"And the new baby replaced him," Stryker finished.

"Sent him over the edge," Connor said.

"So Leah has the baby, and five months later she has questions about his paternity, so she decides to do a DNA test."

"Maybe she agreed to meet with him on Wednesday so she could try to get a DNA sample from him," Connor said. "But he rapes her. So instead, she has to get one from her husband—that'd still get her her answer—so she tricks him into signing the consent form."

"Would've been the easier path for her from the start," Stryker said. "But she's not exactly thinking clearly, right? And then she carries on like nothing ever happened and sends in her DNA test?"

"Well, that is how she operated, isn't it? As if nothing bad ever happened. Her dog gets poisoned, her kids' car seat straps get slashed, and no one even knew about it. No one even knew she filed a police report about the dog. According to Ashley, she just went on with her life. She wasn't sure if her baby was her husband's or her lover's, and she stayed in her marriage. Like I said, appearances were important to her."

"Do you think she knew he was a serial killer?" Stryker asked.

"We have no way of knowing," Connor repeated. "I don't think it really matters at this point."

"You're right. Finding the Strangler should be our main focus. If her ex-lover and the Strangler are the same guy, that just narrows our search. So we need to know where she went on Wednesday, especially if that's when she met with him."

Connor said, "Maybe we can pull video, try to follow her."

"What? From KZLM?"

"From their parking lot. If we know which way she pulled out, we can try to find her route. Go to the next business that has surveillance and see if they've got footage of her driving past. Tail her by surveillance."

"That could take a really long time, not to mention we could hit a dead end at any time."

"We used it successfully on that missing persons last month," Connor pointed out. He flipped to another page in his notebook, searching for the information he had written down about Leah's vehicle. "Wait—hell, the GPS from her SUV. Surely the lab ought to know by now if they can get anything from it. It's been a couple of days."

Connor's phone rang as they pulled up to the division. "I have to take this," he told Stryker. Swiping "Answer," he pressed the phone to his ear. "Claire?"

Her voice was high-pitched. Panicked. "I need you," she said. "It's Brianna. She's—she's missing."

CHAPTER
THIRTY-NINE

"Take me through it again," Connor told her.

They stood outside of Sammy's, Claire near tears. It was hard not to slide into Connor's arms and dissolve into a quivering mess. She drew a deep breath. "We had breakfast here. We walked back toward my car. She was looking through her purse. She said she didn't have her wallet, so she walked back to Sammy's to see if she left it there. I waited ten minutes, then fifteen, and I came here to see what was taking so long, and she was gone. Nancy said she came right back in looking for her wallet, found it under one of the tables, and then left.

"Now she's just gone. I tried calling and texting her—no answer. That's not like her. Something happened. She had a study group this morning. You know, for the bar exam? We had to leave here so she could pick up pastries and get over to it. No way would she miss it, and she wouldn't go to it without telling me. I was going to drive her back to the house so she could get her car. Something is wrong."

Her voice was rising to a squeal. Hysteria poked at the edges of her panic. Connor pulled her into his arms. "Hey," he said. "Stay calm. We'll find her, okay? Let me make a few calls, see if I can pull anyone from the Soccer Mom Strangler case to help us. First, I'll send someone over to make sure her car is still at your house. Do you know where her study group was taking place?"

"I think the UC Davis library."

"Do you know anyone in her group?"

"I know her friend, George. But I texted him, and he said she didn't show up."

"Okay," he said. "Okay. We'll have to canvass, then. Let me see if I can get someone over here to help us."

She nodded her head against his chest. He kept her close to him with one arm and used the other to fish his phone out of his pocket. He made a few calls. She was soothed by the authoritative tone of his voice. This was what he did. This was what he was good at. Finding people. Solving puzzles. Solving crimes.

He pulled away. "Does Sammy have any surveillance cameras?"

She nodded. "Yeah, I think so. Let's ask Nancy."

Nancy was able to pull up footage of the entire morning, from the time they arrived until the time Brianna returned without Claire to ask about her missing wallet. They watched Brianna talk to Nancy and look beneath both tables they had sat at. Beneath the second table, she could be seen scooping up a small, square object and depositing it into her purse before walking out the door. Sammy's didn't have footage of the exterior, but they assumed she had turned in the direction of Claire's car.

"So that means somewhere along those two blocks, she just vanished?" Claire said.

"No," Connor said. He didn't say the words, and for that Claire was grateful. She couldn't bear to hear them out loud: *Someone took her.*

Claire couldn't breathe. Is this how her family had felt when she was abducted?

Connor's hands were on her shoulders, easing her into a chair. He kissed the top of her head. "I'm going to take a look around. I want you to stay put. Don't leave this building, okay?"

She looked into his eyes. "I want to help."

He smiled. "I know," he said. "But I want you to stay here in case she comes back."

In case she comes back.

She wondered if that was code for *We don't want you finding her dead body.* A lump formed in her throat. Sobs threatened to make their way up and out of her body. She nodded because she was afraid if she spoke, the hysteria would come out, and she wouldn't be able to rein it back in. The breakfast rush was over, but a few stragglers lingered, plus the staff.

Connor was halfway out the front door when a blood-curdling scream cut through the air. He turned back to Claire. Their eyes locked and then they both sprinted toward the back of the building. Claire got there faster. Behind her, Connor said, "Claire, wait." She was only vaguely aware of the strain in his voice. He didn't want her to see it. The back door hung open. A small alley ran behind the store. Across the asphalt, Nancy stood, leaning against the dumpster, her face pale as snow, eyes wide and filling with tears.

"No," Claire said.

"Claire, wait," Connor said, louder this time.

They reached the dumpster at the same time. Claire had to lift onto her tiptoes to see inside. "Brianna!" she cried.

Connor leapt into the dumpster in a single motion. Brianna lay face up, sprawled among the trash bags and loose debris. The smell was sickening. Her eyes were closed, lips slightly parted. Claire couldn't tell if she was breathing or not. Connor nearly fell on top of her as he struggled to keep his balance. "Claire," he said, his voice sharp and urgent, cutting through the morass of emotions that threatened to overwhelm her.

She looked at him. His fingers were pressed against the side of Brianna's neck. His eyes looked so blue in that moment. They steadied her, as always. "Call 911," he said. "Tell them we need an ambulance. She has a pulse."

CHAPTER FORTY

"What the hell happened?" Stryker said. He paced in front of the security desk at Sutter General's ER, where Connor and Claire stood. They'd taken Brianna back on a stretcher, still unconscious. Connor had driven Claire behind the ambulance. Now she stood beside him, clasping his hand tightly, more grateful for his presence at that moment than at any other moment since her return. Tears leaked from her eyes, and she wiped them away with her other hand.

"We don't know," Connor said. "There's no surveillance out back. We found her unconscious in the dumpster. No signs of sexual assault. No visible injuries but the paramedics said she had quite a bump on the back of her head. She still had her purse and phone with her."

"The hat was missing," Claire said.

The two men looked at her. Connor squeezed her hand lightly. She sucked in a breath and met Connor's eyes. "You saw the footage. That guy who gave us his table, he gave her his hat—to keep—he said he had ten more at home. He kept asking about why Brianna didn't try to get Leah Holloway out of the SUV, then he left. It was awkward, but Brianna thought he was . . ." She trailed off, face heating at the thought of their conversation. Talk of boys—of men, actually—sex, and relationships. Like the teenage sisters they might have been if Claire had never been taken. "She thought he was hot."

"So had he approached her outside, she would have felt comfortable speaking to him," Stryker said.

"Yes."

Connor was staring at Stryker. "So he hits her over the head and takes his hat back?"

Stryker scratched at the stubble on his head. "Makes no sense, but some people are just crazy. Who knows what this guy was thinking? Maybe he had other plans, but it was too risky in broad daylight. We just don't know. We'll find him, though. He asked about the Holloway crash? How old was this guy?"

Claire shrugged. "I don't know. Early twenties, maybe. But everyone in there was asking about the Holloway crash. It was on the news while we were there."

"I already checked with Sammy's staff," Connor said. "He paid cash. Matt is trying to pull a still of his face to release to the media. When he's done, he'll check with the neighboring businesses, see if they've got any exterior footage of what happened."

The sliding doors whooshed open and Claire's older brother Tom appeared. His face was pinched with anxiety. "Claire!"

He rushed toward her, nearly bowling her over with his hug. He released her but kept one arm around her shoulder. Nodding at Connor and Stryker in greeting, he said, "Where is she? What did they say?"

"They're taking a CT of her head now."

"Oh God," Tom said.

He seemed far more panicked than Claire, and she was the one who had experienced the frantic, desperate moments of searching for her sister without success and then finding her slack body in a dumpster. Today's trauma was so much worse than the Holloway crash. She felt like someone had stuffed her whole body in a washer and put it on spin for an entire day. Somehow, her brother looked worse than she did, his open face flushed and rent with pain, like someone was stabbing him with a thousand tiny needles. Fingers dug into her shoulder.

219

"Tom," she said, hoping to get him to focus. "Did you get in touch with Mom and Dad?"

He pulled out his cell phone and looked at its sleeping screen. "Wherever they are, they're not getting cell service. I called the cruise line. They're going to track them down. I'm expecting a call any second."

"Mitch?"

"Headed to the airport to get on the next flight."

A doctor in dark-blue scrubs and a white coat emerged from a nearby set of closed doors, a grim smile on his face. He looked from Claire to Tom and back again. "You're here for Brianna Fletcher?"

Tom said, "Yes, she's our sister. How is she?"

"The bad news is that she has a subdural hematoma, which is a collection of blood that builds up between the skull and the dura, which is the coating of the brain. This is usually a result of a trauma. It looks like she hit the back of her head pretty hard. Her injury is consistent with a fall of some sort. Subdural hematomas can cause pressure on the brain. The good news is that hers is relatively small, and as of right now, she doesn't appear to have the kind of pressure on her brain that would require us to operate on her. She is comatose, but that's not unusual with this type of injury. We've got her on steroids to reduce any inflammation in the brain and medication to prevent seizures."

Claire's knees had weakened. She must've wobbled, because she felt Tom tighten his grip on her shoulder. "What happens now?"

"We wait. They'll move her to the ICU. You can both stay with her. We'll take more imaging in a few hours to make sure it's not getting worse, keep her medicated, and hope she wakes up soon. If the pressure on her brain becomes critical, then we will try to relieve it by drilling burr holes—"

"Stop," Claire said. "Please. Just . . . I can't . . ." Her breath wouldn't come.

Connor was on the other side of her. He and Tom lowered her into a chair. Connor's hand was warm in hers, his breath on her cheek. "It's okay," he said. "Breathe. She's alive. That's what matters. Breathe."

The doctor stood over them, looking uncertain and regretful. "I'm sorry," he said.

"It's okay," Tom said. "We're both still in shock. Thank you, Doctor. You'll let us know once she's moved to the ICU?"

"Of course."

Claire sucked in several deep breaths until the wave of dizziness that had assailed her passed. She was suddenly aware of Tom, Connor, and Stryker all staring at her. She attempted a weak smile. "I'm okay," she assured them. "I just need to sit here for a minute."

CHAPTER

FORTY-ONE

Once the color had returned to Claire's face, Stryker pulled Connor away, his voice lowered. "Look, I hate to say this, but I need bodies on this Strangler case. You or O'Handley. With Jade gone, we're short. You know I'm not asking you to abandon Claire, but you already know everything about the Holloway case. Leave O'Handley on Brianna's case and help me with the Strangler stuff. But I want O'Handley on her case. No one else."

"You thinking what I'm thinking?" Connor asked.

"That there is an off chance the twenty-year-old hot guy from the bagel shop is the Strangler? Yeah. I don't know what he would be doing coming after Brianna, but we have to cover every base."

"The news footage of Brianna has been running since Saturday," Connor said. "Claire said it was on in the bagel shop. He kept asking why Leah was left in the vehicle."

Stryker frowned. "Yeah, I saw that footage. Noel made it sound like Brianna left her there to die."

"Yeah, and this guy is obsessed with Leah. So if he thinks Brianna let her die out there, he's probably pretty pissed. I don't think it's a coincidence that he was at Sammy's today. It would have been easy enough to track Brianna down, follow her there."

"But why approach her in public? If he wanted to kill her, why not attack her at home?"

"I don't know," Connor said, feeling tired. "Maybe he was following her to see if he could catch her alone at some point. Maybe he just wanted to ask his questions. Who the hell knows?"

"We gotta get this guy, Parks. Now. O'Handley is familiar enough with both cases to handle Brianna's case. I'll brief him on what we just discussed. Either way, I want the guy from the bagel shop rounded up. We need to get a bead on this landscaper. Also, we need to see if the GPS from Holloway's SUV is available."

Connor looked toward the waiting room where Claire sat in deep conversation with her brother. He felt a pain in his chest. He didn't want to leave her, but Stryker was right. He had a job to do, and right now it was more important than ever. He knew Claire would understand, but that didn't make it any easier to leave her.

She glanced over at him and did a double take. She spoke softly to Tom and then weaved her way over to Connor. She was the only person in the room. She stopped inches from him, eyes fixed on his, her face lined with tension and grief. "You have to go," she said. It wasn't a question.

He nodded.

She reached up and laid a palm on his bearded cheek. Her touch was soothing and electrifying all at once. She smiled. "Go," she said. "Catch some bad guys. I'm not going anywhere."

The words seemed to have a double meaning. She wasn't physically leaving the hospital, but she also wasn't leaving him again—he hoped. There would be time to discuss all that later. For now, he needed her to be safe while he went to work, especially if the man Claire and Brianna had spoken with in the bagel shop was really the Strangler. The thought of her having been that close to such a monster turned his blood to ice. He had to get this guy.

He cupped her face in his hands, studying her eyes, her skin, her cheekbones. When this was over, he would go to her house, close the door behind him, and not leave for a week. Or maybe they'd take a trip somewhere. Tiki huts on a beach. Sunshine, blue water, beer, and this woman.

She smiled again, leaned into his right palm. "I'll be fine," she said. "I'm just worried about Brianna."

"I know. Me too. Stay with Tom, okay? Don't go anywhere alone. You and Wilson can come stay with me tonight. I need to know you're safe. I'll feel better if you stay with me for a few days. Call me later, and I'll take you home to pick up Wilson. Just please don't go anywhere alone for now."

She backed away from him, pulling his hands from her face and holding them at waist level. "I'll call you," she said.

"Text me if Brianna's condition changes."

"Of course."

She let go of his hands and turned to walk off. Images of Jade and Brianna—their lifeless bodies—assailed him, mingled with images of the incredible night he had just spent with Claire. Then he saw Claire's face on Jade's body, her beautiful smile a rictus of fear. Her body sprawled in a dumpster.

"Claire," he called, involuntarily, hating the tinge of desperation in his voice.

She walked back to him, rocked up onto the balls of her feet, and flung her arms around his neck. He caught her, gathering her to him, and buried his face in her hair, inhaling deeply. He held on as long as she would let him. He kissed her softly on the mouth as they parted, and she said, "I'll see you in a few hours."

CHAPTER
FORTY-TWO
TWENTY MONTHS EARLIER

"You've got great tits."

That was the first thing D.J. said to her.

Leah had followed the white vinyl privacy fence to its gate and knocked on it. She had to pound on the gate hard for several minutes to get anyone's attention. She didn't even know how they could possibly hear her banging over the music that was blaring. It was some kind of heavy metal/alternative blend. All Leah knew was that it sounded like unpleasant noise. The lyrics contained more *F* words than she'd ever heard in such a short span of time in her life. There was no way she was getting Hunter down for a nap with the music blasting like that.

The gate swung open. There he was, like he'd just stepped out of a Calvin Klein men's underwear ad. He was shirtless, his taut young skin tanned, the muscles of his chest, shoulders, and arms like they'd been chiseled from stone.

So that's what a six-pack looks like.

A thin column of brown hair went from his navel to his crotch, which was almost visible between the flaps of his unzipped jeans. He had thick, wavy brown hair and piercing blue eyes. He was so physically perfect he didn't even seem human. She tried to focus, to remember the tirade she'd been practicing on her way over. Something about decibels and city ordinances and putting her toddler down for a nap. But when she opened her mouth, all that came out was "You can't play your music that loud."

He stared at her for a moment, his smug little smile bothering her even more than the way he looked. He leaned against the fence, as if waiting for her to say more, but she didn't. She couldn't. She hated herself for being so disarmed by this boy. Certainly, he was still a boy. He couldn't be older than nineteen or twenty.

Then he said, "You've got great tits."

Heat stung her face. She tried folding her arms over her chest, but that only jostled her breasts more in the V-neck shirt she wore. Anger and embarrassment hardened her tone. "What do you think you're—"

"I've seen you around," he said, cutting her off. "Leah, right?"

She clamped her mouth shut, not sure whether to agree or continue on with her indignant, how-dare-you speech.

He eyed her cleavage, shook his head, and licked his lips. "Great tits," he repeated.

Beads of sweat popped out along her hairline. She'd had pap smears that didn't make her as uncomfortable as she felt standing in front of this kid. She narrowed her eyes and put her hands on her hips, trying for what Peyton called her "scary mommy pose." With it, she tried her scary mommy voice. She refused to acknowledge his dirty remarks. "You have to turn that music down. It's far too loud. I have a toddler who needs a nap."

It was the best she could do.

And he ignored her.

"D.J.," he said, extending his hand.

She didn't take it. She wasn't going to give him the satisfaction of making nice. "I don't care who you are," she snapped, thankful to sound like her old self. "I just want you to turn your music down."

His smile didn't waver. "We're having drinks by the pool, Leah, if you'd like to join us."

He moved out of her sight line to reveal a stick-thin girl, lying on a chaise, naked from the waist up, her flat little breasts facing the sun, her areolas like two sunny-side-up eggs. She wore sunglasses, and in one hand she held a lit cigarette. On the ground next to her chair was an open beer. The sight of the girl did nothing to help Leah keep her cool.

"Are you out of your mind?" she said. "No, I will not join you. I'm only here to tell you to turn down your music. If you don't, I'm calling the police."

His constant stare was unnerving. His smirk was almost a leer. "Leah," he said, like they were old friends. "Chill. If it means that much to you, I'll turn it down."

He turned back toward the girl. Snapping his fingers, he said sharply, "Yo, turn that shit down."

The girl's head swiveled side to side. "What?" she called.

"I said turn that shit down. It's too fucking loud."

The girl took a drag of her cigarette, ash falling on her bare stomach. "Shit," she muttered, wiping it off. She stood, stumbling, the chair scraping along the concrete as her calves bumped it. She walked unsteadily out of sight. After a moment, the music became dramatically lower.

D.J. turned back to her, his smile still in place. "That better?"

His voice was sweet as honey and soft as velvet. He made her skin crawl in a not-altogether-unpleasant way, which only freshly enraged her. She tried to choke out a thank-you. After all, he had done exactly what she'd asked him to do. She hadn't even needed to go full bitch on him. She had told him to turn the music down, and he had—or his drunk, half-naked waif of a girlfriend had.

Why couldn't she manage a thank-you?

She cleared her throat. She tried to hold his gaze but found she couldn't. She looked down, her eyes catching the "tits" he'd just been admiring. She was easily a *DD* cup. Leah had never been a small woman. Even at her thinnest, she'd still had large breasts and an ample behind. She had never been—could never be—petite. There was just more to her than most women. Still, many men liked large breasts on a woman.

"Thank you," she finally mumbled, hating herself even more.

Before D.J. could speak, she turned and left. She could feel his eyes on her ass as she hurried back to her home. She forced herself not to go any faster, and again, her cheeks glowed with heat. She felt strangely violated, like she had just been coerced into doing something that she really didn't want to do. Like in high school when her brother's friend had talked her into giving him a blow job. She shuddered, pushing that memory back into its compartment: Shitty Childhood.

Why had this boy made her so ill at ease?

She heard Hunter's screams before she even reached her front door. Inside the house, Peyton had dutifully gone to her bedroom for her designated "rest" time, but Hunter wailed, red-faced, in Jim's arms.

"Where the hell have you been?" Jim said, hollering to be heard over their son.

Leah surveyed the living room, which looked as though it had been ransacked in her absence. "I asked you to clean up," she said.

Jim struggled to hold on to Hunter, who squirmed toward Leah, his face pinched. "He doesn't listen to me," Jim said. He thrust Hunter toward her. "Besides, he's hungry. He keeps going into the kitchen trying to get those Gerber meal things."

She took her son, who stopped squirming for her but not crying. "Well, why didn't you feed him?"

Jim waved a hand in the air. "I don't know how to make those things."

Anger rose from Leah's gut, burning right up through her chest. Her heartbeat thundered in her ears. "You read the damn instructions on the box, Jim! It's not that hard."

She left him standing in the middle of the living room, knowing if he said one more word she was going to slap him. She heated a Gerber meal for Hunter and fed it to him in the kitchen. Then she took him to his room, slamming the door behind them so Jim would know she was still angry. It wasn't until Hunter had dozed in her lap while rocking in the rocking chair that Leah realized her thoughts kept drifting back to D.J.

CHAPTER
FORTY-THREE
TUESDAY

"This is ridiculous," Claire said into the phone. "I can get Wilson and meet you at your house. You don't need to babysit me."

She paced Brianna's darkened hospital room, back and forth from the window, where the city slept amid thousands of twinkling street-lights, to her sister's bed, where Brianna lay motionless, hooked up to what seemed like twenty different things. A monitor to measure her heart rate, respiration, oxygen saturation, and blood pressure, with each one reported in a different color on a screen affixed to the wall over Brianna's bed. An IV that slowly dripped medication into her veins. Pallor made the light freckles on her cheeks stand out in stark contrast. She hadn't moved all day—or all night. Even with the steady flow of nurses and doctors coming in to poke and prod her at least twice each hour, she remained completely unresponsive.

"It's guarding," Connor answered. "Not babysitting."

"That's a dubious distinction," Claire told him, but the truth was that she couldn't wait to see him again. She didn't want to leave

Brianna's side, but she longed for Connor. His presence alone would calm her frantic thoughts.

"Besides," he said. "You left your Jeep at Sammy's. I've got to come get you."

She pushed a knot of curls off her forehead and sighed. "I forgot."

"You have to rest or you'll be no good to Brianna. You said Tom is coming back. When he gets there, I'll come for you. We'll go get your car, you can follow me home, and you and Wilson can come home with me. Take a shower, eat something, get some sleep. Then you can go back to the hospital around midmorning."

She almost argued with him. The clock above Brianna's bed read 2:45 a.m., and he was still working, which meant that they were in some critical stage of the Soccer Mom Strangler investigation. He likely didn't have time to babysit—or guard—her, but the truth was that she really did need some sleep and Connor did too. Even more than that, she didn't want to be alone, even with Wilson. In the last seventy-two hours, she had watched a woman kill herself, Connor's colleague had been murdered by a serial killer, and her sister had been found unconscious in a dumpster. Claire felt punch-drunk and delirious from it all. A few stolen hours with Connor would sober her and soothe her anxiety. She didn't have to be alone anymore. That was the beauty of being free. She said, "That sounds good."

"How's Brianna?"

"The same," Claire replied. "Everything is the same. But I guess no news is good news. We finally got in touch with my parents. They're getting a flight from the Bahamas and should be back tomorrow night. Mitch's flight was delayed, but he should be here sometime tomorrow. Tom will stay with her until I get back."

"Call me when Tom gets there," he said. "I'll come right over."

True to his word, ten minutes after Tom returned to the hospital, Connor pulled up out front looking more exhausted than she'd ever seen him and yet still so handsome he made her breath catch in her throat.

In the back seat, Wilson paced and whined with excitement. Guilt assailed her. She usually took him to work. This was the first time in months she had left him alone the entire day.

"I fed him," Connor said as she slid into the front seat and was immediately covered in doggie kisses.

"Thank you," Claire said, scratching behind Wilson's ears.

She wanted to touch Connor, kiss him hello, but they were already moving, Wilson balancing his front paws on the console between them, eager for Claire's affection.

"Any progress with the case?" she asked as they pulled away.

"Stryke is all over this twenty-something landscaper who was having an affair with one of Leah Holloway's neighbors. Took us all day to track him down. He lives in an apartment in South Sacramento. We went there but he wasn't home. We've had someone on his place all night, but he hasn't come home."

"You really think he's your guy?"

Connor's voice was heavy. "I don't know. We'll know more when we talk to him. It feels like we're just taking shots in the dark at this point. We need to figure out where Leah Holloway was when she was attacked by the Strangler on Wednesday. The GPS from her vehicle was damaged but not completely destroyed. They're trying to pull the coordinates for where she went on Wednesday. Hopefully, we'll know more in the morning. There are a couple of other leads Stryke is following as well."

"I saw on the news that you got a grainy photo of the guy from the bagel shop," Claire said.

"Yeah. We couldn't get a great still shot of his face. You might need to work with a composite artist if we don't get any tips."

"This is me," Claire said as they pulled up a couple of blocks from Sammy's.

She took Wilson in her vehicle and followed Connor home. Claire hadn't been there in two years, but it seemed familiar to her, as if she'd only been there yesterday. It was the home he'd shared with his ex-wife, but she loved it anyway. It was where they'd spent their first night together, when she was still a prisoner. She had lied to him then about her situation, but it was the first place she had felt safe since she was taken. It was the first night she had spent in his arms. Every detail was etched permanently in her mind. She knew he had always wanted to move. When they'd first started dating, he had promised her he would sell the place and move into a new house, but his work schedule took precedence over house hunting.

Connor had packed Wilson's bed, a bag of his food, and his favorite rope toy together with a small bag of clothes and toiletries for Claire. Once he carried everything inside, he walked through the house, turning on lights. Wilson followed him anxiously, smelling every corner and beneath every piece of furniture. The place definitely had the feel of a bachelor pad—piles of unopened mail tossed haphazardly on the couch, Chinese takeout in his trash, beer cans in his recycling bin, a sink of unwashed dishes, and his dirty clothes strewn across his bedroom floor. She felt a secret sense of relief. No woman was a regular visitor to this house. He wasn't seeing anyone.

"Why don't we take Wilson for a quick walk?" he said, coming up behind her as she stood in his bedroom doorway.

"Right now? It's the middle of the night, and isn't this where most of your Strangler investigation is focused?"

She felt his smile against her hair, her curls catching on his beard. Warm breath tickled her neck. "I've got a gun, and you've got a big dog."

She turned into him and wrapped her arms around his neck. He pulled her close, and she felt some of the tension of the day leech away. For just a few seconds as she breathed him in, she could forget about

Brianna, Jade, serial killers, little Peyton Holloway, her own horrific memories, and the suffering in the world.

"Not now," she said into his neck. "Come to bed with me."

"Claire."

"I'm serious."

Beside them, Wilson whined. Connor chuckled. "He's been inside all day. A quick walk. We have time."

Tears rose to the backs of her eyes so quickly, she didn't have time to blink them away. She pulled back and looked into his blue eyes. "No," she said. "We don't. We think we do. We say we do, but we don't have time. Jade is dead. Brianna is in a coma. There's someone out there taking mothers away from their kids. They didn't have enough time. We don't have enough time."

He reached up and stroked the back of her hair with one gentle hand. "Claire," he said. "It's okay."

"No, it's not. Nothing is okay."

He cupped her face, kissing away the hot tears as they streaked down her cheeks. "Things may not be okay right now, but we will get through this. Brianna will wake up, and she'll be fine. We'll catch Jade's killer. When all this is over, I'm going to take you away. We'll take a trip. Tiki huts on a beach or something. Just you and me."

She captured his mouth with hers, kissing him softly, running her fingers through his thick hair, feeling arousal stir inside her. She broke the kiss, imploring him, "Come to bed with me. Now."

"We don't have to do this tonight. I don't want you to feel like just because we—"

Locking her hands behind his neck, she pulled him backward, toward his bed. "I want to be with you. Not just like this. Not just tonight. All the time. I want to try again. Be together. For real this time. No walking away. I'll try harder, I'll be—"

He let her guide him, his eyes locked on hers. "Stop," he said. "You don't have to be anything but yourself. You don't have to try to be anything for me. Just stay with me this time. I just want you. Exactly the way you are. There is no one else, Claire. I've loved you since the night we met, since I watched you sleep in this room."

They fell onto the bed, and he rolled quickly to the side so he didn't crush her. Wilson's whine was long and pitiful. Claire felt his nose nudge her feet. She and Connor looked toward the foot of the bed to see two mournful brown eyes staring at them. Laughter bubbled up between them, and they let it come. It felt like an unbearable pressure that had been crushing Claire's body was giving way. Wilson hopped up and army crawled up from the foot of the bed until he was between them. A long pink tongue lapped at Connor's beard.

Over Wilson's head, Claire caught Connor's eye. She said, "I love you too."

CHAPTER
FORTY-FOUR
NINETEEN MONTHS EARLIER

The first time it happened was in Leah's garage. They had thrown a backyard barbecue for the neighbors, something they typically did once a year. It was one of the few times she could count on Jim to help around the house. He took great pleasure in sprucing it up—touching up the paint on the walls, replacing the broken miniblinds, having his friend who was a plumber come and fix the leaky kitchen faucet. The only reason Leah agreed to have the barbecue each year was because it was the only thing that seemed to get her husband off his ass and motivated to do something around the house. He had tended carefully that year to their large backyard, the grass like a golf green, not a weed in sight. Even the flower beds were freshly mulched.

He stood by the smoking grill in his "Grill Daddy" apron, surrounded by a loose semicircle of men, regaling them with fishing stories as he flipped burgers. The women sat in patio chairs in little knots, gossiping and watching their children run through the sprinkler Jim had set up. Jim had insisted, as he did every year, that they have beer and wine.

"Nobody has a party without alcohol, Lee," he had scoffed at her. "Responsible parents do," she had shot back.

He had rolled his eyes at her, told her she was unreasonable, and then convinced her to spend a large part of their entertaining budget on alcohol by reminding her that every family who attended their annual gathering lived within walking distance so no one need get behind the wheel after the party. Drunk driving was only one of the many issues Leah had with parents imbibing, but she let it go. She could trade her neighbors drinking in her house for the toilet in her powder room being fixed.

It was hot that day and the children were getting bored. Leah had dragged two kiddie pools into the yard and filled them. She knew she had a whole basket of outdoor toys—water guns, jump ropes, sidewalk chalk—that would occupy the kids well into the evening. She found it on its appointed shelf, except that the shelf had collapsed, its contents fallen behind the large freestanding freezer they kept in the garage. The freezer came to her waist and opened from the top. It was sandwiched between a large shelving unit and an extra fridge that Jim used for his fishing spoils. She couldn't squeeze behind it.

Leah tried moving the thing away from the wall until a fine sheen of sweat broke out across the back of her neck. She wiped her dusty hands on her capri pants and went to the door leading back into her kitchen. Her garage was accessible through its front door, which was closed, and a heavy door that connected to her kitchen. They didn't use it for their vehicles. Jim's boat took up the largest part of it, and they used the area around his boat for storage. Jim's "baby" sat in the center of the garage, surrounded by storage bins of seasonal decorations, the kids' tricycles, scooters, and various other large toys.

Leah stood at the back door and called Jim. It took several tries before he acknowledged her with a wave—like she was just saying hello. A passerby. She gritted her teeth, muttering, "Son of a bitch," under her breath. As always, she'd just have to figure it out herself. It would probably be faster to drive to the store and buy new toys than to try to move the freezer without help. She was mulling it over on her way back through the kitchen when she ran headlong into D.J.

She screamed. She couldn't help it. She hadn't expected him—or anyone else—to be in her kitchen. She'd just walked through it and it was empty. He stood by her island countertop between her and the door to the garage. She backed away from him, her body already tingling from having accidentally touched him. His chest was rock hard beneath a black "Nine Inch Nails" T-shirt, and he smelled faintly like cologne—something thick and musky. Jim never wore cologne.

D.J. smiled at her—at once making her feel hot all over and completely naked. "Hey." His eyes drifted to her chest, which was heaving and covered by her right hand.

"You startled me," she said.

He seemed more benign in her kitchen—fully clothed, with no angry music or half-naked stick girls behind him. His eyes rose to meet hers again. "Sorry," he said. "Do you need help with something?"

Leah really didn't want to spend one more second in his presence, especially not alone. Sensing her hesitation, he took a step back. He put a hand to his heart, a gesture of sincerity, and flashed her a big smile. "I don't bite," he promised.

She looked to her left, out the kitchen window. The party was in full swing, her guests starting to eat the food Jim was pulling off the grill. It would only take a moment. She was in her own house, for God's sake. Judging by D.J.'s musculature, he'd have no problem shifting the freezer out of her way.

She forced a smile and motioned behind him to the door. "Uh, yeah. Some of the kids' toys dropped behind the freezer. I just need help sliding it out so I can get to them."

"Show me the way."

He followed her into the garage, pulling the door closed behind them.

"Be careful," she said as they made their way around Jim's boat to the other side of the garage. "It's a mess in here."

He said nothing. She sensed him moving closer to her. When she reached the freezer, she turned to face him, again bumping into him. She drew back, the edge of the freezer hard against her hip.

"Oh, sorry," she said involuntarily.

He smiled—that private smile again, the one that made her feel both dirty and aroused.

Yes. There it was.

This boy made her feel aroused, and she hated herself for it. His lips were only inches from hers. How had he gotten so close?

"Show me," he said, his voice husky.

"Oh," she said, for a split second wondering if he was talking about something besides what was behind the freezer. But that was ridiculous. He was half her age. She was nearing middle age, overweight, going gray beneath her blonde dye job, and the mother of two young children, not to mention married. No one who looked like this boy would be sexually interested in someone like her, no matter her age and marital status. Even in her twenties, when she was slimmer, firmer, and single, men like D.J. were not interested in her, which had been fine with her. She'd never much cared for men. She'd wanted a family, a life that she could put on a Christmas card. Choosing Jim for a husband had been a calculated decision, not one based on passion and certainly not one based on arousal. In fact, arousal was a completely foreign concept to her.

Until now.

She sucked in a breath and turned away from him. He didn't move at all. Her hip brushed against him as she leaned over the top of the freezer, pointing behind it. "They're back there," she said. "It's a basket of toys. The kids—"

His hands on her hips froze the words in her throat. He pressed himself against her, and she could feel his hardness against her thigh. She couldn't breathe, couldn't move, couldn't think. "Leah," he said, his breath hot against her ear. "I meant what I said." One of his hands snaked around her front, beneath her shirt, and squeezed her breast. "You've got great tits."

She gasped and closed her eyes as her nipple stood to attention beneath his touch.

"You think you're not beautiful or hot, but you are."

He rubbed himself against her. She trembled in his grasp, every inch of her skin on fire—part excitement, part humiliation. He grinded into her ass, his hand moving down, down, down.

"Tell me to stop," he whispered.

She opened her mouth, tried to make the word come out, but she couldn't. She was completely paralyzed, completely unprepared for this. She'd taken self-defense classes, always thought she would be ready, would know what to do if a man made unwanted advances on her. But men didn't make advances on her—wanted or unwanted. Not like this, and if she was being honest with herself, if she acknowledged the moisture collecting at her core while this perfect male specimen touched her and whispered dirty things in her ear, she could admit that she wanted this, even though it was wrong on every level of morality she could think of—not that she was thinking.

He didn't wait long. She heard his zipper, felt him yank down her pants. Then he was inside her. Just like that.

Nearly ten years of fidelity gone in seconds. She pushed the thought away as he thrust in and out of her, slowly at first. So agonizingly slow. Until she started to tighten and quiver around him, until she could not stop her body from responding. Then he sped up, coming at the same time as she did. He stayed inside her for a moment, lifting her hair and kissing the back of her neck. The tenderness of the act made her shiver. Slowly, he withdrew.

He pulled her underwear and pants back up and pulled her gently away from the freezer. After straightening his own clothes, he moved the freezer easily and pulled the basket of toys out from behind it. He placed the basket on the floor beside him and pushed the freezer back in place as if it weighed nothing. He picked up the basket and handed it to her with a smile.

As if he hadn't just fucked her in her garage. As if nothing had happened.

She took the basket, unable to say the words *thank you*. Unable to say anything.

D.J. looked at his feet, suddenly seeming bashful, and then he was gone, leaving her sweaty, wet, disheveled, and shaken to her core.

CHAPTER

FORTY-FIVE

Connor had been asleep for only two hours—Claire naked in his arms, Wilson asleep on his doggie bed in the corner of the room—when his cell phone woke him. He let it go to voice mail the first time, wishing silently for more time. Claire moaned softly in her sleep, and Connor tightened his embrace, kissing her shoulder and then burying his face in her hair. The ringing sounded again.

"You have to get that," Claire mumbled.

In that moment, he would have paid any amount of money if it meant staying exactly where he was. He would empty his entire bank account. Anything not to have to leave this bed.

"Connor, answer it."

With a groan that bordered on a snarl, he disentangled himself, snatched up his phone, and snapped, "Parks" after answering.

"We got the GPS coordinates of Leah Holloway's vehicle on Wednesday," Stryker said. "Guess where she was."

Sitting on the edge of his bed, hunched over, Connor scratched his beard. "I don't want to guess. I don't even want to talk to you right now."

"Five blocks away from the landscaper's apartment."

Fatigue receded quickly. Connor's back straightened. He glanced at his bedside clock, which read 7:13. "No shit."

"Yeah, and the dude is home now. He came home with a woman around four a.m. Get dressed and get in here. We're going over there."

"How do you know I'm not dressed?"

"'Cause the only time you don't want to talk to me is when you're in bed with a beautiful woman. It better be Claire or I'm going to kick your ass, just as soon as we wrap this Strangler case up."

A smile crept across Connor's face. He glanced over his shoulder at Claire's slumbering form. He had a weird feeling of déjà vu. Of the first night they'd ever spent together. A shiver worked its way through his body. She would be there when he came back, he reminded himself. She wasn't going anywhere this time.

He said, "I'll see you in thirty."

Glory Rohrbach's young landscaper-lover lived in a tiny one-bedroom apartment in a rundown section of the city better known for its number of robberies than its charm. Stryker had assigned several of the other detectives in the division to go door-to-door in Pocket and compile a list of twenty-something men living in the area. Most had already been eliminated by virtue of their alibis, but it would take at least a day or two to cover the entire neighborhood. Given the GPS coordinates found on Leah's vehicle, Connor and Stryker had moved Denny Taggert to the top of their list. The coordinates revealed that she had driven to an intersection five blocks away from Denny Taggert's residence, in front of several old homes, some of which Connor knew were halfway houses. The surrounding buildings were nearly falling down, and the owners offered low-rent rooms to people with bleak prospects. Connor had arrested more than one suspect in this area. Unfortunately, there was no surveillance available that showed Leah parking or getting in or out of her vehicle. They had no idea where she had actually gone, but it was too much of a coincidence that she'd been only blocks from someone who had worked in her neighborhood.

Denny Taggert was twenty-six years old, and hadn't had so much as a parking ticket in his life. He had a little-used Facebook page. He barely existed on paper. He had a half-dozen old addresses, almost all of them apartments in less-than-stellar neighborhoods.

They knocked for several minutes before he flung the door open, shirtless and wearing only boxer shorts. His thick brown hair was in disarray. He squinted at them as though they were shining a spotlight on him.

"Denny Taggert?" Connor said.

The man cleared his throat. "Who's asking?"

Connor handed him his credentials, introduced himself and Stryker, and said, "We're here to talk about Leah Holloway."

He handed Connor's credentials back and squinted up at them again. "Who?"

"Leah Holloway," Stryker said.

Denny's brow furrowed. "Doesn't sound familiar."

"The lady who drove her kids off the I-5 overpass into the American River on Saturday."

Denny's eyes widened. "Oh shit. Yeah, I saw that on the news. What's it got to do with me?"

"You tell us," Stryker said.

Denny put his hands up in a defensive posture. "Whoa, dude. I don't even know her. I never even heard of her before I saw the news."

"You sure about that?" Connor said.

Denny shook his head. "Don't know her, man."

"I know her," a female voice said from behind Denny.

The man turned, revealing a huge tattoo of an eagle across his upper back. "I said stay in the bedroom," he told her.

She was easily twice his age, her deeply tanned skin like wrinkled crepe paper, freckled from too much sun. Her blonde hair was pulled into a loose ponytail. She wore only a T-shirt.

Connor assumed it was Denny's. She was rail thin and smelled of cigarettes. She sidled past Denny, breaking his hold on the doorknob. Up close, in the daylight, she was even less attractive. Connor wondered what Denny saw in her. He could hear Jade saying, *She must be amazing in bed. Older women know how to do more stuff.* He could see her wink, feel her elbow in his ribs. He swallowed and looked back at the woman before him.

"Leah was my neighbor," she explained.

"Glory Rohrbach," Stryker said.

She smiled a rueful smile. "Those bitches over there are still talking about me, huh? Which one of them sent you?"

"Nobody sent us, Mrs. Rohrbach," Connor said. "We're just following up on a lead."

Denny had taken a few steps inside the apartment. He picked up a pack of cigarettes from the coffee table and shook two out. He returned to the door and handed one of them to Glory. In his other hand appeared a lighter. He snapped it open and lit it up in one fluid movement. Glory leaned forward toward his flame. She sucked in a long breath as he held it out to her. On a smoky exhale, she said, "A lead? For what? Leah's dead, isn't she? What's there to investigate?"

Connor and Stryker exchanged a furtive glance. "We have reason to believe that Mrs. Holloway was under duress when she went into the river."

Glory guffawed. The sound, loud and unexpected, startled even Denny. "Duress?" she scoffed. "Please. She was a soccer mom. What kind of duress could she have been under? Did the boredom finally drive her insane?"

None of them spoke. When they all just stared at her, Glory shrugged, took a long drag from her cigarette, and sauntered off. She sat on the couch, which was a futon, tucking her left leg up beneath her.

"Mr. Taggert," Stryker said. "Did you see Leah Holloway on Wednesday?"

Denny looked mildly confused, as if they'd just asked for directions to a place he wasn't familiar with. "What? No. I told you, I never met her."

"Where were you on Wednesday, around twelve thirty?" Connor asked.

"At work."

"Where were you on Sunday night?" Stryker asked.

Denny sat on the edge of his pockmarked coffee table and lit his own cigarette. He seemed unconcerned by the sudden change in direction of their questioning. "I was here," he said. "Sleeping. Glory was here too."

Stryker flipped his pad open and rattled off the dates and times of the Soccer Mom Strangler murders. For each one, Denny answered that he'd been at work. That would be easy enough to check. Connor was already feeling as though this was a dead end although he didn't know how much supervision landscapers were given. It was possible that he had committed the crimes while working. A landscaper wouldn't be out of place at a playground or soccer field. He was the right age, and he had no record. Still, doubt niggled at Connor. They'd either woken this guy from a nap or interrupted him midcoitus and started asking him for alibis, and he showed no signs of nervousness at all.

Glory, on the other hand, was a different story.

"Why are you asking him all these questions?" she asked. "What do all those dates have to do with Leah Holloway killing herself?"

"We have reason to believe that someone might have assaulted Mrs. Holloway before her death. We're trying to find that person," Connor said.

"And you think my Denny here did it? He didn't even know her. He would never do such a thing—to any woman."

"Mrs. Rohrbach, we have to eliminate all the possibilities. We're looking at any man in his twenties who would have had contact with Mrs. Holloway last Wednesday. We know that Mrs. Holloway was in this area at that time," Stryker said. He looked at Denny. "Would you be willing to come downtown and give fingerprints, DNA, and a dental impression?"

Denny exchanged a look with Glory. With a sigh, he said, "Sure. I got nothing to hide. You want me to come with you now?"

Too easy, Connor could hear Jade say.

"Please," Stryker said.

"Am I under arrest?"

"No," Connor said. "We're just talking. Why don't you get dressed and we'll give you a ride."

As Denny disappeared into the bedroom at the back of the apartment, Glory advanced on them. Shaky hands lit another cigarette from the butt of her last one. "So you think because Denny lives in this neighborhood, it was him? He wasn't even here on Wednesday at twelve thirty. He was working in some other neighborhood. You can check that with his boss. Go outside and look around. Lots of degenerates live around here. You need to look at some of them. Did you talk to Rachel?"

"Yes," Connor said. "We spoke with Mrs. Irving."

She stared at him pointedly. "So you talked to her nephew too."

"Her nephew?" Connor echoed.

Glory shook her head. "Rachel is a nasty, lying bitch. I know she puts on this Mother and Wife of the Year thing, but she's not. She didn't tell you about her nephew?"

"No," Connor said. "What do you know about him?"

"I know he's around the same age as my Denny, maybe younger. He came to live with her last year, or it might have been the year before that, I'm not sure. Rachel acted like he didn't exist, but I saw him coming and going all the time."

"How do you know he was her nephew?" Connor asked.

"Leah told me. Her and Rachel were besties. I asked her once if she noticed this kid coming and going from Rachel's house. She said he was Rachel's nephew. That was right before I separated from my husband."

"He have a name?" Stryker asked.

She waved her cigarette in the air. "D.J. Don't know his last name. Leah said he was from back East. Pennsylvania, I think. Came to live with them after high school. Rachel hated him. I still can't figure out why she let him live with them. I think she kicked him out eventually."

"Do you know when he moved out?" Connor asked. "Where he went?"

She shook her head. "Couldn't tell you. I left over a year ago. It was Rachel, wasn't it? She's the one who said you should talk to Denny, wasn't she?"

She looked back and forth between them but they said nothing.

"Forget it," she said. "I can tell by your faces that it was her. She thinks it's entertaining to sit around and judge people. Her husband is never home. She's bored out of her skull. Well, if she's going to point fingers, then so am I."

CHAPTER
FORTY-SIX

NINETEEN MONTHS EARLIER

She couldn't call it rape. She had let him do it. She hadn't tried to stop him. She hadn't even spoken. She hadn't said no or stop. She'd made no effort to push him away or fight him off. She had orgasmed, for God's sake. Afterward, she had cleaned herself up in the bathroom, changed her underwear, and gone back into the yard, acting the gracious hostess. She pushed what had just happened into her Deal with It Later compartment. What else was there to do? A few people at the barbecue remarked that she looked pale, unwell, but she just shrugged and said she felt a migraine coming on.

D.J. hadn't stayed. Thank goodness. Leah was excellent at compartmentalizing, at staying in control, at putting on whatever face the situation called for, but she really wasn't sure she could have kept her composure if he had lingered in her yard, eating the food her husband had prepared, smiling at all the female neighbors undressing him with their eyes. Out of sight, out of mind.

She busied herself playing with the children, cleaning up after people as they ate, and fastidiously restocking the strategically placed snacks as their guests consumed them. When the ice in the coolers got low, she offered to drive to the store and get more rather than asking Jim to do it. She took Peyton with her so she wouldn't be tempted to think about D.J. or what had happened. Peyton was a good girl. Leah realized that she should really reward the girl more for always being so quiet and well behaved.

As they stood in line at the nearest minimart, Leah glanced over at the wall of self-serve beverages partially obscured by the coffee kiosk. She placed a hand on the back of Peyton's neck. Her skin was warm and soft. The girl looked up at Leah, her brown eyes questioning. Leah smiled. She leaned down and spoke softly into her daughter's ear. "How about an Icee and some chocolate cupcakes?"

Peyton's eyes doubled in size. The expression—half delight, half disbelief—burst across her face, making Leah's heart seize. "Really?" Peyton said. "Right now?"

Leah nodded. She should try harder to put that look of wonderment on Peyton's face more often. Peyton took off to the back of the store, singing, "Car picnic" in a high-pitched voice.

It was a private ritual the two of them had started the year before when Leah had to take Peyton for her three-year well visit, and she had taken her vaccinations with the stoicism of a Navy SEAL. Rachel had watched Hunter. Afterward, Leah had taken Peyton to a minimart and let her pick out any snack she wanted. She chose a cherry Icee and chocolate cupcakes. Leah let her sit in the passenger's seat of her SUV while they ate and called it a car picnic. Peyton had loved it. It had been so out of character for Leah, who was normally very strict about staying on some sort of daily schedule, that Peyton had requested it ever since. But Leah rarely gave in. She was too busy or Hunter was with them. Or they just didn't have time.

"Mommy, I want the red," Peyton said when they reached the Icee machine. Leah dispensed two red Icees and bought them each a pack of chocolate cupcakes. They sat in the front of the parked vehicle with two bags of ice melting in the back, and Leah watched her daughter's tiny lips turn red from the cherry drink, watched her scatter chocolate crumbs down her front and onto the passenger seat.

They returned to the party, Leah's Deal with It Later compartment more tightly locked. She was able to get through the next day—the cleanup day—without really thinking about D.J. or what had happened between them. Then work Monday. But it kept pushing its way out of the Deal with It Later drawer in her mind, bringing back the feel of him inside her, the way her body had gripped him and coursed with pleasure. She did her best to pretend it hadn't happened, to deny it to herself, but she became more and more frazzled as the week went on. The energy she had to expend to keep it hidden from her own mind began to be greater than the energy she needed to carry out her daily life.

She was exhausted.

On Saturday, she found herself sitting at Rachel's kitchen table, never more grateful for Rachel's weak coffee. Even though Leah had never been so happy for a weekend to arrive, Jim had been driving her crazy watching his fishing shows and talking about lures, casting, and other things she didn't care about. The moment Hunter went down for his nap, she'd hustled Peyton out of the house for some much-needed girl time for them both.

She knew it was counterintuitive. Considering what she had done, she should want to stay as far away from Rachel as possible, but that would only arouse suspicion, and Rachel was nosy as hell. Leah knew she would not withstand the scrutiny that would come from avoiding her best friend. Besides that, Rachel categorically refused to speak about D.J. Leah had pried countless times, and Rachel had always shut her down. It was not a topic that was open to discussion. The boy had been living with Rachel and Mike for weeks before Rachel even acknowledged that he was there, and that was only because he happened to walk through the television room while Leah and the kids were visiting.

Rachel had had to explain his presence, although it was clear she hadn't wanted to. In a halting tone, she had simply said, "My brother's kid. He's here from Pennsylvania. He just needs a place to stay for a few weeks." Leah had always thought Rachel was an only child. But Rachel had never talked much about her childhood. She occasionally made references to her mother, but never to her father or any siblings. Leah had never pushed because her own childhood had been so traumatic, she had no desire whatsoever to rehash it.

Rachel acting as though D.J. didn't exist made it easier for Leah to act that way as well. She could pretend that he had never come into either of their lives. She could just be a woman having coffee with a friend. So that's what she did.

She'd purposely left her cell phone at home, but that didn't stop Jim from pestering her. He just dialed Rachel's landline. She'd been at Rachel's house for fifteen minutes, and Jim had already called twice.

Both times, Rachel put him off, answering his inane questions herself. She shook her head as she hung up the second time. "This man lives with you, and he doesn't know where to find the bottle opener or the spare toilet paper?" Rachel rolled her eyes and resumed her spot at the table across from Leah. "Even I know where you keep them. Men. You can't live with them and you can't shoot them."

"Or strangle them in their sleep," Leah added.

They both laughed.

"He's driving me nuts," Leah admitted. It was a familiar refrain. When didn't her hapless husband make her crazy?

Yet, when Rachel responded with "Rough week?" it wasn't Jim who came to Leah's mind.

"This has been the worst week of my life," she confessed.

Rachel froze, her coffee mug halfway to her lips, and stared at Leah. Slowly, her eyebrows drew together. She put her mug back down on the table without drinking. She said, "Is there something I don't know?"

She leaned forward, the interest in her eyes bordering on glee. "Did something happen with Jim?"

Anxiety was a vise around Leah's midsection, restricting her diaphragm, making it hard to breathe. She put a hand to her chest. "Oh no," she backpedaled. "Jim's fine. Everything's fine."

"No more fallout from the day care–pickup fight?"

Leah tried a smile, her skin feeling tight, like her face was sunburned. "Oh no," she said.

Rachel's shoulders slumped just perceptibly, as though she were disappointed. Leah was glad she had chosen not to tell her friend anything more about the "day care–pickup fight." Jim was due at work by four, and Leah got done working at three. The kids had to be picked up from day care by three. Leah thought it worked out perfectly. Jim could pick them up before work, and Leah would be home in time for him to leave. But the moment she'd proposed the arrangement, Jim suddenly had to be at work by three. She'd accused him of lying, which he hadn't taken well. They'd had a huge blowout over it, which Leah had initially told Rachel all about. But Jim had started going in at three each day. Because Leah couldn't afford aftercare—she was already paying an exorbitant amount of money for before care—she had to leave work early each day. It was hugely inconvenient, and she'd promised her boss it was only temporary.

What she hadn't told Rachel was that she'd driven past Jim's work one day after picking up the kids and seen him sitting in his truck, eating a sandwich and listening to the radio. She'd driven by three times after that to find exactly the same thing. When she confronted him, he told her he kept forgetting something in his truck. They'd fought, but eventually, she'd given up, too worn down by the absurdity of it all. She'd revisit it with him when he brought home a paycheck that didn't reflect the extra hour a day he swore he was working. Of course he'd probably still deny it. Her husband was the type of person who'd throw his dirty underwear at your feet and then vehemently deny having done so. And what could Leah do? Leave her husband because he refused to pick up the kids from day care? Was that the type of thing you ended a marriage over?

She didn't know, but until the time came to confront him, she would put it out of her head. She had to. She simply couldn't deal with it. Her mind was too full and her body was too tired. Working full-time, taking care of her children every second she wasn't at work, and managing the household was enough.

Now there was D.J.

Rachel's heavy sigh brought Leah out of her jumbled thoughts. "Well," Rachel said, taking a sip of her coffee, "you look tired."

Leah racked her brain, searching for something to cover, something Rachel would believe. "Work!" she said too loudly, the word coming out more as excitement than as a complaint. Leah swallowed and adjusted her tone. "I meant it was the worst week of my life at work," she said more quietly. "A big contract fell through."

"Want to talk about it?"

Leah shook her head. "No, no. It's just work. I shouldn't have brought it up."

But it had slipped out.

She was fraying at the edges, her mental compartments opening unexpectedly like the drawers were spring-loaded, scattering her unwanted thoughts all over the floor of her brain. She tried picking them up, stuffing them back into place, but it wasn't working. The more she tried not to think about what had happened with D.J., the more vivid and all-consuming the memory became. The entire week she was convinced people could see it on her face—all the conflicting emotions raging inside her. Above all, anger—at him, but mostly at herself. Men were essentially primitive creatures. They'd always do just whatever the hell you let them get away with. It was her job to set boundaries and to stand firm.

"Tell me to stop."

Her face burned.

Rachel waved a hand at her. "Did you hear me?"

"N-no. I—" Leah stammered.

Rachel leaned forward, resting both elbows on the table. She lowered her voice even though it was only the two of them in the kitchen. "I said, 'Talk about the worst week of your life. Glory Rohrbach got caught cheating on her husband.'"

So scattered were Leah's thoughts that it took her a moment to pull up their neighbor's face in her mental Rolodex. Glory was notoriously snobby. They often joked that she thought she was a Real Housewife of Pocket.

"Really?" Leah said, hoping she sounded interested. For once, she didn't care at all about Glory's antics, especially where it concerned infidelity.

"Oh my God," Rachel said. "Wait till you hear this. She was screwing the kid who cuts her lawn! You know, the kid who always looks like he's all strung out on something? What is he? Twenty-five? Twenty-six?"

"I—I don't know," Leah mumbled.

Rachel thought of a man in his midtwenties as a kid. My God, what did that make D.J.? Leah's cheeks flamed. The skin at her throat itched. Luckily, Rachel was so enthralled by the story of how Glory's husband caught her that she didn't notice.

There was a time when Leah surely would have reveled in Glory's downfall, but now she only felt her own guilt, her own shame, like a coarse, heavy coat, making her sweat and her skin itch.

How could she? She had betrayed her husband and her children, broken her vows, and defiled their family home. She'd thrown away years of careful, steadfast fidelity, a thing she valued, a thing she expected of Jim.

For what?

A single sexual encounter with a boy who was wildly inappropriate for her?

An orgasm? She could give herself those. God knew, she usually did. Jim liked sex, but like most things in their relationship, it was about what he got out of it and not so much about pleasing Leah. But she hadn't married him for sex. She never cared about physical pleasure, had never enjoyed sex any more than she enjoyed a cup of coffee or a chocolate bar. It was fine but not necessary. She'd married Jim because he was a man who would never cheat on her and never leave her.

"Can you believe that?" Rachel was saying. "Her poor husband. He gave her everything. He works so hard to support her and their kids, and this is what she does? Cheats on him with a druggie landscaper?"

Leah made a noise of agreement, taking a long sip of coffee. Jim had never been as attentive as Glory Rohrbach's husband, but it was his short attention span that precluded cheating. He barely managed to spread his attention among his own wife and children. No way could he handle a mistress. Leah had always counted herself lucky. She would never be that woman. Humiliated, duped, left behind. She had a good husband.

But *she* had cheated.

Which made her the other kind of woman. The kind she'd always judged so harshly. Like Glory Rohrbach.

"I heard she would invite him in, and she'd have sex with him in exchange for OxyContins," Rachel went on. "Remember how we always used to see her kids sitting out in the driveway?"

Leah had always felt immediate and unforgiving hatred for cheaters. No exceptions.

"She was locking the kids out while she did this guy for some pills. Can you believe that? What a bitch. I mean really. I hope he leaves her with nothing. She shouldn't even be allowed to see her kids, don't you think?"

Leah blinked, Rachel's earnest face coming into focus. "What?"

The vise around her torso tightened. *My kids. Oh God. My kids.*

Rachel looked at her strangely, one brow raised just a little. "Don't you think she should lose custody of her kids?"

In front of her, Rachel was eclipsed by an image of D.J.'s face, smiling suggestively at her in the kitchen. She heard his words in her ear again. *"Tell me to stop."*

Why hadn't she stopped him?

Leah blinked again and Rachel reappeared, frowning now. "Leah?"

She scratched the skin at her throat. "I don't know. That seems harsh to me. People make mistakes. Sometimes things just happen."

Rachel erupted into loud laughter. She slapped the table. "Oh my God. Who *are* you?" She raised her voice, her tone mocking. "'People make mistakes.' Please. Not those kinds of mistakes. You're the one who's always saying how inexcusable cheating is. What's going on with you today?"

Her expression remained jovial but Leah knew she was really asking. Leah leaned back in her chair, licked her dry lips. She could never tell a soul what had happened. Not anyone. Especially not Rachel—the boy's aunt! She had to lock it away. It was done, and she couldn't undo it. She could only move forward and act as though it hadn't happened. She had to pull herself together. She gave a wan smile. "I'm fine. Really. Just tired and the thing at work—I'm just stressed. That's all."

Rachel didn't look convinced, but before she could interrogate Leah further, the phone rang. Rachel stood and answered it, the corners of her mouth drawing downward. She held out the receiver to Leah. "It's Jim. Can't find his own ass to wipe it, probably."

CHAPTER

FORTY-SEVEN

Rachel answered the door wearing jeans, a tank top, and a burgundy bolero sweater. Connor was shocked to see her in something besides yoga pants. Her hair was pulled back in a ponytail but one side hung loose over her cheek, which Connor swore looked red. Had they wakened her from a nap?

"The girls aren't home," she said without preamble. "Mike took them to his parents. They're really bored here, and with all the commotion—the police and media—it was just too stressful."

Too much of an explanation, Connor thought. Offering too much too soon. "We're not here to talk to the girls," he said.

Rachel put a hand to her chest. With her other hand she tucked the loose hair behind her ear. "Oh," she said. "Okay, well, I—"

"Can we come in?" Stryker asked.

Connor expected hesitation, but she flung the door open and let them into the formal sitting room to the right of the foyer.

"Who's D.J.?" Stryker asked, going right for it.

Her whole face dropped. The color drained from her skin. Then she looked around the room. Looking for a life preserver, Connor thought.

"I—uh—I don't—"

"Don't say you don't know," Stryker said. "When you lie to a police officer about an investigation, that can be considered obstruction of justice. I will charge you because I'm sick and tired of being lied to—I have a case to solve before someone else gets killed. Now, who's D.J.?"

She looked around the room once more. Then her shoulders slumped. Her hand went to her "#1 Mom" charm. "He's my . . . nephew."

Connor's phone buzzed in his pocket. He pulled it out and looked at the display. Lena Stark. "Excuse me," he said. "I need to take this." To Stryker, he added, "Stark."

CHAPTER
FORTY-EIGHT

Claire dozed fitfully after Connor left. When it became apparent that restful sleep was going to be impossible without Connor there, she got up and called Tom, who was still at the hospital. Nothing had changed. Brianna remained comatose. Tom urged her to go back to bed, get some more sleep before she relieved him at the hospital, but Claire knew it was a lost cause. Instead, she showered, rummaged through Connor's near-empty refrigerator for anything edible, and decided to take Wilson for a nice long walk to make up for the day before.

She hesitated before putting Wilson's leash on him. Connor had been overprotective and on edge since Brianna was attacked. He had explained to her that there was a possibility that the man they'd met in the bagel shop, Brianna's attacker, was the Strangler. He had also shared his theory that the Strangler had tracked Brianna to the home she shared with Claire and then followed them to Sammy's. She knew he didn't want her going anywhere alone. But Claire had been prisoner to a psychopath before, and she was not doing it again. She refused to give up something as basic and mundane as walking her dog.

Besides, she reasoned, she was at Connor's house, in Connor's neighborhood. If the Strangler decided to come after her, how would he find her here? How would he even know to look? And why would he look for Claire in the first place? Brianna had been the one on the news. Brianna had taken credit for saving the Holloway and Irving children—and the blame for leaving Leah in the river.

Guilt on that score was a heavy stone on Claire's chest. Stryker and Jade had been right when they warned about lying to the press. It had done a lot more than bite them in the ass. Brianna had almost paid for the decision with her life—and it was Claire's fault. She felt tears forming behind her eyes and quickly grabbed Wilson's leash from Connor's kitchen counter. Tugging Wilson along, she plunged outside, as though getting out of the house would get her away from her feelings.

They meandered through the streets of Pocket. The neighborhood was quiet. Claire tried to keep track of the turns they made and how far they went so she could find their way back to Connor's easily. Wilson sniffed this new territory with intense vigor, finding every blade of grass endlessly fascinating. He kept looking back at her like he expected her to abruptly end the newfound fun at any second. She smiled at him. This was what she loved about dogs. There was no grudge for having been left alone for over twelve hours. Wilson was just happy to be with her and be on a walk. She had, of course, met rescues who had been abused and had triggers just like she did, but much of the time dogs were able to live gloriously in the present.

She was thinking about that, watching Wilson's tail wag happily, when she rounded a corner and saw little Peyton Holloway playing in the front yard of a brown-and-white two-story home. She sat in the grass wearing shorts, a tank top, and a pair of flip-flops. Her blonde hair looked as if someone had brushed it hastily and missed the back where a tangle of knotted hair peeked from the girl's collar. She had what looked like Barbies in each hand, making them talk to one another. In front of her sat a purple Barbie car. Claire watched as she positioned each doll inside and pulled it back out again. She talked so softly, Claire could not make out her words. As Claire and Wilson got closer, Claire noticed a very familiar vehicle in the driveway of the neighboring house. She wondered if Connor and Stryker were there. Claire looked back at the Holloway's front yard. As if sensing her presence, Peyton looked up. Her eyes widened in recognition and Claire smiled, giving her a small wave.

The girl stared for a moment before she abandoned her dolls and walked slowly to where Claire and Wilson stood. Claire looked at the house. She could see through the screen door that the heavier door was open, but no adult stood there or peeked from any of the windows. Rage unfurled inside of her as though she were generating it on a cellular level, her body warming uncomfortably from the inside out. Small beads of sweat popped out along her hairline. She knew stranger abductions were rare. She'd heard the statistics, read all about how the odds of what had happened to her were so slim as to be negligible.

When her case broke, and last year when Jaycee Lee Dugard was recovered after eighteen years in captivity, alive after having borne her abductor two children, Claire got to hear all about how rare stranger abductions were, on the news. In other words, don't worry about this because it will never happen to your kid. But it did happen. It had happened to Claire when she was much older than Peyton and better able to outsmart an abductor, or fight back, and Claire had not been able to do either of those things. Claire realized that most normal people could not live their lives as though a pedophile lurked around every corner just waiting to snatch their child, but leaving a little girl like Peyton alone, unguarded like this, seemed tantamount to putting her tiny hand in a blender, plugging it in, and then asking every person who passed to please turn it on. Eventually, some sicko would be happy to shred her tiny hand.

Beside Claire, Wilson whimpered.

"I like your dog," Peyton said. "Can I pet him?"

"Of course," Claire said, pushing her anger down. "Thank you for asking me first."

Peyton shrugged and gently stroked Wilson's back.

"Peyton, where's your dad?"

"Asleep."

"Oh. Where are your brothers?"

The girl didn't look up, just kept running her hand over Wilson's fur. "Grandma had to take them to the doctor."

"So you're alone out here?"

Another shrug. "Daddy's inside. I used to have a dog."

Claire swallowed. "Oh yeah?"

Peyton scratched behind Wilson's ears. "His name was Lucky, but then he died. He ate a bad thing."

"I'm so sorry, Peyton. That must have been very hard."

Peyton didn't look at her. "Yeah," she said. "I guess Lucky and Mommy are in heaven together."

A lump formed in Claire's throat. "Yes," she croaked. "I'm sure they are."

Wilson lay on the ground and rolled onto his back so Peyton could scratch his belly.

"My grandma says my mom is burning in hell, and she got what she deserved."

Peyton's tone was flat and emotionless, as though she were just relating a fact. Claire felt her rage ripple again. What kind of person said that to a six-year-old who had just lost her mother? Though Claire understood the sentiment: What Leah had done was horrible, shocking, unforgivable. Impossible to comprehend. Leah had killed people, had tried to kill her own children and her friend's children. What would make a mother do that? People were confused and angry, especially the people closest to Leah, who had had no indication that she had been remotely capable of something like this. Moving forward, it was going to be difficult for her kids to live with what she had done. It was something they would struggle with their entire lives. Demonizing Leah to her young children, though, seemed cruel to Claire.

Claire looked down at Peyton's feet. Her toes were painted hot pink. "Peyton, what was your mommy like?"

Peyton thought about it for a moment. Then she said, "She was nice."

"Did she paint your toenails?"

The girl nodded, looking down at her feet. "Yeah. She liked to paint my nails and brush my hair. She said I was pretty."

Claire smiled. "You are pretty."

Peyton pursed her lips as if considering something. "She was a good mommy," she said finally, with the proud, simple conviction of a six-year-old.

"I'm sure she was."

"She wasn't mean, not like Grandma. She got mad a lot, though, mostly at Daddy."

"Well, that happens," Claire said. "Grown-ups get mad at one another sometimes. That's pretty normal. Haven't you ever been mad at someone you love?"

Peyton thought about it. "I get mad at my brother a lot 'cause he breaks my toys, and he cries a lot, and he is really annoying."

Claire laughed. "But you still love him, right?"

"I guess."

From the corner of her eye, Claire thought she saw movement in the Holloway house, but when she looked up, the door and windows were vacant.

"But one time my daddy said if we were bad, Mommy wouldn't come back. Do you think I was bad?"

Claire's heart ached. She wanted to touch the girl but wasn't sure how she would take it. "No, Peyton. I don't think you were bad at all.

I think you're very smart and sweet and brave, and what happened to your mommy had nothing to do with you. I think something bad happened to your mommy," Claire said, thinking of Leah's terror-stricken eyes. "And it had nothing to do with you at all."

Peyton looked down at Wilson. She'd stopped rubbing his belly. He turned over and nuzzled her hand gently. She scratched the top of his head again. Then she said, "It was D.J."

Claire squatted next to Peyton. "What's that, Peyton?"

"I saw D.J. pushing Mommy in the kitchen."

Claire stayed very still. The whole world seemed to stop. She knew Peyton hadn't talked to anyone since the accident. Now here she was telling Claire something that, from the sound of it, could be crucial to finding out what sent Leah spiraling out of control. Furtively, Claire looked back at the Holloway house, hoping Jim Holloway would not choose this moment to wake up and come looking for his daughter.

"Somebody pushed your mommy?" Claire coaxed.

"Yeah. D.J. I was supposed to be asleep, but I got thirsty. I went to the kitchen but then I saw him pushing her on the table."

"On the table? You saw him push her into the table?"

"He was pushing her on it. He . . . he didn't have any clothes on, and he kept pushing her. I thought it was a bad thing. Molly said he showed her and Maya his nub, and Miss Rachel said that was very bad and made him go away forever."

Claire couldn't have moved if her hair caught fire. She was trying to think of what to ask next. She wished Connor were there, but then again, he had attempted a few times to interview Peyton without success. So it was Claire, then.

"Peyton, did your mommy know that you saw her and this . . . D.J. on the table?"

Peyton shook her head. "No. Mommy didn't see me. I got afraid. I went into my room and hided. I thought the police would come, but then Mommy woke me up and it was a new day, and she didn't look like she was hurt."

"Did you ever tell anyone?"

"No. It's a secret."

"When did this happen?" Claire asked.

"I don't know, like five years ago or five days ago."

Five years or five days. "Was it last week? Like, before your soccer game?"

"Yeah, it was before my game. Like three years ago."

"Was it a long time ago? Do you remember how old you were when you saw it?"

"Sure. I was four or five or six."

"Okay," Claire said, resigning herself that pinning the time down was a dead end. "Did you know D.J.? Had you met him before?"

"Yeah. He lived with Miss Rachel and Maya and Molly and their daddy, except Maya and Molly said Miss Rachel made him live on the garage in the backyard."

"You mean on top of their garage?"

"I guess."

"Is D.J. related to Molly and Maya? Like a cousin or something?"

"I don't know. I guess. Molly said when he showed his nub, Miss Rachel was mad 'cause that made it unrest."

"Do you mean incest?"

Peyton shrugged. "I don't know. What's incest?"

Claire licked her lips. "Never mind. What else did Molly tell you?"

"Molly said D.J. is gross and that he's mean too. Maya said his nub was big and gross too."

Claire felt sick. "Okay," she said. "Peyton, did D.J. ever show you his, uh, nub?"

"No," she said simply.

Relief flooded Claire. Then she felt a prickle along her spine. A low thrum, the feeling of impending harm, started at the base of her spine and worked its way up to the base of her neck, where the fine, downy hairs stood straight up. Wilson sat to attention and growled. Peyton jumped back, but Claire caught the girl's arm. "It's not you, honey. He's not growling at you."

Peyton looked around until her eyes found him. The man from the bagel shop. Claire felt Peyton tense beneath her grip. "That's him," she hissed. "That's D.J."

CHAPTER

FORTY-NINE

Connor moved to the doorway and took the call from Lena Stark. Once she had filled him in, he rejoined Stryker and Rachel in the sitting room. Stryker had his notebook in hand and was already firing off questions. Connor stood aside and watched the exchange.

"What's D.J.'s last name?"

"North. His full name is Dylan John North."

"How old is he?"

"Umm, nineteen. No, twenty."

"Where is he?"

"Where? I, uh, don't know where. He left like a year ago. I haven't seen or heard from him since. We didn't—we weren't really getting along."

"You have his phone number?"

"No. We had put him on our cell phone plan when he came here. When I kicked—when he left, I took him off. I didn't get a forwarding number."

"You have some kind of problem with him?"

"He was just—he used to curse a lot and say inappropriate things in front of the girls. When I asked him to stop, he became abusive toward me—verbally, I mean—so I asked him to leave. I didn't want him here in the first place. I hadn't seen him since he was five years old. We never had a relationship. It was a favor, letting him stay here until he found a job."

"He ever find one?"

She shrugged. "Not that I know of."

"How long did he stay with you?"

"Maybe six months?"

"You did him a favor letting him live here, but you put him on your cell phone plan?"

"Another favor. Only temporarily. Look, I tried with him. It didn't work. He's not . . . he's not a nice person. He is out of our lives now, and I'd like to keep it that way. I'm sorry I can't help you, but I haven't seen him since he left over a year ago."

"He's your brother's kid? Your sister's?"

Her fingers twisted the charm. "Brother?" she asked, seemingly confused by the question. Then she gathered her composure, took a deep breath, straightened her shoulders, and said, "Yes, my brother. He's my brother's son."

Stryker marked something on his notepad. "Your brother's name?"

"My brother's name?"

"Yeah."

"Oh, um, Sebastian."

"Where does he live?"

"Pennsylvania, out on the East Coast."

"I'm going to need his phone number and address."

The charm twisted again. "Oh, I don't have—"

Stryker raised an eyebrow. "You don't have your brother's address and phone number?"

She smiled weakly. "We're estranged. Dylan—I mean D.J.—he called. He was out here. He needed a place to stay. So we let him stay above the garage in the back. It was temporary."

"D.J. came here from Pennsylvania?"

"Yeah."

"You haven't seen him in over a year?"

She glanced at Connor. "Um, yeah. I mean I think so. I don't really remember."

Outside, a dog barked. The sound was strangely familiar. Connor walked back to the foyer. Something down the hall, in the kitchen, caught his eye. An overturned chair. Broken glass twinkled on the tile floor. Connor's heartbeat thundered in his chest. He turned and stepped back into the room. "You saw him today," Connor said. "Where is he?"

Rachel stepped back, away from him. Connor could feel Stryker's eyes on him. The barking outside intensified. Stryker kept his eyes on Connor but moved toward the window.

"I don't know what you're talking about," Rachel said.

"Stop lying," Connor said. "Where is he? Tell me where he is right now."

CHAPTER FIFTY

Wilson's growls had rapidly turned to barks. He put himself in front of Claire and Peyton and strained against his leash. D.J. was still several yards away, wearing the hat he'd given Brianna that morning. He had come from the direction of the Holloways' neighbor. Claire prayed that Connor and Stryker really were nearby.

D.J. smiled at them as he approached. Welcoming, nonthreatening. Charming, even. But Claire was pretty sure she knew what lay beneath that smile. There was no doubt in her mind that Brianna lay in a coma because of this man.

As he moved closer, Claire tried to decide if he would really attack them in broad daylight. It was a huge risk, but so was attacking Brianna and putting her body in a dumpster in broad daylight. No, she decided. He cared little about risk at this point.

D.J. stopped about five feet away. The smile never left his face. "You better control your dog before I fucking kill it," he said. He had to speak loudly to be heard over Wilson's barking, but even his tone was without menace. Even so, Claire knew he was deadly serious. At the sound of profanity, Peyton turned her head and buried it in Claire's hip. Claire held tightly to the girl with one hand and gripped Wilson's leash with the other.

"Did you hear me?" he said. "Calm your fucking dog down. You want me to kill him or what?"

Peyton clung harder to Claire. Slowly, putting both hands on Wilson's leash, Claire knelt and spoke into Peyton's ear, hoping D.J. couldn't hear her. "Peyton," she said. "This is very important. When I say go, I need you to run as fast as you can into your house. Lock the door, wake up your dad, and tell him to call the police. Can you do that?"

The little girl nodded. Claire looked back at D.J., who was closing in. Claire didn't see a weapon in either of his hands but that meant little. He was still a threat. Claire knew the damage a man could do with his bare hands.

She could scarcely hold Wilson back now. His hackles were up. Foam flew from his mouth with each fevered bark. She didn't want to put Wilson in harm's way. She didn't want Wilson anywhere near this man, but she had little choice. She had to make sure Peyton was safe. Besides that, there would be no talking Wilson down if he perceived a threat to her. Either D.J. walked away or he got mauled. Claire was certain that his first line of defense would be a heavy kick to the dog's side or head, which meant she needed to distract him before she set Wilson loose. She hoped Peyton running toward the house would draw his gaze away from the dog for the precious second that Wilson would need to get the upper hand.

"Go!" she shouted, her voice sharp and loud.

Like a starting pistol had gone off, Peyton sprinted toward the house. Claire released Wilson while D.J. watched Peyton. Wilson flew through the air. Large, furry paws hit D.J. square on the chest, knocking him to the ground. His hands flew up, trying to block Wilson from biting his face and throat. They rolled back and forth, a blur of golden fur and blue jeans. The whole confrontation lasted only seconds, ending when Wilson moved his bulk to the side in an effort to bite the arms that punched him. D.J. flipped onto his side and roundhouse kicked Wilson in the ribs. The dog yelped, and Claire's whole body went loose with fear. She ran toward Wilson as D.J. stood on wobbly legs, holding his throat and face with both hands, and ran off, leaving droplets of blood behind him.

Claire dropped to her knees. Wilson lay on his side, his breathing labored. A small whine issued from him. Tears fell from her face as she touched him gingerly. He definitely had some broken ribs but she hoped that was all.

"Hold on, buddy," she said, chest tight with anxiety. "Just hold on."

At the Holloways' door, Jim appeared, eyes misty with sleep, a phone pressed to his ear. Claire reached into her back pocket and pulled out her cell phone. With trembling fingers, Claire started to dial Connor, but the commotion had already brought him and Stryker outside of the house next door.

Connor knelt down next to her. "Oh my God, Claire!"

Claire looked up at Stryker. "He went that way. It's the guy from Sammy's. Follow the drops of blood. His name is D.J."

Connor and Stryker exchanged a look. Then Stryker ran off in the direction D.J. had gone, and Connor followed. "Call 911," he shouted over his shoulder.

CHAPTER

FIFTY-ONE

"Are you okay?" Jim Holloway asked.

He had wandered barefoot to the edge of his driveway, Peyton's little hand in his. With his other hand, he held out his phone. "Peyton just told me what happened. I called the police."

Claire looked up at him. Hot tears streamed down her face. "Thank you," she said. "It's my dog, he—" She couldn't finish. Wilson shook beneath her hands. He wasn't making any sounds now. But he was breathing. She turned back to him and stroked his face gently. "You're such a good boy," she told him. "You'll be okay. You're a good dog."

I'm sorry.

"Daddy," Peyton said in a tiny voice, "is the doggie going to die?"

"No, honey," he said.

"I just need to get him to the animal hospital," Claire said. "I have to go—to go get my car." A sob shook her body as she realized how long it would take her to retrieve her vehicle.

Jim Holloway's feet appeared next to Wilson's head. "I can take you," he said. He moved toward Wilson's back and knelt down, his hands poised to slip beneath Wilson's body. "I'll put him in the back of my truck, okay?"

Claire wanted to throw her arms around the man, but there was no time. She managed a husky "Thank you" instead. A moment later, Wilson was safely stowed in Holloway's truck bed, nestled in a *Toy Story* blanket that Peyton had brought from inside the house. Claire lay down in the back with him as Jim, wearing sneakers but no socks, hopped into the cab. He strapped Peyton in beside him and threw open the small center window between the truck cab and bed.

"You'll have to give me directions, okay?" Jim called.

"Of course," she said. "Thank you."

CHAPTER
FIFTY-TWO
EIGHTEEN MONTHS EARLIER

She tried to forget about it. Of course she did. It would never happen again. Of course it wouldn't. It was a terrible mistake. One of the few things in her life she wished she could take back. Something she desperately wished she could undo. But D.J. didn't make it easy. She didn't see him at all those first couple of weeks after it happened, but then he was everywhere. He appeared whenever she was struggling with some task, like dragging her trash cans to the curb or carrying the huge box with Hunter's new car seat in it from the back of her SUV into the house.

Then there was the day she herded the kids out to the car at seven thirty in the morning only to find that she had a flat tire. Jim was snoring away in their bedroom, just as he did every morning until ten or eleven, having worked the four-to-midnight shift—or three to midnight, as he now claimed—and gone to bed late. She wasn't keen on waking him, but she couldn't change the tire and watch the kids at the same time. Peyton, maybe—she'd sit in whatever spot Leah told her to and stay there until Leah released her—but Hunter was another story.

While Leah stared hopelessly at the flat, Peyton said, "Mom." When Leah turned to her, she found her pointing down the street. Her two-year-old son was already halfway down the block.

"Shit," Leah said. Then to Peyton: "You didn't hear that." She chased after her son, who giggled when she scooped him up and carried him back to her driveway, as if it were all a game.

D.J. seemed to materialize from nowhere, leaning against her car, looking like Mr. April from a hot-mechanics calendar. Not that he was a mechanic. As far as Leah knew, he did nothing and had never attended any college or trade school. Apparently, for now, he got by on his parents' money and his good looks. He wore jeans and a clingy black T-shirt. His hair was mussed, and she saw small circles under his eyes, like he'd been up all night. He smiled, making her feel naked, dirty, and aroused all at once. She wished she could melt into the pavement. From the grass beside the driveway, Peyton stared up at him in perfect silence.

"I can fix this for you," he said. "Have you on your way in no time at all."

Leah swallowed. She said nothing. She couldn't. Her mouth, her throat—none of it would work. Hunter squirmed in her arms, wanting down. D.J. just stared, that smirky, knowing smile on his face. Leah felt a tremble start in her legs. She hoped he wouldn't notice. Why did he keep showing up? What did he want from her? He couldn't possibly think she'd let him have sex with her again.

They'd never discussed what had happened. The last two or three times he'd appeared to help her in her time of need, he'd left without saying anything at all. Although he always made sure to touch her somehow, to brush against her or accidentally grasp her fingers when she handed him something. It was like he was taunting her. Thank God Jim was never around when he showed up. Leah would never be able to keep her composure.

Today, D.J. simply laughed, shaking his head as though they were sharing some private joke. He held out a palm. "Leah," he said, the sound of her name on his lips sending a shock through her entire body.

"Mommmeeee," Hunter whined.

"Give me your keys," D.J. said. "I'll see if you've got a spare."

She had no conscious control over her body. Her traitorous hand reached into her pocket for the keys and dropped them into his hand.

He said, "You look nice."

She mumbled a thank-you, pushed Peyton back inside the house, and waited nervously until D.J. finished changing the tire. She'd driven over a nail, he told her when he knocked softly on the door to return her keys. That was it. That was all. He walked off. She was only ten minutes late for work, a minor miracle.

She had no idea what he was doing, what he was after. She hated seeing him, hated the way he made her feel, hated being reminded of what she had done, and yet . . .

"You look nice."

When was the last time Jim had paid her a compliment?

What happened was nearly imperceptible. Leah didn't see it, didn't fully understand how it had happened until it was too late. D.J. waged a war of attrition, and Jim seemed to help D.J.'s cause at every turn, the two of them chipping away at her resolve—D.J. purposeful and Jim oblivious as always.

It started with D.J.'s good deeds, his general smoldering, and his compliments. They were far less crass than his initial "You've got great tits," which only confused her more. But her fights with Jim, which were not unusual, were the nails in the coffin that housed her tenuous fidelity.

The first fight they had post-D.J. was after Jim called her at Rachel's house because Hunter had woken from his nap. Another weekend, another coffee klatch with Rachel while Peyton played with the twins. Leah was growing increasingly uncomfortable around her best friend, especially after what Leah had done, but D.J. never appeared while she was there, and Rachel's house offered some slight, desperately needed respite from her nonstop pace as a mother and wife. It was blessed grown-up time with someone who understood and sympathized with all the challenges of Leah's daily life—her sordid sexual encounter notwithstanding. Plus, as she kept telling herself, avoiding Rachel would be extremely suspicious, and she was trying not to arouse suspicion in any way, shape, or form. So, she dealt with the raging discomfort by doing what she did with everything unpleasant: she tucked it away in a secret compartment in her mind and pretended it didn't exist.

She'd only been there ten minutes when Jim called. Rachel handed her the receiver. "What?" Leah snapped.

"Hunter is up," Jim told her.

She wondered how her husband had managed to wake the boy so soon after she put him down, but she didn't ask. If Jim had woken the baby, he should have to watch him. Leah said, "So?"

Jim made a noise of exasperation. "So, he's awake from his nap."

He said the word *awake* slowly and loudly as if she were hard of hearing and stupid to boot.

"Why are you calling me?"

A sigh. "'Cause I want you to come back over and take care of your kid."

For a split second, her breathing stopped. Her rage was so complete that it seemed to instantly pause every physiological process in her body and then kick them back on all at once into overdrive. Her breathing and heart rate quickened. Her skin blazed so hot that sweat formed instantly in every crease of her body. It was like a white-hot sickness consuming her. Her voice went up an octave. "My kid?" she said. "Did you just say 'my kid'?"

Another sigh. "Jesus Christ, Leah. Just come home and take care of him. He's asking for you."

She slammed the receiver down. Rachel didn't ask questions. She put Leah's coffee mug in the sink. "I'll keep Peyton for a few hours," she said.

Leah nodded and stalked off to her own house. Her rage diminished slightly when she walked in to find Hunter sitting on the couch, sippy cup in hand, watching *Secret Agent Bear*. He leapt up and ran across the room to her. "Mommy!" he said gleefully, wrapping his tiny arms around one of her legs.

She scooped him up, managing a smile for him. "Hi, baby." She kissed his cheek and smoothed his sandy-brown locks back from his face. "Where's Daddy?"

He pointed a chubby finger toward the kitchen. Leah set him back on the couch. "You stay here," she told him.

Her husband was in the kitchen standing before an open fridge, studying its contents. Leah stood behind him, arms akimbo, her rage like a heartbeat pumping adrenaline through her entire body. "What is wrong with you?" she said.

He glanced over his shoulder. "Oh, good, you're here. He's in the living room. He might be hungry."

Her vision narrowed to Jim's face, everything else around him a blur. She advanced on him and slammed the fridge door closed.

"Hey," he said.

She poked his chest. "Hunter is your son too, or did you forget that? What is wrong with you? You can't be alone with him for an hour? You can't feed your own son?"

Jim rolled his eyes at her like she was acting crazy, like she was being so unreasonable. "Leah, he doesn't want me. He wants you."

"Because you never spend any time with him, Jim. Of course he prefers me. I take care of all his needs. But you're his father. He needs a father."

Jim put his hands to his chest. "He's got a father. I'm here, aren't I? He's still a baby. He still wants his mommy. Wait till he gets older and I can really do stuff with him. When he gets older, I can take him fishing."

For a split second, she softened, thinking of Jim and Hunter alone together, out on Jim's beloved boat. But that wasn't going to happen overnight. She needed his help with the kids now. "Jim," she pleaded. "You can't just start being a father when it's enjoyable or convenient for you. These are really important years in a child's life. The kids need to know that you're here for them, that you care about them."

Again, he rolled his eyes. "For God's sake, Leah, I am here. I'm here every fucking day. I work my ass off for you and the kids. You think I like working all week at a job I hate? I do it for you and the kids. Why are you all over my ass right now?"

Leah closed her eyes, tipped her head back, and sucked in a deep breath. She counted to three in her head, willing herself not to strangle this man she had pledged her life to. Opening her eyes, she looked at him again. "Because, Jim, I need help with the kids. I need you to help me with them—feed them, bathe them, pick them up from day care, help potty train Hunter. Watch him while I have coffee with a friend. I need a break, Jim."

His face reddened. He threw his arms in the air. "Oh, *you* need a break? Well, I need a break too, Leah. You act like you're the only one who works hard."

She cut him off. "That's not what I meant. You get breaks all the time. You go fishing, get away. You sleep in. You don't have to pick up or drop off the kids. You get away from everything. When I'm not working, I'm with the kids nonstop. I can't even go to the bathroom without the kids barging in—"

He was shaking his head as she spoke. He wasn't listening to her. It was all about him, as usual. He said, "You know what? Fuck this. I'm going out."

"Jim!"

But he had already turned away from her. She watched as he left the kitchen. Before she could fully process what had just happened, the front door slammed, and she heard his truck roar to life and tear out of the driveway.

Leah walked slowly, zombielike, to their front door and looked outside.

Hunter said, "Mommy, I'm hungry."

As she stared at the empty space where Jim's truck had been, she felt it for the first time: the lessening of her epic guilt over what had happened with D.J. Like the loosening of a belt. Just a notch. It made it a little easier to breathe, a little easier to function, easier to face Rachel, and easier not to walk out on her family and drive off the nearest cliff.

CHAPTER

FIFTY-THREE

Wilson had three broken ribs and some abrasions, but he was stable. Dr. Corey wanted to keep him overnight. Claire didn't care. He would survive—that was all she needed to know. Jim and Peyton Holloway stayed in the waiting room long enough to hear the good news, and then Claire insisted that she could get home on her own. As the door swung closed after them, she heard little Peyton cry, "You saved the doggie, Daddy!" She smiled, then returned to the exam room to sit with Wilson, one hand tangled in the fur on the back of his neck while he slept. Dr. Corey had given him something for pain. He seemed comfortable.

When Claire had rescued him as a puppy, she'd done so because she had always wanted a dog. From the time she was a little girl, she had asked for one, but her father was allergic so they could never have one. When she returned from captivity and moved in with Brianna, she'd gone looking for one. Her post-abduction life was all about doing the things she wanted to do because she could. She was free. She was in control. It had taken less than a minute for her and Wilson—then more fur than anything else—to bond.

She'd never considered that a dog would make an excellent body-guard until Wilson got a little older and became protective of her. Even then, he wasn't exactly intimidating. His temperament was better suited to serving as a therapy dog. But today his instincts had taken over. He had sensed D.J.'s evil and gone after him with a ferocity Claire hadn't even thought him capable of—all for her. To protect her, to keep her safe. She was so grateful, she still couldn't stop crying, even after Dr. Corey assured her that he would be just fine.

She continued to weep quietly at Wilson's side when her cell phone rang. Connor's face lit the screen. Her heart leapt into her throat as she pressed "Answer."

"Where are you?" he asked without preamble.

She brought him up to speed, assuring him that she and Wilson were both fine. "Did you get D.J.?" she asked.

She could hear the frustration in his voice. "No," he said. "I'm sorry. Not yet, but we've got everyone looking."

"Connor, I need to talk to you about what Peyton Holloway told me."

Fifteen minutes later, they hung up.

As the morning wore on and Claire sat alone with her injured dog, she picked up her phone three times without even thinking, ready to dial Brianna so she could tell her about the crazy shit that happened at Leah Holloway's house before remembering that Brianna was in a coma at Sutter General.

She wished everything would just stop. She wanted to go back to this morning, when she was snug in Connor's arms, and start the day over. She wouldn't tell him to answer the phone. She would convince him to stay in bed with her. Convince him to never leave. The thought, impossible though it was, brought her some comfort. She looked at her watch. It felt like an entire day had gone by, but it wasn't even noon. She was ready for a hot bath and bed, and the day hadn't even started yet.

She was going to have to leave her injured dog and find a way back to her vehicle so she could return to the hospital and relieve her brother.

Next to Wilson, her cell phone rang again. This time Tom's face lit up the screen. She had called him twenty minutes earlier to let him know what had happened. Butterflies took flight inside her stomach as she pressed the phone to her ear.

"Tom?"

"She's awake." His voice was thick with tears but high-pitched with joy. "She's awake," he repeated. "She's talking and everything."

The butterflies gave way to a rush of relief. "Thank God. How is she? Does she remember anything?"

Laughter filtered through the phone. "She's pissed. She doesn't remember anything after leaving Sammy's. She remembers having breakfast with you and that's it. She has no idea what happened to her. She's in a lot of pain. She's asking for some of her own clothes, and also, they need her insurance card and some form of photo ID. I don't see her purse here."

"It's evidence. They found it in the dumpster. I'll call Connor, but I'm not sure he'll have time to track it down today. She might have another card. I think she keeps another one at home with her passport. I think Dr. Corey's son is coming by here in a little bit. I'll ask him to take me to get my car at Connor's, and then I'll go home and get some of her things."

She hung up, buried her face in Wilson's fur, and sobbed, the tension leaving her body with each shuddered breath. Brianna was okay. Claire knew she was okay because pissed was her natural state. When she called Connor to let him know, his joy quickly gave way to seriousness. "Get Derrick to follow you home," he said. "Keep me posted. I'll feel better once I know you're at the hospital. Tell Brianna I said hi."

CHAPTER
FIFTY-FOUR
EIGHTEEN MONTHS EARLIER

Their next fight was over Peyton's fingernails.

"Jesus, Leah," Jim had said. "Peyton's nails are really long. You need to cut them."

It was one of the rare times they'd all sat down to dinner together. A Sunday night. Leah was surprised by the instant rage that overcame her. She threw down her fork. It clattered onto the table, drawing stares from her children. They didn't like it when Leah got angry. For a moment, she felt guilty—she knew she was dangerously close to flying off the handle right in front of them.

She always strove to stay calm even when she was enraged, to stay present even when she felt like fleeing. That she constantly had to check her anger only fueled it further. Jim never tried to curb his temper. He routinely walked out during their fights. She didn't have those options. She was a mother. She couldn't walk out on her kids just because she was angry with Jim. She couldn't bear to think of them frightened and upset, wondering where she had gone and if she would come back. She knew they would blame themselves even though it was really their father's fault. Plus, they were two and four. Someone physically had to be there for them, and Jim wasn't doing it. So, she stayed, she stuck with them, and she curbed her temper.

She knew it wasn't healthy. All that anger would get pushed down into her My Feelings Come Last compartment, only to spring back out at a later time as depression, dark and harpy-like. The depression used to threaten to consume her, like an inky blackness overtaking every corner and compartment of her brain. But at some point it became like background noise or a wall hanging. A great tapestry. It was just there. She learned to live her life in spite of it, even though she never forgot it was there. She had been spinning her anger into depression since childhood. A counselor she'd been forced to see in her sophomore year of college had told her she was what they called a high-functioning depressed person. The scariest kind, the woman had said, because high-functioning depressed people rarely gave an indication of the true depth of their sadness or pain. Meaning Leah could fantasize about suicide on a daily basis, but still carry out all the tasks necessary to maintain her daily life.

It was usually after fights like these that Leah lay in bed, indulging in her fantasies of suicide the way other people fantasized about going on vacation. It wasn't the act that she thought about. As a teenager, she had imagined every scenario she could think of and none had held any appeal. She didn't actually want to hurt herself. She just didn't want to deal with life any longer. She didn't want to *be*. She didn't want to wake up to an endless litany of demands that she somehow never fulfilled, no matter how hard she tried. She felt like the guy in that Greek myth who rolled a boulder up a hill each day only to have it roll back down, causing him to start over the next day. Sisyphus.

She loved her children. Indeed, they provided the only joy in her life. She even loved Jim, in his way. But she did not love living. It was difficult, messy, and largely joyless. Watching the news for even a few minutes left her wondering: What was the point? There was so much evil in the world, and there was no escaping it. Sooner or later, it found you. It had found her early in life. Sure, she was long past it—the evil visited on her was now a distant memory—but she didn't feel any better or happier.

Why bother? Her mind often repeated this question in her quietest, most private moments. Why was she—or any of them—even bothering to scratch out a life? What was the point? She longed for a sweet release from the absurdity of living. But she kept living anyway. These, she told herself, were the silly, idle thoughts of an exhausted mother. She would never actually do anything like kill herself. Her own mother had committed suicide. Leah had no intention of following in her footsteps. Unlike her utterly self-centered mother, Leah would never do such a thing to her children. At least, that's what she told herself.

Which meant that she usually had to talk herself into somehow accepting what life threw at her. Rationalization was her biggest ally. Sitting across from her husband as he shoveled food into his mouth, Leah struggled to rationalize airing just a small amount of her overwhelming rage. Then something came to her. Rachel had read on a parenting blog that sometimes it was okay to fight in front of your kids. It helped them learn conflict resolution and showed them that people could fight but still love one another. Not every fight signaled the end of a relationship. Fights were a normal part of a relationship.

With that in mind, she glared at her husband. "You know where the nail clippers are too. If they bother you that much, you can clip them yourself. You are her father."

Jim said, "That's your job."

Rationalization was crushed instantly beneath the spiked boot of her rage. The fight went nuclear in seconds, leaving both children crying as Jim stormed out of the house. For a moment, while Leah soothed her weeping children, assuring them that their father still loved them and would come home eventually, she was so angry at Jim that a little, tiny part of her felt glad she had betrayed him.

It was sick, she knew it. A base impulse. She tried to stow it in her mental drawer of Thoughts That Should Never See the Light of Day, but it kept popping back out. Mainly because each time she and Jim fought or disagreed, the ugly knowledge that she had somehow settled the score—albeit secretly—gave her some relief from her all-consuming rage. She could bear her marriage if she had some relief. She had been able to bear her horrendous childhood because she knew one day it would end. One day she would get to leave, strike out on her own, call the shots in her own life.

Maybe she should leave Jim. She had often considered it. But what would she say to Jim? What would she tell other people when they asked why she was leaving? That he irritated her? That he didn't do as much around the house or with the kids as she would like? Did people leave their spouses over such trivial things? Leah's mother had endured unspeakable abuse from her father and she hadn't left—unless you counted her suicide as leaving permanently. Leah had always thought that in spite of her issues with Jim, they had a good marriage. He wasn't abusive. He never hit her. He wasn't an alcoholic. He had a job and he went to it faithfully. Leah had always considered herself lucky. She'd seen a truly bad marriage. Her parents were a glowing example of the worst marriage ever. Leah's marriage was not even close to that nightmare.

Most of the women she knew had similar issues with their husbands. Many had more serious problems—husbands with gambling addictions, husbands who traveled 90 percent of the time and were never around. Husbands who didn't work at all and refused to contribute at home. Those women stayed, just as Leah did. She remembered one woman she was friendly with at work used to say, *"Sometimes I wish he would hit me. Then I'd have a reason to leave."*

Leah had never felt that way, but she understood the sentiment. What would she tell the kids if she left her husband? She'd ruined their lives and disrupted their home because Jim got on her nerves? She couldn't do it. She had chosen Jim, chosen to bring her children into the world. She'd committed to giving them a good life, a happy life. She was determined to keep her family intact for their sake.

She began to feel guilty for not feeling so guilty about what had happened with D.J. But the awful truth was that a part of her was glad she'd had sex with him. In her secret, vindictive moments, she was glad. She thought it would stop there. She tried to reconcile herself to the fact that she was a horrible person: not only had she done something inexcusable, there were secret moments when she didn't want to take it back. She tried maintaining—balancing her inner world somewhere between her shame and her spite. Even with D.J.'s ubiquitous presence and his unwanted help. The knowing smiles and light touches. The temptation.

Then came the weekend of the retreat. Her boss had scheduled it at some vineyard. No spouses or kids, just the staff. It promised to be a relaxing weekend, and Leah hadn't had one of those since she first got pregnant. She hated being away from her kids, even for one night, but the prospect of a break from her harried life, from the demands that seemed never ending, from the bickering with Jim, was too good to pass up. By that time, she had confronted Jim over his obvious lie about not being able to pick up the kids from day care. His check showed no extra hours. Caught in his deception, he tried several lame excuses: "The kids don't want me, they want you." "I'm not really comfortable being alone with the kids. What if there's an emergency?" "They don't listen to me."

Leah had told him to man up, and in a tone that brooked no opposition, told him that he would be watching the kids overnight while she went on her work retreat. He'd taken it amazingly well—silent and sulky. Really the best reaction she could've hoped for.

She should have known it would never work. She'd been at the retreat for four hours, and he'd called four times. On the last call, he'd asked when she was coming home, as if she hadn't made it clear to him a half-dozen times. Leah sighed. "Tomorrow, remember? That was the deal."

She heard Hunter wailing in the background. Jim said, "Leah, I'll never get these kids to bed. They're upset. They keep crying. They've never been away from you this long."

"Jim," she snapped. "It's been four hours. I leave them alone for eight hours a day, Monday through Friday, when I'm working. For God's sake, play with them, take them to the park or for ice cream. Be a dad."

The next call came two hours later. This time it was little Peyton, her voice tremulous. "Mommy, when are you coming home?"

"I'll be home tomorrow, sweetie."

Then Peyton lowered her voice, as if she didn't want Jim to overhear her. "Mommy, Daddy said you might not come back."

It was like a spike right through Leah's heart. Again, she told Peyton she'd be home the next day. When Jim got on the line, she lambasted him. He had a ready excuse, as always. She was blowing things out of proportion. All he had said was that he didn't know why Leah would want to come back to two crying kids. He had spoken without thinking. "The kids were acting up. I didn't mean anything by it. I'm sorry."

She tried to go back to the retreat, to relax, to enjoy her time away, her time alone. But she kept hearing the tremor in Peyton's voice. She couldn't let her daughter believe that she might not come home.

The ride back gave her plenty of time to stew over Jim's behavior. She didn't believe for one moment that he had said such a thing to their kids without thinking. He'd done it on purpose, she was sure. Her guilt was his trump card.

And he'd won, she realized as she was driving home from the retreat after only six hours—less than a workday. Here she was, driving back to be with her kids because her husband could not or would not watch their children alone. Once again, Jim got his way. Once again, Leah had to put herself last in order to pick up his slack.

She seethed, white-knuckling the steering wheel. She pictured herself arriving home, bursting through the door, and demanding a divorce. Jim, of course, would act like she was being crazy and unreasonable. Nevertheless, she tried to imagine her life as a divorcée. It would be exactly the same except for Jim's paycheck and the bickering. She'd still be responsible for all the childcare, all the housecleaning and cooking, all the finances, all the decisions. Jim just wouldn't be there. She wondered if he would even see the kids if they got divorced.

She knew the answer, of course. If he couldn't handle them overnight now, there was no way he'd suddenly want to see them on a regular basis. Then what? Her kids would resent him for being an absentee father. She would resent him even more than she already did. The fact was that practically, financially, she was better off staying. Plus, she really wanted her kids to grow up in a two-parent home. It wasn't their fault that she wasn't happy with Jim. She'd have to stay. Even though she wanted to strangle him half the time.

The drive was forty minutes, but it was long enough for her rage to reach its boiling point. She replayed their last few fights over and over again, growing angrier each time. Tension in her shoulders, arms, and hands turned to an unbearable ache.

"Come back over and take care of your kid."

"That's your job."

"You act like you're the only one who works hard."

When she came to the turnoff to her street, she kept going. She parked her car a few blocks over, on a side street that didn't get much traffic. She walked briskly in the dark, cutting through backyards until she reached D.J.'s garage-top apartment. She crept up the steps like a criminal, every nerve in her body on edge, humming with fear and anticipation. She couldn't stop, couldn't allow herself to think about what she was doing. She let her rage propel her to his door, hoping both that he would be there and that he wouldn't. She knocked softly.

Someone moved around inside, and Leah's heartbeat thundered so hard, it seemed to rock her entire body. The door swung open. D.J. stood before her wearing nothing but a pair of boxer shorts. A small lamp lit the room, casting a golden glow over his perfectly sculpted body.

Her breath hitched in her throat.

He smiled. "Leah." His hand circled one of her wrists, tugging her toward him. He said, "Come here."

Afterward, she snuck back to her car, a thief in the night, and drove home.

Jim and the kids had fallen asleep together on the couch.

CHAPTER

FIFTY-FIVE

O'Handley babysat Rachel Irving while Connor went back to the division to get the Genechek file, then released him to help Stryker. They had a lead on D.J.'s apartment. Connor doubted they'd find him there, but they might find something that would help them track him down.

Connor stood just outside the doorway to the Irvings' kitchen, watching Rachel. She sat at the table, a half-finished cup of coffee in front of her. She had made some effort to clean up the room, although he still saw some stray pieces of broken glass glinting from beneath the table. Other than her incessant twisting of her "#1 Mom" charm, she showed no signs of nerves. If anything, she seemed bored and impatient. Her gaze found the clock on the microwave just about every two minutes. She rolled her eyes in its direction and then collected air in her cheeks, like a chipmunk storing nuts, only to blow it out loudly.

In his mind, Jade was at his elbow, matching Rachel eye roll for eye roll. *Can you believe this smug bitch?* he could hear her saying.

Connor patted the pocket of his suit jacket to make sure his phone was there—he would be waiting for text updates from Claire throughout the day—then entered the room and pulled out a chair across from Rachel, placing the Genechek folder on the table.

Rachel smiled at him, like she was in a restaurant awaiting her dinner date. Like she'd been expecting him. With a small chuckle, she said, "I really don't know why that other detective insisted on staying here with me, like I'm some kind of criminal. I've been more than cooperative."

Connor wasn't doing pleasantries today, nor was he interested in trying to justify O'Handley's presence to her. He launched right into his interrogation. "We need to talk about Leah again. One of the last phone calls she got before she drove her car into the river was from an outfit called Genechek. Do you know what Genechek does?"

Rachel's familiar smile faltered. The "#1 Mom" charm disappeared in her fist. "No," she said.

"Mail-in DNA tests."

She swallowed, her throat quivering, the first sign of nervousness. "Like paternity tests?"

Connor nodded. "Yeah, like paternity tests. And maternity tests as well."

"Maternity? Why would you need a maternity—" She stopped talking and clamped her mouth shut.

"You know why, don't you, Mrs. Irving?"

"Please," she whispered. Her air of complete confidence shattered, her eyes suddenly sad and pleading.

"It's time to stop lying," Connor told her. "Women are dying. You understand that, right?"

She looked down. Her mouth worked, as though she was trying on various responses, but none were appropriate, so she said nothing.

"You have a hairbrush go missing last week?" Connor asked.

Her head snapped up at him, eyes wide. Still, she said nothing.

"I thought so," Connor said.

"I swear I didn't know what he was doing," Rachel whispered.

"You didn't? Your best friend figured it out. You couldn't?"

She didn't respond. Connor tapped the file folder on the table between them. "Leah Holloway sent in two tests to Genechek. A paternity test and a maternity test. For the paternity test she used buccal swabs—scrapings from the inside of the cheek, which I guess is possible to get when someone is sleeping. Anyway, she listed Tyler as the child and Jim as the potential father. It came back as a positive match, except that Jim has no memory of submitting to a DNA test. He probably signed the form because he always signed whatever Leah put in front of him. But he doesn't remember giving her the buccal swab.

"The only problem with that is that the DNA profile from the Genechek paternity test doesn't match Jim Holloway's actual DNA profile. Jim gave us DNA. Our lab tested it. Chain of custody and all that. So we know for a fact that the DNA sample that Leah sent in under Jim's name wasn't Jim's DNA at all. Do you know whose DNA it was?"

Rachel didn't speak. Connor had the feeling that none of this was coming as a surprise to her. He said, "It was the Soccer Mom Strangler's. Leah had DNA from the Soccer Mom Strangler, and she sent it to Genechek under Jim's name. You know what that means, right?"

She stared at him.

"Tell me you know what that means. Tell me you're following this."

She licked her lips. "The Soccer Mom Strangler is Tyler's father."

CHAPTER
FIFTY-SIX

SIX DAYS EARLIER—WEDNESDAY

Leah was about to orchestrate her own rape. At least, in her mind it would be rape, since she didn't want to do it. But she would consent to it because there was no other way to get the information she needed. She had tried to figure out a way that would not involve having to see D.J. again, but she couldn't come up with one. One time. She would see him one last time, and then she would know the truth.

Leah stood outside the door of D.J.'s studio apartment, trying to still the tremble working its way through her whole body. Walking into his building had been hard enough. The gossip on her street was that this was the same neighborhood where Glory Rohrbach was shacking up with her landscaper. That was just what Leah needed, to be found out by Glory Rohrbach.

She tried to calm her shaking limbs. She didn't want D.J. to see the fear or disgust she felt for him now. It would make him rougher with her. He seemed to thrive on that. She hated the look of excitement on his face when he was hurting her. It terrified her.

She sucked in a deep breath. It had taken her weeks to work up the nerve to do this. She had worked so hard for so long to erase him from her life, but he would not leave her alone. He would not let her go. This might at least placate him for a while. If he thought she was still interested in him, maybe his assault on her life and her children's safety—or at least his incessant calls and texts—would stop, even if temporarily. But in the long run she knew this would make things worse, so much worse. It was going to take a long time to put the distance between them again. She didn't know if she would ever be free of him.

The hallway was dark and gray, water stains peeling the paint from the ceiling. She'd never been inside a prison but she imagined this is what it felt like—close, gloomy, and wholly depressing. She knocked softly on the door to 1A. Her heart pounded in her chest. What if he wasn't there? Part of her wanted him not to be—to spare her from the hour ahead, from the disgusting things she would have to do. But another part of her prayed that he was, because she didn't think she could work up the nerve to come here again. She was taking a huge risk—again.

Finally, she heard rustling behind the door. She let out a breath she hadn't realized she was holding. The door swung open and there he stood. He looked like he hadn't slept in a few days. Circles smudged the skin beneath his eyes. His thick brown hair was mussed. He had no shirt on and, as always, her eyes were drawn to his well-muscled chest and abs. For the first time, she didn't feel the heat and discomfort of arousal when she saw him. She didn't admire his deeply tanned skin, the sharply cut grooves of muscle that lined nearly every inch of him and rippled every time he moved. She was finally, mercifully impervious to the smolder in his deep-brown eyes.

"Come in," he said, moving aside to let her enter.

She felt like she was stepping over the threshold to hell. But she'd done that eighteen months ago, hadn't she? Without so much as a word of protest. The things she'd let this boy do to her—surely she deserved to go to hell.

The place was small and dark, its whitewashed walls scarred with stains and scuff marks. Yellowed squares marred the walls where someone had used scotch tape to hang things beside nail holes that had never been patched. It was a single room with a mattress on the floor. Beside the bed lay a pile of clothes and a cardboard box with a small lamp atop it. At the foot of the mattress a television sat positioned precariously on an overturned plastic storage bin. Behind the television was a door to the bathroom, judging by the swath of white shower curtain visible. The room smelled sweet and sour, like marijuana and old sweat.

The sound of the door closing behind her made her jump. D.J. laughed softly. "Why are you nervous?"

She tried a smile but the corners of her mouth would only go up so far. "I—I'm not nervous."

I'm terrified.

He moved closer, his movements fluid, snakelike. His smile sent a shiver up her spine. Like a predator smelling her fear, he moved in closer. He wrapped a firm hand around her neck and pulled her into him. She tried not to recoil. Sensing the tension in her body, his fingers tightened, digging into her skin. Tears stung her eyes.

"D.J., I—"

"Shh," he breathed into her ear. His other hand had already found its way up her skirt. She wanted to clench her legs together but she couldn't. She had to do this. It was the only way to find out what she needed to know.

"This is the last time," she said.

His lips found her throat. "You always say that," he breathed between hungry kisses.

He moved his hand from her neck, down her back to her bottom, squeezing hard. She closed her eyes. Her voice was weaker this time. "I mean it, D.J. This has to end. No more phone calls. No more texts. You have to leave my children alone. No more . . ." She trailed off.

"No more fucking?"

Abruptly, he tore at her shirt, popping two buttons on her blouse. An involuntary cry tore from her throat. His teeth clamped down hard on her shoulder. She hissed a breath. He withdrew, his tongue making a trail across her collarbone to the hollow of her throat.

"It hurts when you do that," she told him.

With a single swift motion, her skirt was around her ankles. "It hurts when you leave me," he whispered.

She let him push her down onto the mattress. She stared at the brown water stains on the ceiling while he did everything he wanted to do. When he hurt her, she prayed it would end soon. She promised herself she would never do this again.

After he exhausted himself, he lay propped against the wall, smoking a cigarette. She snatched her clothes and purse from the floor and locked herself in the bathroom. Her hands shook as she dressed and pulled out the Genecheck kit from her purse. She nearly knocked the whole thing onto the floor when D.J. rattled the doorknob.

"What are you doing in there?"

Quickly, she tore open the wrapper and positioned the swab so it was easily accessible by simply reaching her hand inside her purse. "Just cleaning up," she called.

The door rattled again. "I have to piss."

She zipped her purse and straightened her clothes. As soon as she opened the door, he pushed past her and lined his body up with the toilet. "Don't leave," he told her as he relieved himself.

She stood in the doorway, staring dumbly at him. It had taken Jim months to be able to pee in front of her. D.J. had no such issues. In fact, the level of comfort he showed with her was downright alarming. It put a fine point on his months of harassment. She still couldn't even think about her poor dog without breaking down.

"D.J.," she said as he moved back into the bedroom. He rifled through the pile of clothes beside his bed until he came up with a joint. He plopped onto the bed and patted the space beside him. She wished he would put on some clothes. Her body ached all over from the hour she'd just spent beneath him. She didn't want him getting any ideas about a second round. Lucky for her, the marijuana lulled him quickly into a deep sleep. She waited a full fifteen minutes before she retrieved the Genechek kit from her purse, moving slowly and carefully so she didn't wake him. The only good fortune she had that day was that D.J. slept with his mouth open. It was difficult to keep her hand still as she took the swab. What would she say to him if he woke up while she was trying to swab the inside of his cheek?

She didn't have to find out.

The moment she had what she needed, she snuck out. She made it halfway back to work before she had to pull over and vomit on the side of the road.

CHAPTER
FIFTY-SEVEN

"Tyler Holloway is the Soccer Mom Strangler's son," Connor confirmed. When Rachel didn't speak, didn't move, he said, "You know, if I found out my kid was the son of a serial killer, I might want to drive into the nearest river. So Leah was having an affair with the Soccer Mom Strangler. Had his kid. Figured it out. Went berserk. Case closed, right?"

Rachel licked her lips again but went silent.

"Except that Leah also sent in a maternity test. I kept asking myself why she would need a maternity test. Surely she hadn't forgotten giving birth five months earlier. I double-checked the medical records. She definitely gave birth to a baby boy five months ago. Maybe she thought there was a mix-up at the hospital. Maybe the nurses accidentally switched babies. That's happened, hasn't it? Switched at birth. Maybe that explained how Tyler could be the son of the Soccer Mom Strangler. Except for the hairbrush."

She looked away.

"Leah paid over three times as much for the maternity test than she did for the paternity test. Do you know why?"

No response.

"Because the sample she submitted was from a hairbrush, not a swab. The DNA had to be extricated from the hair on the brush. It's harder to do, takes longer, and so it's more expensive. So I ask myself, 'Why would Leah send her hairbrush and pay three times as much for the results of the test when she could simply swab her own cheek?'"

Rachel sank down in her chair, arms folded over her chest. Her "#1 Mom" charm lay untouched on her chest, its shine dulled from all of her fidgeting.

"You and I both know why. She used your hairbrush. Guess what else? The sample she sent in for the maternity test for Tyler wasn't Tyler's. The profile doesn't match the profile Genechek has on file for Tyler for the paternity test. But guess whose profile it does match?"

Again, no response.

"Ding, ding, ding!" Connor hollered, simulating a bell and startling Rachel into meeting his eyes. "Jackpot! It's the Soccer Mom Strangler. Congratulations, by the way, you're officially a grandmother."

Rachel closed her eyes. Tears leaked from the corners. Her shoulders shook.

"Does your husband know that your son is the Soccer Mom Strangler?"

She opened her eyes. Her expression was both tortured and resigned. "He doesn't know that D.J. is my son. Please. No one knows."

"Please what?" Connor barked a laugh. "You think there is a scenario here where no one finds out that this kid is your son? For all we know, you're in collusion with him. You could be going to prison. He's killed five women, that we know of, including one of my colleagues. He is never going to stop hurting people until we catch him. So I need to know what you know. Now. No more lies."

CHAPTER
FIFTY-EIGHT
SEVENTEEN MONTHS EARLIER

She hated herself, before, during, and after. Even as the pleasure of the earth-shattering orgasms coursed through her, she hated herself. Daily, she weighed the pleasure against her shame: the satisfaction of somehow besting Jim against the cost, should she get caught. The whole affair didn't last long. A few months. The sneaking around, alone, was enough to give Leah a heart attack. She didn't understand how other people did this. D.J. seemed completely unaffected by the stress of it, although they never discussed it.

They didn't talk much. It wasn't that kind of relationship. Besides, Leah was usually rendered speechless by him—by the way he looked, by the confidence with which he touched her, took her, by the hunger in his eyes when he gazed at her. She was torn between feeling like some sort of centerfold model and defenseless prey. She didn't understand his insatiable desire for her. No one had ever wanted her the way D.J. did. A part of her was always waiting for the punch line. Was she on some sick version of *Candid Camera* or *Punk'd*?

At first, the intensity of his lust was electrifying. He would wait until she got the kids down for bed at night, and then he would sneak into her house while Jim was at work. She rarely heard him enter. There were nights she even locked the doors, but still, he found his way in. She would be putting in a load of wash or clearing off the perpetually messy kitchen table, and suddenly he'd appear behind her, his hungry mouth on her neck, his hands all over her. He'd do whatever he wanted with her body, speaking only to give her instructions:

"Take off your shirt."

"Lie down."

"Ride me."

Occasionally, he would pay her a crass compliment that made her skin burn like she had just jumped into a pit of lava:

"You're so fucking hot."

"I love your tits."

He said other, dirtier things to her too. Things she could never repeat to another human being. Even thinking about the things he said after the fact gave her hives. She had never watched pornography, but she wondered if that's where he learned such things.

One night, they had just finished an especially acrobatic session in the laundry room when little Hunter wandered in. His tiny face was foggy and scrunched with sleep, his hair flattened on one side of his head. He carried his stuffed T. rex in one arm. The room was dark, thank goodness. Leah shrieked when she saw him, pushing D.J. away from her. Thankfully, he disappeared into the shadows as Leah scooped Hunter up and made a beeline for the door. She held him against her naked skin and hustled him back to his room.

"Mommy," he said. "I was looking for you."

She couldn't catch her breath. "I was doing laundry, Bug," she said in a shaky voice.

He poked her breast. "You're naked."

She smiled tightly. "I spilled soda on my clothes and had to put them in the washer. Now you stay here while Mommy goes to her room for pajamas."

"Mommy, there was a man in our house."

Her skin felt like ice. She was certain her son could feel her heart pounding in her chest. "Oh, honey," she said. "There was no man. You were just dreaming, okay, sweetie?"

He rubbed his eyes. "Did you check?"

She smoothed his hair away from his face with one hand. "I sure did. There was no man. It was just a dream. Go back to sleep, okay, Bug?"

"Okay, Mommy."

She tucked him back into his toddler bed, which was just a twin mattress on the floor. They'd done away with his crib a few months earlier after he kept climbing out of it. She kissed his forehead and went to her bedroom to put some clothes on. Once she was sure Hunter had fallen back to sleep, she went in search of D.J., but he was gone.

She didn't see him for three days after that. Every time Hunter spoke in front of other people, Leah held her breath, just waiting for him to talk about the man he had seen in their house, but he didn't bring it up again. Apparently, he believed it really was a dream, or he simply didn't remember.

The next time D.J. snuck in, she managed to sidestep him before he could touch her. She had been at her kitchen sink, washing dishes, ears pricked for the sound of him creeping up on her. She put the kitchen table between them in what, to anyone else, might look like a child's game of keep-away. D.J. laughed. "Leah," he said.

She extended a soapy hand in his direction. "Stop," she said. "You stay over there."

Again, he laughed, but she needed him on the other side of the room if she was going to talk to him. "We can't do this anymore," she told him.

A grin remained on his face. His eyes wandered from her face to her breasts. She could practically feel his gaze, like two hands groping her. She tugged at the collar of her T-shirt.

"Why?" he said. "'Cause your kid saw us? What is he—one? He won't remember."

"He's two and he does remember things. All I need is for him to tell Jim that he saw you here with me."

D.J.'s eyes drifted back to hers. "So what?"

Her cheeks flamed. "So what? My marriage—"

This time his laughter was sharp and derisive. "Your marriage? Really, Leah? You expect me to believe that you give two shits about your marriage? You expect me to believe you care if that dumbass you're married to finds out? I know he's never fucked you properly."

"D.J."

He moved around the table and she moved in concert, maintaining the distance between them. His tone shifted. "I like the way you say my name. Say it again."

"No."

"Leah."

"Why are you even with me?" she blurted.

It was the question that had plagued her from the very first time he'd screwed her in the garage, but that she did not want the answer to. She thought of the half-naked twit he'd been with the first time she'd met him. He could have any woman. With his male-model good looks, his mysterious little smirk, and those muscles that rippled every time he moved, any straight woman would swoon instantly over him. He could have a young, scantily clad idiot for each day of the week if he wanted to, and yet he was visiting Leah every night, doing things to her she didn't even know were possible.

His gaze swept downward, toward the table. Instantly, she thought of the time they'd done it on top of the table and shivered. He looked back up at her from beneath long eyelashes, taking on a boyish, almost shy look. "Why don't you believe that you're sexy?"

It was her turn to laugh. "Please, D.J. I know what I am. I just don't think you do. You could have any woman. You could have a different woman every night if you wanted."

He placed both hands on the table and leaned toward her. "I don't want other women. I want you, Leah. Maybe that doesn't make sense to you, but it does to me. You're a beautiful, sexy, smart, sophisticated woman with the hottest ass I've ever seen."

She had to look away from him. Her skin was on fire. His sneakered feet appeared inches from her own bare feet. With one hand, he tipped her chin, trapping her with his gaze. "What do you want, Leah? You want me to be more careful? I'll be more careful."

His fingers crawled around to the back of her neck, pulling her in, pressing himself against her. She felt his erection straining against his jeans. She was aquiver with the memory of the last time he'd been inside her.

"You can keep your dope of a husband, and I can keep fucking you."

"D.J.," she protested, but his mouth crashed down on hers with a force that drove all reasoned thought from her mind. That night, she went to bed raw, sore, and hating herself more than ever.

CHAPTER

FIFTY-NINE

Rachel broke down, sobbing loudly, her whole body shuddering. It went on for several minutes. Connor left the room to retrieve a box of tissues he had spotted in their den, then came back, and she didn't seem to notice. He pushed the tissues across the table. She plucked one out and blew her nose. Her chest heaved. She took several more tissues and dabbed her eyes before balling the tissues up in her fists.

"I was fifteen, okay? D.J.'s dad was older—like, a lot older. He was a professor at the college. I used to walk my dog past his house. The dog was the worst. It never listened. Walking it was a nightmare, but my mom made me walk it. 'You wanted it,' she always said. D.J.'s dad saw me struggling. He had dogs. He was good with them. He helped me train that little asshole of a dog. Then, you know, things started to happen."

"Did he rape you?" Connor asked.

She smiled ruefully and blew her nose again. "That would make things so easy, wouldn't it? If I just claimed rape. I was the neglected teenage daughter of a single mom with more daddy issues than there are stars in the sky. I was the perfect target for a pedophile, right? Lonely, attention seeking. It probably would have been more accepted if I said he raped me. But he didn't. He was kind and patient and caring, and I thought I loved him. When I got pregnant, he promised to care for us—for me and his child."

Here, more tears streaked her face. "He promised, and he kept that promise. He didn't have to, but he did."

Connor frowned. "But you were fifteen. I'm not clear on the law in Pennsylvania, but in most states the age of consent is older than fifteen."

She nodded and dabbed her eyes. "We tried to keep things secret. We knew he'd be in deep shit if anyone found out. Of course, eventually, my mom figured it out. I was very stupid back then—if you didn't already guess that—so I confessed everything to her, thinking she would understand."

"But she didn't?"

"Not even a little bit. She immediately kicked me out, and then she called the police. Accused him of rape. Lucky for us, we lived in a small town, and he was very friendly with the police chief and the DA. I was already staying with him because I had nowhere else to go. If they prosecuted him, I'd be on the street with a newborn. I refused to testify, anyway. They made it go away, kept it out of the press. He kept his job. I moved in. We were going to get married the day after I turned eighteen."

She sighed and looked up at the ceiling. "Such plans we had. Then Dylan—D.J.—came. I was wildly unprepared for a baby. You have to understand: I was sixteen years old. I'd gotten swept up in the drama and excitement of it all, this intriguing older man who was willing to move heaven and earth to be with me. The wild and crazy sex. The plans. So many plans. He wasn't wealthy, but he had some money. We were going to travel the world together. Make love in a dozen different countries."

"Well," Connor said, "a baby will throw a wrench into those kinds of plans."

"No kidding. It was awful. And D.J. was the worst baby. I think I knew something was wrong with him right away. Sebastian—that's his dad's name—thought it was postpartum, and I always wondered if he was right, but then I had the twins and it was completely different."

"You didn't bond with D.J.?"

She shook her head and lowered her voice. "It was more than that."

Connor waited for her to continue, but when several seconds of silence slipped past, he said, "Rachel?"

She looked at him again. "You said no more lies, right?"

"No more lies."

She looked him dead in the eye, and without blinking, she said, "I hated him."

CHAPTER SIXTY

SIXTEEN MONTHS EARLIER

Jim became an afterthought, his complaints and demands white noise. For once in their marriage, she was happy they worked opposite shifts. She left him a plate of food for when he came home at one in the morning. He handed the kids off to her at three thirty, and they saw each other on weekends. He still climbed on top of her some nights, waking her with sex that was as unremarkable as it was undemanding. She didn't care. For once, she didn't want to punch him in the face every time she saw him. For once, she didn't have knotted muscles across her shoulder blades every second of the day. She laughed more and started to enjoy dinner with her children each night instead of dreading its hectic and unpredictable nature.

One night, Hunter told her she was silly. They'd been making mashed potato sculptures on their plates, all three of them. They'd gone on until their sides ached from laughter, until their dinners were cold and small clumps of mashed potatoes were strewn all over the place, even in Peyton's hair. For once, Leah wasn't annoyed that she'd have to give them both baths after dinner. She was having fun with her kids.

Peyton said, "I love Silly Mommy."

Leah laughed, molding a head for her mashed potato turtle. "Oh yeah? You like her better than Regular Mommy?"

Peyton shrugged. "Yeah," she said with a guileless four-year-old's honesty. "Regular Mommy is mad all the time. Silly Mommy is happy."

Hunter smashed his fork into a pile of mashed potatoes he claimed was a dinosaur and hollered, "Silly Mommy!"

Of course her newfound silliness came with a price. The stress of compartmentalizing her affair was enormous. When D.J. wasn't screwing her, she had to pretend that he didn't exist. There was no other way. The alternative was to deal with what a horrible person she'd become—a liar and a cheater. She simply couldn't. During the day, she locked thoughts of D.J. into her mental Did Not Happen drawer. There were more than a few lies in that drawer, most of them from her childhood.

Of course, it took enormous effort to keep that drawer closed. She pictured herself in some musty, old room filled with drawers, driving her entire body weight against that one drawer. It was mentally exhausting. She started forgetting things at work. Important things. At home, she forgot to pay the electric bill; she burned casseroles in the oven, left lights on, left water running in the tub until it overflowed, forgot to take Hunter to his well visit. Flightiness became her new normal. One morning, after she drove to work with both kids still in the back—bypassing day care altogether—she knew she was in trouble. Thank goodness the kids were old enough to say, "Are we going to work with you, Mommy?"

She had a flash of herself as one of those parents who left their children to die in hot cars. Her kids had always been foremost on her mind. Even at her most sleep-deprived, she never forgot about them. She never understood what the hell happened with those parents who forgot about the kids in their cars. How did you forget about the single most important thing in your life?

Like this, a voice in her head said. *Exactly like this.*

Like an idiot, she didn't ascribe her newfound mental fog to D.J. at first. She figured it was a physical problem: chronic fatigue syndrome, lupus, early onset Alzheimer's, a stroke, maybe even a brain tumor. Okay, so maybe she shouldn't have googled "memory loss" before she went to the doctor. Her family doctor gave in and ordered an MRI of her brain. When it came back normal, he told her that her symptoms were merely the result of stress.

"Has anything changed in your life in the last couple of months?" he asked. "Any recent stressors?"

There was only one thing that had changed. She didn't tell her doctor about it, of course. The fleeting moments of satisfaction she got from her trysts with D.J. were not offsetting the enormous stress of carrying on the affair.

It just wasn't worth it.

Her next attempt at ending things between them didn't go well. They were locked in her laundry room. The kids were asleep. D.J. had snuck over under the cover of darkness as usual. He was pawing her, tearing at her clothes like he was desperate to be inside her. She still didn't understand it. Every time he touched her, the questions niggled at the back of her mind. What did he see in her? Why did he want *her*? Was this some kind of cruel prank?

She had to wait until he was finished. The sex was becoming rougher, faster, more like rutting. At first, he'd been very concerned with her pleasure, often taking his time with his mouth and hands, bringing her to new heights of satisfaction every time they did it. Lately, she felt like she didn't even matter; he just needed a warm body to pump himself into.

"D.J.," she said as he pulled his boxers and jeans back up. "We need to talk."

The only light was seeping under the door from the kitchen, but she saw the glint in his eyes. "No, we don't."

She bent over, fishing around for her panties. "Yes, we do. This—this thing between us, it really has to end. I—I can't do this anymore."

He grabbed her hips, grinding himself against her, laughing as she slapped him away. "Oh, come on, Leah," he said, sounding remarkably like Jim. Dismissive.

Her hand seized on her panties and, nearby, her shorts. She leaned against the dryer and pulled them on. "I'm serious. I cannot do this anymore. D.J., you're a—" She paused. What was she going to say? He was a nice boy? He didn't act like a boy. A nice guy? The things he'd done to her were as far from nice as one could get. She was still appalled at what he reduced her to at times.

"I'm a what, Leah?" D.J. coaxed. "You're going to say I'm a great guy? I could have any girl I want? It's you, it's not me?"

He wasn't taking her seriously. Leah stalked across the tiny room, flicked the light on, and put her hands on her hips. "I'm married, D.J. I have a family. I'm nearly twenty years older than you. I mean, you had to know this wasn't going to last forever."

"Leah," he said. His face had transformed as she spoke, his smirk giving way to a more serious expression. She couldn't quite tell what it was. She barely knew him. Of course she couldn't read his expressions, but it looked like confusion. Maybe just a bit of panic.

"Really," she continued. "You had to know this was just . . . just . . . a fling. There was some kind of attraction between us, we've explored it, and now it's over."

He held out a hand, beseeching. "Leah, please."

She shook her head. "I'm sorry, D.J. I am. I should never have allowed things to go this far between us."

He stepped toward her and tried to touch her face. She turned away. "There is something between us, Leah."

She smiled weakly. "Yes, something physical, and it's been . . . amazing, but I—"

He pressed himself against her, pushing her against the door. "Because you're amazing. Please, Leah, don't leave me."

She pushed him gently, alarmed by his tone. Gone was the über-confident, ultramasculine lover who had handled her body so deftly the last two months. Before her now stood the boy he really was. Her skin felt clammy and cold. A coil of dread unfurled inside her.

"D.J.," she said, trying to sound soothing. "I'm not leaving you. You do understand that we were never committed to one another, right? This was just an affair. This was just sex."

"Incredible sex," he said. This time, it was less an assertion and more of a question.

"Sure, yes. Incredible, but it couldn't go on forever. You're young. You'll find someone else, someone your age who isn't married. You'll forget about me."

His eyes glistened. Were those tears? Her heartbeat ticked up. Could he really be that infatuated with her? She knew he was young, but was he really so inexperienced in relationships that he had developed a serious emotional attachment to her in such a short time, without ever having had a real conversation with her?

His voice was high-pitched and reedy. "Leah, please don't do this. I don't want anyone else but you. I don't care if you're married."

"Well, you should. What you think you feel for me, it's just a crush. It's not real."

Abruptly, his hands cupped her cheeks. He stared into her face. There were definitely tears now. "It's the realest thing I've ever felt."

She put her hands on his wrists and tried to pull them away, but he held fast. "No, D.J."

His voice took on a new urgency, a firmness born of desperation. "Yes," he said. "It's real. How can you say it's not?"

She tried again to loosen his grip but couldn't. Fear tickled the back of her throat. One of his hands snaked down, slipping beneath the waistband of her shorts, between her legs. "This is real. You know it just as well as I do." His fingers worked, and in spite of herself, her body responded. "See?" he breathed into her face. His breath smelled like cigarettes and mouthwash. "You feel it too."

Her body raced toward climax, but she resisted, twisting away from him, prying his hand away. She knocked him back, against the washer. "No," she said firmly. "We can't do this anymore."

"But, Leah, I need you," he pleaded.

"No, you don't, and I don't need you. This is over. Finished. I want you to please leave and do not—do not come back again. I'm sorry, D.J."

He dropped to his knees, hands raised and clasped together, crying openly now. "No, Leah, no. Don't do this."

She pointed to the door, trying to keep the tremor out of her voice. "Leave."

He wrapped his arms around her legs, pressing his face into her stomach. "I'll hurt myself," he blurted.

The temperature in the room seemed to drop by twenty degrees. She arched her back away from him. "What?"

"I'll hurt myself. I'll kill myself," came his muffled voice. "I have a friend, his dad has a gun. I'll put a fucking bullet in my head."

"D.J., no."

"Rachel has Xanax. I've seen them. I'll take the whole bottle."

She touched his head. His lustrous brown hair was stiff with hair gel. "D.J., stop. What about your family?"

"Family? You think my family gives a shit about me?"

"Well, I don't know what your situation was before you came here, but what about your aunt Rachel? She took you in—"

He spit her name. "Rachel? You think Rachel gives a shit about me? You really don't know her, do you?"

"I know that she—"

"You don't know anything about her. You should ask her sometime about the people she left when she moved here."

Baffled, Leah searched for a response. She had no idea what he was talking about. As a rule, she and Rachel rarely discussed their upbringings—Leah because hers was so traumatic and Rachel because she maintained that it was completely unremarkable. Nothing to tell.

D.J. pressed his face deeper into her abdomen. His hands clutched the backs of her thighs. For once, there was nothing sexual about the way he touched her. This was pure neediness, and it scared the shit out of her.

"I'll do it," he promised. "If I can't be with you, I don't want to live."

"No."

She didn't know what else to say. His sudden turn from a man with endless swagger to the boy begging on his knees before her gave her whiplash. Was he serious? Would he really try to kill himself? Did he have some kind of mental illness? Again, the realization that she knew nothing about him other than what he looked like naked stung her. What had she gotten herself into?

"D.J., please," she tried. "Don't hurt yourself. Not over me, not over this. You're so young. You've got your entire life ahead of you. You'll find someone so much better than me. Someone you can start a life with."

He was shaking his head against her stomach as she spoke. "I only want you," he mumbled.

Feeling nauseated, she tipped her head back and closed her eyes. Her mind raced. What could she say? If she took a hard line and threw him out and he really did kill himself, could she live with that?

No. She couldn't.

Even though Leah had long held mixed feelings about her mother's suicide, it had been devastating, especially for Leah's brother. Leah's own abstract suicidal fantasies aside, she knew that suicide had long-lasting, horrific effects on those left behind. She would never wish such a thing on D.J.'s loved ones. Her mother's voice crept into her head, rising like mist from the Shitty Childhood drawer of Leah's mind.

"People who really mean to kill themselves don't talk about it."

Leah had been sixteen and depressed, and had threatened to off herself in front of her mother.

"So, if you're gonna do it, get on with it and shut up."

Her mother had been right. Leah was still alive and her mother was not. But could she trust that D.J. was all talk and no action? Could she take that chance?

The laundry room door rattled. Leah yelped. She tried to push D.J. away but he held fast. Peyton's voice sounded from the other side of the door, thick with sleep. "Mommy?"

"Just a minute," Leah called.

Panicked, she pushed again at D.J.'s shoulders, trying to disentangle herself. "Let go," she hissed.

He raised his tear-stained face to hers, looking very much like a lost little boy. Her resolve weakened.

"Mommy?" Peyton called.

"Coming, sweetie." She looked down at him. "Okay," she whispered. "Please, D.J., don't hurt yourself. Nothing has to change right this second. We can talk later, okay?"

"You promise?" he said, a hopeful lift to his brow.

She touched his cheek. "Yes, of course. I promise. Let's not talk about this now. Everything is fine, okay? You go on home, and I'll see you tomorrow, okay?"

Finally, he released her. She tried not to sprint through the door. She didn't look back, slipping out of the room before he could respond.

CHAPTER

SIXTY-ONE

Connor stared at Rachel, keeping his face blank, saying nothing, letting her fill the silence.

"It sounds horrid, I know. What kind of mother hates her own child? But you don't know what it was like. Sebastian left me alone with him all day. I had no idea what I was doing. All he did was cry. It didn't matter how much I fed or changed him, whether he was hot or cold, lying flat or in a swing. He just cried, endlessly. Only Sebastian could get him to stop. Sebastian loved him. Instantly. Crazily. I didn't even matter anymore, except for whether or not I was fulfilling D.J.'s needs, which of course I couldn't."

"What about when he got older and was able to tell you his needs?"

She rolled her eyes. "His needs were endless, and when I didn't snap to, the tantrums were just unbelievable. When he was three, he chipped my tooth throwing a coffee mug at me because I wouldn't let him play with an electrical socket. When he was four, he poured my hot coffee on one of Sebastian's dogs. He liked that so much that he found other ways to hurt the dogs until we had to put one of them down and find homes for the others. He hurt me too. Endlessly. Always finding ways.

I was lucky that he was so small or he probably would have put me in the hospital."

"What did Sebastian think of all this?" Connor asked.

"It was a phase. Just a phase. He loved D.J. so much, he couldn't accept that he was . . . evil."

"That's a strong word to use about a four-year-old."

Rachel closed her eyes again, took another deep breath. "You weren't there," she said. She opened her eyes and looked at him, a pained expression on her face. "At five, in preschool, he pushed a girl off the jungle gym and cracked her skull open. He wasn't allowed back. Sebastian paid all of the girl's medical expenses and then some. The local public school wouldn't accept him into kindergarten. They wanted him tested." She used air quotes around the word *tested*.

"I told Sebastian that D.J. needed to be institutionalized, but Sebastian wouldn't hear of it. Not at first anyway. By the time I left, D.J. had become so violent that Sebastian began making arrangements to have him housed in a facility, to get mental health treatment."

"You still left," Connor said.

"I had to. I was so unhappy. D.J. going into a facility wasn't a given. Sebastian was very conflicted. The truth is that I read stories about mothers who killed their own children, and I understood why. I thought about how much easier our lives would be if D.J. were dead. Even if he were in a facility, Sebastian would always be drawn to him. Would always want to visit. Would always want to try bringing him home. When I started having those thoughts, I knew I had to leave. Then an opportunity arose: My mother died. She had cut me out of her will, which was fine since the only thing she owned was a ten-year-old Honda hatchback. But she had forgotten to remove me as the beneficiary of her life insurance policy. I had five hundred thousand dollars. Enough for a new life. So, one day while Sebastian was at work and D.J. was napping, I left. I never looked back. I went as far as I could get from that life, that place."

CHAPTER

SIXTY-TWO

SIXTEEN MONTHS EARLIER

Leah didn't see D.J. for a week. She felt relieved, then guilty for feeling relieved. What if he had really hurt himself like he said he would? No, she would have heard about it. Rachel didn't like talking about D.J. but surely she would have told Leah if he had done something terrible to himself. Leah reassured herself that wherever D.J. had gone or whatever he was doing—he was alive and unharmed. She couldn't ask anyone about him. It would look too suspicious. As far as anyone knew, Leah and D.J. had only ever been in the same room together a handful of times and that was only for social functions. She didn't even have his cell phone number.

The absurdity of it struck her. For three months she'd been more physically intimate with this kid than with anyone else in her entire life, Jim included, but she didn't even have his phone number. She knew he had a phone. Rachel had complained about having to put him on their plan when he arrived. It was less than a month later that she insisted he get his own plan. Mike didn't want him on theirs, she had said. It was one of the only times she had ever acknowledged D.J.'s presence in their home. The new phone was a prepaid one. Leah knew this because she'd had a brief conversation about it the first time she'd seen it in his hand. They'd talked about his phone, but he'd never given her the number. He'd been sneaking into her house nearly every night, and she had no way of reaching him.

Now she wondered if he was staying away on purpose—to make her worry, to make her feel terrible about the last time he'd been with her, for trying to break things off with him. She wondered how calculating he really was—had he meant it when he threatened suicide, or did he only say that to try to keep the affair going? How would she ever know?

She couldn't take the chance of him harming himself. She wasn't that monstrous.

By the time that week was over, she was torn between worry for D.J. and relief that she hadn't seen him all week. It felt so good not to worry constantly about being caught, not to wrestle with her guilt, not to spend hours castigating herself for every time they had sex. She hadn't realized how much energy she'd been expending by carrying on with him. For what? So she could feel better about having chosen a shitty husband? That week without D.J. just confirmed for her that she needed to end things. The whole thing was crazy. She'd lost her mind. Had some kind of break with reality. Temporary insanity. It wasn't worth her marriage, her family, her friendship with Rachel, her life as she knew it. She would have to break things off if he came back. She had no idea how, but she'd have to.

Of course, faced with him in the flesh once more, she could barely catch her breath. She hated her physical response to him. He snuck in on Monday night, after the kids were in bed, settling near her feet as she dozed on the couch. She woke to his hand sliding up her thigh. She sprung upright, heart pounding. "D.J.," she said.

He smiled at her. "Miss me?" he murmured. His hand reached between her legs. At once, she wanted to both push him away and melt into his touch. She did nothing. His smile froze on his face. His hand stopped moving. "Leah," he said. "I think we've been going about this the wrong way. I mean, I think I get what you were saying before."

Slowly, she shifted away from him. He pulled his hand back. She licked her dry lips. "Oh?" she said.

His gaze dropped to his lap. "We should get to know each other."

"Oh, D.J., no, I don't think—"

He cut her off, meeting her gaze with an earnest look on his face. "What's your favorite color?"

She smiled and touched his forearm. "Oh, you're sweet, but—"

"I want to know things about you. Tell me, what's your favorite color?"

"D.J.," she said. "Relationships are based on more than just knowing each other's favorite things."

"What's your husband's favorite color?"

She was taken aback by the question, but his steady gaze said he fully expected an answer. "Blue," she said.

"Rachel's your best friend, right? What's hers?"

"Red," Leah answered slowly. "But, D.J., that's not how relationships work, and this, what we're doing, this isn't a relationship."

His brow furrowed. "But you said everything was okay between us. That we could keep going. I want you, Leah, and I want to know more about you."

She couldn't deny the warmth she felt break open in her chest, even as she fought it. No man had ever said such things to her. Her husband had never even said such things. He had never shown that much interest in her.

"I want you."

She tried to be sensible, but while she was trying to put aside the schoolgirl euphoria he inspired in her, he draped himself over her, a snake coiling around its prey. His mouth began finding every bare inch of her skin, kissing softly, his tongue flicking, sending pleasurable tingles through her. She succumbed, pushing her concerns about the affair and D.J.'s neediness into her mental Deal with It Later drawer.

"So tell me," D.J. whispered. "What's your favorite color?"

He gathered information from then on, peppering their lovemaking with so many questions, Leah felt as though she were being interviewed or taking a survey on some dating site. She had no idea what he was going to do with all of the information he was cataloguing in his brain. Did he really need to know that her favorite type of food was Mexican? It wasn't like he was going to take her out to dinner. Did he need to know that her favorite flower was a carnation? It wasn't like he would or could ever get her flowers. But she answered his silly, schoolboy questions, all the while trying to figure a way out of this . . . she dared not call it a relationship. This entanglement.

The longer it went on, the more he insisted on knowing about her, the more insatiable he became. Not just for more inane facts about her, but for her body. What went on between them had lost all traces of lovemaking and degenerated into mere fucking, returning to the rutting type of sex they'd been having before she tried to break it off with him. He appeared every night, jumping on top of her and pumping into her with the relentless force of a freight train. It became unpleasant. He did things she didn't like, and he never asked if they were okay. It was as though he thought interviewing her afterward made it all okay. She started to wince at his touch. She didn't want to do it anymore. It was too dangerous, too stressful, and too hard on her body.

Then there was the biting.

The first time he did it, she howled, more from shock than pain. Instinctively, her hands pushed him off her. Chest heaving, she felt along the rounded contour of her shoulder for broken skin. It was intact, but sore and tender. Awkwardly, she hefted herself off the table and planted her feet on the tile floor. D.J. stood a couple of feet away, completely naked, staring at her in confusion.

"What the fuck?" he said.

A flush started at the roots of her hair. She stared at him as though he were a complete stranger—which he was, really. He'd given her his phone number the night he asked her about her favorite color, but she'd yet to use it. She couldn't risk it. She didn't know this boy, didn't know what circumstances had brought him here from somewhere that Rachel only vaguely referred to as "back East." Her voice trembled when she said, "Don't do that. I don't like it."

A hand closed over her breast. He pushed her back onto the table, his knee forcibly spreading her legs. "You don't like it when I mark you?" he whispered, his voice teasing, but with a low undertone of menace.

His chest was rock hard beneath her hands. "No, I don't. I'm serious. Don't do that anymore. I don't—I don't like it."

He pushed inside her. Her breath was gone. In her ear, he said, "I know what you like."

But she didn't like it any longer. Any of it. She just wanted it to stop. It was all too familiar. This man doing whatever he wanted to her whenever he wanted to do it, in her own home. The place that was supposed to be her sanctuary. It didn't matter what she said, what she wanted or didn't want. She had to take it. Wait for it to be over. Then clean herself up and stuff it all into her This Never Happened compartment.

It was making her sick. In fact, she came down with the flu for the first time in fifteen years. It was that day that she had finally had enough. It was a weekend. Jim was off fishing. Rachel had come over to borrow some children's Benadryl, taken one look at Leah, and immediately herded Peyton and Hunter out the door.

"I'll take all the kids to the zoo. You just get some rest."

Leah had been so happy. So blissfully happy to be completely and utterly alone in her misery. She lay on the couch in mismatched pajamas and a thick, baby-blue fuzzy robe. A nest of used tissues surrounded her. Cough-drop wrappers littered the floor beside the couch. She was taking a swig directly from the bottle of NyQuil when D.J. appeared in her living room.

"No," she said simply, her voice hoarse. Her throat felt like she had swallowed a pack of razor blades. She held up a hand, waved him off. "Go away. I'm sick. So sick." Her head fell back onto the couch cushion. Her eyes wouldn't stay open. Hands tugged at her pants. She batted them away. "No. Please. I'm sick."

Hot breath tickled the nape of her neck. D.J. said, "I know what will make you feel better."

"What will make me feel better is sleep."

"Not today."

What followed was one of the worst days of her life. She was too weak, too sick, and too exhausted to fight him off. Even when she cried and pleaded with him to stop, he ignored her. He used her. There was no other way to describe it. He took her clothes off, positioned her in all the ways that he wanted, and fucked her like he was trying to win some kind of contest. She was a rag doll. She was so relieved when he finished quickly, thinking he would leave, but he didn't. He stayed. He was young and virile. He could get it up several times in a matter of hours. Through her delirium she remembered how she used to take pleasure in this fact. This time, her body felt like a giant bruise, and every touch intensified the pain a thousandfold. When he finally finished, what seemed like an eternity later, he left her without a word, naked and bruised. She had never felt more like an inanimate object in her life. She didn't matter to him. Perhaps his threats of suicide had just been a ruse to keep her from ending things. She wished she had never entertained them at all.

She managed to pull her pajamas back on, but landed on the floor, which was where Jim found her an hour later.

"Leah," he said, his voice sharp with urgency. "Are you okay?"

Sobs erupted from her body as he lifted her onto the couch. "I'm sick," she cried. "Jim, I'm so sick."

He stared into her face, his bushy brows kinked with concern. "You look like hell. I'm taking you to the hospital."

She gripped his arms, fear seizing her. No one could see her like this. "Please, no. No hospital. I just need my bed. I just need to be left alone."

Jim looked around the room for the first time. "Where are the kids?"

"Rachel has them. Please, Jim. Just take me to bed."

"Let's get you cleaned up first. How about a bath?"

She couldn't think of anything more inviting than a hot bath, but then he might see the bite marks that D.J. had left on her. "No," she said. "I mean thank you, but right now I just want to lie down."

Within moments, he had her tucked into their bed, a cool, wet washcloth across her forehead. "I'll make you some tea," he said.

She caught his arm as he stood. "No," she said. "Please. Just stay here with me. Just lie down next to me. Please, Jim."

Without protest, he kicked off his shoes and lay down next to her. Leah's hand crept across to his side of the bed until it found his. She laced her fingers through his. "Thank you," she said.

For the next few days, Jim fussed over her—cooking for her, bringing her meals in bed, taking over the child care with help from Rachel. He stayed home from work to tend to her. For the first time since her daughter was born, Leah slept the days away with total abandon and watched whatever she wanted on television. Jim's constant presence at home kept D.J. at bay. Her husband seemed to enjoy her newfound clinginess. At night, after the kids were asleep, they lay in bed together talking like they had when they first started dating. As soon as she felt better, Leah initiated sex with him, subtly encouraging him to touch her and move in ways she had discovered she liked. Their lovemaking was slow and deliberate but also more passionate than it had ever been. She relished Jim's light touch after having been handled so roughly by D.J.

In the dark, he never noticed the marks the boy had left on her.

A week later, D.J. came back. She was ready for him. She used her scary mommy voice to tell him that it was over—for good this time—and that he was no longer welcome in her home. She braced herself for his backlash. For the begging, the tears, the threats of harm to himself. But it never came. He simply stared at her, his eyes dark and stormy, his silence so palpable, it felt like another person in the room. He spun on his heel and left. The slamming of her back door caused her to jump.

She should have known it wouldn't be that easy. It took two weeks, but she finally heard from him again. This time it was a series of text messages.

You think you're the only bored housewife I fucked? Talk to your neighbors.

I gave all you bitches syphilis.

Good luck explaining that shit to your asshole husband.

This development was completely unexpected. Leah had been pre-pared for him to threaten suicide again. She had even been prepared for him to threaten to tell everyone they knew. To out her. But this . . . she was not prepared for this. Was it true? Had he really been sleeping with multiple women?

Of course he had.

She had been a fool to be so easily manipulated by him—not to mention that she'd been stupid enough to have unprotected sex with him the entire time they were carrying on. A birth control shot didn't protect against STDs. Her gynecologist had made a point of reiterat-ing this fact to her each time she'd had the shot after Hunter was born. Each time she bristled at how ridiculous it was for the woman to even bring that up. Leah was as straight, narrow, and vanilla as they came. Her records clearly showed that. She'd never have to worry about STDs. She was a faithful wife, a loving mother.

Except that now she wasn't.

Now she was a liar, a cheater, and a colossal idiot. She wasn't an unwitting participant in a hidden camera show, she was just one of a long list of conquests. Had those conquests really been her neighbors?

Or was he just saying that to upset her more? Did she really have syphilis? What else had he given her?

She went four days without sleeping before breaking down and making an emergency appointment with her gynecologist. Once there, she couldn't bring herself to tell them that she had been having an affair. It would go in her records. There would be an official admission somewhere, even if no one would ever see it. So when the doctor asked her why she wanted to be tested for STDs, she blurted out that Jim had had unprotected sex with another woman. She wept through the invasive exam, ignoring the pity in the eyes of the staff. She had to know if D.J. was telling the truth.

She didn't have a sexually transmitted disease.

She was pregnant.

The greasy lubricant the doctor had used during the exam made her crotch stick to the paper covering on the exam table. Shifting only made the paper rustle and tear. Leah clutched the ends of the equally fragile paper gown over her breasts. "That's not possible," she told the doctor. "The shot, the birth control shot—I can't get—"

The doctor's smile was both pitying and condescending. "Your shot was due to be repeated two months ago. We called you several times but you never called back."

Stunned, Leah stared at the woman. The doctor kept talking—something about prenatal care and due dates. Leah heard nothing. The words kept swirling in her mind: *"two months ago."* Right about the time of her D.J.-induced brain fog.

She had no memory of getting dressed or checking out at the reception desk. Somehow, she ended up in her vehicle with an appointment reminder card in one hand that said she was due back at the doctor's office in one month.

Pregnant.

They'd told her the due date. She used the calendar on her phone, counting the weeks up, and was horrified to realize that the baby could be D.J.'s or Jim's. She'd never stopped having sex with her husband. Of course, she'd had sex with D.J. almost every day during that time, sometimes multiple times a day. The odds were in his favor, not Jim's.

She tried to concentrate on her chest moving up and down, on her breath going in and out of her body, because it felt like she couldn't get any air. Unfocused eyes took in the other vehicles in the parking lot coming and going, giant blurs of color. Women walked to and from the doctor's office. Some were visibly pregnant. Others were mere teenagers, just starting out. Probably there for their first exams or because they needed birth control for the first time. Tears spilled down her cheeks, and her vision slowly came back into focus. She watched a young girl with luxurious, straight brown hair flowing down her back exit the office, a brown paper bag clutched in one hand. An older woman followed behind her. As they got closer, Leah could see the resemblance. Mother and daughter. The mother said something, and the daughter tipped her head back and laughed uproariously.

Leah's hand pressed into her chest. She thought of her own mother, and for the first time, she truly understood why the woman had killed herself. Leah had always hated her. First, for allowing Leah's father to do so many terrible things to all of them, and then for abandoning them altogether. Why hadn't she stopped him? Leah always wondered. Why hadn't she stood up to him? Called the police? Pressed charges—just one time? Why hadn't she done everything she possibly could to protect her children? Why hadn't she packed them up and fled? Why hadn't she stayed with her children? Why hadn't she seen things through? Why hadn't she tried? It had seemed so cowardly and yet so fitting that her mother should simply wrap a rope around her neck and instantly get a free pass. No more pain. No more struggle. No more agonizing over whether or not to do the right thing. No more abuse. No more torture. No more.

Leah was worse than her mother. Her mother had found herself in an impossible situation. Getting out of an abusive marriage was not a simple thing. Her mother had had so many things going against her. But Leah. Leah had everything going for her. She had just chosen to throw it all away. Didn't that make her worse than her mother? Was she destined to follow in her mother's footsteps? Was that what this was about? Had she unwittingly sabotaged herself? Was it purposeful, on some subconscious level? What had she done? What was she doing to her children? She'd been so angry for so many years, blaming her mother for ruining her life, but here she was, actively ruining her children's lives, just in a different way.

She felt her old feeling of hopelessness like a hollowness in her stomach. Like her belly was filled with air—so full that there wasn't room for anything else, least of all nourishment. At that moment, the thought of absolute nothingness, the prospect of *no more*, was so tempting that it shook Leah to her core.

"I'm not my mother," she muttered to herself, which meant she had to make this work.

No one knew about the affair. She would deal with D.J. if he came back, but the entire thing would be stuffed into her This Never Happened drawer. The baby was Jim's. She wouldn't entertain any other possibility, even in her own mind. No one else would ever have reason to question her. No one would even believe that she would have had an affair. That was the beauty of having lived a postcard life up to that point. She had built trust. Besides, not all children were carbon copies of both parents. If this baby looked different, Leah could call on her parents' sides of the family. She only had a couple of grainy photos of her folks. No one really knew what they or their parents had looked like. She could do this. She could pretend that the whole entanglement with D.J. was simply a bad dream.

It almost worked.

She found out from Rachel a few days later that D.J. had gone back East. For months, as the baby grew inside her and she moved on with her life, she waited for a call or a text from him, even sometimes thought she heard him sneaking in, but he was gone. She and Jim and the kids fell into a peaceful rhythm of work and day care and preparing for their new arrival. By the time she started to show, Leah dared to feel almost happy. Just a little. She'd done something wild, crazy, wrong, and horrid. She'd made a mistake, but it was over. She would simply learn from it. She would move on. Her Christmas-card life would remain intact.

But then a few weeks before she gave birth, D.J. came back.

She thought she had seen him coming and going from Rachel's backyard, but when she asked Rachel—casually, of course—if he was back, Rachel said no. Then one day, Leah was doing dishes after the kids had gone to bed when she heard his footsteps. Either he wasn't as stealthy as he had been or she had just learned to identify the sound of him approaching. Her heart started pounding so hard, she could feel it pulsing in her temples. Little Tyler tumbled in her stomach. She turned to see D.J. standing just a few feet away, looking thinner, but as model-like and gorgeous as ever in a fitted blue T-shirt and torn jeans.

"You're not welcome here," she said, trying to keep her voice firm and not betray the panic she felt. She had grown so large with this pregnancy she could barely climb steps. There was no way she could endure his advances—not that she had any desire to anymore. The thought of him touching her made her physically ill. But she needn't have worried.

His eyes fell from her face to her burgeoning belly. Confusion gave way to something she could only describe as disgust. He grimaced as though he had smelled something rancid. For a split second she thought she saw tears gather in his eyes. He gestured toward her. "You . . . you got fat."

He said the word *fat* in a broken whisper, as though he were in great pain and it hurt to speak.

She almost laughed. Had he never seen a pregnant woman before? "I'm pregnant," she said.

His eyes went from her belly to her eyes and back to her belly. "Preg—you mean you're having a baby?"

Something in the way he looked at her stomach—the way most people looked at cockroaches or dog excrement—made the hair on her arms stand up. She curled both hands around her belly. Tyler pushed a tiny hand against the inside of her distended abdomen. "Yes," Leah said. "A baby."

"That's why you left me."

She shook her head. "No. I didn't leave you. D.J., I broke things off because what we were doing was wrong. We were hurting everyone— my husband, my kids, your aunt—"

He looked puzzled momentarily. "My aunt?"

"Rachel. What we were doing was not fair to anyone. You're so young. I'm married. I have a family. Rachel is my best friend."

His fists clenched at his side. Leah took a step to the side, trying to put something between them. The kitchen table or a chair at least. "Fuck her," he snarled. "And fuck you too."

Her body turned to stone. Only baby Tyler moved freely inside her, completely unaffected by the tension locking every muscle she had. Something old and hideous rose from the Shitty Childhood compart- ment of her brain. A warning. It told her she should run as far and as fast as she could. Back then, she had had nowhere to go. The evil took what it wanted, leaving hopelessness and depression to grow inside her like a malignancy. Now she felt the warning at her back like a hurricane- force wind, pushing her, urging her to get away from this boy. She wasn't aware she had even moved until a doorknob poked her back.

D.J. said, "You'll pay."

Then he was gone.

CHAPTER

SIXTY-THREE

"You moved to California," Connor said. "You left D.J. and Sebastian behind, took your mother's life insurance settlement, and came out here."

Rachel nodded. "Yes. I got an apartment, lived as frugally as I could. Eventually, I started college, that's where I met Mike. He asked me to marry him in my sophomore year. He was graduating, had a job offer here. I said yes, we moved here, and the rest, as they say, is history. Sebastian never tried to find me. I think he knew that I wasn't meant for that life."

"But you married someone else. You have children."

"It was completely different with Mike and the girls."

"You mean it was easier."

She bristled. "No. I mean I was older, wiser, and more self-sufficient. I didn't need to make decisions out of desperation. I was ready to be a wife and a mother."

"You never told your husband about your past?"

"No. I didn't see any point in it. I didn't think that Mike would understand."

No shit, Connor thought, but kept silent. "You never worried that D.J. might come looking for you one day?"

Rachel shifted in her chair. "When I met Mike I started to worry, so I called one of Sebastian's neighbors, an older woman I had been friendly with. She told me that D.J. had been sent away. Evidently, there was an incident where he turned on Sebastian and burnt him badly. After that, Sebastian put him away. Even in an institution, he was problematic. I didn't worry after that. I just thought he would never get out. I thought I was safe."

Connor sighed and spread his hands. "And yet here we are. What happened?"

"He showed up at my house one day. I had no idea who he was. It was so unexpected. He said he just wanted to talk. I made him coffee—Mike was at work. The girls were at pre-K. I thought if I talked to him, he would go away."

"But he didn't."

"He said he needed a place to stay. Just until he got on his feet. I thought about paying him to go away or paying for a hotel room, but I don't work and Mike controls the finances. So we agreed I'd ask Mike if he could stay above our garage temporarily, get him a phone, as long as the story was that he was my nephew from an estranged brother."

"Your husband bought it?"

"Why wouldn't he? He wasn't happy about it, but he's never home so it really had no effect on him. He allowed it, but he never liked D.J."

"And you? Did you like him?"

She shuddered. "I didn't know what to think. I thought the nice-guy thing was an act. I saw him act differently around other people. I kept waiting for his other side to show, but he lived with us for months and nothing happened. He told me he'd been released from the institution at eighteen, and I thought if they released him maybe he'd changed. Maybe the inpatient treatment had worked."

"Did he ask you why you left?"

"Of course he did. That was why he came. I told him that I was young and stupid and not ready to be a mother, and that I knew Sebastian would take better care of him than I ever could."

"Did Sebastian know he'd come to see you?"

"Sebastian financed it. Hired a PI to find me, flew him out here, but told him if he chose to stay, he was on his own, which is why he needed a place to live."

"You talked to Sebastian?"

"Yes. I asked him to take D.J. back, but he said D.J. was an adult and he couldn't force him to do anything. He said he deserved to know about his mother." She humphed. "'About' his mother, he said. Like I'm some kind of monster."

Connor said nothing.

"So he was here and then one day he left. I don't know where he went or what happened to him."

Connor raised a brow. "He just left? Like mother, like son?"

She frowned. "That's not fair."

"You didn't force him out because he exposed himself to Molly and Maya?"

He didn't think she could get any paler, but her skin went a shade whiter.

"No more lies, Mrs. Irving, remember?"

"Oh my God. Please. I didn't want my husband to find out."

CHAPTER

SIXTY-FOUR

Derrick readily agreed to take Claire from the vet's office to Connor's house so she could get her car, and even followed her home, just to make sure she arrived without incident. Derrick waited out front in his car while Claire ran inside to gather some things before she returned to the hospital. D.J. was waiting in her bedroom. Some visceral part of her sensed him as she crossed the threshold, but it was too late to retreat. She was already fully through the door. Her body lunged toward her dresser where her .380 rested in a fake, hollow book. But he sprung out from behind the door and snagged her around the waist. Her elbow whipped behind her, trying to make contact with his face, and missed.

Then she was flying through the air. She braced herself for a hard landing, for the awful loss of breath. She remembered well the feeling of having a man on top of her after she'd had the wind knocked out of her. But she landed on her bed, face in the pillows, the dizzying scent of Connor that still clung to the sheets flooding her senses.

As it had in the river, her consciousness tried to remove itself from her body, this imperfect vessel that had taken so much abuse over the years. Her "No" came out as an actual snarl and she flipped onto her back.

"No?" D.J. had stopped in his tracks at the foot of her bed, fists clenched, the expression on his ruined face equal parts surprise and amusement.

She took a second to study him, revulsion sending bile into the back of her throat. He looked like something out of a horror movie. His once perfectly chiseled features were shredded and bloody. A two-inch gash sliced his forehead. His right cheek bore three red puncture marks that looked as though they went straight through to the inside of his mouth. On his left side, a flap of skin along his jawline hung down, exposing bone and bright-pink tissue. The side of his neck bore several puncture marks and some deep gashes where Wilson had tried to pull the flesh from his body. Dried blood had turned his white tank top almost entirely reddish brown. She could not imagine how badly his wounds hurt, and she felt a deep gratitude toward Wilson for the damage he'd inflicted on the monster before her.

"Why are you here?" she asked him.

He tried to smile, but one half of his face was paralyzed. The side that worked winced in pain. He made a guttural noise—pain and rage. "Before I kill you, you're going to give me what I want."

Slowly, Claire pushed herself up on her elbows. From her periphery, she tried to gauge how quickly she could make it to the gun on the dresser. There was no chance. He didn't look like he had a weapon, but she knew he didn't need one. His rage was his weapon. Claire was well acquainted with that kind of rage, and she had no desire to be on the receiving end of it ever again. He was high on adrenaline. It numbed most of his pain. It would make him stronger, amplify his rage, which, Claire guessed, even at its baseline, was deadly.

She could take a beating. The things that had been done to her had amounted to nothing short of systematic torture, and she had survived it. But the man before her was likely to go straight for the kill. She had to be careful. She had never expected to find herself at the mercy of a psychopath ever again, but here she was, and she had to survive. Her heart pumped so hard that every beat seemed to jar her entire body. Her bones vibrated with fear and the terrible awareness of what this beast was going to do to her.

This time, her "No" came out squeaky and strangled.

D.J. took a step toward the bed. A car horn sounded from outside. He stopped and looked back toward the door, as if he could see out front from there. "What the fuck is that?"

She didn't answer. The beep came again.

He put a knee on the bed and reached for her. Her body betrayed her. She scrambled back, pressing herself against the headboard, hands raised. She thought she could take it—his hands on her—but she couldn't. She was dangerously close to shutting down completely. "It's my friend," she choked out. "He—he's outside. He's waiting for me."

"He brought you here?"

"Yes."

"You have a choice. Get rid of him or he dies too."

With a death grip on her right triceps, he yanked her off the bed and led her to her front door. His instructions were to get rid of Derrick from the doorway. She was not allowed to signal him in any way, or to mouth anything. Her heart sank the farther they got from her .380. She was both relieved and disappointed when Derrick drove off after just a wave and a stiff smile from her. But then she remembered Derrick had no idea of all that was really going on. He knew she had helped save the Holloway and Irving children after the accident on Saturday; he knew Brianna had been mugged and Wilson had been injured, but he had no idea that any of those things were related to the Soccer Mom Strangler case. When she had asked him to take her to get her vehicle, she had only said that with everything that had happened in the last few days, she would feel better if he followed her to her house.

With a sinking heart, she watched Derrick drive away. D.J. dragged her into the living room. He pushed her and she fell, tripping over the coffee table and falling awkwardly on her side, half on the couch and half off. Her knee throbbed as she dragged herself into a sitting position onto the couch.

He started pacing. Fresh blood oozed from two of the puncture wounds in his neck. If he got close enough to hurt her, she would go right for his wounds. She'd rip that flap of flesh right off his face if she could. She just had to hope that the pain would not simply fuel his deadly rage.

"It was you," he said. He stopped and pointed at her. "You were in the river with Leah that day. Not your twat sister."

Claire thrust her chin at him. "You hurt my sister, didn't you? You put her in the dumpster."

"I'll do worse to you if you don't tell me the truth."

"Did you hit her?"

"No. The dumb bitch fell backward and hit her head. All I wanted to know was why she let Leah die. I grabbed her. She told me to stop. Then she said Leah was dead when she got to the car. I knew she was lying. She changed her story. I kept telling her to just tell me the truth. I was sure she killed Leah. That she could have saved her, but she just didn't. She kept saying, 'No, it wasn't me, I wasn't there, it wasn't my fault.' And I'm like, what? What do you mean, you weren't *there*? But then instead of answering, she tried to get away, and she fell. Just, like, out cold. I could've killed her. How was I going to figure out what she was talking about now? But then I did: I've been watching you two for a couple of days now, seen how far up each other's asses you are. I have no idea why, but you two were running some kind of game. Lying about the whole thing. Christ only knows why, but it was really you who swam out to the car."

"She was protecting me," Claire explained. "I didn't want to be in the press."

Claire felt a searing stab of guilt. She blinked back tears.

"So you were there."

"We both were," Claire explained. "But only I swam out there."

"You saved the kids. It was you."

Claire nodded. He started pacing again. A terrible half grimace stretched across what was left of his face. He stopped, slightly out of breath, and pointed an accusatory finger at her. "You let her die."

It felt like a slap. This was about Leah. All of it. He was the one who had been stalking Leah. He had stalked her, raped her, then let her live. He was obsessed with Leah. He'd probably believed it was reciprocated. Claire knew better than anyone how deep these psychopaths' fantasies could run. Reality became a vague, easily discarded suggestion. All that mattered, all that existed, was whatever their diseased minds had conjured, and woe to anyone who did not fully subscribe to it. Claire had to be careful what she said about Leah, lest she contradict whatever fantasy he'd created in his mind.

"It was too late to save her," Claire lied.

"No, no. It wasn't. You saved the kids. You could have saved her."

Claire's cell phone beeped. If D.J. noticed it, he didn't let on.

Claire put her hands up. "No, listen to me. She was in the front seat. She was the only one in the front seat. She took the brunt of the impact. Her internal injuries were extensive."

"You're lying."

She shook her head vehemently. "I swear to you, I am not lying. Why would I lie? You think I wanted her to die? You think I didn't try to get her out? You think I enjoyed watching her die? Having to tell her children that their mom didn't make it?"

He became very still. She hoped she had the attention of whatever piece of him that was capable of processing logic and reason.

"I tried to get her out. The locks were jammed. She was in the front. It filled up with water fast. So fast. Her—her injuries were so bad that she—she was disoriented. I don't even think she knew where she was or what was going on. I'm sorry that she's gone, but please know that I did everything I could." Claire added, "Leah meant a lot to you."

"She was mine," he said. "She came back. She came back to me. She promised never to leave again. She promised me. I came back for her, but she was having a baby. She chose the baby over me. I told her she would pay unless she came back to me. Then she called me. I was with her last week."

Claire tried not to grimace at his language. He talked about Leah as though she were an object he owned. Claire doubted very much that things had happened the way he described them. But there would be no penetrating his delusions. "I'm sorry," Claire said.

"If she was hurt so bad, you should have saved her first," he insisted.

Her cell phone beeped again. His eyes flicked around the room, but he didn't try to find the source of the noise. "You got all those kids out; you could have gotten her out."

Claire wondered if anything she said would satisfy him. Leah hadn't given Claire a choice. But telling D.J. the truth wouldn't feed the fantasy he had so lovingly constructed and violently cultivated. The truth could be disastrous for Claire. The problem was that she had no idea if anything she said would make a difference. He was likely going to kill her no matter what. She needed more time. That was her only hope. When she didn't answer his texts, Connor would come looking for her. Then she would have a chance. Her cell phone beeped again.

"I told you, she was really out of it when I got to the car. She was barely conscious. The locks were jammed. I couldn't get the doors opened."

D.J. loomed over her, one fist clenched. "That's not true. You're lying to me. If the doors wouldn't open, how did you get the kids out?"

"Through the sunroof," Claire said.

"So, you got those stupid kids out through the sunroof and you still left her in the car to die."

"No," Claire said. "Leah lost consciousness. There was no way I could have gotten her out through the sunroof."

He stepped closer. "You left her to die. Did she cry?"

"No, no. She wasn't crying."

"She begged you to help her, didn't she?"

"No," Claire said.

His voice was growing more and more high-pitched. "She wanted to live. We were going to be together. I know she wanted to live. You killed her."

"No."

"She begged you to help her, you ignored her, and she died. That makes you a killer."

"Listen to me—she was very badly injured. She didn't . . . suffer. I promise you, she didn't beg. She was very disoriented."

"You heard her last words," D.J. said. "What were they?"

Claire racked her brain, trying to figure out a way to stall him that wouldn't result in him beating the hell out of her. She thought about all the things Connor had told her about Leah's case. "You know," she told him.

His expression loosened. "Know what?"

"You were the last person to talk to her."

He shook his head. "No, I wasn't. I hadn't talked to her—"

"Your call was the last call she took before she crashed. You used a—what's it called? A burner phone?"

He swallowed. More blood oozed from the puncture wounds in his neck. "Yeah, I guess. A prepaid phone."

"Yes. A prepaid phone. The police call it a burner. What did she say to you before she crashed her car?"

He looked nonplussed. "I didn't talk to her."

"You didn't call her on Saturday morning? Right before she went into the river?"

"No, it wasn't me. I—"

"Did she know about the other women?"

"What?"

"The women you killed. Did Leah know?"

Her cell phone beeped once more. This time he lunged for her, his hands everywhere at once as he clawed at her pockets. She was starting to hyperventilate when he finally came away with it. He stood over her again, staring at the phone's screen. "Who the fuck is Connor?"

"He's my boyfriend," she said.

He read off the texts: *"Did you get home ok" "Where are you?" "Please answer me. Are you ok?"* Then he thrust the phone at her. "Text him back. Tell him you're okay."

"But—"

"Shut up."

He sat on the coffee table across from her and held the phone out. "Keep it where I can see it. I want to see what you're typing. And don't hit 'Send' until I see what you typed."

Her hands trembled as she took it from him. There had to be a way to alert Connor without D.J. realizing what she was doing. She punched out the letters as slowly as she could so he wouldn't realize she was up to something. When she was finished, he snatched the phone from her. "Who the fuck are Miranda and Simon?"

"They're our friends. If he thinks I'm here alone, he'll come over. He doesn't want me alone after what happened with my sister. You said to get rid of him."

He looked at her like he wasn't sure whether or not to believe her. She braced herself for his attack, but instead he pressed "Send" and then looked up at her. "Now you're going to stop wasting my time. You killed Leah, and you're going to pay."

CHAPTER

SIXTY-FIVE

"I shouldn't have to remind you that lives are at stake here, Mrs. Irving. Did D.J. expose himself to your girls? That's why you kicked him out?"

More sobs shook her body. Connor let her cry it out again for another minute or so. He used the break to surreptitiously text Claire for a third time. She should be back at the hospital by now.

Rachel said, "I had run over to Leah's. I needed eggs for something. I was baking. The girls were watching TV in the TV room. Dylan came in to the kitchen to grab something to eat. They saw him and went in to tell him not to disturb my baking stuff. He—he told them to shut up. Then Maya said she would tell me that he was being rude to them. He said of course they would because they were . . . they were little . . . little twats just like me. Then he—then he took out his, you know, his . . ." Her voice seemed to fade, as though she'd suddenly developed laryngitis. She swallowed several times.

"His penis?" Connor supplied.

She nodded. Her voice came back sounding scratchy. "Yes," she said. "He, uh, urinated all over the kitchen. Like a dog. I walked in on the tail end of it. The girls were screaming. He was . . . he was laughing.

Enjoying himself. I told him to leave before I called the police. I told him he was no longer welcome."

"He just left?"

"Yeah. I don't know where he went. He was gone for a few days. Then he came back and he was back over top of the garage like nothing ever happened. So I called Sebastian, and I told him either he convinced D.J. to return to the East Coast or I was going to call the police. I don't know how Sebastian did it, but D.J. was gone the next day. Sebastian called me the day after to let me know D.J. was back with him and to make sure I wasn't going to turn him in for indecent exposure. That was it."

"But that wasn't it, was it?"

She leaned forward, her expression earnest. "But it was—for me. I thought he was gone. Then my friend called, about six or seven months ago. She said Sebastian was in the hospital. He'd had a heart attack. She didn't know where D.J. was. I checked over our garage. He'd been squatting there. I don't know for how long. I waited for him, told him he couldn't stay."

"And he left again?"

She shrugged. "He was upset about something. He didn't even seem to care that I wanted him to leave. He said he wouldn't bother me again."

"That was it? Until today, when we showed up here. The overturned chair, the broken glass. He'd been here."

She drew in a deep, ragged breath.

"He came after you."

She dabbed at a new onslaught of tears. "He started to. He threw some things. Called me every name in the book. Then you guys knocked. He took off, that was it."

"What did he want?"

"His things. He'd left some things in his room, but I'd given them to Goodwill. He had broken into the garage apartment on Sunday

347

night, but he didn't find whatever he was looking for so he came back today. When he realized I had given his things away, he went out of his head."

Sunday night. The night Jade was killed. Connor's cell phone buzzed. He pulled his phone out and stared at the text from Claire, feeling a cold sweat break out across his forehead: *I made it home okay. You don't need to come after work. My friend Miranda is here. Simon dropped her off. Love you.*

Rachel continued, "But I don't know where he is now, I swear."

Phone clutched in his hand, Connor stood, knocking his chair to the ground. "That's okay," he said, sprinting toward the door. "I do."

Outside, he fumbled with his car keys. He dialed Stryker and pressed his phone to his ear. "Stryke, where are you? You need to send everyone to Claire's house now. Send the nearest patrol car immediately. I'll meet you there. He's got her. The Strangler has Claire. They're at her house."

Stryker said, "Wait, what? What are you talking about? I found D.J. North's apartment, if you can call it that. He's not here."

Connor's car roared to life and he tore out of the parking space. "Because he's with Claire." Connor gave him the gist of the text message she had sent. "Miranda Simon," he said. "Stryke, don't you remember? She's the girl Reynard Johnson strangled. Claire witnessed it. Claire and I just talked about this the other day when Jade was killed. She's trying to tell me that something is wrong. That he's there with her. I'm only a few minutes away. I'm on my way."

CHAPTER

SIXTY-SIX

Claire pressed her back into the couch, trying to get as far away from D.J. as possible. The overpowering scent of his blood and sweat was nauseating. He leaned closer to her, and she drew her knees up. He slapped them down. "Don't move."

Frozen in place, her knees halfway to the floor and halfway to her chest, she stared at his mangled face. Her abs ached.

"Please," Claire said. "I'm telling you, I didn't kill her. She wouldn't have survived the crash anyway, even if I had gotten her out first. I told you, her injuries were extensive."

"You're lying."

She was a broken record, but she just had to keep spinning her wheels until Connor arrived. "No, I'm not. She had internal injuries from the crash. Bad internal injuries."

He sprang up, a guttural shriek ripping from his torn throat, and lunged for her, hands outstretched. Instinctively, her own hands shot upward, but it was too late. His hands wrapped around her throat, crushing her windpipe. She'd been choked before by her abductor, but D.J.'s hands felt ten times more powerful. Lungs burning, she fought, kicking against him with her feet as he climbed atop her. He straddled her easily. His angry, mangled face swam in her vision. Her sight dimmed, but not before her brain registered once more the flap of skin dangling from his bloodied cheek. Her hands found his face, searching for the edge of the torn flesh. Seizing on it, she pulled as hard as she could until something wet and slick came off in her hand. Blood poured through her fingers. His howl cut right through her. It was the sound of an animal caught in a trap. For a few precious seconds, his grip around her neck loosened. She reached up and tried to pull his hands away altogether. Unfortunately for her, this only further inflamed him. His hands were slippery with blood as they tightened once more around her throat. They struggled until Claire had no strength left in her body, and every muscle felt permanently clenched. Even as blackness filled her field of vision, her fingers scrabbled for his face again, searching for anything soft, open, or raw she could dig into.

Then Connor's voice cut through the room. "Police," he shouted. "Hands behind your head. Down on your knees. Now!"

D.J. froze. Slowly, he removed his hands from her throat, pulled away, and stood up straight. Claire rolled away from him, coughing and massaging her throat. Connor stood in the doorway, his gun drawn, sighted on D.J.'s chest.

"Who the fuck are you?"

"Sacramento PD. Hands behind your head. Get down on the ground."

D.J. said, "Fuck you."

Claire wasn't sure what happened first, Connor's gun firing or D.J. rushing him, but the thunderclap of a bullet exploded across the room. Instinctively, Claire covered her head and closed her eyes tightly. When she opened them only seconds later, the men were rolling around on the floor, a blur of angry, flailing limbs, punctuated by grunts. A slick of blood had formed beneath them, streaking as they thrashed in it. Claire assumed—and hoped—it was D.J.'s blood and not Connor's. She couldn't tell if Connor's shot hit him, but as D.J. had been with

Claire, his adrenaline made him stronger and more deadly than he might normally be.

Claire stood and staggered toward them on weak, wobbly legs. The room seemed to tip to the side every couple of steps. Her eyes searched the floor for Connor's Glock. Before her, the men rolled from one side of the room to the other, knocking against the furniture. Framed photos and lamps shattered on the floor, leaving glassy debris in the blood, a macabre mosaic. Claire fell to her knees and looked under the coffee table. That was always the first place she looked when she couldn't find Wilson's ball or his rope or his beloved stuffed squirrel.

Connor's Glock was there. Her left hand closed over the handle. She got to her feet again, took a shaky shooter's stance, and aimed the weapon in the direction of the men, her finger resting along the side of the barrel. She was an excellent shot, but she was anything but steady and couldn't risk hitting Connor. With the two of them fighting, there were too many moving parts. She needed to get D.J. away from Connor.

She waited until Connor was on the bottom. Her chest heaving, she raised the gun high above her head, angled away from them, and fired off a shot. The men froze. D.J. straightened his back so he could look at her. Without hesitation, she sighted back in on him and fired two shots into his right upper chest.

His eyes widened with shock. He looked down at the holes in his body. In the seconds it took him to dip his chin, she strode across the room, gun at her side, and kicked him square in the chest. He toppled off Connor with a heavy thud, landing awkwardly. He groaned and flopped around like a half-paralyzed, landed fish.

Connor scrambled to all fours and flipped D.J. onto his stomach. "D.J. North, you have the right to remain silent." He wrenched the man's arms back and squeezed his wrists together. Tearing a zip tie from his rear pocket, he secured his wrists, then continued Mirandizing the man. When he'd finished, he turned away and left him there.

Connor and Claire met in the middle of the room on their knees in a pool of the man's blood. Their embrace was as strong as stone. Claire buried her face in Connor's neck, wanting to smell him, not D.J.'s foul sweat or the coppery scent of blood. Connor loosened his hold on her and pulled back so he could examine her face and her throat. "Are you hurt?" they asked each other at the same time. They answered one another by feel. Claire wept with relief when she was satisfied that Connor had no bullet holes in him. Connor studied the bruises already beginning to appear on her throat. She could see the guilt and regret in his face. "It's okay," she said. "I'm okay."

He pulled her back in, squeezing her hard against his body. She pressed her face into his throat. Relief made her weak, like she hadn't eaten in days. "Just don't let go," she breathed. "Don't let go."

"Never," he said. "I'm never letting go."

CHAPTER
SIXTY-SEVEN
ONE WEEK LATER

Whereas Jade's funeral was a citywide affair with all the pomp and circumstance befitting an officer killed in the line of duty, Leah Holloway's funeral was a simple graveside service with a pastor presiding. The press was still hungry for any news about her, but they were more concerned with the Soccer Mom Strangler having been taken into custody, so only a few members of the media waited near the exit of the cemetery, hoping for a good shot or perhaps an interview with one of the mourners.

A few short readings from the Bible and Leah Holloway was lowered into the ground. Jim stood beside his mother, looking shell-shocked. He wore a brown suit that looked like it had been in his closet unused for the last ten years. His hair was damp and combed to the side. Connor couldn't help but wonder if his mother had dressed him and brushed his hair. Peyton stood beside her father, her hand held loosely in his. A few feet away, Hunter sat beside a tombstone, knees drawn to his chest, pouting. Baby Tyler slept soundly in his stroller next to Mrs. Holloway. On the other side of the coffin stood Ashley Copestick and two other of Leah's coworkers Connor and Stryker had spoken with. Hanging back on the periphery was Rachel Irving, dressed in a smart black pantsuit, hair tied tightly back from her face, arms crossed over her chest.

Claire and Connor stood hand in hand behind the Holloways. Only Ashley wept, the sound unsettling in the sunny valley. It seemed a strange, almost griefless affair, but Connor felt a wave of sadness wash over him. By all accounts, Leah Holloway had tried hard to maintain what she felt was a perfect life. A two-parent family. Parents who were sober, hardworking, and child centered. She had doted on her children, that much was clear. Hapless though Jim Holloway was, Leah had clearly been the center of his universe. He was rudderless without her. In spite of Leah's efforts, her life had ended in scandal and tragedy. It was everything she never wanted.

After the service, Claire lingered, talking quietly to Peyton as the other grown-ups exchanged awkward goodbyes. Seeing Rachel walking slowly toward her car, Connor hurried after her. He caught up with her just as she reached the vehicle, and he leaned against her door so she couldn't get away.

"Excuse me," she said.

"It took me a while to figure it out," he told her.

She stood stock-still, eyes fixed on Connor's shoes as though if she kept perfectly motionless, she might cease to exist or he would forget that she was there.

"It was you," he went on. "You were the last person to speak to Leah."

"You can check my phone records," she replied in a low voice. "There are no calls to her that day."

"Not from your phone, no," Connor conceded. "But you said you'd been going through D.J.'s things, getting rid of them. D.J. had a burner phone, one he hadn't used in months. One he left at your house. You were going through his things and found it and turned it on. You saw Leah's number in there, and you called it. Or maybe you didn't recognize it as her number at first. Maybe you just dialed it and she picked up. She must have been surprised to hear your voice."

Rachel said nothing.

"So it was you, something you said, that drove her into the river—with your kids in the car."

Rachel shook her head.

Connor said, "It bothered me from day one that she tried to kill your kids too. She had a chance to leave them at the gas station, but she didn't. She spoke with you for over ten minutes, during which this woman, who never drank, downed three-quarters of a bottle of vodka, and then she got behind the wheel and tried to kill both your kids."

Rachel's voice was low and hard. "She was going into that river no matter what. She had a psychotic break."

"I forgot, you're an expert on psychotic people."

Rachel's mouth hung open.

"So it didn't bother you that your best friend tried to kill your kids?"

She rolled her eyes. "Of course it did. I never thought she would do something like that. I never thought—I mean, I—"

"What did you say to her?"

Rachel raised her head. Her eyes shone with tears, but her face was lined with revulsion. She looked as though she were holding back a shudder. "It wasn't anything I said."

CHAPTER

SIXTY-EIGHT

Leah was herding Peyton into the smelly gas station restroom when her phone rang. She pulled it out of her purse and looked at the screen. It said: "Lilly, Accounting." It was the prepaid cell phone D.J. had bought when Rachel took him off her plan. She had programmed it into her own phone under a fake work contact. That way if he ever called or texted, and Jim, Rachel, or anyone else saw it, they'd think it was a woman from work contacting her.

He hadn't called her from it in over a year. Not since their unceremonious breakup. Not since she risked everything to be rid of him, only to be shocked when he disappeared entirely. When she was due to give birth to Tyler, and D.J. returned violently and unexpectedly, he'd had a new phone with an East Coast area code. Leah hadn't programmed it as a contact, deciding that if anyone saw missed calls or texts from a Pennsylvania number, they might believe it was a wrong number, a case of mistaken identity. He'd been calling and texting from the Pennsylvania number for months, ever since his harassment campaign began. But she instantly recognized the old number.

She hit "Answer" and pressed the phone to her ear as they passed through the door. Peyton dutifully made for the first stall. The smell of piss and industrial cleanser burned Leah's nostrils.

"Why are you calling me?" she said into the phone.

But the voice on the other end was not D.J.'s. It was a female voice, one so unexpected that it took Leah's breath away. "Why is your number in D.J.'s phone?"

Leah's heart stopped. Then it seemed to explode into action, its beats coming so hard and fast she feared it might burst through her chest and fly away, a heart-shaped hummingbird. "It's his old phone," Leah said stupidly.

"It's you," Rachel hissed. "Leah."

She said Leah's name like a curse, like she was casting a spell. A dark, damning spell.

"It's not what you think."

Before her, Peyton carefully tore off foot-long strips of toilet paper and placed them on the toilet seat. They kept falling off, one side, then the other. Furtively, she glanced at Leah, and Leah realized that the girl was expecting to be scolded. She was like a dog waiting to be struck. Was Leah *that* mom?

"Not what I think?" Rachel snorted. Her voice was thick and throaty. Leah recognized the tone. Rachel wasn't much of a crier, but a few times in the eight years Leah had known her, she'd seen her overcome with painful, raw emotion. When Maya was mistakenly diagnosed with leukemia at three years old, and again, when they found out it was a mistake. The day she found condoms in Mike's suitcase upon his return from a business trip. He'd mollified her by telling her his notoriously womanizing colleague had thrown them into Mike's bag when the man's wife unexpectedly showed up at their hotel. Leah was surprised that Rachel had accepted the "holding it for a friend" defense, but who was she to criticize? You did what you had to do to keep your family intact. You believed what you had to. You looked the other way.

You became a master of self-deception. Now, the sobbing rasp was back, and Leah had a bad feeling about what was to come. A very bad feeling.

Finally, Peyton sat on the toilet. She stared up at Leah, face flushed. "It won't come out," she said in a tiny voice.

"Shhh," Leah said. She turned her back on the girl. Her free hand fidgeted with the strap of her purse, fingers bumping against Alan Wheeler's bottle of vodka.

"Do you think I'm stupid, Leah?"

Leah's hand curled around the neck of the bottle. She had something on Rachel, she reminded herself. That was the whole point of the hairbrush and getting the sample from D.J. She'd been trying to figure a way out of the whole thing with D.J. A way to get rid of him without completely destroying her life. She was willing to give up her marriage to Jim if she had to, but she had to keep her kids and her job. She had figured that the only way to get rid of D.J. once and for all was to come clean to Jim and all the world about everything. It would be the hardest, most painful thing she had ever done, but once everyone knew, she could go to the police freely. She could go to work removing him from her life once and for all. But she needed Rachel in her corner.

She had the DNA test, she knew Rachel's secret, that D.J. was her son. She must have been incredibly young. Given him up for adoption. There was no shame in that, but still, Rachel had felt the need to lie about his true identity—even to her own husband, from what Leah could gather. Obviously, she didn't want people to know. Leah had intended to use that fact as leverage, if she had to. She would keep Rachel's secret if Rachel would forgive her for what she had done. Leah would need *one* friend. Now, though, it was clear from Rachel's tone that any hope of remaining friends was long gone. Now, Leah was thinking she might have to use the secret to combat whatever threats Rachel was about to level against her. Leah knew Rachel. Knew she could and would be vindictive. "She has a mean streak," Jim had always said. She had, in fact, outed Mike's Lothario colleague to his wife at an office party six months after discovering the condoms. With a smile on her face, she'd told the woman to make sure her husband kept his condoms out of Mike's things. "I mean, they're golf buddies, not frat brothers. It's bad enough Mike has to hear about every dirty tramp your husband fucks—how they do it, where, how many times. Honestly, you guys may be into the whole open marriage thing, but some of us are just plain old vanilla."

The woman hadn't had an open marriage. Hadn't had a clue about her husband's infidelities. And she was eight months pregnant. The whole thing had caused quite a stir at work for Mike. His colleague left the company. Mike had come down hard on Rachel for the incident. To his face, she'd acted wide-eyed and innocent, remorseful and repentant, but to Leah she was devilish and gleeful. The whole thing had been calculated on Rachel's part. It had been very much on purpose.

Peyton flushed the toilet.

"There are pictures," Rachel said, in a voice like a death knell.

Leah's body went cold. Her hand tightened around the vodka bottle. "No," she said. She didn't try to lie or to cover it up. "I watched him delete the pictures," she said, voice shaking. She turned to see Peyton wiping herself and pulling her pants up. She looked up at Leah, and Leah was struck again by the look of expectation on her daughter's face. Expectation that she would be scolded for some reason. Leah was no better than her own parents, when she got right down to it. Tears burned her eyes. She reached out and touched Peyton's cheek. "Good job, honey," she whispered, craning her chin away from the phone. The girl's eyes lit up. A smile broke across her face. She skipped out of the stall.

Rachel said, "Screen shots live forever, bitch."

Leah poked her head out the door. The children were all still in the vehicle. She turned back into the bathroom. Peyton looked up at her expectantly. Leah covered the receiver and tried to smile at her daughter. "Wash your hands, baby. Then wait outside the door for Mommy." As

Peyton dutifully turned toward the sink, Leah locked herself inside the nearest stall and leaned against the door. The phone vibrated in her hand. She pulled it from her ear and stared at the screen. Her teeth began to chatter in her mouth. The phone vibrated again and again. Texts were arriving. Rachel's voice punctuated each vibration. "Look," she said. "Look."

There they were. The photos that D.J. had taken of her naked in various compromising positions. There was one of her fellating him. Even one of him entering her from behind, which he must have taken in secret. In fact, there were at least a half dozen she had never seen. Hands shaking, she deleted each one as it came in, but it didn't matter, did it? They were out there. Rachel had them. Her best friend, Rachel.

Rachel with the mean streak.

As she adjusted the strap of her purse, her fingers brushed the cap of the vodka bottle again. In one movement, she freed it from her bag and unscrewed it. She hesitated. She didn't drink. She had the kids. But she also didn't fuck nineteen-year-old boys who turned out to be her best friend's son. She didn't get pregnant with their children and try passing the baby off as her husband's. She didn't let her nineteen-year-old lover take photos of every disgusting sexual thing they had done together. She wasn't that person.

But she was.

And her world was about to be blown apart. Why had she ever thought that she would be okay admitting to the affair and taking responsibility? What she had done was unforgiveable on every level— and there were photographs to prove it. This was ten times worse than anything Glory Rohrbach had ever done.

The vodka seared the back of her throat. It spilled over and dribbled down her chin. Keeping her voice low so that Peyton wouldn't hear her, she said, "I know he's your son."

Silence. Then: "You think exposing me is going to make what you did seem less wrong? You have no idea what you've done. You want me to say it, Leah? Yes, D.J. is my son. I made a mistake when I was a teenager. I brought him into the world, and I left him because he was a mistake."

Again, Leah felt a coldness creep up the backs of her legs. She shivered. "How can you—how can you say that about your own son?"

Even as she asked, Leah knew. She had known early on that something was not quite right with D.J. She had no idea what kind of situation Rachel had found herself in as a teenager—a young teenager, by Leah's calculations—but still, Rachel's words seemed harsh.

"He's a monster, Leah. He's always been a monster."

The photos of the Soccer Mom Strangler victims flashed across Leah's mind.

"They all had hair like yours."

She took another small sip of vodka. It was like gasoline on her esophagus.

"What are you saying?" she croaked.

"You don't know what he's capable of. Do you know why he left last year?"

Because I broke up with him. "No, I—"

"He exposed himself to Maya and Molly."

"Oh my God."

A full-body shudder descended through her. She closed her eyes, thought of all the times she'd allowed him to put his hands on her. She felt even more violated than she had as a twelve-year-old, when her father started sneaking into her room at night. She took another swig of vodka.

"He's a monster," Rachel repeated. "He's a monster, and you fucked him. A lot, apparently. Looks like you enjoyed it. How could you?"

"You don't understand. It wasn't like that."

"I don't need you to tell me what it was like. I've got pictures. At first, I thought no one would believe me, but oh, look, there are thirteen photographs of my best friend sucking my deviant son's dick. How could you? And what I can't figure out is, why you? You're a fat cow. Your own husband doesn't even like you that much. But I forgot—D.J. spent the last eleven years in an institution. He doesn't know any better. You were supposed to be my friend. How could you do this? You, of all people?"

Each word was a new barb in her skin. This woman was supposed to be her best friend. She called D.J. a monster, and if he really had exposed himself to the twins, then he certainly was—not that Leah needed convincing, after he'd killed her dog and tried twice to harm her own kids—but Rachel had refused to acknowledge him long before the incident with the twins. Somewhere, in a far-off corner of her mind, she wondered what Rachel was really angry about. But she kept returning to the word *institution.*

"What do you mean 'institution'? What kind of institution?"

"The kind you put your kid in when he is a born fucking psychopath. The kind you hope he never gets out of. The kind you put your kid in when he pours hot coffee on the family dog at age four and pushes a classmate off the jungle gym at age five. You know the scar on my chin? The one I always tell everyone I got from falling while ice-skating? It's from him. When he was five he bit my face because I wouldn't let him have a chocolate bar for breakfast. Hard enough to leave a scar for the rest of my life. So go ahead and tell people. Rachel has a psychopathic deviant for a son. I'll still come off more sympathetic than you. Once people see these photos, they won't give a shit whose son he is. They'll be too disgusted by the fact that you were having an affair with a boy young enough to be your own son—a boy who enjoys showing his penis to five-year-old girls."

"Rachel."

"Shut up."

"He used to bite you?"

Her own body was still tender from the other day. D.J. had broken her skin. No matter how many times she washed the bites or lathered them in bacitracin, they still ached. She was worried they would get infected and she'd have to see a doctor for them. What would she say? Her twenty-year-old lover had bitten her like a rabid dog? But he'd almost always bitten her. Not this hard, of course, but he was angry and incensed, waging a campaign of terror to bring her back to him. She'd often had to hide the bite marks from their lovemaking.

The bite marks.

It was a detail of the Soccer Mom Strangler case the news media was completely euphoric over. They were high on it, on the sheer gruesomeness of it, as though the way those women had been killed wasn't gruesome enough. Every newscaster had delivered that detail as though they were telling viewers about the trip to Disneyland they'd just won.

A source close to the investigation revealed today that the Soccer Mom Strangler leaves bite marks on each of his victims, usually on their breasts or neck.

The detail had lodged somewhere in her mind, but she had shuffled it off to the drawer marked "If I Don't Look Directly at It, It Won't Become Important." But here it was. Bite marks. A monster. A deviant. Since he was a child. Institutionalized. Leah racked her brain, trying to think back to when the news of the first Soccer Mom Strangler victim broke. Had it been right after his return—after he found out she was pregnant with Tyler? After she sharply rebuffed him? Rejected him? Had he gone out and found a woman who looked like Leah and done all the things with her that he'd wanted to do to Leah? Had he killed her?

Again, the faces of the victims flashed in her head. No, not just their faces. Their bodies too. What had Rachel called her? A fat cow? She was hardly that big, but she was slightly overweight, just as all the Soccer Mom Strangler victims had been.

She took another swig of vodka.

Rachel said, "You want to play this game? The secrets game? Really? You want to go there with me? Fine then. Let's go."

"No," Leah said. "I don't."

She dropped her phone into the toilet. She turned and reached for the stall lock only to discover that she felt a little woozy. Had a few sips of vodka made her drunk already? She held the bottle out in front of her. It was half-empty.

She clutched the bottle to her and staggered back onto the toilet. She needed to think. She would never mollify Rachel. Her mistake had been in challenging her.

"I know he's your son."

That had sealed her death warrant with Rachel. She might not circulate the photos right away. No, she would hold them over Leah's head for a while. Watch her squirm. Savor it. But one day, they would appear on her husband's phone or in her boss's email or her mother-in-law's mail. Rachel had social media accounts, and Leah would not put it past her to "accidentally" post a photo on one of her accounts. Everyone would know. Everyone would see what Leah had done. Those most private moments.

Private moments she had shared with a serial killer. The serial killer she had inspired, if not created.

She didn't want to think it, didn't want to acknowledge it, the thing her mind had been circling around for the last week. But it was true. She knew it in her heart. Had known it the first time she saw the newscasts about the bite marks on the Soccer Mom Strangler victims. That had been the impetus for getting the DNA tests, finally. She needed to know if her son came from a killer. And he did.

Tyler was Dylan's son. She had lied on the DNA test kit because she could forge Jim's signature. It was easier that way. Only she knew the truth.

What had she done?

She thought of people she'd read about whose lives had been ruined over much less, like racist tweets or photos on social media that they only intended as jokes. Even people who'd only worn offensive Halloween costumes found their lives ruined when photos got around.

Leah didn't stand a chance. Her name would always be associated with the Soccer Mom Strangler. It wouldn't take a rocket scientist to figure out that her affair had been going on when she got pregnant. People she didn't even know would question Tyler's paternity—and they'd be right.

Everyone in the world would know what she had done, who she had become, and the shame would follow her children into adulthood. People would wonder about her kids. Little Tyler's father was a savage, remorseless killer. A killer who'd shown violent tendencies as a very young child, if Rachel was to be believed. What if Tyler turned out the same? Would she even be able to look at him the same after this? Would she be wondering about him his entire life?

What about Rachel's girls? Their mother had given birth to a serial killer. Rachel with the mean streak. What if her daughters grew into monsters as well? They would be unstoppable.

Leah slid off the toilet, wedged between the stall wall and the commode. She lifted the bottle to see that only a small amount was left. Had she really consumed all of that vodka? Wriggling and grunting, she freed herself and stumbled to her feet. The stall door banged open, the noise echoing in the tiny room. She dropped the vodka into the trash can.

Peyton stood outside the door. "Let's go," Leah told her. Using every ounce of concentration she had, Leah got her daughter across the parking lot and strapped back into the car. Hunter and Tyler were sleeping. The twins were engrossed in a conversation about something they had seen on *Secret Agent Bear*, which they quickly brought Peyton into.

Leah fled back to the bathroom. She braced herself against the sink. All the compartments of her mind were flying open at once. The vodka was making it hard for her to keep her mind so tightly controlled. She couldn't stop it from happening. She couldn't stop anything from happening. She looked up and saw herself in the mirror. She had her mother's features.

The woman in the mirror blurred out of focus and then returned, looking resolute. She said, "No more."

CHAPTER
SIXTY-NINE
TWO MONTHS LATER

After her return from captivity, Claire had traveled. Sometimes with her sister, sometimes with their mother. They had taken one trip as a family, all the Fletchers together, to Disney World. She had always stayed in budget hotels, especially when she was with Brianna, who was notorious for cutting corners. "The less we spend, the more places we can visit" had always been her reasoning. Claire hadn't cared. She'd enjoyed exploring new places. Places she never imagined she would get to see during the years she'd been chained to a radiator in a shack in the woods. Traveling—even on the cheap—felt like the kind of luxury only A-list celebrities and lottery winners could indulge in. It was a fantasy.

But the resort in Bora Bora Connor had chosen for their romantic getaway was beyond all of her wildest dreams. It literally looked like a version of paradise. It was a cliché, but she honestly kept pinching herself surreptitiously. A small part of her wondered if the Soccer Mom Strangler had actually killed her and sent her to this heaven to spend all of eternity with the man she loved.

She lay on an outdoor chaise lounge in a bathing suit, the warm breeze caressing her bare legs. They'd tanned nicely in the three days they'd been there. Crystal-blue water spread out before her, so clear and clean that she could see to the bottom for miles. In the distance, the green hump of Mount Otemanu rested beneath perfect, cloudless blue skies. She'd spent the better part of the last hour trying to decide which was more blue—the sky or the water? Connor had booked them in an overwater suite that wasn't even a suite, really. It was a Polynesian-style bungalow with a faux thatched roof. There were several of them, spread out along the shallow waters near the bank of the lagoon. They were all connected by a wooden walkway that led to the main hotel building. The inside of the bungalow was decorated in lovely wood decor, a king-size bed the centerpiece of the main room. It also boasted a couch, table and chairs, and the deck that Claire now sat on.

Connor emerged from inside the bungalow, shirtless and beautifully tanned, a margarita in his hand. She tried to think of ways her life could be better in that moment, but there were none. He handed her the drink and sat in the chaise lounge beside hers. Leaning in for a kiss, she caught a whiff of his sunscreen. She'd have to take the bottle home with her when they returned to reality. That way, when things got stressful, she could smell it and remember this. Paradise.

"Tell me again how much you paid for this place?" she said.

Connor laughed. "I'd really rather not." He reached over and took her hand. "Besides, it doesn't matter. I promised you tiki huts."

"Indeed, you did."

"We should have come sooner."

"No," Claire said. "This is the perfect time."

She didn't say it, because she didn't want to talk about any of it—not here—but he had needed time to help Stryker wrap up the Soccer Mom Strangler investigation so that his office could turn the file over to the district attorney. Since D.J. North hadn't died of his injuries and had pled not guilty to the many counts of murder and attempted murder levied against him, there would be a trial, but that was a year or two away. Claire was happy to finally be away from it. The case was still on the news almost daily. Once Leah Holloway's and Rachel Irving's associations with the case had come out, the press had gone crazy. The sordid details had made national headlines. Rachel Irving's husband had taken their twins and left her. Jim Holloway had refused to keep baby Tyler. Rachel hadn't wanted him either—at least, not until D.J.'s father swooped in to take custody of him. Sebastian North had retired and moved to Sacramento to be close to D.J. as he built his defense. Word was that Sebastian had remortgaged his house to pay for a high-powered lawyer for his son. Claire and Connor had noticed that each time the press showed Sebastian coming and going from the courthouse, Rachel was in tow, looking miserable with baby Tyler in her arms. Claire wondered if she was really trying to give the life she'd left behind another try, or if she simply had nowhere else to go and had latched on to Sebastian. Obviously, the older man was the forgiving type. Connor had told her that the district attorney had declined to press obstruction of justice charges against Rachel. They couldn't prove beyond a reasonable doubt that she had known that D.J. was the Soccer Mom Strangler. Besides, Connor had reasoned, karma had taken care of Rachel Irving.

The whole thing was terribly sad to Claire, but mouthwatering to the press.

"Did you email Brianna today?" Connor asked, drawing Claire out of her reverie.

They didn't get great cell service, which Claire found to be a blessing, but the Wi-Fi was fairly reliable. She'd made sure to check in with her sister by email. Brianna had recovered well from her head injury. When she wasn't studying for the bar exam, she was grilling Claire for every detail about her relationship with Connor. She'd asked for daily updates from Bora Bora.

"Yes," Claire assured him. "When I got up this morning. My responsibilities for the day are finished."

"Oh, they're not finished," Connor said.

"Really?"

He stood, pulling her with him, toward the steps that curved from the deck down to the azure water. "You promised me a swim, remember?"

Claire grinned. "That I did."

She followed Connor to the bottom of the steps and watched him dive into the water. Then she plunged in after him.

ACKNOWLEDGMENTS

First, I must thank my readers for your relentless passion and enthusiasm. You keep me going, and, as I've said in the past, I am so grateful for every message, email, Facebook post, and tweet. As always, thank you to my wonderful husband, Fred, and my lovely, inspiring daughter, Morgan, who gave up so many hours of time with me so that I could write this book. I love you both, and I am eternally grateful for your patience. Every day you make me want to be a better person and a better author. I would never be able to write a word without the following folks in my corner, encouraging me and supporting me every step of the way. These people were instrumental in helping me along my journey this time around, always ready to beta read, answer questions, or just offer the words I needed to keep writing: Nancy S. Thompson, Michael Infinito Jr., Dana Mason, Katie Mettner, Carrie Butler, Jeff O'Handley, Donna House, Joyce Regan, William Regan, Rusty House, Melissia McKittrick, MK Harkins, Ava McKittrick, Jean and Dennis Regan, Torese Hummel, Cat Skinner, and my Frostbite and Entrada beta readers. Thank you to my many, many friends and family members who are constantly spreading the word about my books and leaving me Facebook messages asking why I'm on Facebook and not writing my next book. I love you. You are the best! Thank you to Sue Herwig—if you hadn't stayed on me, I would never have finished this! Thank you to Amy Z. Quinn for the wealth of information with respect to journalism. Thank you especially to Sgt. Jason Jay for answering in great detail my endless stream of questions at all hours of the day and night with infinite patience. I can never thank you enough for all of your input and your willingness to help me get things right—or as close to right as fiction allows. Thank you to Jessica Tribble for taking a chance on me. Thank you to David Downing for helping me get to the really good stuff. Thank you to Scott Calamar for helping me work out the kinks. Finally, thank you to the entire team at Thomas & Mercer for making this book shine!

ABOUT THE AUTHOR

Lisa Regan, the author of *Finding Claire Fletcher*, is a bestselling suspense novelist and a member of Sisters in Crime, Mystery Writers of America, and International Thriller Writers. She has a bachelor's degree in English and a master's degree in education from Bloomsburg University, works full-time as a paralegal, and lives with her husband and daughter in Philadelphia, where she writes books while waiting in line at the post office. Readers can learn more about her work at www.lisaregan.com.